P9-DGH-493

Praise for Jennifer Probst's "fresh,
fun, and sexy" (*Romancing the Book*) series

The Marriage Bargain
The Marriage Trap
The Marriage Mistake
The Marriage Merger

"Charming, fast-paced . . . It will hook you and leave
you begging for more!"

—Laura Kaye, *New York Times* bestselling
author of *One Night with a Hero*

"A beautiful story with characters that will stay with
you forever."

—Candace Havens, bestselling author of
Take It Like a Vamp

"Absolutely amazing! I couldn't put it down."

—*Bitten by Paranormal Romance*

"Highly amusing . . . Jennifer Probst is an amazing
author."

—*Fresh Fiction*

"Fiery and wild . . . it goes straight to your heart."

—*Maldivian Book Reviewer*

"Witty, sweet, and sexy . . . very enjoyable."

—*Bookish Temptations*

"Jennifer Probst is quickly turning into one of my
favorite authors!"

—Susan Meier, author of *Nanny for the Millionaire's Twins*

"She is carving her way into the hearts of readers
with each new breath-catching romance."

—Catherine Bybee, *New York Times* bestselling author

Also by Jennifer Probst

THE MARRIAGE TO A BILLIONAIRE SERIES

The Marriage Bargain

The Marriage Trap

The Marriage Mistake

JENNIFER PROBST

THE MARRIAGE
Merger

POCKET BOOKS

New York   London   Toronto   Sydney   New Delhi

Pocket Books
A Division of Simon & Schuster, Inc.
1230 Avenue of the Americas
New York, NY 10020

This book is a work of fiction. Any references to historical events, real people, or real places are used fictitiously. Other names, characters, places, and events are products of the author's imagination, and any resemblance to actual events or places or persons, living or dead, is entirely coincidental.

First Pocket Books paperback edition August 2013

POCKET and colophon are registered trademarks of Simon & Schuster, Inc.

For information about special discounts for bulk purchases, please contact Simon & Schuster Special Sales at 1-866-506-1949 or business@simonandschuster.com.

The Simon & Schuster Speakers Bureau can bring authors to your live event. For more information or to book an event contact the Simon & Schuster Speakers Bureau at 1-866-248-3049 or visit our website at www.simonspeakers.com.

Manufactured in the United States of America

10 9 8 7 6 5 4 3 2 1

ISBN 978-1-4767-4491-9
ISBN 978-1-4767-4496-4 (ebook)

I'm a mom first, a writer second. Thanks to my own special mommy support group, who I've known since pre-K days, and who have entertained me at play-dates, parties, birthdays, and school trips while our children played together: Danielle Nelson, Patti Turner, Susan Hansen, and Amanda Winters.

And, as always, to my family, my own True North.

Chapter One

I t was official.

　　She was a failure.

Julietta Conte stared sightlessly at the buttercream-colored wall of her home. Funny, she'd never taken the time to put any paintings or photos up. Unmarred by any marks or holes by numerous nails, the clean lines usually soothed her. Reminded her of the orderly, controlled life-style she proudly led. Tonight, the pristine perfection of that wall only made her feel empty. Like an imposter. Or a ghost.

A funny sound escaped her lips. She had lost the biggest deal her family bakery had ever been offered, but losing her mind was not a possibility at this point. A month of research, endless paperwork, little sleep, and various social outings had yielded rejection by the esteemed Palazzo Hotel. She'd been so sure of success. Instead, she was left with nothing but the image of confessing her failure to her team in the morning.

Tugging her cocoa silk robe tighter around her, she crossed the lush carpet over to her trendy kitchen and poured herself a glass of Bolla. Low voices on the television chattered behind her, but the stark silence of her home screamed.

What was wrong with her tonight? She'd lost deals before. Rarely did she allow herself to stumble on her failures—she'd learned to toughen up and head toward the next beacon of profit. It wasn't like La Dolce Famiglia was in any financial trouble. This wasn't life or death. Yet, the lure of making her mark on the business world and in her family was the only thing she had left to give. And now, she couldn't even accomplish that.

A demanding buzz rose to her ears. Julietta scooped up her phone and glanced at the text. Her sister. Again. Was this the third or fourth text tonight?

Did you do it?

Impatience nipped at her nerves. Her youngest sibling was happily married to her longtime crush and insisted a ridiculous love spell had brought the whole thing together. If only. How much easier would life be if you just made a list of all the qualities needed in a man, burned it in a fire to Earth Mother, and sat back and waited? Of course, Julietta gently tried to explain, it probably wasn't the book but the simple fact they were meant to be together. Carina refused to believe it.

So Carina had pressed the violet fabric book into Julietta's hands during her last visit and made her swear on their sisterhood she'd try the spell. Carina believed if Julietta cast this silly love spell, Mr. Right would show up at her door and change her life. After an hour of being verbally abused regarding her inability to see past her spreadsheets toward the future, Julietta agreed, certain her sister would forget the ridiculous conversation and move on.

Two weeks now. Twenty texts. A dozen phone calls. And no end in sight to forgetfulness.

Her fingers punched out two letters.

NO.

The crisp fruity taste of the wine danced in her mouth. Opening the refrigerator, she grabbed a handful of grapes and made her way back to the living room to stew. Why didn't anyone understand or accept that a single woman could be happy? And she *was* happy. Damn happy. Ever since that ridiculous purple fabric book bullied its way into her place she'd been tortured nonstop. Carina swore the spell had worked with both Alexa and Maggie to match them with their soul mates.

A massive wave of hopelessness pressed down on her. She fought sudden panic, dragged in a breath, and coldly analyzed the emotions. Of course, she was a bit envious of her siblings. All of them had settled down into married bliss, chattering about families and get-togethers. She was looked upon as the single female who should entertain them with stories of love gone wrong and hot affairs burning up the sheets.

The flashing screen saver on her laptop advertising the logo of La Dolce Famiglia mocked her. Instead, Julietta spoke of figures and sales and the next deal to bring greatness to the family name. Even Mama began to look at her with concern and perhaps a shred of pity.

She bit down hard on a grape. Tart juice exploded on her tongue. *Merda*. Who cared? Wasn't this the time women did not need men? Sex was overrated and not something she was interested in anyway. Her inability to experience an orgasm or a deep connection with a man had frustrated her for years until she vowed to cut out that part of her life in order to keep her sanity. Her mind might have craved physical intimacy, but her body was steeped in ice. After many failed attempts to feel something—anything—from the opposite sex, she stopped whining and started living. Without sex.

Her sleek, trendy space bespoke her wealth, taste, and success. Though her sisters preferred warm Tuscan furnishings, Julietta favored clean modern lines with a ruthless efficiency that appealed to her sense of order. Bright white paint set off the edgy black and glass tables, bone loveseats, and plum cushions under sky-high ceilings. The huge windows allowed light to flood the rooms in the daytime and offered spectacular views of a lit-up Milan at night. Her kitchen consisted of red leather bar stools and black granite countertops. No need for a massive table since she always ate alone. If there was a new gadget out, she bought it. The place was wired with the latest in all technology, from her various computers and lightning Internet access to a theater-version television, and sound systems that piped music into every room.

She may not own her sister Venezia's flair for fashion drama, but her tailored suits were always designer and beautifully cut. She appreciated well-made clothes and lavished her girly side with a walk-in closet full of leather, suede, silk, and satin. She could have easily bought a mansion on her salary, but she preferred her luxury apartment in the middle of Milan—close to work, people, and activity. Too much silence in the mountains might make her go insane. She chewed on more grapes as her phone vibrated again.

What are you afraid of?

Julietta grabbed the phone and did the unthinkable: hit the power button and punished her sister in the only way possible—forcing her into a void of silence.

She feared nothing except failure. Fortunately, she'd learned that hard work and ruthless control led to success. The only thing she'd been unable to change was her body, so she'd done the next best thing. Accepted it and moved on. Now a few texts from her sister rattled her like chattering teeth on a bony skeleton.

Her gaze swung around and settled on the book. The fabric cover seemed to pulse, somehow demanding, almost begging her to cross the room. She'd shoved it on the shelf next to the biographies she favored, but the odd violet color refused to blend with the other spines. Maybe she'd glance through the book and tell Carina she did the spell. Then they could move on and get over this ridiculous subject.

She placed her wineglass on a coaster, walked to the shelf, and plucked the book from the row. The small, square book seemed innocuous enough. *The Book of Spells*. Hmm, no author noted. As she flipped through the worn, delicate pages, no witches' smoke puffed out. The room didn't shake, and no cold wind blew through the space.

Julietta settled back against the cushions. Strange, just one love spell made up the entire book: Make a list of all the qualities needed in a soul mate. *That certainly didn't promise marriage or happily ever after.* Place a copy of the list under her mattress. Burn the original list in a fire. Chant something silly to the entity of Earth Mother. *Finito*.

That's it?

Julietta shook her head, and with a muttered curse, she grabbed the ledger pad she always left next to her laptop. The dark ink bled on the stark white pages as she scribbled furiously, refusing to linger. No pondering or analyzing this time. Just an emotional dump she rarely allowed herself, a list of everything she always wanted in a mate and knew was impossible to achieve.

Julietta didn't read it over. She folded both papers into four quarters and placed one under her mattress. Then she trudged to the kitchen. Whipped out a stainless steel bowl, grabbed a match from the drawer, and lit the paper.

The edges blackened and curled. She fanned her smoke detector and watched the list disappear. Her lips formed the silly chant to Earth Mother, and her cheeks burned in humiliation at the act. She was going to kill her sister for making her an idiot, but at least she'd kept her vow. A few deep breaths and nothing was left in the bowl except for scattered ashes.

An odd sense of doom came over her. Her heart skittered. Why had she written such a list? She should've stuck to clear, cold qualities in a mate rather than the stark need pulsing from every word on that paper.

Didn't matter. No one would know or suspect. And since Earth Mother wasn't talking, Julietta was safe.

She grabbed her phone, punched the power button, and hammered out her message.

It's done. Now leave me alone.

A second passed. A smiley face popped up on the screen.

Thank goodness. Now she'd get back to her life and put the whole episode behind her.

Julietta ignored the emptiness that clenched her gut, and she pumped up the volume on the television to break the silence.

Chapter Two

Julietta adjusted the knot in her sage green scarf, smoothed down her skirt, and opened the gilded double doors. She walked to the receptionist's desk, where a matronly woman took her name and told her to have a seat. Hmm, surprising. She'd expected a young starlet in killer heels who rocked her boss's world at lunchtime. Shame on her for assuming. Perhaps Sawyer Wells would be a pleasant surprise.

She shrugged out of her lime green trench coat and settled her briefcase on the floor. The ringing of phones drifted in the air as she took in the lush corporate surroundings of Wells Enterprises. The giant logo of a scripted W@E hung in polished brass on the front wall, and the reception area had comfortable leather chairs and royal blue carpet. The massive main desk was of glass and boasted a variety of high-tech equipment along with assorted drawers and compartments for organization.

Julietta had done her homework, but it hadn't given her much. A quick call placed to her brother-in-law Max informed her Sawyer was a friend of his, true to his word, with razor-sharp business skills. His name was well-known in the hotel industry where luxury hotels courted him to run their establishments for certain lengths of time. Sawyer stepped in, turned the businesses around, and gracefully removed himself without another word. His main headquarters was housed in New York, but ten months ago a brand-new satellite office appeared in Milan. Uneasiness rumbled through the business industry as rumors exploded. She bet even the famous Hotel Principe di Savoia kept a close eye on the man. His record was impeccable, and he possessed the golden touch to change a crumbling resort into a treasure trove.

The mysterious phone call had taken her completely off guard. Why would the biggest hotel connoisseur request a meeting with her at nine-thirty on a Monday morning? She'd tried to gain further information, but a curt voice had informed her there would only be only one opportunity to meet with Sawyer, and he'd explain the terms of the meeting in person.

Julietta despised secrets and business cloaked in mystery. She had agreed to the meeting, but had immediately begun digging. Funny that such a powerful man who traveled the world bailing out expensive hotels seemed to have no past. Almost as if he'd been a ghost until his mid-twenties. The last decade showed his steady rise in power, and other than the gleeful press regarding his colorful love life, nothing else interested her. An endless line of women was expected when it came to rich businessmen. She couldn't care less who he slept with or when. She only cared about what he wanted with her company. Unfortunately, Max had only advised her to take the meeting, vowing he knew nothing about his friend's intentions.

"You may go in now, Ms. Conte."

Julietta smiled and grabbed her Pineider briefcase. She was led down a short hallway to a heavily carved cherry-wood door. She reached for the knob, but the door swung open without a sound. A shiver raced down her spine, and she hesitated. Odd—she felt that if she crossed the threshold, her life would never be the same. Almost like being invited into a haunted house by the owner, who craved your soul.

"Come in."

The husky drawl whispered against her ears. She took the necessary three steps in. The door swung closed soundlessly behind her.

Her hands clenched around her briefcase. What was wrong with her? Usually she dominated a meeting from the first moment, but she stood rooted to the floor staring across the room at one of the most powerfully sexual men she'd ever seen in her life.

No wonder his receptionist was a grandmotherly type. There wasn't a woman alive who could work for him without getting tongue-tied and stumbling over herself in an effort to please him. His inner sanctum was decorated in dark wood, wine reds, and rich gold trims. Floor-to-ceiling bookshelves took up the wall behind him with endless leather spines amidst odd figures and sculptures in various materials. Smooth marble, gleaming silver, twisted copper. The left wall was painted red and displayed an assortment of art with an erotic flavor. She longed to study the artwork closer but tucked that information to the back of her mind for future reference. His sprawling cherry desk took up half the room in an effort to intimidate. His chair must have been elevated for a dominating visual impression, because there was no way a man could be that tall. Perched on his red leather throne, he studied her with an assessing air that stripped her of niceties and social barriers, somehow leaving her bare. Exposed. And a bit vulnerable.

His wavy blond hair held so many shades of color, the light danced and played on the strands as if lighting up a halo. That halo brushed his shoulders and tempted a woman to twist her fingers in its length as he ravaged her. She catalogued his features in an itemized list: Gracefully curved brows. High, defined cheekbones. Strong chin with a bit of a cleft. An angel or God himself must have given him those eyes, because they seemed almost pure gold, splintering radiance and piercing past the surface straight to the core. As stunning as hidden treasure, those eyes saw things no woman wanted revealed. Julietta bet most females had little choice in the matter. This man took what he wanted and how he wanted without apology.

Then the angels shot screaming up to heaven and abandoned him to hell.

His mouth was a carved, sensual feast with a wicked sneer that spoke of hot sex and no rules. A brutal scar took up the right side of his face, hooking from brow to chin. The line was clean. She imagined the slice of blade as it tore open skin, and she tried not to show any sympathy. This man didn't need it.

The hard twist of good and bad played to women like the Pied Piper. A cold awareness rippled her nerve endings. Good thing men didn't affect her. She'd be burnt toast before they even negotiated on whatever the damn meeting was about. Julietta straightened her shoulders and met his gaze head-on. "Good morning, Mr. Wells. It's a pleasure to meet you."

She closed the distance between them and stuck out her hand. He stood and grasped her hand in his. The handshake was impersonal while being too intimate. His skin was warm and rough to the touch, and he engulfed her hand as if claiming her body on his own terms.

Startled at her bizarre thoughts, she withdrew first and didn't realize she'd been holding her breath. Those gorgeous lips curved upward in a half smile. She didn't know if he was amused or pleased. Either way pissed her off. Julietta immediately sensed the man was accustomed to winning. Comfortable in his own skin. And entertained by mankind, as if humans on a stage put on a show in which he refused to partake. Hmm. She needed to go on the offense quickly. Defense would bore him to tears and get her nowhere. Julietta took a seat, crossed her legs, and settled back in the chair with a relaxed sense of camaraderie she didn't feel.

"I see you like games."

He cocked his head. The flare of surprise soothed her temper. "Depends on the game."

She offered a cool smile. "Chess." She pointed to the beautifully carved figures of a king and queen flanking a shelf of impressive leather books. The carved ivory and ebony pieces held exquisite detail and bespoke a man interested in mental challenges. "They're quite beautiful."

Sawyer rested his elbows on the polished surface and steepled his fingers. She refused to cower under his stare that threatened to shred the surface. When he finally spoke, his deep voice cloaked and stroked dark places she didn't realize she owned. "Do you play?"

"No."

"Why?"

She spoke in a clipped voice. "Games don't interest me. I prefer a straightforward exchange of information for mutual benefit."

He quirked a golden brow. "Yet you are the CEO of a powerful company. Surely you must acknowledge there must always be a winner and a loser."

Ah, yes, he loved to spar. A deep satisfaction hummed through her. How rare to be able to match wits with a man who was completely unafraid. Most cowered under her chilly words or blustered like idiots to get a point across. No, she preferred a subtle wit as fine and sharp as a samurai's sword. She danced just out of his reach with her answer. "If you do your job well enough, your opponent won't even realize he's lost."

"I disagree. If your opponent is worthy, he will always face the truth that one party tops another. The queen must be stolen in order to win all."

She clicked open her briefcase as if bored now by the turn of conversation. The ruffle of papers cut through the pulsing silence, and she realized her palms were damp. How odd. Not nerves. Something else she couldn't quite pin down. "Queens may be sacrificed. She's the power player, but it all rests on the king. With a smart enough backup plan, the queen doesn't have to destroy the entire board."

His eyes darkened. Oh, yeah, no way could a woman work for this man. He should be the poster board image of what to avoid in teenage pregnancy. The balance between light and dark was just enough to tempt a female to jump over the edge of reason, no matter how hard the recovery from the fall. Fortunately, Julietta despised heights and avoided them at all costs. "I thought you didn't play chess," he murmured.

"I don't." She raised her chin. "But that doesn't mean I don't study the rules. Just in case."

His low laugh slid through the room and stroked between her legs. She acknowledged her body's physical reaction even as her mind remained detached. "You are a fascinating woman, Julietta Conte." His tongue rolled over her name and gave it a whole new meaning. Normally she cringed in the boardroom at the mention of her birth name. Too many men used romance and intimacy to demean women in business. But Sawyer combined respect with a leashed sensuality, keeping her off-balance. "I'm glad I followed my instincts to give you the first opportunity to work for me."

She closed her briefcase and settled it back on the floor, then thumbed through the file in a deliberate power play. "While I appreciate being first in line, I would have preferred knowing the details of the offer. I do hate wasting my morning on a deal not worthy of my time. I'm sure you understand, Mr. Wells."

"Sawyer." He rested his chin on his fingers. "After all, I already met most of your family. Am good friends with your brother-in-law. The least we can do is be on a first-name basis."

"Fine."

"Say it."

She looked up. "Excuse me?"

An odd tension stretched between them, as if a preliminary game was being played, and she didn't know the stakes. "My name," he instructed softly. "Say it."

Julietta blinked. Warmth flooded her body and made her skin itch. Her tummy dropped, then settled. She didn't want to and opened her mouth to gloss over the whole weird exchange, but found herself responding to his command. "Sawyer."

His name stumbled across her lips and she cursed herself for the move. Satisfaction and something deeper flickered over his face, but he only nodded in approval. "Thank you."

She cleared her throat and refocused on the file. "Now that we're properly acquainted, I'd appreciate moving forward. It seems your reputation precedes you."

"In a good way, I hope," he drawled.

"Mostly."

Another short laugh. "You are quite different from anyone else in your family."

She ignored the throbbing wound and managed a tight smile. "In a good way I hope."

He frowned and leaned a bit closer. "Did that comment bother you? I only meant your focus proved an asset for Michael. Your sisters weren't meant to take over the family business. Everyone is lucky to have you."

The wound softened to a slight bruise. Why did he seem so concerned about upsetting her? As if he held the ability to poke at her secret insecurities without the drive to expose and hurt? As if he just wanted to *know*.

"Of course I'm not bothered. I consider myself lucky to run La Dolce Famiglia. I don't think I realized you had met most of my family."

The harsh lines of his face softened into affection. "Max and I ran in the same circles and we became close. He's told me about Venezia, and I was lucky enough to meet Carina in Vegas last year. I attended their wedding."

The memory of her sister's quick nuptials flickered past. She hadn't had the time to fly in and had always regretted not being there. Mama was the only one in the family able to witness the exchange, but the idea of Sawyer seeing such an intimate ceremony bothered her. "Interesting," she murmured. "And my mother?"

All expression smoothed out to a blank canvas. "I had the pleasure of meeting your mother many years ago. I respect her greatly."

There was a story behind his words, but she figured he was a master at secrets. Julietta motioned to the manila folder in her lap. "It seems you have the advantage. My research began when you started taking over hotels and transforming them into profitable entities. There's no mention of family, birthplace, or anything else. Almost as if your life before twenty-three never existed."

The darkness flared and swallowed up the light in his whiskey eyes. Her breath hitched at the rage and raw pain she saw, and just as quickly the emotions were gone from his face. "It didn't," he said. "That will have to be enough for you."

Julietta respected his demons. After all, she hid her own. Slowly, she nodded. "That's enough for me."

He smiled. His teeth were dazzling white but crooked slightly in the front, which kept him from looking pretty. "Good. Let's talk business. I have a proposition for you. A merger of sorts."

She crossed her arms in front of her chest and didn't respond. He seemed intrigued with her control and patience. Julietta wondered what type of women he was used to dealing with in his world. "I'm about to unveil a chain of my own signature luxury hotels. For the past few years, I've bought property in prime locations in main cities throughout Europe and the United States. The plan is ambitious and begins with hotels opening up in Milan, Rome, Venice, and Florence. I'll move into England with three locations including London. Then the United States, where I'll build in New York, LA, and Chicago."

He waited for a comment. She remained silent.

"The hotel chain will be called Purity. I've been working on the concept for years—a dream, so to speak—and have a team ready to move fast. I've decided to begin in Italy for a variety of reasons. The statistics are quite high for travelers in those areas and the need for something extra, especially for many Americans. I'll be combining a line of exclusive spas and catering. I prefer to work with specific vendors who can sign an exclusive contract to my line. My intention is for the people I do business with to work for some of the most sought-after companies in the world. Travelers will beg to experience the uniqueness of Purity's assets. I'll launch this in three main components: One, the linens will be handmade and exclusive to Purity. Luxurious robes, slippers, towels, beds, and sheets. Similar to Frette, but we've been able to create a new line that Armani can't boast of. There won't be one thing a customer touches that he doesn't crave to curl into. Component two is the spa and restaurants. I've already signed contracts to incorporate the finest dining and best relaxation methods in the world. The two chefs I stole turned down television deals to come with me. The third component is delicacies: shops with fine gold, customized jewelry, designer fashion, and of course, desserts."

Julietta leaned slightly forward. Her heart hammered as she hung on his next words.

"I want to sign a chain of bakeries to provide exclusive catering at all Purity hotels. This will encompass catering events of all kinds, including weddings. I need an exclusive, high-quality bakery that can provide product to all restaurants, room service, and a pedestrian shop for impulse buys."

Her mind sifted through the possibilities. The plan was

risky. Almost crazy in the current economy. Yet, the simplicity of exclusiveness and the locations screamed genius. If the components worked together, Sawyer could launch one of the most successful brand names in the world. She pursed her lips in thought. "Do the chefs you contracted understand the terms? Most want total control of all food, including the desserts."

"They all know the rules. I don't want some great cooks who can bake good desserts, or one pastry chef. I need a well-oiled chain that can give anything my clients want in a variety of outlets. And I want the best. La Dolce Famiglia is the best."

Pleasure cut deep, but she ignored it. The man was a genius, but she'd learned early there were always hidden clauses in the deal of a lifetime. "I'm impressed. Of course I'll need to see your development plans, timetables, and locations to get a better feel if this would be right for us."

"Of course."

"Estimated profit margins are key."

"Yes."

"There's just one word that's bothering me in your proposal."

"What's that?"

"Exclusive."

His gaze dropped to her mouth. The hungry predator look surprised her. She wasn't a woman who normally inspired lust. Challenge, yes. But in a business meeting, she was always able to detach the feminine part of her, so attraction never became a problem. For the first time, a matching need flared deep in her belly in an attempt to claw free. What would it be like to be on the receiving end of all that pent-up male attention? He stroked his chin in contemplation while he studied her. Those tapered fingers skimmed lightly over a clean-shaven jaw and right under his plump lower lip. Was his skin as golden toasty brown everywhere under that black Gucci suit? Would his fingers play a woman's body and coax a delicious river of need from between her thighs?

She pushed down a sigh. Just a fantasy. The moment he kissed her and found she wasn't the normal weak-kneed female he preferred, he'd lose interest. They all did. And Julietta didn't blame them. *Dio,* what was she doing thinking about him naked anyway? Had she gone *pazzo*?

"You have a problem with being exclusive?" With a lean, masculine grace he pushed back in his chair and hooked his ankle over his knee. The casual gesture contradicted the steely question wrapped in fuzzy cotton. Her mouth dried up. Why did it suddenly seem they were talking about a whole different meaning of the word?

Julietta gave a delicate shrug. "Sometimes. Multiple partners even out the risk."

A wolfish grin spread over his mouth. "Exactly. The risk of failure. Making a commitment to the right partner pushes the percentage of success to a higher level."

"Or the attachment can equal bankruptcy." The blood pounded and rushed through her veins as they thrust and parried in round two of their mental game. "It's happened too many times."

Sawyer dropped his voice. Sticky honey and hot oil mixed and slid together in a delight to her ears and the pulsing center between her legs. "You chose wrong before and got screwed. But that won't happen with me."

Her skin prickled and her breasts ached behind her proper white bra. Julietta had the sudden urge to rip off her clothes and offer herself to him on his desk. Spread her thighs and bend to his will. Horror mingled with surprise at the primitive reaction he coaxed. Thank God she'd learned early to control her breath to calm her nerves in public situations. She forced a small smile. "Confident, are we? Good, I look for that in a partner. I assume you have a formal proposal I can go over?"

He pushed the black leather binder across the desk. She scooped it up, gave it a cursory glance, and tucked it away in her briefcase. "I'll get back to you this week."

"No. Tomorrow."

Julietta frowned. "Impossible. I need lawyers to look it over. I have to bring it to the board members. Talk with Michael."

He cut his hand through the air. "Michael runs La Dolce Maggie, and I intend to give him the same deal with my local operations in New York. If this is going to work, I need to know you're my point person for everything. You make the decisions. Democracy is good, but sometimes a monarchy gets better results." Something flashed in his eyes—deep and sexual and wicked. "I'll have to prove that to you soon."

Julietta refused to clear her throat or act timid. "You run the risk of me saying no to the whole thing."

"Yes. But I still need an answer tomorrow. I'll take you to dinner."

She shook her head. "No need, Mr. Wells, I—"

"Sawyer."

Her belly dropped at his commanding tone. "Sawyer. I'll need till five p.m."

"Perfect. Whatever your decision is, we'll celebrate over wine and pasta. I'll pick you up at seven."

The situation tilted, and she grabbed for footing. "I don't think that's necessary."

"I do. Whether or not we do business, I've spent time with most of your family and would like to share one meal with you. Talk about Max. Your sister. Is that too much to ask?"

She felt like an idiot. How did she fight such a reasonable request without looking like a total bitch? But something told her she didn't want to be alone with him, especially in her apartment. Inviting him in seemed deadly. Her tongue stumbled over the words. "Fine. You can pick me up at the office; I'll be working."

He bowed his head as if it had been her idea the entire time. "Very good. I'll be looking forward to your decision."

She rose from the chair and decided to avert the whole handshaking thing again. Her cowardly move caused his lip to quirk in a half smile, but he stayed behind his desk and watched her leave. Once again, the door swung silently open, as if finally allowing her escape. Did he have a remote under his desk so he could screw with his clients? The whole meeting rattled her usually calm nerves.

Juliettta dug deep, straightened her shoulders, and marched out of the office without a glance back.

. . .

He wanted her.

Sawyer stared at the closed door and tried to make sense of his rioting emotions. Her scent lingered in the air. He dragged in a breath and tried to capture her essence. The sweetness of vanilla. The exotic kick of coconut. A heady contradiction like the woman herself.

Shit. This was going to be more complicated than he thought.

He rose and paced. Wondered if he should withdraw the offer. He expected certain things from the oldest sister of the Conte family. A reserved demeanor. A sharp mind. A ruthless sense of organization and leadership. Assets he admired and needed in a business partner long term. His conversations with Max and Michael had convinced him La Dolce Famiglia would be the perfect fit, and that Julietta was fully capable of making all the decisions.

He'd never expected to be attracted to her.

Sawyer knew he possessed an uncanny ability with women. Part gift, part training. Every nuance of expression was analyzed. Body language, words, gestures. Especially the eyes, which he believed were the window to the soul. Except his. The inviting golden color was a trick of the light meant to throw an enemy off guard. Once someone dove in, all she'd discover was a black pit of hell.

He shook off the gloomy thought and yanked himself back to the problem. The moment she walked in and greeted him in her cool, possessed tone, he wanted to claim her. Her surface image screamed look, but don't touch. Glance, but don't study. Question, but don't ponder.

Her voice reminded him of tinkling ice squeezed in the heady warmth of an Italian accent. She wore her hair pulled back from her face with only a few strands allowed to escape and cradle her cheeks. When she turned her head, the light caught the glimmer of dark red wine strands glistening like rubies in the midst of proper conservative pearls. Those dark eyes were large and dominated her face, but a swirl of actual gold around the irises gleamed with a hidden depth he bet most men never caught. A strong nose, chin, and defined cheekbones set off a mouth so soft and plump he wanted to spend hours just sucking and licking. The fact that she didn't even accentuate them with lipstick made her mouth even more tempting.

She wore her clothes with the command of a woman who liked classic, expensive fashion and knew how to carry it off. Her long, lithe frame had set off the Vera Wang cream suit: the pencil skirt skimming her hips and hitting midcalf. She had walked across the room with purpose in her bone leather pumps, as if her body were only along for the ride, and almost a separate entity. As if her mind and body were completely disconnected in a dueling battle. The thrust of her small, high breasts under her suit jacket and the smooth peek of warm brown skin as she crossed her legs revved his body to immediate attention. Full staff. Thank God the desk was high, because wouldn't that have been an embarrassing moment. He couldn't remember the last time a woman turned him on by just walking into a room. Not since Carina.

The memory of Julietta's younger sister flashed before him. Before his friend Max made his claim, he'd been fascinated by the earthy need and innocence Carina exuded in Vegas, but he realized immediately she was in love with Max. Never one to settle for second place, he'd let her go because she wasn't meant for him. Not long term. Perhaps a brief affair, but she'd never look at him the way she did his friend. Sawyer was glad they were happily married after such a long journey. But even his reaction to Carina was a slight buzz compared to the roaring in his dick when Julietta entered the room.

Her fingers were strong, smooth, and trembled ever so slightly in his grip. She dominated the challenging conversation that most men wouldn't have been able to follow, and she never lost her footing. Yet when he'd made his comment about her being different from her family, she'd stiffened and pain had flared in her cocoa eyes.

Beneath that tight, buttoned-up demeanor was a tangle of passion, emotion, and mess. The best decision lay before him. Cancel the dinner. Back away from the deal. Move on. A woman like Julietta had the power to wreck his concentration, screw with his business, and make his life miserable.

Yet something pulled him to her. Twisted his insides with a raw need to strip her surface bare and make her face who she really was. The way she responded to his demand that she say his name spoke volumes. She had natural submissive tendencies, which intrigued his dominant side. What would she be like in bed? Her mind was so bent on constant control, he bet she had a hard time focusing on the pleasures of her body.

He could teach her.

His blood pounded and heated through his veins. She wouldn't be an easy match, though. She'd be one major pain in the ass. Did he have time for this now? His long-held dream of building his own hotel empire lay right before him. Tying her up in his business could prove risky. But damn, tying her up in any way, shape, or form was too fucking tempting.

Sawyer realized the past few years he'd been skimming the edges with women. He played at relationships to a point he wouldn't know a real connection if it was advertised in blinding neon. Work had been his driving force for the past decade, and it remained his sole demanding mistress. His forays into pleasure were set ahead of time with ironclad rules. But many women slipped into clinginess and emotion he couldn't handle, forcing him to end the relationship quickly. Julietta might be able to offer him a bit more depth, with the ability to keep business separate from pleasure. Most women couldn't handle the limitations.

He bet Julietta Conte handled any challenge thrown at her.

Sawyer tapped his finger against his lips and analyzed all the options. Such a delicate line to walk between business and pleasure. Snakes twisted in a pit beneath him, ready for even one misstep. She'd need to be handled with kid gloves at first, before he switched to the delicious sting of the whip. He needed to learn what drove her, what she hid, and how best to yank away years of barriers. Was it too risky, especially when he was about to unveil his dream and his only reason for survival all these years?

The answer coursed through him with a bone-deep knowledge he never questioned.

And he made the decision he'd wanted to from the moment he met her.

Chapter Three

Julietta glanced up: 4:58 p.m.

The papers were spread neatly in front of her on the conference table. The room was quiet, and just the hum of low chatter and ringing phones drifted in waves. She had informed the board. Spoken with the lawyers. Made a call to Michael. Pounded out numbers nonstop through the night and refused to sleep. And came up with one decision.

She'd be crazy not to take the deal.

It would be her opportunity to do something on a global scale for the company. Though she'd been acting CEO, it had only been a few years ago she'd been given full control. Her brother had true intentions but still kept the reins on her leadership role until he married Maggie and saw the error of his ways. Finally, she had leapt forward and started making deals on her own. When Michael had begun infiltrating top hotels in the States, Julietta had burned with the desire to push the bakery chain to a new level in Italy. She'd already conquered the street market, but she wanted to go after the hotels. The big ones. The failure of her last deal with The Palazzo still stung. She'd been completely prepared, and every pore of her body had craved a final deal. She hated the simmering knowledge that The Palazzo's executive team didn't believe a woman could give them what they desired. Oh, in bed, yes. But in business?

No. Instead, they gave the deal to her competitor who boasted no vision and an Italian patriarch grandfather. Julietta realized too late The Palazzo wanted full control over her. Once they'd realized the little woman had a strong voice, they'd dropped her contract without another word.

But now she faced a resurrection of her dream. Sawyer's contract could launch La Dolce Famiglia into the world of luxurious hotels.

There were risks, though. With an exclusive contract, she'd be unable to install any other bakeries. She'd be locked up with Purity, and if Sawyer failed, so would she. The gamble lay before her in all shades of gray. Excitement pulsed through her. When was the last time she'd gotten fired up about a deal? She desperately needed a challenge to focus on to launch her out of the current self-pity tour she hosted every evening. There was nothing better than a shot of adrenaline on a new contract.

Five p.m.

The intercom buzzed. She hit the button. "Yes?"

"Ms. Conte, Sawyer Wells is on the line. May I put him through?"

She shook her head and fought a smile. "Yes, thank you."

The connection hummed. His voice spilled like gravel and silk over the phone. "Have you made a decision?"

"Prompt, aren't you?"

"Always." He paused, "We can play another round and drag the discussion out over dinner. Or I can persuade you in the manner you need. I'm quite good at persuasion."

His arrogance was overwhelming and sexy as hell. Damn, he'd be fun to work with. "No need. I've been wined and dined by the best. Never made a decision based on such techniques either."

His dark laugh was like a subtle threat. "You're not familiar with my moves."

"I've found most male moves overrated."

"Delightful. A challenge."

Julietta gave a long-suffering sigh. Better to get the truth out over dinner. If Sawyer thought he'd get some extra side benefits while they worked together, he was quite mistaken. She hoped he wouldn't get cranky and surly like the other rejects. "Trust me, it was simple truth and not meant to wave a red flag in front of you. My answer is yes."

Silence fell between them. She waited him out. "Yes?"

"Do I need to repeat myself? I'll sign the contract. You can still meet me here at headquarters at seven so we can celebrate. A pleasure conversing with you, Mr. Wells."

She clicked off her earpiece. Satisfaction surged. Her tiny rebellion with his name may have been childish, but well worth it. Obviously, he was way too used to women jumping at his call and throwing off their clothes. Time he realized he couldn't get anyone he wanted because the angels bestowed him the gift of hotness.

Regret nudged her. What would it feel like just once to have a strong physical reaction to a man without worrying about freezing up? For it to be simple and clean. Just nakedness and orgasms and an early morning getaway.

Pathetic. If that was her only deficiency in life, she could call herself blessed. At least she had a juicy new deal ahead of her, with long hours of work and a deep satisfaction that called to her.

Success.

Completion.

Achievement.

It was enough.

She repeated the mantra to herself as she got back to work. The hours flew by. Julietta took her last two minutes to smooth back her hair, re-knot her scarf, and tuck her folders away. He arrived on time and in full male glory. Her gaze raked over him with a hint of crankiness. He stood in the doorway and refused to say a word. His quiet arrogance radiated in waves around his figure, and she fought the need to drop her head in recognition. Weirdness.

He wore a charcoal-gray pin-striped suit with a purple tie. The ruthless severity of the suit contradicted with his surfer hair tied back in a short ponytail, setting off the hard lines of his cheekbones and the red scar. The combination of raw sex and power cloaked in masculine grace transfixed her for just a moment. Julietta mentally shook herself. No more drooling. Defenses up. Game on.

"You like being in charge, don't you, Julietta?"

The stroke of her name was deliberate and effective. She forced a pleasant smile. "Doesn't every woman?"

"You won't let me see your apartment. Not even your private office. I've been delegated to picking you up for dinner in your conference room."

Julietta grabbed her red Fendi bag and closed the distance between them. His body pumped out heat, and she had to tilt her head back a few inches in order to meet his gaze. God, he smelled good. Like coffee and spices, rich and all male. Her height usually gave her an advantage. At almost six feet, she usually towered over her competition, but he topped her by several inches. She realized now the sheer breadth and size of his massive shoulders stretched in his proper suit jacket was another contradiction. He was a primitive wrapped up in civilization. The veneer scared her the most, but she wouldn't let herself be in such an intimate position with him. She had to set boundaries immediately, or he'd swallow her whole. "I may have agreed to the contract, but I never invite anyone into my private space."

Sawyer didn't budge. "Ever?" he asked softly.

"Our working relationship doesn't guarantee a friendship, Sawyer. You may have met my family, and we may be going to dinner, but I don't know you well enough for anything more."

He seemed to analyze her words. Nodded. "Fair enough. I figured we'd walk to Piazza Repubblica."

"Perfect."

He ushered her out of headquarters as if he were in charge. His hand rested on the curve of her elbow, his fingers strong but gentle as he guided her over the uneven cobblestone pathways as they walked toward the restaurant.

The familiar sights and scents of Milan rushed past her. She breathed in the heavy, fogged air that made the city unique, and she settled into a comfortable silence. The bustle of cars and pedestrians crowding the streets and sidewalks lent a purposeful atmosphere that soothed her soul. Motorbikes roared by. Beautifully clad women in designer suits and high-heeled shoes weaved in and out amidst the crowd with elegant grace, and sidewalk café tables spilled onto the sidewalk with the scents of espresso and baked goods.

She'd seen videos of New York City and always felt Milan must be a close second cousin except for the grayish mist that cloaked the city and made it seem almost muddy to a viewer's eye. Instead of towering glass buildings, the ancient architecture of the Duomo reigned.

They finally reached the elegant archway of Repubblica. It was already crowded, but they were immediately ushered to a red booth in the corner, and Sawyer ordered a bottle of champagne. The simple clean lines of the restaurant pleased her—the crisp white linens, polished floors, high ceilings, and candles scattering throughout the dimly lit interior. She chatted with the waiter, ordered appetizers, and began to relax.

"No briefcase?" he noted. He lifted the delicate champagne glass to his lips and took a swallow. The imprint of his mouth made a strange shudder squeeze through her. The heat rushed through the vents to ward off the chilly winter evening. She unbuttoned her suit jacket and hung it on the chair.

"No need. I already memorized most of the figures."

Sawyer grinned. "Bet you have. Did you have the support of the board?"

"Enough to move forward. It's a risk, but calculated. You have an ambitious plan for opening. Will you be ready in six months?"

"Yes."

She tilted her head and reached for a piece of crusty bread. The warm dough broke open, and she drizzled fruity olive oil over the edges. "A dozen things could go wrong and delay your plans."

He watched her with a fierce intensity she wasn't used to. Most men never gave her such full attention. Julietta wondered if it was one of his trademark moves he used to seduce women. "I've planned for all contingencies," he finally said. "There will be no mistakes."

His words dug deep. He needed this as much as she. The knowledge soothed her nerves, and she reached for her glass. Perhaps they were more similar than she'd originally thought. Sawyer wouldn't lose his focus over a silly challenge to bed her. Women were definitely a low priority for him. She smiled with relief. "Good. Then we both have something to prove."

"Yes, it seems we do." Golden eyes gleamed. "The question is why?"

Her fingers closed around the last chunk of bread. She hoped he didn't spot her tremble. "Doesn't everyone want to make a fortune in business? Take over the world? It's the human condition."

Sawyer refused to follow her lead. "Is that what you want, Julietta? To make your mark?" His eyes burned. "Tell me, why did the deal with The Palace fall through?"

She kept her gaze averted and focused on the bread. "I'm surprised you don't know the details already. Especially since you were researching La Dolce Famiglia for a while."

"Oh, I do know. I would like to hear your version of the events."

Her temper nipped, but she answered with calm. "They

decided I wasn't the woman they originally believed I was. The team had specific ideas and wanted no challenges. In other words, I wouldn't have a say in my own company."

"But you would have received prestige. Profits. Growth." A tiny frown marred his brow, and she had the uneasy feeling he was digging for something she couldn't understand. "Isn't that a big enough payoff? Worth the sacrifice?"

"No. I haven't gotten to this point to step back and let others take over." She sipped her champagne to settle her nerves. "I'll agree to be exclusive. But I won't give up my rights of control. Ever."

A strange flare of lust heated his eyes, then disappeared so quickly she swore it was just a trick of the candlelight. She wasn't a woman to inspire such devotion, especially with such a primal force of man. "I don't intend to partner with someone who has no opinion or spine, Julietta. Like I stated before, I need a leader who is my go-to person on all aspects. I will use every bit of intellect and talent you have. By surrounding myself with such a team, I'll be able to lead us, but be warned: Final approval will always be made by me."

Her heart hammered, and she squeezed her thighs together as a jolt of arousal penetrated her core. Holy crap. What was with this crazy reaction to his chauvinistic demands? She always hated men who thought they could command others just because they owned a penis. She ignored her body and pushed on. "Understood, as long as there is always a discussion with anything affecting La Dolce Famiglia."

"Of course. So, once we show The Palace what fools they were for letting you go, what next? Will this deal finally be enough?"

Her throat tightened. How dare he try to probe as if he had a right to know her thoughts? When she was finally able to gather her words, her voice was laced with ice. "Still invading personal space? My motivations are mine and not your business. How about you share yours? Will Purity finally be enough for you if it becomes a success?"

The emptiness in his eyes spoke volumes. Julietta clenched her hand in an effort not to reach across the table for contact, as if the feel of flesh on flesh could possibly soothe the gaping wound she knew nothing about. What demons rocked his past? Maybe it was better to never know. "God, I hope so," he said. "But I won't know until I get there."

The waiter interrupted with a variety of steaming plates. Crispy octopus paired with buffalo mozzarella and salty anchovies and capers; bite-size beef ravioli in a creamy butter and thyme sauce; grilled eggplant and zucchini drizzled with oil and an array of salts. An odd intimacy buzzed around them, as if sharing secrets at the back of an Italian restaurant bonded them. What was going on? She'd gone on hundreds of business dinners to discuss contracts. Met many attractive, dynamic men who initially interested her. The outcome always made her back away, but Sawyer challenged her at every turn and seemed to crave something more than the others. As if he not only wanted to strip her clothes off to view her naked body. Almost like he wanted to delve into her soul.

Ridiculous.

She fought a shiver and bit into her eggplant. The toasty skin swirled with the pungent flavors of garlic and tomato sauce, soothing her temper. "Why did you pick Milan to unveil your first hotels? Wouldn't you be more comfortable back home?"

He waited to respond, obviously enjoying his food, which gave him extra points. Most Americans appreciated vast quantities with too much garnish and detail. She preferred the simpler, richer ingredients in a meal that satisfied a deeper hunger in the body.

"I don't have a home."

His simple confession ripped past her ears. Her fork paused midair. "What do you mean? Max said you lived in Vegas and New York for a while."

One broad shoulder lifted in a half shrug. "I live in whatever hotel I'm working on. It allows me freedom, a luxurious lifestyle, and expertise." Shadows flickered over his face. "I stayed in Milan when I was young and learning the business. I've also spent a few years at the Carlton, so I'm quite comfortable in New York. I decided it would be poetic to begin here. I usually stay still for about a year. Longer than that and I'm ready to bail."

Her heart flinched. Family and home were part of her blood, and she couldn't imagine not having a built-in support system. Her brother and sister might have fled to New York, but Julietta gained most of her strength from the crooked pavement under her feet and the vast Tuscan sky overhead. She had no desire to move anywhere else. Sawyer's casual reference to his wandering tendencies only confirmed a deeper loneliness he didn't seem to care about.

There was no reason for her to care either. The man didn't need any extra female support. He'd use any weakness to his advantage, including the possibility of her attraction. Julietta tamped down on an inner smirk. If only he knew such a road would lead him nowhere.

"You never want more?" she asked. "A place to call yours?"

She immediately regretted the impulsive words. Heat flared and crackled with amber flames, hotter than the one-hundred-proof whiskey Papa used to sneak in when he thought Mama wasn't looking. Sawyer's lips twisted in a sensual sneer. "Overrated. I've learned to appreciate the present in all aspects. Taste, texture, sight, smell. I revel in everything given to me, because there's no guarantee it'll be there tomorrow. My home is my current location—nothing more, nothing less." Raw passion flicked from across the table and singed her like droplets of burning water. "Except Purity. It's the one thing I want to say is a constant. Everything else eventually withers."

"Even love?"

The words flew from her lips, and she almost gasped in horror. Her cheeks heated. *Dio mio,* what had she done? She must be having some kind of midlife crisis. Her normal temperament and control slipped around this man in a way that terrified her. She waited for his fury at such an intimate question, but his fork paused midair, as if he was just as shocked as she was. "What did you say?"

Julietta forced a half laugh. "I'm sorry—please disregard that question. I don't know what came over me."

"I think I do." His gaze stripped, probed, tore. It took all her strength not to buckle from the intensity "I appreciate a woman who asks whatever is on her mind. There is more strength in honesty than in pretty words that never scratch the surface of what's real."

"There's no need to—"

"But I will. No, Julietta, I do not believe in love. Never have. I believe in passion and lust, honesty and loyalty. I believe in hard work and sacrifice. I believe in enjoying the gifts of this world. But I do not believe in love."

Her fingers trembled. She reached out and drained her glass, trying not to show him how his words affected her. Had she ever met another man with such a powerful presence? As if no topic was off-limits, and he was willing to explore every dark hidden corner of her body and soul with a fierce pleasure? Yet he calmly shared one of his secrets like a gift.

He did not believe in love.

Julietta waited for the rush of relief but only experienced an odd uneasiness. Why did his confession bother her? An answering grief rose in her gut to mourn for a man she did not know, a man who asserted he experienced no gentler emotions. She ached to know more, but the longing could only end badly. He watched her, unblinking, from across the table. And she made her decision.

Their relationship must be held strictly to business. Nothing more.

It was time she laid out the ground rules.

She pushed her plate away and snapped back to attention. "Thank you for sharing, but my question was uncalled for, and I apologize. I think moving forward we should keep the topics of conversation to work."

His lip quirked and just like that, his emotions shifted back to distant amusement. Damn him for confusing her. Damn him for making her act like a fool. "Such politeness. I'm sure I made you uncomfortable talking about things that are . . . messy."

She managed not to flinch, but her temper rose. "This will be a long journey, and we need to work closely together. Distractions from either of us would be unwelcome at this point."

"Such as sex?"

This time, she jerked. Her glass tipped, but she grabbed it in time and righted it. Naked humor carved out the lines of his face. "Do you like to shock women, Sawyer?" she mocked. "You won't find me that easy to manage. I've been harassed, propositioned, and insulted, and I've dealt with an array of masculine temper tantrums. I've seen it all and can handle it. I *prefer* to keep our relationship mutually beneficial for all involved, but if you want to play hardball, that's fine, too. *Capisce*?"

• • •

Sawyer studied the woman across the table. Her gorgeous brown eyes snapped with leashed anger and a banked sensuality she kept ruthlessly in check. It was official.

He was nuts about her.

Her mind alone brought him to ecstatic heights he'd missed. The thrust and parry of conversation engaged his intellect, while his body hummed with pleasure from her physical presence. She was his feminine equal in all forms except her refusal to admit she wanted him.

But she did.

Every hitched breath she tried to mask played like Mozart to his ears. Her control was fierce, but he spotted breaks in her armor in ways she hadn't counted on. The quick flare of interest in her eyes at the mention of the word *sex*. The slight tremble in her fingers as she gripped the fork. Didn't she know her proper white bra against a silk white blouse was a man's private fantasy? The barest shadow of her nipples pushed against her bra and begged for freedom. She had a delicious habit of running her tongue over her bottom lip that forced a man to imagine what she'd taste like. And that damn red scarf? He'd put it to much more practical uses then entwining it around her delicate neck for fashion purposes. Namely making sure she couldn't move while he stripped her of that very proper blouse and bra and pleasured her breasts. Slowly. On his terms.

Of course, the most intriguing part was her refusal to acknowledge any of it.

Her body was in lockdown. How sweet to imagine breaking her out of that prison and being the one who reaped the benefit? He wondered what asshole convinced her to ignore her physical need. Why else would a vibrant, sophisticated woman hide behind work?

He'd pushed during dinner because he needed a full analysis. She was right, though. He'd never risk the contract to scratch an itch, and he bet she dealt with a lot of men who treated her like crap. Perhaps it was time to tell her a bit more of his truth so she clearly knew his motivations.

For now, she deserved an answer.

"I never meant to offend you, Julietta." Her name melted over his tongue like a Godiva truffle. Sweet and dark and rich. "Let's get something straight. I have no need to threaten or bully a woman into bed. I enjoy sex and giving pleasure. I find you fascinating, complex, and hot as hell. I also think you may be the only woman I've met in the past few years who made me crave to break a few rules just to put my hands on her. In her. Over her. But if you go screaming foul play and harassment, I'll politely back away and leave you alone. *Capisce*? Now breathe."

At his command, the air let loose from her lungs in a rush. She sat frozen in her chair, eyes wide with a combination of shock, confusion, and a touch of fear. The fear mixed with a flash of pure longing. Yes, she wanted him, too. Interesting. Why wouldn't she act on it? Why did a man showing interest freak her out so much?

The waiter glided by, cleared their plates, and asked if they wanted dessert.

"No," she said firmly.

"Tiramisu, please," he countered. "Two espressos with sambuca."

She tossed him a dirty look, and he struggled with the instinct to kiss it right off her. How could a woman who used no lipstick have such a succulent mouth? All pouty and pale pink. "I hope this isn't going to be a precursor of your need to run things," she said. "Though I appreciate your forthrightness regarding the initial attraction to me, I assure you it will fade. I have no time to engage in affairs."

Her prim tone made a surge of lust hit his gut and spread. He shifted in his chair and adjusted the napkin. "Why do you think it will fade?"

Her gaze shifted. She threw back her shoulders, but he

caught the tension in each fine bone of her body. "It always does."

"Do you want me?"

This time, she couldn't hold back a gasp. "We just met yesterday. I don't go jumping into bed with strange men or make decisions regarding my attraction after one dinner."

"Sometimes that's the best time to trust your instincts. The moment we rationalize chemistry, we risk losing it forever."

His words seemed to strike a chord. Regret dimmed the light in her eyes. Protectiveness surged through him and rattled his calm. He ached to pull her into his arms and hold her, rock her, soothe the sadness lurking beneath the cool surface. But she didn't belong to him, so he had no rights.

Yet.

Dessert arrived, and she chose to keep her silence. They nibbled on the cocoa biscuit and savored the rich cream of soaked ladyfingers and cinnamon. The sting of liquor in the dark espresso brew hit Sawyer's belly hard and heated his veins. He watched as Julietta's thoughts scrambled, evident in the slight frown marring her brow and the concentration stamped on her face. The bill came and he paid, sparing her a quick warning glance when she opened her mouth to protest. When the dessert plate was scraped clean and the cups emptied, she patted her lips with the napkin and met his gaze.

"I think we're going to make a great team," she said

slowly. "But I'm not interested in bringing this into the bedroom. I have my reasons, and I appreciate your candor. You're an attractive man, and in other circumstances, I would jump at the chance to engage in a hot affair. Please respect my decision, and don't push me any further. Just . . . don't."

Her voice broke slightly on the last word. His heart squeezed with a need he didn't recognize, but he knew the rules. Created the rules. Both parties must be willing in order to move forward. An element of trust proved key to keeping the relationship burning at a high flame without blazing. The alpha wolf in him howled with lust and challenge to change her mind and make her beg for torturing him. Sawyer waited for the mess of emotions to finish racing through him before he wrested control and blanked out his thoughts.

A smile curved his lips. "As you wish," he murmured.

Her body loosened. Her tongue flicked across her lower lip again, and she smiled. "*Grazie.*"

He nodded, and she rose. Shrugged on her jacket. Grabbed her purse. Sawyer guided her out of the restaurant with a hand at her elbow and tried to calm the rush of adrenaline tightening his muscles and strangling his breath. His last thought flashed like a mantra over and over again.

Let the challenge begin.

Chapter Four

Julietta picked her head up and stretched the kinks from her neck. The stack of files was only half cleared, and her cup of cappuccino had long grown cold. A dull throb behind her eyes warned her time was almost up. *Mio Dio,* how long had she been working? A quick glance at her watch confirmed four steady hours with no break. A sigh broke from her lips and surprised her. Usually she enjoyed her Saturday mornings in her apartment, taking care of all the loose ends she had no time to close during the week. Coffee, paper, her laptop, a little music, and she was content. Except . . .

She stared out her window. The gleam of sun rarely seen in the moody month of February strained from the thick clouds in a screw-you gesture. Julietta unfurled her legs from her chair and strode over to the window, peering at the scene below her. The roar of motorcycles and mopeds echoed from the streets in an attempt to squeeze in as much riding as possible on a nice day.

She pressed her palm to the cool pane and pondered the idea. Funny: Since her last encounter with Sawyer, the rare edge of wildness nipped at her usual logical self, daring her to break routine and echo the sentiment of the current weather.

Screw it. Work could wait.

She made the decision and didn't look back. She was going riding for the rest of the afternoon. Her fingers itched to grab the bars of her bike and stop thinking for a little while. With her consistent workaholic tendencies and slight OCD, she tipped the scales of exhaustion too many times. At least she'd found an acceptable outlet other than therapy.

Motorcycles.

She paused to fix the slight tilt of the three photos on the mantel and headed to the bedroom. She changed in record time, donning supple Prada pants, boots, and a simple cashmere sweater. She shrugged on her leather jacket, took her helmet down from the top of the closet, stuffed her phone in her hobo bag, and left.

She walked the necessary blocks until she came to the small storage garage where she kept her bike. The wind was frisky, but she'd layered enough to stay decently warm for the trip. Mentally calculating the miles she wanted to accomplish, she decided on an easy route toward Navigli.

Julietta stepped in front of her secret obsession and her skin tingled as if she gazed at a lover.

Perfection.

Naked twisted metal and sleek black made up the machine, which was in a class by itself. The brand-new Moto Morini Corsaro had all the elements she admired and demanded in a bike. Speed. Lightweight. Agility. And raw, sexy, growling hp.

Her tummy dipped, and she tugged on her leather gloves. Her hidden obsession with fast bikes came straight from her brother, Michael, but her sisters just didn't understand it. Especially because she was the straitlaced one in the family. How many times had she picked Michael's brain about his racecars and tried to steal his motorcycles for a ride? She'd dreamed of having the bike of all bikes on her own terms, and finally she'd achieved her goal.

She lifted her leg to slide over the seat, and her cell rang.

Porca vacca. She almost ignored it, but too many years of habit took over, so she had to at least glance at the ID. She reached in her bag and pulled the phone out. After looking, she let her finger hesitate on the button only a second before pushing it.

"Yes?"

"*Ciao bella.* Why don't you sound happier to hear from me?"

She tamped down on her impatience and reminded herself this was the deal of the century. Politeness was key. "I'm sorry, Sawyer, I was just getting ready to go out for a bit. How can I help you?"

"Oh, good. I need to go over something in the contract. Why don't you stop by my place and we'll finish it up?"

Julietta scowled at the phone. "It's not a good time right now. Perhaps tomorrow?"

Silence hummed. An irritated masculine silence. "I'm not one to invade a business partner's personal life, but this is a huge undertaking for Purity. I need to know you're on board in this delicate time. One hundred percent."

She practically spit into the receiver. "I've just spent the bulk of my Saturday at the computer. I'm completely on board, so to speak. Can we settle it over the phone?"

"No. Where are you going? Can I meet you?"

She stared at her bike with a lustful need that shook her bones. "I'm going riding for the next few hours. How about I stop by afterward and we'll settle the items up for negotiation?"

"Riding what? A bicycle?"

She couldn't help the automatic scoff that came from her mouth. "No: motorcycle."

He paused for a beat. "Perfect. Give me fifteen minutes and I'll meet you at the Duomo."

Julietta gaped. "What? No—no, you can't go with me. I'm going motorcycle riding."

"I heard you the first time. I promise not to bully you with my bike. See you soon."

The phone clicked.

She blinked and tried desperately to keep her sanity. This was not happening. Her peaceful, stress-blowing bike ride was turning into a business trip with a man she needed to avoid at all costs. She analyzed the options of not showing or calling back to cancel, but she already sensed the domineering man wouldn't answer. And if she didn't show up for their impromptu meeting, he could decide to pull the contract.

Julietta blew out a breath of disgust and climbed on the bike. The low thrum of the engine kicked into gear, and she took off toward the center of town, weaving expertly through traffic and keeping her speed down until she hit open turf and let it rip.

She gave him credit. Her watch just hit the fifteen mark when she saw him pull up. Julietta tried hard not to show any surprise at his choice of ride. She'd expected a brash American Harley, but damn him, he'd managed to up his game without even trying.

She flipped up her visor and flicked him a cool glance. "Nice bike. Where's your Harley?"

The total hotness of male perfection on the MV Agusta F4CC was criminal. In faded, tight jeans, a leather bomber jacket, and vintage riding boots, he cut a bad-boy-meets-surfer figure that almost killed her. Almost. He slowly unbuckled his helmet and slid it off his head to cradle in the crook of his arm. Then shook out his shaggy blond hair. His quick grin flashed that crooked front tooth. "You're not cutting up on the American phenomenon of the Harley, are you darlin'? That could get you shot in the U.S."

She gave a delicate shrug. He never needed to know she secretly loved the American classic. "Good thing I'm not there. How'd you get one of those? There were only one hundred made."

He dropped his voice to a dirty whisper. "I know people. They owe me favors."

Her spine tingled with anticipation. The hungry look as his gaze roved over her body caught her hard, but she rallied. "What do we need to discuss?"

He laughed low. "Nothing at the moment. Where are we going?"

She drew her brows together and tried to be firm. "Nowhere. We'll discuss business, and then I'm going riding."

"Where?"

She shrugged. "Wherever I feel like."

"Sounds like a plan. We'll stop for a break and talk business later. You lead."

Julietta squirmed with the need to wipe the smug look off his face. "I'm trying to be polite here, but you're making it difficult. I don't feel like making social conversation today."

"Who said anything about conversation?"

Her spit dried up and she held back an actual pant. Those full lips quirked as if he knew her body's reaction. "If you can't keep up, I'm not waiting for you. This is my time," she said.

His slow grin taunted and pushed all the right buttons. Or the wrong ones. "I'll admit my surprise at your choice of The Pirate. But can you handle her, little girl? Perhaps I'll be the one waiting for you to catch up."

Julietta snapped her helmet down, kicked her bike into gear, and gave him a pitying look. "See you on the other side."

She took off.

They rode through the city, battled traffic, and finally hit stride. The streets opened up and spit them out as the city rolled by and the gorgeous hills of the Alps shimmered in the distance like a mirage. The sun fought like the king it was and triumphed over the grayness for a few hours. Traffic was lighter than normal for a Saturday, and she headed toward Navigli. Julietta rode hard, pushing the machine into full gear and squeezing out more horsepower. The flash of the road underneath the wheels, the tug of the cold wind in her nostrils, the whiz of vivid blue and green and yellow of the colorful buildings all rose up and mixed together in a symphony of sweetness to her soul. For a little while, on a fast bike, in her beloved land, she was truly free.

They stopped for a break at a small café near the canal and bought lunch. They parked their bikes and stretched their legs in a leisurely walk. The market was open and bustling, and a boat slugged slowly down the water, charming the tourists with an old-world yet Bohemian influence. Filled with endless trinkets, clothes, food, and jewelry, Navigli boasted one of the most wonderful markets in Milan. In the evening, the place came alive with a variety of hip-hop nightclubs, cafés, and shopping. With sunset approaching soon, the crowds would build, so Julietta stuffed their water and uneaten wrapped food into her saddlebag and took off again

She gave him credit. Sawyer never said a word.

But his gaze followed every swing of her hips and caught her sneaky half glances. The man's ass was comparable to David's, and Michelangelo's statue had brought her to tears.

Julietta looked at the sky. Not too much longer before dark hit. She craved the bite of adrenaline she usually achieved from the closure of a good business deal. But she'd just found another way to get her hit.

Julietta stopped her bike, cocked her hip, and made the offer. "I'm heading toward Castello Sforzesco. There's a nice open road to let the bikes breathe. Let's see who gets there first."

Surprise skittered across his face. "You wanna race?"

"Call it what you want. I plan on welcoming you at the gate."

He threw his head back and laughed long and hard. The

sound was sweeter than Mozart and sexier than Pavarotti. "You've got to be kidding. This baby has more balls than most bikes on the market."

She smiled sweetly. "I'm sure you both do. See you there."

Julietta's skin prickled with anticipation, and the blood in her veins heated and rushed with the challenge.

She took off toward Castello Sforzesco in a race to beat the dying sun and the man beside her. Julietta hated to admit he rode like a pro and handled the meatiness of the bike with a grace most men couldn't imitate. She'd ridden with many men throughout her lifetime: some family, some friends, some lovers. Usually she was disappointed in the aggression and selfishness of the rider.

Not Sawyer. He respected the power of Claudio Castiglioni's prized possession, never trying to reach the 196 mph the bike was reputed to achieve, and instead using the mechanics like a lover, coaxing the best with a seductive skill that made her soaking wet between her thighs. He was also a dominant driver, fully in control through each bend of the road, fiercely concentrating on his goal.

Brash for brash, he should've won. But Julietta had been racing for years, knew the streets like an old lover, and excelled at weaving in and out through obstacles in the bustling city. She eventually took the lead and held it tight, pushing the limit of speed and agility as the rush burned through her and took command.

When she finally reached the castle, she was a few beats

ahead. The towering stone ruins dominated the view, but the quiet park behind the structure was her main focus. She cut off the bike, unfastened her helmet, and waited for him to cut his engine.

Sawyer slid off the now-quiet bike. She waited for his response and prepped for a cutting remark. Or a joke. Or an excuse.

But he didn't speak. Just grabbed her saddlebag with their lunch and allowed her to lead him through the cobbled pathways to an open area. The ground was still cold, so they settled for the carved benches scattered amidst the towering trees and picked a spot where the Castello was perfectly positioned for study.

She loved riding along the road where the stunning clock tower thrust into the sky, surrounded by a mass of carved stone. A massive water fountain welcomed visitors in, the multiple streams of water spitting out in the marble circle and catching the last rays of light. The cobbled paths wound in an intricate pattern where tourists could stroll, shop, or grab a quick bite from a market vendor. Being close to such antique beauty reminded her that life was long and many things didn't last, but the things that mattered would.

Sawyer remained silent, as if he too was under the spell of a good ride. He unwrapped their sandwiches, and they shared the food: hard, crusty bread; fat, salty olives; and the delicious small salami *strolghino di culatello,* paired with creamy sheep's milk Gorgonzola blue cheese. The scone with strawberry butter added a bit of sweetness to complete the meal.

Her shoulders relaxed even more and she ate in perfect solitude, looking out at the view. Her mind was finally blank, as if she had just departed from the ashrams of India after a weeklong meditation.

"Hell of a bike for a hell of a rider. Mind sharing how you learned to handle that thing, let alone know what it can do?"

Pride etched her face. "My brother, Michael, raced cars on the circuit. His love of good and fast machinery extended to motorcycles, and I got hooked. He was kind enough not to tell me good girls don't ride bad bikes, and he taught me everything he knew."

Sawyer shook his head and took a long slug of water. "Nice. Most women overcompensate for their lack of brute strength. But you used it to your advantage. It was like watching a poetry slam. Heat and beauty and grace at top speed. What's the best bike you ever owned?"

"I still have it. The classic Moto Morini three and a half Vintage."

"No. Fucking. Way."

She leaned forward. "Yes way. Bright red, classic lines, and if you ever heard the motor, you'd swear you were dreaming. Took years to restore, and people are begging to buy it all the time." Julietta pursed her lips. "Like I'd sell to anyone who wouldn't ride it. That would be a tragedy."

His gaze dropped and rested on her mouth. Her next

breath came at a struggle, but she dug her nails into her palm to ground herself. This man was dangerous, and she refused to mix business with pleasure. Even though he had a love and respect for bikes.

"I agree. Beautiful things that are underused is a crime."

The double innuendo stole her sanity and immediately her nipples peaked to attention. He leaned forward and lifted his hand. Slowly, he closed the distance, obviously reaching out to touch her. Mesmerized by the hunter he was, she took a few seconds to react to his intentions.

"Don't." She jerked her chin away. "I thought we agreed to stick to business."

He lifted his palm up. "Sorry. You have a smear of butter on your cheek. I was just going to wipe it off."

She ducked her head to hide the faint blush and grabbed a napkin. Again, that distant amusement emanated from his aura. Like he cared. But didn't. Like he was above all the messiness of emotion and drama, and she was the current plaything. "What was the issue with the contract?"

"Section B, clause three. You forgot to initial."

She stared at him. "You hunted me down, bullied me into a bike ride, and it was about my signature? Our lawyers could have handled the issue in a second."

"I like to use a hands-on approach. In all aspects."

Julietta snorted. "Where do you come up with this stuff? It's like a landmine of a conversation with you, all roads leading to sex."

That got him. He lifted his brow and shifted his weight on the bench. "Is there something wrong with sex?"

She couldn't help it. The dare was all over his face, and his desire to play her for a fool using business as an excuse burned within. Julietta moved in slowly and stopped inches from his mouth. His breath caught, then the sweet rush of air from him released over her lips, smelling of mint and sugar and sin. Her tongue slid out to lick her lower lip, and a tiny groan escaped him. Her hand rested on the hard muscle of his thigh and squeezed. "Nothing wrong with sex. When the situation calls for it."

His voice dragged like the scrape of gravel. "How about this situation?"

A husky laugh escaped her. "Not gonna happen when we're working together."

"You didn't initial. Technically, the contract is void."

She caressed upward over the sweep of denim, hit his belt buckle, and slipped her hand under the leather jacket. This was now fun. Teasing a man and walking away was a game she rarely played, but he needed a lesson. Washboard abs tightened under her touch, and those amber eyes darkened. "Still not gonna happen."

"Care to tell me why?"

She grinned with pure satisfaction, seduction, and a hint of tart. "The one with the biggest balls doesn't always win, Sawyer Wells."

He muttered a curse. "So who does?"

Julietta pursed her lips. "The one who can go the distance."

Satisfaction poured through her. How was that for an innuendo? Heady with getting the last word, she began to pull back out of the danger zone.

Too late.

He moved so fast she never had a chance. With a strength that amazed her, he lifted her off the bench and onto his lap, holding her arms tight at her sides so she was a bit off balance. Her struggle was instinctual but quickly faded under his calm, implacable demeanor.

She had made a fatal mistake.

And now she was gonna pay.

. . .

The woman was driving him mad.

He was uncomfortably hard, his erection torturing the hard denim and roaring for freedom. The wind caught her scent—full of leather and musk and cocoa— and drenched his nostrils, wrecking his brain and his dick in one effective swoop. Her body was trim yet full, from the curves of her breasts to the lush swell of her rear, now firmly cushioned in the notch of his thighs. Her face reflected the uncertainty of her position and a slight regret at pushing him too far. Good. At least the woman sensed his need to dominate and take. A crazy lust swirled through his system from the mind-blowing twist of hidden sensuality, cool snarkiness, and razor wit of the woman on his lap.

He had almost hit the floor when he pulled up on his bike and caught sight of her. Dressed in bad-ass black leather with thigh-high boots and her hair stuffed up in a red helmet, she was droolworthy. He didn't know any woman who rode a bike, let alone appreciated them. The way she bore down in their race showed the hard-core spirit of a woman who enjoyed winning, and her ability to pick through every obstacle in front of her without slowing almost made him have an embarrassing situation.

Almost.

And she'd won. He revered a good competition and rarely lost. The idea she was even able to cross the finish line before him made him want to rip off her clothes and win in another way. A much more pleasant one.

He tightened his grip. He figured she wanted to taunt him, but now his goal was to make her mad enough to lose some of that precious control. For some reason, his gut told him anger would get past her barriers and allow some of that seething sexual energy to spout out. She held back big-time, and there was something else other than the obstacle of business between them. Until he found out what, he wouldn't be sleeping soundly at night.

Her hair had come undone—her clip had broken. Sawyer had only before seen the coal-black strands neatly twisted up on the top of her head. What he now spotted sealed his decision to get her into his bed at all costs.

A shimmering waterfall of silk spilled past her shoulders and hit her waist. Rapunzel hair. He had nasty visions of holding all that hair while she was on her knees taking him deep, of the glossy pin-straight strands brushing his thighs, his stomach, and his chest as she reared up over him. For a second, his mind blanked, and he didn't know if he was capable of not taking her right here in the public park.

Her clipped words dragged him back to the moment. "What do you think you're doing? Let me go; this is unprofessional."

Damn, she was hot. He kept hold and chuckled. "And what you did was professional? Taunting me?"

She stuck out her chin. "You deserved it. You need to stop talking about sex in hidden meanings."

"Fair enough. You're wet, aren't you?"

A combination of shock, outrage, and lust glimmered in her eyes. "You did not just say that to me," she hissed. "You go too far."

"Your body gives you away." He slid a hand over her rear, under her jacket, and around to her front where he cupped her breast. Her nipple stabbed into his palm past the fabric of her sweater, past the barrier of her bra, and demanded freedom. "I can see your pulse hammering at your neck. Your nipples are stiff, your pupils are dilated, and you can't catch your breath."

"It's cold and the ride was hard."

His dick twitched. She was fucking magnificent, refusing to surrender even a bit. She could be his greatest challenge. "I know another thing that's hard," he muttered.

"See! Another innuendo. Let me up."

"One kiss."

She stilled. Was that fear or regret on her face? What was she so nervous about? "Why?"

"Prove it. Prove you're not interested right here, right now."

She rolled her eyes. "You've dated too many blondes. This has 'sucker' written all over it."

Sawyer fought a grin. "You kiss me. Just once. You're not into it, or me, I won't push anymore. You hold the reins."

"You won't try to touch me?"

"Nope." Regretfully, he removed his hand from her breast and dropped his arms to the side. She shifted her weight so she wasn't off balance, and Sawyer swallowed a painful groan.

"My terms? Then you leave me alone?"

"Yes."

A tiny frown creased her brow. He waited patiently until she finally nodded. "Okay. Then we move on as business partners. No weird stuff."

"Agreed."

As if preparing for a test, she dragged in a breath, shut her eyes, and leaned forward. Her lips touched his, super soft and sweet, like the spun cotton candy he lusted after as a kid and beyond. Tentative. Honest. Pure.

Her body softened on his lap, and all the signs of her arousal flared to life. It took every ounce of power in his being to accept her kiss on her terms, but when she finally lifted her mouth, the surprise in those dark eyes told him more than he'd learned about her so far.

Oh, yeah, she was afraid. Of him. Of her reaction. She wanted him as badly as he wanted her. But she didn't know what to do with it, and there was a major blockage in the way of her physical reaction, as if she didn't allow herself to ever slip over the edge of not being in control.

Another piece of the puzzle slid into place.

She drew back. Her tongue slid over her bottom lip and probably caught his taste, since her body gave a tiny little shudder. Sawyer realized that chaste kiss was sexier than an openmouthed, tongue-mingling mating, because it was the first time she'd given him something on her own.

He swore she'd be giving him a hell of a lot more.

"Okay? Satisfied?"

"Yes."

She hesitated, as if not trusting him to give up so easily. But she quickly pulled herself together, scrambled off his lap, and began packing up the bag. "We better go. It'll be dark soon."

He didn't answer. They threw out the trash, walked to their bikes, and donned their gloves. "Thanks for letting me ride with you. I'll express the page to your office and have my assistant come get it when you're done."

"Fine." She tried to stuff her glorious hair back into the helmet, and Sawyer caught the tremble in her fingers. "I assume you'll stick with your word and not bother me again in a—personal way?"

"No."

Her head shot up. "What?"

He rocked back on his heels, enjoying the hell out of her. "I said if you didn't respond to that kiss, on your terms, I'd leave you alone. But you did. You want me just as badly as I want you."

Her mouth dropped open, then closed with a snap. She fisted her hands. "I didn't respond! I told you I'm not interested in taking this relationship into the bedroom, and you need to respect that. *Porca vacca,* you are unbelievable!"

He grinned. "That kiss proved a lot of things, including your interest. Something's holding you back though; I'm just not sure what it is. But your comment made a lot of sense to me. It's not about having balls."

"Huh?"

He gave a wink. "It's about going the distance. Which I intend to go with you. See you Monday."

He slid onto his bike, revved it up, and roared down the pathway, leaving her standing by the castle in the dying sun with a shocked look on her face.

Chapter Five

Sawyer stared at the current shithole, which used to be his pristinely kept kitchen, and tamped down his impatience.

Again.

Soda spilled on the counter. A bag of chips open and growing stale by the hour. His gleaming stainless steel stove smeared with some type of dark liquid and spots of burnt cheese. His boots crunched on the white marble floors as he shoved the chips back in the cabinet, recycled the soda bottles, and dragged a sponge over the stove.

Didn't parents usually count to ten when they were about to explode? Okay, he liked his place clean, but he was a guy, and even this was tough. Ever since the kid moved in, his already thinning patience stretched to epic proportions.

The original plan to stay at a hotel didn't make sense. He'd be in Milan for a while and needed to oversee each part of the construction of Purity, so he decided to rent an apartment close to headquarters. Back in New York, his new apprentice stayed in an adjoining suite at a five-star hotel, so they both had privacy but remained close enough so Sawyer could play guardian. Of course, the benefits of a hotel included constant maid and room service, so he rarely worried about the state the kid kept the room or if he was properly fed.

When he got to Milan, he decided to rent the luxurious loft and move the boy in with him. After all, he was too young to trust alone, though he acted like a twist of an old bitter man and a young biker gone bad. And the space was pretty damn big, which should have meant plenty of room for both of them.

Wrong.

Sawyer threw the sponge back in the sink and wondered for the billionth time if he was nuts for getting a kid he didn't know off the streets of New York City moved in with him, and involved in his business. After all, he had enough on his list of things to do without including helping a homeless teen with a sarcastic wit who challenged him at every turn. Maybe it was the angry, lost look in his eyes that dragged Sawyer back to his past and made him want to prove someone could give a shit in this world. That maybe he could help and make a difference. God knew his foster brother Danny had never gotten that chance.

Sawyer only planned to assist Wolfe for a few weeks and get him on his feet. Instead, eight months rolled by, and Sawyer made no move to get rid of him. Of course, the teen proved to be wicked smart and a big help in getting Purity off the ground. Before long, Sawyer decided to hire him as a permanent fixture as his assistant and see what happened.

If they didn't kill each other first.

Sawyer made his way past the living room—decorated in simple masculine tones of beige and brown and currently strewn with dirty underwear, jeans, and socks—and followed the smell to the back room. Silence greeted him, but he knew the iPod earbuds were stuffed in Wolfe's ears, so he'd hear nothing anyway. Instead of knocking, Sawyer pushed open the door.

A pair of surly blue eyes stared back in rebellion. Sawyer ignored the look and tapped his ear in a demand for the kid to take the earbuds out. Vincent, now named Wolfe, shifted on the bed and muttered a curse. Ripping the bud from his right ear, above which his hair was shaved, he glared. "What?"

"How about cleaning up your mess?"

A snort. "You got a cleaning lady, so why do you care?"

"She only comes once a week, and it already smells. Ever hear of a hamper?"

"You leave your stuff out."

Sawyer refused to sigh; it was so cliché. "Yeah, but not clothes that are breeding. I'm letting you crash here so you don't have to pay for a room. The least you can do is buy food once in a while."

Wolfe's response was a long sigh. "Sure. Sorry."

"Why don't you get out of this place for a while? Take a walk. Shop. Do something."

The kid looked at him as if he'd won the dummy award of the year. The gold hoop in his brow and in his ear winked in mockery. Why did Sawyer suddenly feel like shuffling his feet? How could a nineteen-year-old boy intimidate the crap out of him? He reminded himself to be patient. Patience and understanding would eventually allow him to win. The kid had been through a lot, and he was supposed to be helping. "Why? So I can wear those ridiculous clothes you bought me and parade myself around like I'm some kind of designer toy? Or sip espresso and pretend I've got my shit together to score a supermodel? No, thanks. I'll stay here."

Sawyer glanced at his regular uniform that rarely changed. Faded jeans with a hole in the knee. Battered black boots. White T-shirt. The matching leather bomber jacket completed the look of bad-ass, young Johnny Depp wannabe in the current century. Not that he cared what the kid wore, as long as he cleaned it up a bit for the office. He tried to change the subject. "You don't have to wear the clothes if you don't like them. I thought you'd enjoy getting out to explore. Your Italian is amazing—you picked it up faster than I ever did."

"It's a sissy language."

Sawyer bit back a laugh. The kid was a pisser. "Fine. Stay here, but don't steal my last bottles of Peretti—you're still underage. And don't use my house as a base to get women. Did you contact the sales team for me on those issues I pointed out?"

"Yeah, it's done."

"Thanks, Vincent."

The name slipped from his lips before he remembered. Hot blue eyes narrowed with rage, and the boy's fists clenched. Sawyer stood still, as the kid battled with his inner demons. Demons Sawyer knew way too much about. "Don't ever call me that again," the kid hissed. "Ever. My name is Wolfe."

He threw his hands up. "Sorry. Still getting used to it."

Sawyer turned on his heel and left the boy alone. Shit, talking to him was like crossing a viper pit. One wrong step and you lost a fucking leg. He must have been crazy to think he could make some sort of difference. Even worse, he'd had a big enough ego to drag the kid from New York all the way to Italy to show him the business. They shared no blood. Didn't owe him a thing. And the kid—Wolfe, as of now—had stolen from him, then spit in his face when he threatened his ass with jail time.

The legal court records stated his name was Vincent Soldano. Three months ago, the boy told him he would no longer answer to the name and requested to be called Wolfe.

The significance of his appeal burned deep and stirred bad memories that Sawyer still battled. Hell, he'd done the same exact thing. Remade himself and taken a new name in an attempt to start fresh. Creating a new identity helped him let the old crap go. Still, he occasionally slipped and the old name Vincent escaped. He needed to try harder to remember.

A half smile tugged at his lips. But damn Wolfe had fire in the pit of his belly. Sawyer realized immediately fire like that took a person one of two ways: toward a life of crime where a sharp brain and some decent skills could score money to deaden enough of the pain. Or to the high road.

Which usually sucked, wasn't as profitable, and hurt a hell of a lot more.

He offered the high road. The kid took it. The rest was fucking history. And a dirty home.

His cell phone buzzed and cut off his thoughts. He didn't recognize the number but punched the button anyway.

The familiar voice drifted across the line, and Sawyer froze. Memories shot past: a tangle of good, bad, and a turning point that he'd never forget. He switched to Italian and exchanged a few words of greeting. She spoke for a while and he listened until she fell silent, awaiting his answer. He closed his eyes and dragged in a breath. Tension squeezed the sides of his head, but he refused to take a stroll into the past, which reminded him of a jacked-up Tim Burton movie rather than Disney.

"Yes. Thank you for the invitation. I'll be there."

He hung up the phone and went to change.

• • •

Julietta walked up the cobblestone pathway and began to truly relax for the first time in the past week. The muscles in her neck and shoulders eased with each tap of her heel, and the warmth of her family home embraced her in a comforting hug of familiarity.

The three-tiered terra-cotta villa held simple lines and soaring archways. Michael had urged Mama to leave so he could buy her a castle befitting the empire she built, but she laughed and announced she'd die in the home that Papa had lived in. Julietta didn't blame her.

More than five acres of land sprawled in every direction and allowed an onlooker to gaze upon the sweeping beauty of the Alps. Bergamo was the perfect place for her family to grow up in, a combination of old and new world split into two tiers—Citta Bassa and Citta Alta—the lower and upper cities. This home boasted wrought-iron balconies, cooly shaded patios, and endless gardens of lemon and olive trees. Julietta opened the door and made her way toward the kitchen.

Heavily carved pine tables and chairs dominated the space that called for long family dinners and endless courses, and stood as a witness of time gone by. Hand-sewn rugs accessorized the wooden floors. The warm Tuscan colors of red, gold, and green swirled before her and tantalized all of her senses. The sharp tang of citrus and salty olives, sweet basil and rich red tomato. An endless length of granite countertop slashed down the right side of the kitchen and held various jars and baskets of fresh fruit. Steam wafted from pots of boiling water; platters contained rolled-up meats; and slices of Italian bread crowded the table. A smile curved her lips, and peace settled over her.

She was home.

"Mama?"

Mama Conte turned from her station in front of the stove. "Oh, my goodness, I didn't even hear you. Damn ears. I used to catch the click of the window from miles away when your sister tried to sneak out to meet Dominick. Now I can't even hear when my front door slams."

Julietta laughed and gave her a hug. After birthing four children, launching a successful bakery empire, and burying her husband, her mother still possessed a driving force built into her core. Her long gray hair was always twisted back in a bun, and her arthritis was serious enough to warrant a cane to help her walk. She'd had a few scares with her heart problems, but she'd held strong the past few years.

She wore her favorite apron—taken out each Sunday—marked with various stains from years gone by but always freshly laundered. The logo of La Dolce Famiglia was imprinted on it, and it had been given to her as a gift from

Papa after their first bakery launched. For a little while, wrapped up in her childhood home with her mama at the stove, Julietta was happy. Safe.

She stowed her bag away, grabbed her apron, and settled herself at the table to chop tomatoes and peppers. "Is Uncle Brian coming over for dinner?" she asked, expertly dicing the vegetables.

"No, he's taking the kids somewhere after church."

"Is all this food just for me?" she teased. "Stop trying to fatten me up, Mama. I'll have to buy a new wardrobe."

Her mother paused, as if thinking about her next words. "We shall have one guest for dinner."

"Who?"

"You will see. For now, tell me what is going on at work. Did you close the deal with The Palazzo as you had hoped? I know you've been working on it for months."

Julietta tried to fight off the disappointment of failure and squared her shoulders. "No, they made their decision a few weeks ago. I lost the deal."

"I'm sorry, sweet girl. I know that meant a lot to you, but it is not needed. Everything happens for a reason. A better deal will be presented."

The truth of her mother's words struck home. An image of Sawyer sprang before her eyes: those sculpted, devilish lips quirking in amusement, as if he knew she'd eventually end up in his bed. At least he had backed off and hadn't tried to push. Still, she needed to be on guard at all times. She didn't trust him to play by any rules. Julietta cleared her throat. "Umm, actually, I'm signing a pretty big contract, Mama. For a new hotel chain called Purity. We'll be exclusive to the hotels, and the first one launches in Milan within the year."

Pride etched out the lines of her mother's face. "Well done. Why don't we celebrate with some Moscato? I have a bottle chilling in the refrigerator, and we'll open it at dinner. Perhaps, now that this big deal has been signed, you will finally ease up the workload?"

Julietta's confidence slipped a notch and she avoided her mother's gaze. Of course. Business was never enough when compared to marriage and love and babies. She swallowed back the ridiculous sting of tears, wondering if she was getting her period. What was up with her lately? She was so emotional and . . . girly. "Actually, I'll need to work harder," she said lightly. "But I enjoy every moment. I'm doing exactly what I always dreamed."

Mama Conte sliced off a piece of fresh mozzarella and handed it to her with bread. The rich, creamy texture sank into the warm dough, and Julietta swallowed in pleasure. "I know you enjoy your career. Without you, I don't know if La Dolce Famiglia would have succeeded, even with Michael at the helm. You have a gift. I just want you to share it with someone special."

She lifted a shoulder in a half shrug. Typical motherly dream. Still, the comment bit hard, as if what Julietta had done with her life wasn't enough. It wasn't as if she could confess to her mother something was wrong with her, and she couldn't connect with a man. She pushed the depression to the back of her mind and tried to concentrate on enjoying her visit. "Perhaps one day," she said brightly.

"*Si.* One day."

A knock at the door saved her from further inquiry. She wiped her hands on the towel and grinned. "Ah, our mysterious visitor. I bet it's Father Richard; he's always happy to eat your cooking." She moved to the front door and opened it.

Her mouth fell open.

Sawyer Wells stood in the entrance. His business suit had been replaced by a pair of comfortable khakis, a thick cableknit cream sweater, and Versace leather croc boots. His hair swung free and touched his shoulders in a delicious mess of golden waves. He held a bouquet of freshly picked flowers and a bottle of red wine. "Hey."

She stared.

He cocked his head and seemed to fight amusement. "Umm, can I come in?"

She recovered her voice and lowered it to a hiss. "What are you doing here?"

One brow shot up. "I guess you didn't realize I was invited to dinner."

She blinked. "Huh?"

"Real wordsmith out of the office, aren't you? Your mother invited me to dinner."

Julietta jerked back. "Impossible."

A voice from the hallway drifted to the open door. "Julietta, stop torturing the man and let him in. He is correct."

Sawyer grinned. "Told ya."

He stepped around her and waltzed past. Her fingers clenched around the door in an effort to keep standing. After a few deep breaths, she followed him in. "How beautiful," Mama Conte crooned, inhaling the scent of roses and lilies. "Julietta, can you put these in the vase from the living room? Sawyer, can you open the bottle of Moscato? It's in the refrigerator. I was just told Julietta closed a big deal, and we're celebrating."

Sawyer rocked on his heels, obviously amused at the whole scenario. "Big deal, huh? Of course."

"Mama, what's going on? I didn't know you and Sawyer were . . . close?"

Her mother's head snapped around. "He is a friend of Max's, and it is Sunday. Of course, I would invite him to dine with us. My home is open to all, especially one known to my family. I am sure you agree with me, correct?"

Julietta licked her dry lips. Ouch. Her mama's anger was something to be reckoned with, and nothing pissed her off more than the idea of people not being welcome in her home. *Mio Dio,* why was this happening to her today? She only wanted some peace and quiet, and now the symbol of her distress would be breaking bread in her family home. She forced the words out. "Of course. Let me get the vase."

She busied herself with the flowers as Sawyer uncorked the champagne and poured. Small talk fluttered back and forth between them, but her skin burned under the scorching heat of his gaze. How did the man manage to shrink the room? He carried himself with a powerful dignity that stole all the air around her. Vulnerability shot through her. She wished suddenly for her business suit and high heels. Her current Sunday outfit consisted of jeans, a purple T-shirt under a zippered sweater, and black suede flats. Her hair was loose and a bit tangled from the breeze, and she rarely wore makeup when hanging with her mother. She pressed her lips together and swore not to let him make her feel uncomfortable. He was the outsider—not her.

"Both of you sit and relax. I have everything under control. Have some antipasto." The tray of prosciutto, crackers, cheese, and pepperoni looked inviting. There was something intimate about eating in her mama's kitchen. The heavy pine table was large, but the space evoked a cozy atmosphere. The huge arched window over the sink allowed light to pour through and showed off the view of the rolling golden hills. The rich colors of burnt orange, scarlet, and gold shimmered in welcome from the pine floors to the colorful pasta bowls and trays hand painted in bright tones. Hand-stitched linens and mats made a presentation for every plate served. The scents of gravy, steamed garlic, and lemon hung heavily in the air and wrapped them in warmth. Julietta knew her mother wouldn't let her help when there were guests here, so she filled her plate to bursting, sipped her champagne, and tossed her business partner a glare.

He didn't seem intimidated. More like fascinated by her outfit, greedy appetite, and surliness.

"I'm so honored you invited me to dinner, Mama Conte. I assume Julietta shared the good news about our deal?"

"No, we didn't get to the details yet. My goodness, you mean you're both working together?"

Sawyer grinned. "Yes. I'm building a new chain of hotels called Purity, and La Dolce Famiglia will be my exclusive supplier. Of course, Max will take care of the U.S. hotels but the big launch is Milan. Julietta will be key to helping make this a success."

She tried hard not to make a face at him, which was extremely juvenile and beneath her. How dare he steal her thunder? As if he bestowed his contract as a gift without her having a say in the matter. Screw him. She jumped in. "Of course, negotiation was involved before I'd sign the contracts. Some of the clauses were unacceptable."

"Of course." His ready agreement only pissed her off more. Why did he continuously annoy her?

"She makes this family proud. And you've done well for yourself, Sawyer. Tell me about this hotel chain."

As he talked about Purity, she caught the glow of pleasure on his face. Odd, she understood him in some basic ways. The need to succeed and prove oneself. The fierce satisfaction of building something of your own in a world where nothing was permanent. She rarely analyzed where the drive came from. She was too afraid to know the truth.

It had been a full week since the kiss. As if he had sensed she needed to retreat, he had allowed her the distance and stuck to a few phone calls and a short visit that focused entirely on business.

But the damage had been done.

She thought about the kiss all the time. The texture of his lips, the scent of his skin, and the promise of his mouth, open and hungry on hers. She had tossed and turned at night and had cursed him. How could such an innocent peck affect her so deeply? If she didn't know her body, she would've thrown away her reserve and her principles and dragged him into bed.

Unfortunately, she knew what would happen. The burst of flame and lust. The promise of satisfaction. And eventually, the withering of heat as her body pruned up and chilled under a man's hand. Sawyer would be no different, and she didn't intend to have him figure out her secret.

She just needed to get over it.

Julietta focused on conversation. "How did you meet Sawyer, Mama?" She made sure her direct question completely cut out his answer. He stiffened. A whirling array of emotions flickered in those tiger eyes, but they cleared so fast she wondered if it was her imagination.

A short silence fell over the kitchen. She knew then there was a story here—and waited for her mother to tell it.

Finally, she'd get a piece of the missing puzzle that made up this mysterious man and maybe gain some leverage.

"I was having a drink with Max's mother at the Prospect Hotel. Sawyer was at the bar with his boss. My goodness, it was so long ago I barely remember, but I think there were harsh words exchanged. His boss was being quite abusive. How old were you? Twenty-two?"

"Yes."

His tone was flat, and his face held no expression.

"Anyway, his boss left, and I couldn't get the bartender's attention. Sawyer bought me a drink, and we began chatting. He reminded me so much of Max: young, ambitious, ready to conquer the world."

Julietta waited. Silence fell. "That's it?"

Mama Conte glanced at her with surprise. "Yes. Why, how did you think we met?"

Her gaze locked with Sawyer's. Heat crawled up her body, scratched under her skin, and dampened between her legs. This weird sexual power he commanded was too much for her, but damned if she'd let him win this staring match.

"Sawyer was quite mysterious about your meeting. I just thought there was more to the story."

"Not that I recall. Did anything else happen, Sawyer?"

He paused only a moment. Her gut screamed something big had occurred in that bar with her mother, but she was letting him hold the reins. Finally, he gave a tight-lipped smile. "No. That was it."

Her shoulders slumped in defeat. Damn, she needed some ammunition. No matter how hard she dug, his past was a blank canvas before he stormed into the business world. She hated the idea that he knew more about her. What was worse?

He realized it.

Mama kept talking. "It's amazing how life works. You met Maximus on a business venture, and now you will be a permanent part of our bakery with Julietta. Almost as if you were meant to be with our family."

Alarm bells rang in her head. Hell, no. She refused to share her quiet Sunday dinners with a man who only wanted to press her sex buttons. Their relationship had to stay firmly in the office, where it belonged. She cleared her throat. "Umm, Sawyer probably likes to keep his work life clearly separated. We need to respect that."

Mama Conte snorted and cut her hand in the air. "Nonsense. As I tell you all the time, you need more outlets besides work. Dinner with friends and family are neces sary in this lifetime. Money and success are not everything. Happiness is."

Julietta crammed another cracker stacked high with pepperoni in her mouth to keep herself from screaming. Sawyer steepled his fingers and watched. Humor danced in his eyes. "I agree," he said slowly. "In fact, I told Julietta I'd love to spend more time with her on a personal basis. I don't know too many people in Milan."

She swallowed the dry crumbs and barely fought off a choking fit.

"A wonderful idea. From now on, you will join us for dinner on Sundays. I'm sure Julietta will make time from her busy schedule to introduce you to some of her friends."

"Thank you."

Her eyes widened. Mama placed heaping bowls of manicotti and fresh salad in front of them and beamed. "Isn't this wonderful? Now both of you. *Manga*."

Sawyer winked and picked up his fork.

. . .

"Why are you bothering me?"

They sat on the back terrace with cups of cappuccino and a plate of freshly baked honey almond biscotti. Open and airy, with a view of the lagoon-type pool and lush gardens, the wrought-iron furniture added to the old-world appeal of Mama Conte's villa. Terra-cotta pots lined the colorful cobblestones and burst with various herbs and fruit plants, just waiting to sprout at the first sign of spring. The last sting of winter hung fiercely on, but the bite in the air cleared Sawyer's lungs and sharpened his instincts. The mountains shimmered in the distance, and the sound of bubbling water from the sculptured marble angel soothed his ears. He propped up his legs on the opposite chair and dipped the cookie into his coffee. "I'm not. Your mother likes me."

She rolled her eyes. "My mother likes everyone. She'd invite a serial killer to supper."

"Nice."

"What really happened between you and Mama? It feels like there's something else you both aren't telling me."

Oh, there was. Not that he'd confess such a big piece of his past. Mama Conte had saved his life and put him on a new path that changed everything. The memory of their most recent encounter flickered before him.

She'd come to see him when he scored his first big coup with La Principe Hotel. Proud of what he had accomplished with her help, drunk on the victory of leading a life he only dreamed about, he'd treated her to lunch, and then he'd taken her in his arms for a gentle hug. He spoke in Italian to her and made a vow—a sacred promise from his very gut and soul—and whispered in her ear.

"*La devo un grande debito. Se lei mai ha bisogno di me, farò che lei chiede.*"

"*I owe you a great debt. If you ever need me, I will do whatever you ask.*"

He intended to honor that promise if the opportunity to do so ever came. Sawyer stuffed back the memory. "Let's just say I knew immediately she was an extraordinary woman. Must run in the family."

"Look, I don't want our relationship blurring from business to personal. I've told you over and over, though you seem not to listen. I'm not interested."

"So you did." He swung his head around and studied her. He loved the slight vulnerability she showed today. In her casual clothes, with her hair blowing loose and sexy, she looked approachable. Young. Her bare feet were tucked under her legs, which seemed tiny for such a tall woman. The ice queen image was packed away for a bit, and he wondered at the raw need rising in his gut. He ached to tug her onto his lap, clasp the back of her head, and feast on those pale pink lips. Thrust deep until moans were ripped from her throat and she begged for more.

The woman was a mass of contradictions. Savvy businesswoman. Bad-ass motorcycle rider. Sweet and domestic in her mama's kitchen. When she had shrugged off her sweater during dinner, he had spotted a purple lace strap beneath that conservative T-shirt, and he'd gone hard instantly. Holy crap, the woman wore sexy underwear. Somewhere, underneath all that proper restraint, lay a hidden temptress dying to escape. He bet she wore thongs. Probably a matching violet. Would she be bare and shaven? Or hidden by a silky triangle of dark hair, trying to mask her secrets?

"Hello? Earth to Sawyer?" She snapped and scowled in his direction. "Why do you have that weird look on your face?" The woman shifted and he caught a flash of cherry red toenails. Not clear gloss or conservative peach. Fire-engine red. Yep, he was a complete goner.

"Just thinking." He reached out and caught a section

of her hair. It rippled and clung to his fingers like a lover. Strands of fiery wine threaded through the brown and played a sexy game of peekaboo. "Your hair is beautiful. So long and silky." He loosened his grip and allowed the locks to drift softly back to their position. His fingers brushed her cheek. "And your skin is flawless. Golden and smooth. If I ran my tongue over you, would you taste like chocolate and coconut?"

Her breath hitched, but she never surrendered. "Here we go. Are my eyes like dark pools of desire, awaiting you to drown in them?"

Sawyer shook his head. Damn, she was sharp. "Not bad. I was sticking with the chocolate reference, so I was going to go with cocoa."

Her lip twitched. "Overdone."

"Maybe. I've been thinking about your breasts a lot, too."

"Hmm, let me try. Milky globes of flesh?"

"Awful, just awful. No, they're high, firm, with long, sensitive nipples that push against your bra. I've been dreaming of the color, though. Pale pink like cotton candy? Or ruby red like a delicious strawberry?" Her eyes dilated, and he took advantage by trailing his finger along the line of her lips, pressing against the pouty curve with his thumb. Like a doe caught in the middle of a grassy field, she held perfectly still and waited, as if sensing danger. "I imagine they'll swell and tighten when I take them between my teeth. I'd enjoy biting your nipples, Julietta. Sometimes the edge of pain blurs into pleasure and takes you higher. I'd like to explore that edge with you."

"Stop—"

"Why?" He lowered his voice to a whisper and leaned in. His breath rushed over her moist mouth, and the blood rushed to his dick in cranky demand. "Hasn't a man ever told you what he wants to do with you? Verbal foreplay is key in getting a woman ready. The brain is the greatest sexual tool, and many don't use it to its potential." His other hand dropped to her jeans-clad leg and stroked over her knee. "Your legs were made to wrap around a man's hips as he thrusts deep. Long and muscled, with those pretty red toenails. Except I may ask you to keep on those high heels you love so much. I think I'd enjoy the sting of your heel in my thigh as you demand your pleasure."

Heat tinged her cheeks. Aware that she was completely under his spell—for a few seconds anyway—he inserted his thumb between her lips, looking for entry. She paused only a moment. Then opened her mouth.

His finger slid in and her wet tongue lashed out. He sucked in his own breath.

"But I'd make you wait," he murmured. "Because I imagine you've tortured me for far too long. I'd slide my fingers into your tight, slick pussy, tease your clit, and make you beg."

Her teeth bit down on the fleshy pad of his thumb.

Arousal exploded inside of him. "Fuck this," he growled.

He removed his finger, grabbed her head, and slammed his mouth down on hers.

He devoured and took her the way he wanted to since the moment he met her. This was no game of tease-and-seek, no gentle touch of lip to lip. Sawyer followed his gut and pushed hard in sheer demand, for everything.

She tasted of sugar and honey as his tongue dove deep and possessed every dark, silky crevice. He swallowed her moan and sank into female heat. For one moment, she gave it all back to him—thrusting her tongue against his, her nails digging into his shoulders. For one moment, she burned bright and true and so hot he almost decided to rip off her jeans and take her right here in Mama Conte's back-yard.

And then she changed.

He felt the shift immediately. The slight coolness of her flesh, the rigid tenseness of muscles that had been soft and giving a minute ago. He eased the pressure of his mouth as she changed from willing participant to reserved recipient. The fire blew away, leaving a trail of smoke, ashes, and dying heat.

He lifted his mouth from hers and gazed into her eyes.

Loathing.

Not at him. Not for the kiss. More of a disappointment and self-loathing. The rip of pure feeling was immediately locked up and shoved somewhere else deep inside. An icy reserve coated her, and it was as if he looked upon a distant stranger and not the woman who burned up in his arms.

And then Sawyer knew.

The knowledge slammed through him, but he had no time to process it. She pushed him away with a quiet dignity and lifted her chin. "Please don't do that again," she said cooly. "I'm sure you needed that experiment, but as I told you before, I'm not interested in a physical relationship with you."

He allowed the retreat because he needed time to sift through this new information. "I apologize. All that talking of food and body parts spun me out of control."

She gave a tight smile, obviously desperate to push past the awkwardness of the encounter. "Apology accepted. This won't work, Sawyer. I want you to beg off dinner on Sunday. It's the only time I get to relax during the week and spend quality time with my mother. Surely you can respect that."

"I like seeing you this way," he murmured. "Softer, more approachable. I liked the way you helped your mom in the kitchen, and the way you gorged on dinner without a care, and the way you looked at her with such love and respect." His thoughts slid into the past. He had always wished for a family to love. A family to love him. It was such a mysterious concept he couldn't understand, and watching the close relationship with Julietta and Mama Conte set off a fire of emotion and longing he rarely let escape. He remembered when he had come home from school with a black eye from a bully on the playground. When his foster father had asked who won, and he'd told the truth, he got a slap that almost knocked his teeth out. He wasn't allowed to eat for two days, because losers deserved nothing.

What was he doing?

He wanted to seduce Julietta Conte and take her past her comfort zone. He wanted her savvy business skills to make Purity the best. He did not need to be immersed in her family or be reminded of gentler feelings he had no place or time for. They existed for her, but he knew better. They weren't meant for him. Thinking about what he couldn't have wouldn't help.

He had to get out of here.

She drew back in surprise when he stood up from the chair. "You're right, of course. I won't bother you at dinner any longer. I'm going to say good-bye to your mother, and I'll see you at the office tomorrow. I'll need you to meet the other suppliers for Purity and go over some initial plans."

"Yes, yes, of course."

"Very well. *Buona sera,* Julietta."

He left her on the terrace and tried not to run like evil zombies were on his tail. She was right about one thing: Dinner was a mistake.

But not the kiss. Definitely not the kiss. He knew now

what she needed, craved, and how to get her there. No way was he giving up the opportunity to show her what she'd been missing and initiate her into the dark world of erotic pleasures.

Sawyer tightened his lips and his resolve and went to find Mama Conte to say good-bye.

Chapter Six

What had happened last night?

Julietta sat at the conference table with the other members of Sawyer's team and tried to focus. He'd managed to outmaneuver her for a moment, but when she got back into control, something had changed between them. A certainty glimmered in his eyes that scared the crap out of her. Suddenly, he reminded her of a hungry predator ready to swallow her whole. The scary part was that the outcome didn't seem so bad.

She thought she'd regained her footing, and then that other look had crossed his face. Regret. And a hint of longing. He'd left so fast she'd known he'd been hurt in some way she couldn't understand. The knowledge she could wound a man like Sawyer Wells kept her up all last night. Thinking about that kiss. For a few seconds, her body came alive and was ready to play hard. For a moment, she thought he'd cured her, and she would've gratefully climbed on his lap and impaled herself on him faster than he could imagine. The idea of an orgasm thrilled her, beckoned like a shining beacon of light she never seemed to be able to reach. But, as with all the others, her mind finally clicked back on, and the desire drifted away.

It had only been a mirage.

The failure had mocked and burned as she tossed and turned in her tangled satin sheets. If Sawyer couldn't get her to respond, no man would. She knew that in her gut. He'd given off all signals of recovery. Of course, at least she didn't have to torture herself anymore about what-ifs. They could go back to business, and she wouldn't be tempted any further. Sure, it was a bit embarrassing to think Sawyer pitied her, but maybe he just thought she wasn't attracted to him like other women. Maybe he didn't see her as deficient but as more of an exception to a rule. Hopefully.

She turned her attention back to the other suppliers who crowded around the table. Tanya, the interior designer and fabric expert, seemed a bit snobby but extremely talented. Her short red bob, bright makeup, and tendency to wear all black told Julietta she had a keen sense of style and how to put things together. Ricardo, head chef of Purity restaurants, exhibited an even temperament key to the hotel industry, and he fleshed out his ideas in businesslike fashion. Evelyn, the spa expert, was extremely new agey, with blond hip-length hair and dressed completely in organic, breathable earth-tone fabrics. Her voice was low and melodic, with glowing, fresh skin and a lean body she trained with hours of yoga. Each brought something new to the table, and thank goodness she felt as if they could all work well as a team, yet own their individual flair.

She watched Sawyer from under half-lidded eyes. He was magnificent in action. Completely in charge, but with a relaxed ease that invited opinions and discussion. Ruthlessly organized and well spoken. He reminded her of Michael, but he vibrated on a lower key, as if skimming the surface but always retaining tight control. His slate gray suit molded to his muscled length in loving attention, and when he turned toward the PowerPoint presentation, her gaze fixed on the hard, tight ass her fingers longed to explore. Amazing how badly she craved his touch from a distance. Already her panties were damp, and that burning need throbbed between her legs. Too bad she froze once contact was initiated.

He turned and shot her a knowing look. She tried not to flinch and concentrated on not letting her face grow hot. How embarrassing. Staring at his rear like a silly teenager crushing on her teacher.

The door opened and a young man walked in. He whispered something to Sawyer, nodded, and pulled up a chair to join the conference.

Everyone stared in shocked silence.

Dressed in a tame navy blue suit and tie, he seemed the typical employee from the neck down. That's where it ended. His hair was half shaved on the right side, revealing the gold loop and various piercings in his ear and brow. The left side of his hair was jet black, arranged in an array of spikes that stuck straight out like a hairstyle gone horribly wrong. Surly blue eyes stared back at each of the suppliers, as if challenging them to say a word about his appearance. A tattoo of some snake/serpent thing was etched around his neck like a permanent collar. Julietta pegged him as nineteen or twenty at the most. What was he doing here?

Sawyer cleared his throat and spoke up. "I'd like to introduce you to my assistant, Wolfe. He's been interning with me, and I'm assigning him to helping you with whatever you need. I know you already have a full staff, but he will be your main contact person for daily issues that crop up."

No one spoke.

A sneer twisted Wolfe's lips. "Don't all jump at once," he shot out. The warning look Sawyer cut him elicited a shrug; then the kid leaned back in his chair like he couldn't give a damn.

Tanya spoke. "Sawyer, I don't think a young boy still finding himself will work for me. My associates are well trained. I'll take care of things on my end, but if there's an issue, I'm going straight to you."

Ricardo nodded in agreement. Evelyn looked at Wolfe with a curious stare, as if studying him for a project. "Fascinating," she whispered. "But I agree with Tanya; we only deal directly with the head of the project. If you disagree, I'm afraid we'll have a problem."

Wolfe shook his head. "I told you," he said. "This wasn't going to work. They only want you."

"I assure you Wolfe is completely capable of helping and knows everything we need to achieve with Purity. I've been training him for months; don't let his appearance throw you."

"Yeah, I can count without using my fingers," Wolfe added.

Julietta bit her lip to tamp down a laugh. Damn, he was full of angst. She remembered Carina at that age; even with her sweetness, she was surly, miserable, and hated life. Why would Sawyer ever hire someone like him? The mystery fascinated her.

Tanya gave a brittle laugh. "No offense, Mr. Wolfe, but we refuse a middleman. Too many mistakes are made that way. Take it or leave it, Sawyer."

"Agreed," Ricardo spoke up.

"I'll work with him." The three shut up and stared at Julietta with astonishment. The kid narrowed his eyes with suspicion. "That is, if Mr. Wolfe would like to work with me. I'd love someone on this end I can pass information through. Sawyer will be busy implementing all the puzzle pieces, so I appreciate the help."

"It's Wolfe. Not Mr. Wolfe."

Julietta smiled. "*Mi dispiace*. Wolfe, I mean. Thank you for your assistance."

He gave a nod, crossed his arms in front of his chest, and stared at the table. Pleasure and relief carved out the features of Sawyer's face. Her heart lifted. How odd. He seemed to care about this boy more than a normal employee. She needed to dig and get the story.

They finished their meeting and broke for lunch. Julietta made her way over and stood beside Wolfe. "Thank you again for offering your services." She stuck out her hand. He hesitated, as if anticipating she'd jerk her hand away at the last minute and start laughing. Then he shook her hand with a firm grip, letting go so quick she wondered if her palm was sweaty.

"Welcome."

"How long have you worked for Sawyer?"

He shifted his feet. "Why?"

She shrugged. "Just wondering. Purity means everything to him. If he trusts you to have a hand in it, he must believe you're good."

Wolfe looked over his shoulder at Sawyer speaking with Tanya. "I have a photographic memory," he grudgingly admitted. "And a weird thing for figures. We met in New York and he asked me to come work for him."

His jaw unclenched and blue eyes softened a shade. Interesting. They cared about each other. Saving the rest of her questions for later, she nodded. "I'd love for you to come to La Dolce Famiglia and meet some of my team. I have a specified list of things to get moving, and someone who can add without his fingers would be a huge asset."

His lip quirked. "Cool."

"See you later." She turned on her heel and headed toward the door when her name rang through the room. Her feet stuck to the carpet at the commanding tone, and her belly flipped and sank low. She turned her head. "Yes?"

Sawyer pinned her with his hot gaze. "Stay, please. I need to discuss something with you."

She opened her mouth to tell him no, but he'd already turned to finish his conversation with Tanya. Julietta was tempted to walk out, but she figured she'd let him win this round. He quickly dispersed the other conference members and Wolfe, shut the door, and pressed a button on his desk.

The door slid closed without a sound and locked them in. Oh, no. Not again.

Temper flowed hot and clean through her veins. How dare he do that intimidation thing with her? She wasn't his lackey, and he had no right to order her around. She tilted her chin and marched toward him. "The magic lock thing is a nice touch, but it doesn't work on me." Who cares if she lied? "Next time ask me nicely to stay. I don't take well to being bossed around."

He smiled and shifted his hip so he was leaning against

his desk. With a lazy, assessing air, he unbuttoned his suit jacket and shrugged out of it. The crisp white shirt pulled against his broad chest, and the red tie just made him look hotter. "Funny, I disagree. I think what you've been missing is a man who will tell you what to do. What he wants. And how he wants it."

The air whooshed out of her lungs. The room tilted, then steadied as his meaning finally penetrated her ears. Had he gone *pazzo*? "Have I just dropped into a badly directed porn movie? Listen, I'm not one of these repressed feminists who needs the right man to unlock her hidden desires. Been there. Done that. Now, unlock the door or I'll spring a lawsuit on you so fast your head will explode."

He shook his head and grinned. "This is completely separate from work and you know it. I thought you were braver than that, Julietta. Don't try to hide behind our contract."

She sputtered with outrage. "You're pinning this on me? Oh, that's priceless. Let me try to be crystal clear. You kissed me last night. I allowed it. Fireworks didn't explode, the earth didn't tilt on its axis, and now we're moving on. How about you tuck your ego back in your pants, and we put the episode behind us? Maybe you can target Evelyn—she looks like she's into that tantric thing, which might be a real hoot for you."

A delighted laugh broke from his lips. The cool sophistication she prided herself on slipped under her scrambling fingertips and left her with a hot mix of emotions she didn't know how to handle. "Damn, you're perfect for me. Okay, let's get past the slow getting-to-know-you phase and get to the good stuff." Suddenly, his relaxed demeanor changed. As if a switch had been turned, he pushed away from the desk and focused his attention on her. His eyes gleamed with heat and a touch of menace.

She remembered watching a show on snow leopards. The sleek grace of their bodies as they stalked their prey was a bit teasing at first, before they revved up the intensity to such a high level that the prey was unable to run and just stood there waiting to be eaten.

That's how she felt. Julietta didn't even realize she was retreating until her back slammed against the wall. The satisfied smirk on his lips told her he knew how he affected her, and he intended to do everything possible to prove his point. Slowly, he caged her in by pressing his palms flat against the wall beside her head. Her body lit up and begged to play. The lace of her bra scratched against her sensitive nipples, and a drugging heat pulsed through her body.

Furious at her weakness, she rallied. "Move any closer and you'll regret it."

One golden brow arched. "Like this?" With one graceful motion, he eased her legs apart and pressed his hips to hers. His heavy erection stole her breath.

"You're a bastard." She craved to slide her fingers into those thick waves and surrender. The knowledge that her body would eventually freeze up and torture her made her blink back furious tears. "Why are you doing this? Do you have to conquer a woman's 'no' to feel like a man? Fine, get it over with. Let's have a repeat of last night so I can prove to you we don't have the right chemistry."

His eyes softened a bit, and he stroked her cheek with tender motions. "My sweet, we have the perfect chemistry. I have never wanted a woman as badly as I want you. How long has it been since you responded to a man?"

She pushed against his chest but he didn't budge. "Last week."

"Tell me the truth."

Humiliation flooded her in waves. *Mio Dio,* she couldn't do this any longer. Knowing her honesty would finally make him leave, she spat the words in his face. "Never! I can't respond to any man, and I never have. Are you satisfied now? Will you leave me alone and stop playing these games?"

He pressed his forehead to hers in a soothing gesture. "Thank you, Julietta," he whispered against her lips. "Thank you for telling me the truth."

She kept her body stiff and waited for him to finally pull away. When he began pressing tiny kisses to her brow and down her cheeks, she bit back a sob. "Please let me go."

"No. Not yet." He tortured her with slow caresses over her hips, sliding his hands under her jacket and stroking the thin silk of her blouse. His touch was heated and strong as he kneaded her muscles. His mouth drifted near her ear and played with her lobe, licking, biting gently, until a slow burn simmered under her skin. "You've been screwed, baby, and not in a good way. Assholes have made you feel there's something wrong with you. Tied you up in so many knots that your body is stuck."

She took a deep breath, quickly twisted and brought her knee up. Unfortunately, he anticipated the move and kept her tightly pinned. His rock-hard erection pressed against her core, and a low animal moan escaped her lips. Where had that come from? His soft laugh stirred the strands by her temple, and unbelievably, she grew wetter. "I could show you things you've been missing," he taunted. His tongue licked the inner shell of her ear and a stream of hot breath caused goose bumps to pepper her flesh. His hands continued to massage her hips and slide behind to cup her buttocks, forcing her to arch on tiptoes. "Things that can free your delicious body and let you surrender to pleasure."

She panted. "Like sexual discrimination and harassment? Oh, goody."

"Let's put that mouth to better use, shall we?"

His lips traveled across her cheek and took her mouth. He nipped at her lower lip. The quick pain startled her and she allowed him full access. This time, he didn't claim and possess. No, he teased and cajoled, his tongue playing and slipping in and out, pairing the invasion with little nibbles that kept her off balance. Automatically, she reached up to try and push him away, but he grabbed her wrists in one hand

and dragged them over her head. His easy grip was unbreakable. Her breasts strained against her blouse as she struggled for breath. She fought for equilibrium, but he held her legs open within the confines of her pencil skirt. The combination of pleasure and pain, restraint and control, swarmed within and around until her senses took over completely. Her brain scrambled for clarity, but she couldn't seem to surface. His fingers plucked at her tight nipple, rolling the tips through the thin fabric and lace, but never enough to satisfy her. Her blood roared and her hips arched for more.

"That's it," he murmured. "Strong women like you need a way to turn off their thoughts. Surrender completely to me and I'll make it so good for you, you'll beg for more."

She stiffened. Surrender? What was he talking about? She wasn't weak, she was—

"Ah, back to thinking, are we? My mistake, I let you wander." He deftly unbuttoned the top three buttons of her blouse and slid his hand inside to cup her breast. Those warm fingers hit her skin and she held back a gasp. His thumb swiped her aching nipple against the lace, forcing a shudder. She craved more pressure, but he wouldn't give it to her, wouldn't give her the full-body contact she needed to feel satisfied. Back and forth, over and over, until she gritted her teeth and wiggled in his grasp, trying to get loose. He only tightened his hold, and the erotic torture made her hotter. That sexy laugh again, as if he knew exactly what she wanted and refused to give in. "You like that, huh? But you're not ready for more. You have to learn to ask for what you want, baby. Ask nicely."

Her eyes widened. "What?"

"You heard me." His gaze drilled into hers until she was caught up in hot golden flames. "You know what I want? I want to push up your skirt, pull down your panties, and slide my fingers into your wet heat. I want my mouth on your nipple, your thighs wide apart, and your honey flowing over my fingers. I want to watch your face when you come so hard you scream, and then I want to strip off your clothes and do it all over."

Her heart thundered in fear and lust. How could he say these things? So raw and lurid and . . . carnal. No one had ever dared to speak with her in such a way. It wasn't proper. "Don't say things like that." Her voice came out hoarse and ragged.

"Why?" he murmured, coaxing her nipple tighter. He watched every motion until she felt stripped naked and vulnerable. "Because it's not proper? You've done proper already, and it hasn't worked. It's time you do dirty."

"No, it won't work, it will—oh!" He bit down hard on her neck, then licked the tender flesh at the same time he squeezed her nipple. Shudders wracked her body and her thoughts spun out of control.

"You're wet, aren't you? Wouldn't it feel so good if I slipped my fingers between your legs? Rubbed your clit until all that tension just exploded?" His outrageous words should have embarrassed her, but social niceties took a nosedive under the sudden crazed demand of her body. She panted and twisted for one final desperate attempt at sanity.

"I can't have an orgasm, okay? Let me go."

"No." The shock of a man not listening to her commands threw her off. "For the next few minutes, your body is under my control." Butterscotch eyes burned with clear direction and blistering heat. "You have no say over what I do. You can't touch me or worry about what comes next." His hand left her breasts and slowly tugged up the edges of her skirt so it bunched around her upper thighs. She couldn't move, completely transfixed by his words and voice and demand. "You are not allowed to think about the business deal, your schedule, or what you're cooking for dinner." He nudged his knee up behind hers so her left leg was lifted and open to his touch. "Now let's see how hot and wet this little episode got you."

She gasped at his crudeness but he crashed his mouth over hers.

He invaded her mind and body at once. His tongue pushed through the seam of her lips and dove deep, while his fingers found the edge of her panties, slipped under, and found home. A strange noise broke from her but he only swallowed the sound with an expertise that robbed her breath. Talented fingers parted her swollen flesh and dove into her drenched core. Confused, Julietta could only respond to a variety of demands, as her nipples begged for the lash of his tongue, and his delicious taste of coffee, spice, and male hunger urged her mouth to open wider for more. She clenched around the push-pull of his pumping fingers until the unbelievable sensations of a looming orgasm hit every muscle. She reached, trying to hold on to it with her mind. Her fingers curled into his, and his thumb pressed over her throbbing clitoris, the nerves screaming for release. He ripped his mouth from hers as she teetered on the edge, caught between the hazy place where logic was dead and physical need trumped every lesson she'd ever learned. His gaze drilled into hers and demanded surrender. *Yes.* Yes, she would do anything right now. The slightest bit of pressure would throw her over. Just a little more and—

He was gone.

Julietta blinked, panting hard as her brain tried to make sense of what had occurred. The few inches of space that separated them brought a sudden chill to her overheated flesh. Her body ached from raw need, and she stared at him with growing horror as the scene crystallized before her. No, this couldn't have happened. He only meant to torture her, show her a horrible lesson, then leave her stranded so he could laugh and make fun of her. With clumsy fingers, she pushed down her skirt and straightened her clothes. Humiliated tears stung the back of her lids, but she gritted her teeth and fought through the emotion, going back to her safe, cold place where nothing could hurt her.

"Don't you dare," he ripped out. "You will not demean

yourself anymore in my presence. Look at me. Look at how badly I want to take you against that wall like an animal." His erection seemed huge and looming from the tight fabric of his pants. "You think this was a goddamn lesson for my ego? I needed to show you what it could be like between us. I can take you further, all the way, but you have to make that decision."

Frustration ripped through her. "I'm not some sort of project for you, Sawyer. You wanted to show the poor frigid spinster you can get her off once? Congratulations—close enough. Thanks for the sampler platter, but I'll pass on the meal. Now leave me the hell alone."

She headed toward the door, but he blocked her so fast it reminded her of the Twilight movies where Edward whizzed in front of Bella with vampire grace. "Not before you listen to me, or I'll push you back against that wall and damn the consequences." Her thighs trembled at the threat. What the hell was wrong with her? She was sick to be so turned on by his caveman tactics.

"You're not sick," he said gently.

His ability to read her thoughts only enraged her more. She crossed her arms in front of her chest and lifted her chin. "Talk. You have two minutes, and then I'm leaving this room. I swear if you try to stop me again, I'll scream the building down."

"Fair enough. Simply put, you respond to a more dominating sexual manner than other women. Your mind is so strong and in charge, your body doesn't get a shot. You'll probably get more excited by restraints or a lover who you can surrender control to in the bedroom."

"And how do you know all this?"

His face tightened, as if remembering painful memories. "I had some issues to work out, and I learned a bit about domination and submission."

She rolled her eyes. "I don't need to *submit* to any man."

"Not submit. You couldn't be any man's plaything or slave, baby. Though in traditional roles, the one who submits is the one who always holds the power. No, I'm talking about simple surrender. Giving up control in order to get sexually excited and stay there." He took a step toward her and his scent rose in her nostrils. She fought the urge to close her eyes and drag in a deep breath. Just his closeness turned her on like no other man ever had. "I want to show you that world. Give you pleasure. Since I met you, I've imagined you in my bed with your legs wrapped around my hips while I thrust inside you. Your face when you come. But I need you to trust me on some level first. Give me a chance."

The fight sagged out of her body, and she was left with the bruising knowledge she didn't believe him. Sure, he was able to get her close to orgasm, but she hadn't managed to finish. She was probably caught up in the moment. Another planned encounter would never work.

"One night, Julietta." His voice stroked and probed

every dark corner like crushed velvet. "I want you, and I'll do anything to get you. If I can't give you an orgasm in one night, I'll leave you alone. In fact, I'll give you an incentive."

A humorless laugh escaped her lips. "An orgasm and an incentive? How much better can it get?"

"I'll put you in charge of the entire operation."

She stilled. "What?"

"I said you had free access but I was the one with the final decisions. If you spend the night with me and you're not satisfied, I'll give you final approval over anything to do with La Dolce Famiglia."

The consequences of full control when it came to her bakery flooded her with adrenaline. She had so many ideas that he might fight her on. This way, anything she wanted to try would be all hers. If she disagreed with his actions, she'd be able to overstep his command. It was almost a guarantee of success, because there was no way to lose—she'd never have to depend on his approval.

Sawyer laughed. "Ah, I knew you would like that. Think about it."

"What do you get out of it? You'd lose one of the most important aspects in this deal—the ability to veto any decision."

"I get you."

His gaze locked with hers. Julietta was unable to keep her body from trembling or to mask the raw lust for more of him. To have him naked and demanding in her bed, pushing her to places she'd only dreamed about. *Mio Dio,* what was she going to do?

"Only for one night." Her quick words reeked of defeat. He remained silent and studied her. Julietta shifted her weight onto her other high heel and tried to think. "What if I lose?"

His lip lifted. "Then we both win, don't we?"

The intercom buzzed and interrupted the electricity zinging in the air. "Mr. Wells, your one o'clock is here."

He never moved or answered. She envied his control over the situation, even as she realized he was still fully aroused. Time to retreat and get herself together. The man oozed pheromones that fried her brain. "I'll think about it."

Sawyer nodded, as if they discussed a business arrangement rather than a night of sex. "Very well. I'll wait until you give me an answer."

Julietta veered around him and gave up a small victory. No matter. She'd have time to regroup, but right now his nearness needed to be avoided. His low chuckle confirmed he noticed, and she cursed under her breath as she scurried out the door in full cowardly retreat.

Damn him.

What the hell was she going to do?

• • •

The demons were back.

Sawyer rubbed the nape of his neck and pushed away

from his computer. Hours of work usually focused him, keeping him primed and targeted toward his main goal. But after his encounter with Julietta, and trying to balance too many requests with the looming opening of his Purity, his nerves were shot.

He couldn't get her out of his head. How long had it been since a woman had crawled under his skin and stayed there? Sure, he'd gone after particular females who interested him before, but he'd never experienced the intensity that encompassed not just his body, but his mind and emotions. The gorgeous flushed look on her face haunted him. Sawyer lifted his hand and pressed his fingers against his mouth. God, he still smelled her. Musky—with hints of vanilla and coconut swirled together. He remembered her soft lips relaxed, hips arching for more, completely in the moment with him and surrendering to her body.

He'd realized immediately after their first kiss she needed a man to control her in the bedroom. No wonder she had trouble responding. A woman so fiercely independent and in charge of a huge empire would loathe the idea of surrendering her body, and he bet her past lovers didn't own steel balls. Hell, that was what it'd take to challenge her, and most men had fragile egos. Coaxing a lukewarm response from a lover usually added to frustration for both parties. He bet she tried to lose her inhibitions and only received humiliation for trying. A woman like Julietta would cut her losses and move on, accepting full responsibility for her failure in the bedroom.

Assholes. They took everything passionate within her and forced her to believe she was frigid. Instead, she was a fucking dormant volcano ready to explode, all hot, creamy lava and lusty noises. The way she bit her lip hard to control her cries and tightened her muscles told him enough. She'd give him everything she got and more if she let herself go.

A smile tugged at his lips at the memory of her inner battle. He loved how she challenged him on every level and made him work for it. Sawyer had learned early that many of the aspects of BDSM called to him, and he'd dived into the experience once he had enough money to indulge his eclectic tastes. With his midthirties approaching, he now admitted he liked aspects of the push-pull of dom/sub, but it wasn't a lifestyle he wanted to commit to. His normal play in private and some exclusive clubs tamed the beast for a while, but work began to feed his insatiable appetite in a more soothing manner. So far, women had been a temporary enjoyment.

Until Julietta came on the scene.

He liked control. Needed it at all times in order to negotiate his life now. But for just a moment, he almost lost it, unbuckled his pants, and slid into her wet heat without a thought. And that, as he learned, was dangerous. How many years had it taken him to finally curb the violence and anger? The frustration of being dependent on people whose only goal was to let him down? Only two people in his world ever gave him a glimpse of something more.

Jerry White.

And Mama Conte.

The familiar twinge in his gut drove him to his feet and toward the back of his office. Toward the hidden door behind the mass of bookcases where a slice of peace and sanity were close enough to yank him from the abyss.

Fuck, he hated such weakness.

Sawyer stepped into the room. He took in the surroundings made for physical torture—soundproof so no grunts of pain were ever heard. The mats were thick beneath his feet, and the various instruments were there for one single purpose.

Sweat.

He toed off his shoes, stripped off his clothes, and changed into a pair of shorts and a T-shirt. He tied his hair back with a rubber band, shoved his feet into the sneakers, and donned the gloves. He started with the bag first, warming up with some jabs and letting his brain empty out into his body, ready to ease out the poison.

One. Two. Three.

The memory flickered.

"You're a fucking pussy, you know that." It was Christmas Eve, but there was no tree, no lights, and no warmth in the hellhole. His foster father drank from a rapidly declining bottle of Clan MacGregor and the smell drifted sickly sweet and sharp to his nostrils, making him gag. He kept quiet, knowing the trick of the game was to say as little as possible.

He was chained to a chair in the dirty kitchen. The cheap yellow linoleum held an array of scratches and stains. He let his mind go and focused on the tiny circle by the broken chair leg. Round and round his gaze followed the pattern and his mind began to drift. The other kids were asleep in the basement. He'd locked the door behind him so Asshole couldn't get in, knowing the holidays were one of his favorite times to play. It was easier to piss him off and get him to go after him than sacrificing the rest of the crew for a group party.

Unfortunately, it worked better than he planned.

Sawyer tamped down the trickle of panic. His feet were still free, and the more Scotch that disappeared, the worse Asshole's reflexes. No problem.

The burning sting of the cigarette pressed into his forearm made him jerk, but he kept his gaze down, on the circle, round and round.

The laugh was pure mean. "You like to play the hero, don't you, boy? Always thought you were better than us. Time to teach you some life lessons and take you down a peg."

He ignored the taunts. The first punch cracked him hard and he knew it would be a long night. . . .

Sawyer moved, ducked an imaginary opponent, and slammed his fists over and over into the bag. Lightning swift, he fought the memories gouged in his head until the sweat poured off his skin and a sliver of light shone from the grunge of his past.

Oh, Asshole had made him pay that Christmas Eve. The broken rib was taped up later, and the burns left scars he didn't give a crap about. What he gained that night was more important.

Hope.

He was growing bigger and more dangerous. Of course, if he didn't take it, the younger ones suffered, and he'd rather have physical bruises than an ache in his gut that'd eat him alive. No, it was easier to take the punches, but time was running out. He'd be free in nine months, five days, and four hours. Eighteen years old meant freedom. Escape. Maybe he'd be able to go to social services then about the others. Maybe . . .

The raw fury choked him, so he punched harder, kicked higher, and fell to the brutality of the streets, where winning was so much more than a competition: It was a matter of survival. So stupid to think he'd be able to outrun his past. The last shred of innocence ripped from his soul when the knowledge he'd failed almost killed him. Almost. Instead, he accepted that he'd killed his foster brother Danny out of his own greedy need to escape. Forced the acceptance into the dark closet and locked the door. Then decided to live.

"Sawyer?"

He spun around and crouched, still only half in the present. Breathing hard, he recognized Wolfe standing by the doorway. The kid was rarely surprised by anything, but it seemed discovering Sawyer knocking the shit out of the bag in his private chamber threw him off. Sawyer straightened and walked to the bar. "How'd you get in here?"

The kid thrust out his chin. "Door wasn't completely closed. Found a weird notch in the bookcase, so I checked it out. I wasn't spying."

"I know." He guzzled a half bottle of cold water, then wiped his mouth with the back of his hand. "This is private space—no one else knows about it."

A strange expression crossed the kid's face. Hurt? "Like I give a crap. I won't gossip at the next tea party. Just wanted to tell you I'm heading over to La Dolce Famiglia for a few hours before dinner." He turned halfway. "What is this anyway? Your secret Batcave?"

Sawyer swallowed a laugh and grabbed a towel. "Kind of. You work out?"

Wolfe studied the walls of free weights, punching bags, and bars around the room. A bad-ass sound system was wired to an array of hard metal that Sawyer loved. A flash lit those blue eyes, almost like longing. "Nah, not into it."

Sawyer wiped off his forehead and studied the boy. He'd been with him almost eight months now and still knew relatively little about his past. Of course, he knew enough. The abuse was evident, like a beaten dog that cowers at loud noises and growls to warn off strangers. Wolfe's tattoos, shaved head, and piercings showed he searched for his own sliver of peace and probably hadn't found it yet. Sawyer only meant to give him an opportunity in the business world and get him off the streets. Instead, he became his mentor, dragged him to Italy, and put him in charge of his biggest operation. He even lived with him, for God's sake.

The memory flashed before his vision and played out in slow motion.

He'd been staying at the Waldorf hotel in Manhattan—an elegant queen set amidst the class of Park Avenue in midtown. The exquisite richness of service and class New Yorkers demanded from a top-class hotel was achieved with marble floors, antique furniture, rich tapestries, and golden, dripping crystal chandeliers. He'd been consulting on a project and was walking down the hallway to his next meeting. An employee passed by with his head down, and though he was distracted, Sawyer immediately realized when his wallet was lifted from his suit pocket.

Quick as a snake, he reached out and grabbed the man's hand. Someone else probably wouldn't have noticed—the guy was good—but living on the streets had given Sawyer an edge most didn't own. The quick indrawn breath and frantic tug made Sawyer squeeze harder, until a pair of blazing blue eyes lifted and locked on his.

A kid. Maybe eighteen—dressed in the hotel uniform. Before he had a moment to process the information, the kid shoved him hard and he fell back. The kid raced toward the end of the hall with his prize. And slammed right into one of the hotel managers.

The next few hours blurred as they discovered he'd been living in the janitorial quarters, stealing uniforms, and basically living off the guests. Taking food from the room service trays. Washing in various bathrooms around the hotel. As the story came full blown, the memories of his own childhood choked him mercilessly. Trying to find a safe place to sleep and knowing the shelters were the most dangerous places to hole up. Finally getting smart enough to target one of the big hotels and learning the ins and outs of the system. My God, if Jerry had never taken him under his protection, he'd be in jail, too. And now, years later, he looked upon another teen in the same position. He'd be endless trouble and a huge complication Sawyer didn't need. Better to walk away from the whole mess and not look back. He'd get the hotel to drop the charges and make the whole thing go away. Then wish him luck.

Instead, he made a bargain. Got the charges dropped. Then offered the kid a job where he could keep an eye on him.

Sawyer never thought it would work. After all, this kid was surly as hell and full of scars. He was a minefield ready to explode or implode. He traced the paperwork to a boy named Vincent Soldano who had been linked to numerous foster homes and a list of complaints. At eighteen, he was now on his own with nowhere to go. Sawyer got him a room at the hotel he stayed in and offered to train him as his assistant. Hell, he figured the kid could at least learn to file, copy *things, and be a general errand boy. With his full black hair, blue eyes, and classic features, he'd polish up nice in a suit and tie.*

Sawyer shook his head at the memory.

Oh, yeah, he remembered that polite conversation all right. Vincent had nodded and told him he'd give him his answer in twenty-four hours. When he returned the next day, he had a gold ring piercing in his brow, a snake tattoo around his neck, and he had shaved off half of his hair. He confronted Sawyer with a snarl and a comment that changed Sawyer forever. "This is what you're really getting. I'm fucked up now inside and outside. Do you still want me now?"

Sawyer realized it was both a challenge and a plea. His gut lurched as he glanced at the kid's freakish appearance and admired his stubborn spirit.. "You can never touch drugs or I throw you out. And no stealing. That's nonnegotiable."

"I'm not a user. And I won't steal from you."

The truth gleamed in those blue eyes. And Sawyer gave him his answer. "Yes, I still want you. We need to buy you some clothes. You start tomorrow."

Sawyer figured he'd get him on his feet and the kid would move on. Eight months later, they were still together, with a fucked-up relationship both of them were afraid to probe.

He had tried setting him up with a shrink, but the kid almost bailed on him, so Sawyer decided just to keep him close and see what happened. Looking at his homemade gym, he realized he might be able to show Wolfe another way of slaying the monsters. He chugged the rest of his water and slammed it back on the bar. "Come with me; I need a spotter."

The gold bar in Wolfe's eyebrow caught the light as he arched it. "No, thanks."

"Don't think you can pull your own weight?"

His lips twisted in a snarl. "I could take you any time, old man."

Sawyer grinned and tossed him a pair of shorts and a tank. "Prove it. You may wear some pretty jewelry, but I don't think you can lift."

His taunt worked. The kid disappeared to change, then trudged to the bench press. Sawyer noticed he didn't wear the tank, but had replaced it with a long-sleeved tee that covered his arms. Wolfe loaded on the weight, lay back on the bench, and put his gloved hands elbow width apart. "Count it down."

He did a full set, rested, then did another. They switched on and off, while the sounds of classic Guns N' Roses blared around them and drowned out any attempt at conversation. They worked the circuit together, pushing, pulling, grunting, and sweating, until Sawyer's mind was clear and his body exhausted. He threw Wolfe a bottle of water, and they guzzled it down with sheer greed. "You did good," Sawyer said. "Those skinny arms surprised me."

Unbelievably, the kid half smiled. Sawyer realized he'd

rarely, if ever, seen any type of emotion cross Wolfe's face. Especially a hint of laughter or happiness. Sawyer's heart did a weird little flip that almost embarrassed him. "I'm surprised a man your age can still box."

Sawyer snorted. "I studied boxing for years. It's more than just punching a lousy bag. It's about balance, flexibility, controlled power." He remembered sparring in that hole of a gym. He did the shittiest jobs so the men would keep him around. Cleaning bathrooms, washing disgusting towels, taking punches as a sparring partner, all in the hope of a few hours of staying in a place that made him feel safe. Practicing for hours in order to make sure he survived on the streets. "I'll teach you."

The kid's head swung around. Suspicion gleamed from his eyes. "Why?"

Because he needed something to help him empty out the pain. Because he had to start living and stop just existing. Because Sawyer didn't know what else to do to reach him.

He shrugged. "Because I get bored by myself. I'm here by five a.m., then I go back to shower and change for work."

"Five fucking a.m.?"

"You like your beauty sleep, huh? No wonder you're a bit soft."

The snarl was back, but this time it came with a spark. "You wish. Fine. I'll join you, but just because you need a challenge, old man."

Sawyer grinned and tamped down the impulse to squeeze the boy's shoulder. He'd learned a few months ago touching was off-limits to the kid. "Welcome to the Jungle" pounded through the room. Sawyer threw the bottle across the room and made a perfect dunk shot into the garbage. "Let's get back to work."

They left the gym together.

Chapter Seven

Julietta stared out the window and looked at the gray, misty scene before her. Motorbikes whipped in and out of the roadways and fought with the crowds. Almost lunchtime. Many people held cups of cappuccino in hand, smoking furiously and ducking their heads from the drizzle of rain. The Duomo rose in the distance, and for a moment, she wished she were one of her younger sisters. Venezia would bound toward the elaborate shopping galleries and get lost in Prada, Armani, and Dolce & Gabbana. Carina would take a stroll on the uneven pavements, nibbling on a buttery pastry and enjoying the scene before her, rain and all.

She bit back a sigh and glanced at the massive stack of papers on her desk. Not her. She'd eat again in her of-

fice, soothe some cranky egos from the board since allowing
Wolfe to be her liaison in the project, and crunch numbers.
The advertising plan needed to be nailed down soon in
order to prepare for a quick opening. Sales were down in
Firenze for some strange reason, and she needed a confer-
ence call with the chef.

She pressed her palm flat against the cool pane of glass
and thought again of the other offer before her.

One night with Sawyer.

It had been nearly a week since their encounter. Five
full days of no close interaction—just a glance from the end
of a conference table. Five days since he touched her and
kissed her and boldly propositioned her with sex. Her rational mind raged at his crudity and obvious dismissal of the
polite rules of society and work.

The other part of her relished the dark freedom.

She turned from the window and adjusted the few
frames on her desk that kept getting misaligned. What was
wrong with her lately? Usually work satisfied every aspect
in her life. During yesterday's meeting, she found her gaze
attached to Sawyer. Especially the tight ass muscles his custom Calvin Klein suit enhanced. And damned if he hadn't
turned around and given her that dirty little smile. Like he
knew what she was thinking. Imagining. Fantasizing about.
And what he refused to give her until she agreed to his
ridiculous terms.

So embarrassing.

She told herself over and over he played a game of ego and ruthlessness. Why did he want to give her an orgasm so badly? Why did he care? And yet . . . the lure of one night with him taunted her sanity. Maybe if she gave him the opportunity, everything would go back to normal? Couldn't it be a win/win for her?

She paced back and forth and analyzed the details. Maybe there was room for negotiation. He'd do his best to give her physical pleasure, and if she couldn't . . . well, climax . . . she'd have full control over the bakery's terms in Purity.

Asset number one.

Sure, it could be a bit awkward, but she'd already warned him about her inability to relax, and a few hours of being uncomfortable would be worth the reward. Her mind sliced through the options and switched to devil's advocate. What if she did have an orgasm?

Her belly dipped at the tantalizing image of pleasure. Well, that would be great, right? Maybe she'd finally get her head back in the game of business. After all, couldn't one orgasm last her a long time? Kind of like inventory. Her body would be more loose, she'd have the satisfaction she was normal, and she'd move on. Yes, he'd still retain full rights of final approval. Unless . . .

What if she raised the stakes? Made it more difficult for him to achieve his goal?

After all, if he was able to rise to the new terms, she'd

deserve to lose. Her gut said it'd be an impossible task for him to accomplish. Even if he managed to get her to slide over the cliff once, he'd never, ever make her come twice. Right?

She tapped her fingernail against her bottom lip and scanned all possibilities. Could she get him to agree? Yes, challenging his ego and giving him an unreachable goal would call to his sense of dominance. A shiver raced down her spine. And she knew he'd be dominant in private. Just the way he'd restrained her wrists and gotten that gleam of lust in his eyes made her wet. She sensed he'd go for the new terms and lose. Maybe she'd get one orgasm and score the contract also.

Win/win.

As if her thoughts conjured him up, her secretary buzzed her. "Mr. Wells is here to see you. Can I send him in?"

Julietta tamped down the girly impulse to check her hair and makeup, though she hardly wore any, and cleared her throat. "Yes, please."

She didn't have a magic door, so she settled back in her burgundy leather chair, straightened herself to full height, and pretended to be engaged in her folders. He entered silently, as if he practiced burglary in his spare time, and the only way she knew he was in front of her was the pull of his body heat and the delicious smell of spice he carried on his skin. She lifted her head, a polite smile on her face, and froze.

He was so gorgeous. Would she ever get used to that face?

His smoke-gray cashmere coat set off a red plaid scarf and the golden halo of his wavy hair. His tall, lean length held a restrained strength she found both appealing and intimidating. As if he didn't need to show off for anyone because he possessed the real thing. The slash of his scar only emphasized the graceful lines of his face, reminding her that underneath his civilized, graceful veneer, something savage lurked. Her throat grew dry as she tried to find some spit and found it had disappeared. Without missing a beat, Sawyer crossed the room, propped two hands on her sprawling mahogany desk, and leaned in. Butterscotch eyes delved straight into hers without hesitation or apology. As if he'd been patiently waiting for her answer and was now done.

"Well?"

Some weird noise squeaked from her throat. She dropped the folders she was holding and rallied. "Well, what?"

His lip quirked. "Have you approved the final layout? The builders need to set up the proper space for equipment for the pedestrian store."

Disappointment tweaked at his focus on business. Stupid to believe he'd come here for something else. She shook off her thoughts and squinted in consideration. "I prefer the right corner. Studies have proven that locations in lobbies propel more impulse buys."

"Not in this case. La Dolce Maggie owns the same spot in the Venetian and sales are rocketing."

"This isn't America," she retorted. "Milano is a hard city to conquer, especially with a hotel with American influences. You may get the tourists, but pastry buyers prefer a window shop on the right."

His teeth flashed from the wolfish grin. "Perhaps. But I already have a use for that prime space. You can make it up in other ways—you don't have to rely on passersby for main profits any longer."

Irritation pricked her nerves. "An interesting but completely inane opinion."

One golden brow arched. "Inane, huh?"

She smoothly continued. "The impulse buyer happens to bring a high level of profit we don't want to lose. Especially since, as you Americans like to say, we have our eggs in one basket."

"But it's a hell of a basket."

The wicked curl of seduction tipped his words. She ignored it, but her heart pounded anyway. "Perhaps. Though a bit small."

His bark of laughter startled her. Julietta fought a flush of pleasure at her ability to make him laugh. He drew his hands back and slowly unknotted his scarf. Slid off his coat and hung it neatly on the back of the chair. Why did this basic stripping of outer clothes affect her like this? As if she was in his private bedroom waiting for the finale. Her gaze probed his clothes as she wondered what type of body he sported beneath the thin fabric. His muscles seemed tight in all the right places. When he'd pinned her against the wall, everything felt rock hard and powerful.

"Now that was an interesting thought," he murmured.

This time, she blushed. Hurriedly ducking her head, she pretended to neaten the pile of papers before swiveling the chair around. The massive desk hid most of her body and gave her a layer of protection she badly needed. "So, can we adjust our original location?"

"No."

She stiffened. "Why not?"

He adjusted his cuffs as if he had all the time in the world. "Because I don't want to. My plan will work better."

"What if I disagree with your opinion?" She rolled the last word around in mockery to make her point.

He gave a half shrug. "I don't care. Final approval, remember?"

Julietta sucked in a breath. "Are you using this as leverage for your ridiculous offer?"

Humor glinted in his eyes. "I don't need leverage, Julietta. Personal relationships do not have to affect my business ventures. In this case, I want you badly enough to take a gamble." His obvious ease with admitting he wanted to take her to bed reminded her she was sparring with an expert. And for one crazy moment, she wanted to play in a different arena. Wanted to leap and take a chance on something that scared the crap out of her.

Her protective stance behind her desk suddenly seemed like a prison. She got to her feet and moved, keeping a safe distance between them. His obvious amusement raised her hackles again and she blurted out the words to push him off guard. "Let's negotiate terms."

"I told you. The space decision is final."

"I'm talking about our night together."

That did it. Surprise flitted across his carved features. "You want to discuss bullet points?"

She ignored his question and sank into the world where she was most comfortable. Business. Her heels tapped on the polished wood as she paced with slow, steady movements. "Of course. I've been thinking about your offer. At first glance, it seems like a solid compromise due to my inability to reach certain physical aspects most other women are able to achieve."

He shook his head, crossed his arms in front of his chest, and stared. "I hear a 'but' in there."

"But I feel it's too easy of a mark for you to hit. I think by raising the terms to two orgasms, it will be a fairer competition for either of us to win."

His mouth opened but nothing came out. Satisfaction coursed through her at his sudden inability to speak. About time she finally grabbed the upper hand. He finally found his voice. "We're negotiating the number of orgasms now?"

She frowned. "Of course. I didn't limit your option

clause to specified use of any toys, so really, you may pull out an advantage. And let's be honest, shall we? Achieving one orgasm may be difficult but achievable with the focus of an estimated eight hours. Two would be much harder and bring us on a more equal playing field."

"Holy shit. You're not kidding."

Annoyance fluttered through her. "I'm sorry, perhaps I was mistaken. Was this a negotiable, valid offer or not?"

He let out a deep belly laugh, the rich tone booming and pumping the room with life. "God, you're magnificent," he murmured. Suddenly, the laughter faded and was replaced by a glimmer of hard lust. Her toes curled in her bone-colored pumps. "You are correct, Julietta. This is a valid offer and negotiations are definitely in play."

Her confidence wobbled. Why did it feel like he was back in charge? She reminded herself to stick to business and not get distracted by his sexiness. After all, he probably used such assets to his advantage. "Very good. I believe we should raise the limit from one to two."

"Done."

She blinked. Way too easy. Why did he seem so danger-ous? His tongue wet his bottom lip as if imagining her taste when he finally pounced. "Oh. Well, good. Then I guess we have a deal."

"Oh, we're not finished." Sawyer moved toward her a few steps and studied her face. "I assume, first off, this will not be a written contract, but verbal?"

She fought the blush this time and won. "Yes, I trust your word and would rather this deal not be in ink."

"Agreed." One more step in. She slid her foot back in a casual manner and gained another inch of distance. "Time is important. You mentioned eight hours. I think we should be more specific—let's say eight p.m. to eight a.m. for a full twelve hours."

"Uh, I don't think I should be staying overnight. Or sleeping in your bed. How about eight to two?"

"Nonnegotiable. I'll need a certain amount of intimacy to have a fair shot at getting you two orgasms. You will stay the night."

She hated the idea and had been hoping to scurry out before the morning light. "I'll agree to six a.m., but no later."

Was that pride reflected in his face or her imagination? "Agreed. Let's discuss location. Where shall this take place? Your apartment?"

Julietta frowned. "No. It should be on neutral territory."

"I'll book a hotel."

She dragged her other foot back. "I don't want any gossip. Discreetness is key."

"I promise to take care of it. Do you trust me?"

Did she? Did she trust him to keep her secret safe, along with the use of her body? Yes. The word floated from her gut and she didn't question it. Julietta had learned the hard way to always trust her instincts, whether she wanted to or not. "Yes."

Satisfaction gleamed from his eyes. He moved forward three steps. "Thank you."

Her fingers curled into tight fists. "*Prego*. Anything else?"

"Yes. Methods."

Mio Dio. "What type of methods?"

An intimate smile curved his lips. "Am I allowed to use toys? Or just my fingers and mouth?"

Her heart thundered so loud she heard the *boom, boom, boom* echo in the room. The idea of him using a vibrator on her was too much to handle. She shook her head. "No, no toys. It gives you an unfair advantage."

"Hmm, I'm tempted to fight you on this point. I can further your pleasure and take you higher."

Perspiration dampened her palms. "No, thank you."

"Very well. It will give me something to work for."

Not able to take his closeness, she pivoted and practically raced back toward the safety of her desk. "Good. I think that's it. I should get back to work."

His voice was whisper soft. "When?"

She dived into the chair. "Saturday night?"

"Done. Oh, and one more thing, Julietta. It's a rule and I won't bend on this one."

Her stomach dropped. "What rule?"

Slowly, he moved toward her. Her haven became a prison as he came around the desk, grasped the supple leather arms of the chair, and swiveled her around to face him head-on. Thoughts emptied from her head and turned her into a wide-eyed idiot. His scent swarmed her nostrils, and he dragged the chair a few inches forward. Leaned in. Stopped a hair's breadth from her lips.

"I'm in charge. The moment you enter that door, your body belongs to me. I tell you to do something, you must agree to do it."

She trembled. "That's ridiculous. I'm not going to do everything you say."

"Then no deal."

His gaze drilled hers and confirmed there was no backing down. All or nothing. "What if I'm uncomfortable or scared?"

His face softened. He ran an index finger over the curve of her lip. "I'd never hurt you. I'll give you a way to slow things down, or stop, but you need to trust me."

There was that word again. *Trust.* Trust a man with a savage scar and no past, who was a sexual force to be reckoned with. Again her gut screamed the answer, and the word broke from her lips.

"*Va bene.*"

The triumph in those butterscotch eyes almost made her withdraw her consent. Almost. He must have known she was tempted, because with one last stroke of his fingers, he pulled back and gave her space. "Saturday night, then. I'll let you know where to meet me." He shrugged on his coat, twirled the scarf around his neck, and headed toward the door. "Let me know if you have any problems with Wolfe. I'll be in touch."

He walked out without another word.

Julietta shuddered and wondered if she'd just made a bargain with Hades himself.

. . .

"I don't want this kid involved."

Julietta held back a sigh and faced her long-term, opinionated director of marketing. She'd never particularly cared for him, even if he was good at his job. She found him a bit snobby, with his designer clothes, his perfect posture, and his tendency to pass judgment on everyone. He was probably the biggest gossip in the place, and most of the female employees panted after him. She took in his crisp blue suit, Gucci boots, and stylish Stone Rose pink shirt. Dark hair was cut ruthlessly short to accent riveting green eyes and a sculpted mouth. Julietta found that so-called sensual mouth quite sulky and his voice whiny. He liked getting his way just to say he could.

He adjusted his diamond cuff links and jerked his head toward the closed door of the conference room. "He looks like a criminal. I'm certainly not working with a teenager with an attitude problem."

Julietta tamped down her impatience. "You don't have to work with him long term, Marcus. He'll have little to do with marketing—he's here to help us transition and get on board with the Purity vision. We sell Purity, we sell La Dolce Famiglia. Simple math."

The famous pout appeared. "I run my team and don't need interference. The campaign with your mother as the main draw was a big seller. Moving into the hotel industry and targeting a larger catering, leisure audience will be a challenge, so we'll need to come up with something fresh. I have an idea in the works."

"Fine. Can you have your presentation ready for next week?

"Absolutely."

She nodded. "Let me know if you run into any problems." He glided out of the office and stopped short as the door swung open before him. Wolfe trudged in. His large gold hoop earring winked, and crazy spiked strands of hair shot toward the sky. The shaven-clean half of his skull only added to the bizarre effect. Funny, she was beginning to like having him around. Besides adding some local color, he seemed amazingly sharp and to the point, and had no ego to deal with.

Marcus backed up as if he was afraid to get pickpocketed. A sneer curved the younger man's lips. "Hey, Mark."

Marcus shuddered delicately. "It's Marcus."

"Whatever." Wolfe bumped into her director without apology and took a seat at the table. Marcus brushed his clothes off and glared. "Listen, Enzo doesn't want to work with me. Says he can't trust me with the latest sales figures. Probably thinks I'll sell them to Princi Bakery and finance my new tattoo." Julietta bit her lip and held back a laugh at Marcus's horrified expression. "This isn't gonna work. I respect you for trying, but I'm not up for a fight every time I go into a new office and ask for information. I'll go back to headquarters and let Sawyer know."

Marcus muttered something under his breath in obvious relief.

"Absolutely not."

Both males turned toward her. She pivoted her headset closer and tapped a button. "I want heads of all departments in my conference room now. Pull them out of any meetings and be here in fifteen minutes."

Her secretary responded immediately. "Yes, Ms. Conte."

Julietta directed her attention to Marcus. "Do you think I would throw someone I don't trust into one of the most important deals this bakery has ever made?" Her frosty tone hit the mark. He blanched and glanced down at Wolfe in distaste. "Do you think I care he's a decade younger and has a penchant for facial jewelry? He's worked with Sawyer and is willing to help us move forward. He knows the vision we're after, and I need everyone to get on board."

Marcus stiffened. "I don't appreciate his rudeness, unprofessionalism, or your willingness to shove a stranger into a tight family circle."

Julietta nodded. "Fair enough. I respect you, Marcus, and I agree. We need to work together in a strong environment." Her gaze settled on the young man currently slouched in his seat and sporting a classic, conservative black suit that only made him stand out more. "Wolfe, you don't need to like everyone here, but I expect you to respect a department head's position. Agreed?"

She waited. Wondered if he'd walk out with a surly insult. Instead, he seemed to analyze her words with an assessing air that told her he'd be brilliant in the business world when he grew into his own talents. He held the same type of restrained wildness Sawyer did, but Wolfe was young and hadn't yet been able to weave it into the fabric of society. The kid turned and faced her director.

"I apologize."

That was it. No more excuses, whining, or explanations. Marcus still didn't look happy, but he gave a curt nod. A strange rush of pride filled her for the boy's courage. "Good. Can you leave us alone for a few minutes, Marcus?"

He left the conference room. Wolfe shifted in his seat, obviously expecting some sort of retribution. The uneasy silence thickened the air. Julietta studied the boy. How far could she push? A level of trust was needed in the relationship between them if they were to move forward. Odd, a work bond was just as important as a personal one—sometimes more so. Long hours, stressful situations, and endless decisions regarding money and time were key. She handpicked her employees and made sure they bonded, or the end result was failure and messiness. She had ten minutes to decide before the employees came in.

Julietta plucked the headset off and settled in the chair opposite him. Every muscle in his body stiffened as if he were preparing for a beating. Her heart squeezed. She wondered if he had the stamina to push past his distance and give her something precious. Something that might hurt.

"I want to work with you, Wolfe. I'm ready to back you to my team so you'll never have trouble here again. You'll be part of the group and be involved in all decisions with La Dolce Famiglia and Purity. You'll earn their respect if you're good. But I need to know if I can trust you."

He gave a bitter laugh. "Yeah, sure. Like anyone's gonna trust me anyway. This whole thing was a mistake. I don't belong here."

The ravaged emotion in those blue eyes hit her like a sucker punch. But he didn't need her pity or her sympathy. His past was clearly a minefield of crap, and he'd do best if she kept it straight and to the point. "I don't know your history, and I don't care to. How you deal with me and my staff is all I care about. Make yourself belong if this is something you want to do."

Wolfe lifted his head and studied her. She had gained his full attention and didn't plan on squandering the time.

"Sawyer probably didn't belong either, but he forced his way in. When I faced a wall of male employees who told me I couldn't run a business because I didn't own a penis, I didn't belong either. I carved my own place. You can, too."

"How?"

His honest question gave her hope. "I'll give you my full support on one condition."

A frown marred his brow. Suspicion laced his tone. "What condition?"

"Give me one reason to trust you. Just between us, and everything stays here at this table. Why should I let you help lead a multimillion-dollar deal?"

He flinched. "What kind of question is that? You either trust me or you don't."

She shook her head. "No. Trust is earned. Give me something—a piece of truth—an admission no one else knows. Tell me why you should stay on your own accord and not because Sawyer is letting you play on the business ground."

Seconds ticked. His face clearly showed the struggle to either share something he didn't want or walk away. He shifted in his chair, got to his feet, stopped, and cursed under his breath. Julietta made her own leap and gave him the push he needed.

"I was twenty-two when I started working with my brother. I knew I had a lot to prove, and I swore I'd make him proud of me. I worked harder and longer hours than anyone else, studied the industry, and took a lot of crap from the executives who didn't think I belonged here. One night I was working late and an exec from advertising followed me into my office." God, she still remembered the scent of his overpowering cologne and the fake smile on his lips. His eyes gleamed with a coldness that froze her in place. Even as he pretended to make small talk as he sat on the edge of the desk. Touched her hair. Focused his greedy stare on the edge of her skirt. Hot breath against her mouth and grabby hands on her thighs.

"He tried to force himself on me. I got lucky. One of the cleaning people heard me and burst in before anything happened." Her composed tone contradicted the deep shudder that wracked her body. "I pressed charges, but they were dropped. The executive got fired. And I learned the lesson. It didn't matter if I was smarter, worked harder, or was even more deserving. It only mattered what he saw—a silly female sex object not worthy of this company or his respect." She shrugged. "That episode made me stronger. I can't change anyone's opinions, but I sure as hell won't let them screw me just because they think they can. That's my truth."

Wolfe didn't move. She locked her gaze with his and waited. His fingers fisted, and she watched as the memories struggled to surface—watched his internal struggle—and the control he used to compose himself. He clenched his jaw. "I've been to hell. I got out. I'm never going back." Wolfe swallowed. "I had no place to go, so I tried to steal from Sawyer and got caught. Most rich guys would've locked me in jail and pressed charges. Instead, he offered to take me in. Gave me a job and a chance to learn the business. He didn't even know anything about me, yet he gave me more than anyone had in this lifetime. A chance. You can trust me because any other way is back to hell."

"Is it just about a job? Or something more?"

Again, he gave her the priceless gift of truth. "It started as the job, but now it's more. We've been together almost a year now. He's the smartest man I've ever met, and he's fair." He ducked his head and his voice broke. "I don't want to disappoint him."

Her chest hurt, so she breathed carefully, kept her face impassive, and nodded. "You won't. You show the skills of someone much older and wiser, and you've seen the other side, so you'll never take anything for granted. You're the type of man I want on my team."

He looked up. Nodded. She caught the tiny smile on his face as he sat back down in the chair, making his own decision to stay. "*Grazie*."

Damn, she liked him. Bristly and honest and real. "*Prego*."

"Julietta?"

"Yes?"

"What's the name of the guy who hurt you? Maybe someone should pay him a visit?"

Startled, she laughed with delight at his sudden protectiveness so ingrained in the male species. Another thing to like about him—once he trusted, he'd be loyal to the core. "No worries. Michael allowed the charges to be dropped for a good reason. Let's just say my older brother knows people. At least the exec's hospital stay was quite short."

"Good." He gave a half grin. "Italians are definitely the

best in the area of payback. I've watched the *Godfather* and *Goodfellas* a bunch of times."

She was still laughing when her employees streamed into the room. They threw odd glances at both of them as they took their seats and waited for her to speak. Julietta moved to the head of the table and smiled.

This was going to be fun.

Chapter Eight

Sawyer did a quick survey of the rooms to make sure everything was in place. The Bulgari Milano hotel was perfect for their first encounter, offering an old-fashioned luxury that was both visually and physically arresting. The sitting room was intimately set up with a Brera stone fireplace, and the rich woods of teak and oak blended with deep vanillas and buttery colors that soothed the senses. The refined elegance of the eighteenth-century palazzo reminded him of Julietta. The display of ornate jewels and tasteful antiques throughout the suite added an extra touch. The open carved archway led to the bedroom, where a magnificent canopy bed dominated the room. Ice blue silk pillows matched the ridiculously expensive thread count of the pulled-back sheets, and the glass doors opened to a private balcony that overlooked the gardens. A bottle of champagne chilled in the silver bucket across from a tray of finger foods to keep any hunger at bay.

He hoped he'd finally elicit a different type of hunger. Anticipation bit through him in sweet agony and stiffened his cock. Their negotiations over this night still turned him on. He'd never met a woman so worthy of pleasure. The sharpness of her intellect was as much of a turn-on as her luscious body. A body she didn't know how to use or to take pleasure in. The dom in him howled to release such a prize and claim it for himself.

The possessiveness surprised him. He'd shared women before without a thought—not to hurt them but to make sure he didn't restrain them with false expectations. Sawyer realized long ago he'd never be whole enough for a healthy, long-term relationship. With a past filled with abuse, neglect, and mental games, there was nothing pure or good in him to offer. He made sure women knew there was no future going in so he never gave fake hope. But since Julietta, his inner caveman broke out with a primitive impulse to mark her as his.

He'd just have to get over it.

Still, he couldn't believe he'd persuaded her to spend the night. When she calmly informed him he'd only get a few hours and she'd leave before dawn, the need to claim her till morning shocked him to the core. Usually it was the other way around. A rueful smile touched his lips. Guess he got a taste of the other side. And it sucked.

A knock sounded on the door.

His fingers tingled as he opened it and wondered if she'd obey his first request. His scrawled note with the gift box probably intimidated her. Had he gone too far? Sawyer flung open the door.

Instead of a trembling lover, he faced a pissed-off ice queen.

A scowl settled on her brow. "You actually think women like wearing this crap? Do you know how humiliating it is to have people think you're not wearing anything under your coat? I got stares from the taxi driver and doorman."

She stalked in wearing a short cream-colored wool coat. Stiletto heels. Black stockings. And not much else.

Loose mahogany waves fell past her shoulders and continued to her waist, emphasizing the nakedness of her collarbone, teasing an onlooker to try to take a peek. Her skirt was so short it disappeared under the hemline and gave the impression of erotic hide-and-go-seek.

Oh, yeah. She obeyed perfectly. His gaze roved over her with pure greed, even as he fought a grin at her entry. She was so different from any other woman—he was endlessly fascinated by the twist of confidence and vulnerability she exhibited.

"You didn't like the stares of the other men?" he challenged. "Doesn't it make you feel desirable? Sexy?"

"Dirty," she quipped, dropping her purse on the chair and glancing around. She obviously wasn't ready to lose the coat. "*Puttana*?"

He poured her a glass of champagne and crossed the room. The scent of rich coconut and mocha drifted from her skin. "Slut, huh? Ah, you are judging by society's expectations again. Why shouldn't a powerful woman want to be a slut in her own bedroom? Such a negative connotation for a woman who demands pleasure and will do anything to get it." His words caused a delicate shudder to rip through her body. Good. She liked the verbal images, and it reached her on a deeper level.

She dived into a change of subject. "I don't know if I feel comfortable at this hotel."

"Why?"

She nibbled at her lower lip. "The rooms are close. People may hear us."

He handed her the delicate flute. God, she was adorable. One moment a lioness, the next a shy virgin. "I'm glad you're thinking you'll enjoy yourself enough to scream, but I've taken care of the problem."

"How?"

He smiled. "I bought all the rooms on this floor. We are completely alone."

She blinked. "Oh. Good thinking."

"Thank you." He dropped his voice. "And necessary. Because you will be screaming, Julietta. A lot."

Her fingers tightened on the stem of the glass, but she refused to cower. She tipped the glass up and took a long sip. Then met his gaze. "If you're lucky."

"Why don't you take off your coat?"

"Not yet. So, tell me, Sawyer. Is this what men fantasize about women wearing? Because I'm here to tell you it's uncomfortable as hell and not much fun. This thong is riding up my rear in a permanent wedgie. And my breasts are held so tight together it's hard to breathe. Not the best way to get me in the mood."

He reached out and touched a glossy wave. The heat from her body burned and pulled him in, making a mockery of her calm demeanor. Oh, yeah, she was definitely aroused. She just didn't know what to do with it and hoped to lock it up in a neat little closet. He looked forward to causing her much discomfort in the next few hours. His cock twitched in his pants.

"You're not pushing past the surface," he murmured. "Behind the vague discomfort is the opportunity to let your body take over. The corset I picked out for you pushes your breasts out and makes your nipples more sensitive. Every breath you take is controlled and earned, so you're aware of the rush of air in your lungs." He kept up the slide of his fingers over her hair, tugging gently to wake up her scalp. "When you're aroused, your nipples will harden and poke against the lace. The scratch will be a reminder of what my stubble may feel like against your breasts. The edge of your panties separate the globes of your buttocks and barely skim your mound. As you get wet, you'll be aware of each sensation. Discomfort brings awareness, Julietta. It's all part of eroticism."

Her pupils dilated. Yes. He knew she dampened at the stroke of his voice, her body finally letting go enough to make the connection with her brain. He imagined the tightness of her nipple under his tongue and the sweet arch of her hips as she opened for him. But first, he needed to strip all of her mental defenses.

He released her hair and took a deliberate step back. "Now, back to my original request. Take your coat off."

Surprise flickered across her face. "I'm cold."

His lips twitched. "I'll warm you up soon. For now, let this be a gentle reminder to the terms of our agreement. Full command. Full surrender."

His queen rallied. Crap, she was magnificent. Her eyes snapped cocoa brown heat and her fingers tugged open the buttons. "This is ridiculous." One. Two. "I can't believe I agreed to this sex scene. Just so you know, this is not turning me on, so I hope at least you get a thrill from this episode." Three. Four. She shrugged off the barrier and threw it on the velvet chair to cover her purse. "Satisfied?"

Oh, yeah.

He took in the fine black lace of her corset, which nipped in at the waist, squeezed her breasts, and lifted them up like a gift to the gods. The minuscule black skirt barely covered her ass. Her skin was flawless and a golden brown that begged for a man's touch. Endless legs clad in sheer black hose ended in a pair of four-inch fuck-me heels where her fire-engine-red toenails peeked out in rebellion.

Time to reel in his stubborn lover-to-be. He switched to his dom voice, which vibrated with a confident power, and whipped through the room like a lash. "Turn around."

She jerked. Blinked. But obeyed immediately, turning in a full circle so he could feast on the full globes of her rear, where the wisp of fabric hugged her most intimate body parts. His fingers clenched to touch the lush flesh and warm it to a nice pale pink. Instead, he crossed his arms in front of his chest and studied every inch of her. A delicate flush bloomed in her cheeks. Good. She was aware of his full attention and was off balance. "Have you ever had a man look at you like this, Julietta?"

She shook her head.

"Answer me, please."

Pure resentment and something deeper flickered. "No."

"When I ask a question, I want a verbal answer."

"Fine."

He kept the humor from his face and continued his appraisal. "A man is a visual creature. When a woman takes off her clothes, she's stripping her barriers and giving a precious gift. Her vulnerability. Do you know how that makes me feel?"

"How?"

"Honored. Aching. Like the anticipation of opening up a present, peeling off the paper and bow and uncovering a treasure. Let me tell you what I see when I look at you." His voice deepened and he let the yawning want for her show on his face. "I see breasts that are already swelling and peaking, begging for my fingers and tongue. Your belly is quivering ever so slightly. I'd run my tongue down your stomach and over that tiny piece of lace. Feel your heat and wetness and smell your arousal. Your legs are long and graceful, and I can imagine them wrapped around my hips and squeezing tight as I thrust inside you." Her chest lifted as she sucked in air. "I want to discover every hidden secret of your body and a thousand ways to make you scream my name." His eyes glittered and he moved forward. "A reminder of the basic rules. Do everything I say. No talking unless I ask a question. And absolutely no thinking. I'll do that for both of us tonight." He paused so his words had a moment to sink in. "Let's begin, shall we?"

. . .

Julietta burned. Her skin prickled as if she stood near to a raging fireplace while wafts of heat hit every exposed part of her body. She squirmed in discomfort and tried to lock onto the strange feeling that her body had separated from and left her mind behind. Her nipples ached behind the constricting binds of the corset, and the thong between her legs emphasized an achy pulsing between her thighs. Odd, she'd been aroused before. Even believed she neared climax a few times. But never had she been so turned on by a man who hadn't even touched her yet.

He stalked her slow and steady, letting her know she'd be under his command in a few minutes and there was nothing for her to do to stop it. A thrill shot through her. There was no one on this floor, and nobody knew she was here tonight. She was completely at his mercy for him to do anything to her body. Utter any outrageous comment he felt like. She had no clue what his next move would be— if he'd be gentle or cruel.

The knowledge turned her on. Big time.

He was still fully dressed, in a snowy white button-down shirt, tan chinos, and bare feet. She ached to touch the mass of honey waves that framed his face, a fascinating mixture of white to dirty blonde. She wanted to see his bare chest and run her hands over his skin. Was he covered in light hair or bare? He smelled of a mix of rich scents that made her dizzy: coffee beans, spice, and musk.

Julietta kept her position and refused to back down. If this was the beginning of round one, she'd be damned if she'd make it easy. He settled his palms on her naked shoulders and stroked down her arms, as if checking the muscles of a racehorse he contemplated buying. The thought helped ground her. "Do I pass muster?" She managed to keep her voice calm and cool.

"A broken rule already? No speaking unless I ask you a question."

She snapped her mouth shut and glared. Humor lit whiskey-colored eyes, but he kept his face impassive as he touched her. He interlaced his fingers with hers and pulled each one in a sensual massage. Her muscles tensed, waiting, but he took his time. He moved from her fingers to the swell of her breasts that pushed out to meet him. Caressed the erratic pulse at the base of her throat. The curve of her cheek. The sensitive line of her neck. Every inch exposed to his view was explored by his fingers until a melting sensation dropped in her belly.

She began to relax.

He knelt in front of her.

A strange noise bubbled from the back of her throat. What was he doing? *Dio Mio,* he grasped her thigh and kneaded the muscles in her legs, exploring behind her knee, sliding down her calves to her ridiculous heels that screamed sex. Up and down, until goose bumps peppered her flesh and every muscle clenched waiting for his next move.

"Take off your skirt."

Julietta hesitated. A roaring filled her ears, and her clothes suddenly felt as if they were strangling her. His gaze drilled into hers and commanded her obedience. Before she could analyze the request, her thumbs hooked under her waistband and she dragged the material down her hips. The skirt fell to her feet.

His warm approval washed over her. He lifted one of her heels, then the other, and tossed the skirt to the side. "Very good. Now, don't move."

A gasp fell from her lips as he lifted her foot and placed one sharp heel on his shoulder. He pressed his mouth to her inner thigh, rubbing his cheeks back and forth over the sensitive skin. Her center throbbed and begged for more, but he seemed content to breathe her scent in and take tiny nibbles over the expanse of one thigh, then the other. She leaned against the wall for balance, and her fingers auto matically came down to rest on his head. The sensations were exquisite: a swirl of his tongue, a nip of teeth rising higher to the place she needed it most. Why was he going so slow? Did he want her to participate? She always sucked at this part, wondering how long she'd have to reciprocate with any oral sex given when she really didn't like it much. If she got this over with quickly, maybe they'd get to the real sex part sooner.

His mouth moved higher along the edge of the lace and his hot breath blew over her swollen lips. *Merda,* they needed to move this along. Julietta fisted her hands in his hair and urged him to the spot she needed him to touch the most.

He backed away. She trembled and let out an irritable sigh. "What are you doing?" she asked. "Why did you stop?"

He shook his head with disapproval and rose from his knees. "Obviously, you are not one made to obey rules. So let's help you along, shall we?" Sawyer walked over to the small writing desk, slid open a drawer, and withdrew a set of handcuffs.

The outrageousness of the scene appalled her, and she threw her hands out. "Hell, no, you are *so* not using those on me."

"Do you trust me?"

"That's not what this is about."

One golden brow arched. "It's what this entire night is about. Trust. You trust me to get you where you need, and I trust you to obey."

"But I, I—"

"Do you, Julietta?"

If she lied she could go home. Screw the contract. She didn't need an orgasm or more business control. Her mind screamed for her to grab her coat and get out. Instead, her hormones slapped her brain in a knockout punch. "Yes. I trust you."

"We're doing the cuffs. Hands out, please."

Her tongue dragged across her lip, but she held out her wrists. In some crazy way, she got wetter, her nipples nearing the edge of pain in a stark need to escape the corset. He clasped the cuffs, checked the fit, and stepped back to survey her. "Much better." The fur lining encased her flesh with luxury. He tipped her chin up and took total control of her gaze. "You can't touch me. You don't have to wonder what move to make or what you need to do to make me happy. I own your body and I'll do whatever the hell I want with it now. Understood?"

A raw sizzle cut through her. She nodded, past the point of wanting to talk. A strange relief sagged her muscles as if reaching a new level; the complete truth of his statement shook her foundation. Suddenly, there were no more choices. No decisions to make. No right or wrong. He'd stolen it all and left her with nothing.

Nothing but freedom.

Satisfaction and raw lust flickered in his eyes. "There we go," he murmured. "That's what I want." He lowered his head and claimed her mouth.

She opened her lips, nowhere left to hide, as he swept his tongue and conquered every dark crevice, thrusting in and out while he held her head still. Julietta moaned under the savage attack, unconsciously looking to touch him or help guide the kiss. Her handcuffs clinked together. The sound drifted to her ears and caused a rush of wetness to trickle down her thigh. *Mio dio,* she ached for him, but every time she tried to scissor her legs together for relief he held her tight against him, one thigh trapping her wide and open to his touch. He commanded every sensation, wracking shudders from her body while his tongue mated and tangled with hers. His fingers moved from her hair and dropped to her breasts. He stroked and teased the edges of her nipples, still imprisoned by the delicate bones of the corset, until she twisted wildly in an attempt to get more.

He bit down on her lower lip. "What do you want?"

"Touch me."

He kissed her long and deep and hard, ignoring her request. Then finally broke away. Golden eyes seared and commanded her to reach for more. "Where? If you want something, ask."

Embarrassment disappeared under a craving need to get what she wanted. "Take off the corset. Touch my breasts."

"Very good." He reached behind her and with deft skill unfastened the long row of hooks that held the fabric together. She sucked in a breath as sweet air rushed into her lungs, and her breasts sprang free. He cupped them in his warm palms and rubbed her tight nipples. Julietta arched for more. "Like this?"

"Oh, please—"

"Tell me."

"Suck on them." With a lusty groan of approval, he dipped his head and took one nipple into his mouth. The hot wetness as he pulled and swirled his tongue around and around ripped a cry from her throat. Julietta twisted and once again reached out to hold on to something, but she was bound and at his mercy.

Just like she wanted it.

The thought skittered past. Her nipples throbbed under his talented mouth as he moved from one to the other, but the realization she loved being handcuffed and ravaged like some sort of weak, pathetic female exploded in her consciousness. What was she doing? How could the CEO of the most powerful bakery in the world beg a man to do dirty things to her while she was helpless? A cold ball of ice settled in her gut, and she was dragged back to the familiar scene. Her body began to shut down, her arousal lessening with every second until—

A slight pop sounded in the air as he lifted his head from her breast. Sawyer studied her face. "God, you're stubborn." His lower lip quirked. "Thinking too much again, baby? Better up my game."

"Sawyer, I don't think this—oh!"

With no transition, softness, or warning, his hand slipped under the lace of her thong and plunged inside.

Her hips bucked in demand and her body wept. The delicious friction of his fingers pumping inside her tight channel contrasted with the light, teasing stroke of his thumb over her clit. She tried to close her eyes to hide from her raw response, but he held her gaze with a fierce demand that refused to let her cower. Every naked expression and moan was his. And he reminded her of it with each stroke of those talented fingers.

The combination pushed her toward the edge. Julietta strained toward the rapidly nearing orgasm, frantic to grab on before it shimmered away. Her clit swelled with each flick. The cuffs clinked. Sawyer slid his hand away, curled, and dove deep.

Oh, yes. Right there.

"*Mio Dio!*" She shuddered, tipped on the edge, and—

He backed away.

The climax slid out of reach.

She shook with frustration and anger. "Why did you do that? I was so close!"

"No talking or I'll gag you." Her eyes widened. "You're not even close to ready. As gorgeous as you look right now, I need more. Let's get you out of these clothes."

Temper simmered and coiled like a pissed-off snake. She lifted her bound hands. "I can't do much with these on." The slight whine in her voice filled her with humiliation. He didn't seem to mind—in fact, he looked quite satisfied with her reaction.

The corset hung down by her tied wrists. She waited to see if he'd unlock her, but he took the piece of fabric and ripped it right down the middle. "That was expensive!"

His expression snapped her lips closed. No way did she want to be gagged. "Your clothes belong to me just as you do. I do what I want with them." He tossed the garment aside. Then grasped the edges of her soaking thong and pulled it down her legs. The heavy scent of her arousal filled the air. He stood back and surveyed her naked body, his gaze probing every inch of her as she stood still under his inspection like a slave girl at auction.

Her belly clenched in lust. She had this weird need to please him, give herself over to anything and everything he wanted. After all, she had no choice anyway. Each step led her deeper into a dark, twisted world she never knew existed.

"Fuck, you're beautiful. More beautiful than I imagined."

The truth of his words struck home. The erection that pressed against his pants. The burning heat in his eyes as he looked at her. For the first time in her life, she knew this man wanted her as badly as she wanted him. Before, she only experienced the motions of sex, the thoughts of arousal and give-and-take. Now, there was nothing but the bare bones of want, messy and vulnerable and alive. Her chest squeezed with a strange sadness and longing.

Sawyer gave her no time to analyze the emotions. In one quick motion, he bent and slid her over his shoulder and marched down the hall into the bedroom. He placed her on the bed. Cool satin sheets pressed against her overheated skin. Her legs hung over the edge, feet still clad in her stiletto heels.

"Scoot back, baby. Head against the backboard. Keep the shoes on."

Julietta inched her way up. He nodded in approval, lifted her hands, and clipped the hook on the cuffs to a chain coming from the wall. It happened so fast, she never thought to protest, until she found her hands bound high over her head. He had chains above the bed? This was a respectable hotel. "I don't think—"

"I do." His voice snapped out and silenced her. Again, that crazy rush of liquid heat throbbed in her pussy from his dominating tone. He pulled open the bedside drawer and removed a condom and a rubber band. He laid both to the side and climbed on the bed. She tensed, but he only grabbed the rubber band and slowly tied his hair back. Her legs whipped closed, but he grinned and shook a finger at her. "Bad girl. You never close yourself to me. Ever. Unless of course you want me to tie you spread-eagled on the bed."

Heat sizzled to her core. A moan rose to her throat.

Sawyer clasped both of her ankles and pried her legs apart. He knelt between spread thighs. "Hmm, I think you would like that. Maybe next time."

Next time? This was insane; she had to get out of here. She couldn't be who he wanted, give him the satisfaction he needed with his partners. She was only playing a role, and soon her body would dry up like it always did. Her skin prickled with awareness. This road would only lead to more frustration and humiliation and pain. She had to get out of here, had to—

"Look at me, Julietta. Eyes on me." Her panicked gaze swung to his, and she gulped for breath. "You have nothing to be afraid of with me. I would never, ever hurt you."

The fear faded, leaving only uncertainty. "I can't be what you want." she whispered.

His eyes blazed fire. Oddly, his face seemed to soften with a possessiveness she'd never glimpsed before. "You

don't have to be anything, baby. You have no choices left—
I've taken them all away. I'm about to play with your delectable body, and there's not a damn thing you can do."

Relief loosened her muscles. Her arms sagged within
the hold of the chains.

There was nothing she could do. . . .

Whatever she felt or didn't wasn't up to her any longer. As she accepted the fact, Sawyer slowly unbuttoned
his shirt. She took in with pure greed the gorgeous lines of
his chest and shoulders. His pecs were clearly defined, the
lean muscled strength of his meaty biceps and arms told
her he worked out. Hard. The snowy shirt fell away, and
she sucked in her breath at the tight six-pack of his belly. A
light smattering of hair dusted his upper chest, but most of
his skin was a toasty brown and hairless. She noted several
strange marks and scars scattered in various places but had
no time to wonder. He lowered himself onto his elbows between her spread legs. Looked up at her naked body. And
smiled.

The room tilted at the sight of his wolfish, purely masculine grin. Oh, he was about to feast all right. On her. Every
part. The knowledge gleamed on his face, and the promise
shimmered from his eyes. The sheer vulnerability of her position horrified and excited her. The image of her wet inner
lips pulled open for him. Her pulsing clit on display for
whatever he deigned to give her—his fingers, tongue, teeth,
lips. Her skin pulled so tight over her bones she fought the

urge to pull against her chains and twist with raw need for him to do his worst.

"I've spent nights wondering how you'd taste. Dying to dip my tongue into your heat and make you come against my mouth. But I won't make this easy on either of us." He paused in the pulsing silence. "You'll have to beg long and hard before I give you what you want, baby. I've earned it."

He dipped his head.

Julietta had experienced oral sex before. Mostly, she remembered how conscious she was about every action performed, constantly worried about how she smelled, and how she tasted, and if her lover was even enjoying it. She'd faked her orgasms in half-assed, weak ways that men noticed until the only way to gain relief was to break up with them.

Sawyer caressed her trembling inner thighs as he nuzzled her cleft, moving his face back and forth over the small patch of damp pubic hair. The slide of his roughened cheek stung just enough to cause a delicious burn. Her channel clenched around emptiness, begging for more, but he only played for a long time, breathing her in, murmuring dirty words against her pussy, and rubbing her clit with light strokes evenly on each side.

Julietta dragged in breath and fought for her slipping composure. She wanted to worry about a thousand different things, but her body wept for more—something to take away the growing tension that twisted her muscles and throbbed under her skin. Her vast world began to shrink in tiny increments until all she could focus on was Sawyer's next move. It seemed as if hours had passed before the first flick of his wet tongue coasted up and down—tiny tastes that only caused more frustration.

Julietta moaned and pulled at the cuffs.

"You're not giving up that easily, are you?" he teased, using his thumbs to part her even wider. "Ah, your clit is poking from the hood, wanting more. Would you like more?"

She curled her fingers and grabbed desperately for sanity.

"I knew you'd be a worthy opponent." His eyes glittered with mad lust. "I was right. You taste exactly like an Almond Joy."

He opened his lips and devoured her.

A long, high shriek ripped from her throat. All expectations of what oral sex was and should be disappeared forever under the demanding lash of his tongue. He rotated different strokes in ways that made her toes curl in her fuck-me heels. Licking his way over her entire pussy, he laved the sides of her clit but never dragged his tongue over where she needed it most. His teeth nibbled ever so gently, causing just an edge of pain that tilted her toward climax, but never enough to get her there.

"Please." Her voice broke but she didn't care anymore. "Oh, please, I need more."

"Not yet." She let out a long string of vulgar curses her

mother would have whipped her ass for. His wicked chuckle drifted to her ears. "I just learned some new words. Did you just call the man who controls your orgasm an idiot?"

Her head thrashed from side to side on the plump pillow. His thumb dragged across her turgid nub again in punishment. Sweat pricked her skin. "*Mi dispiace*. Please, Sawyer. I need—oh, God I need—"

"I know what you need."

He dipped two fingers into her dripping channel. She clenched around him and tried to pull him in, but he moved too slowly, using her wetness to coat her clit and gently massage her aching flesh. Madness threatened. She needed that orgasm more than she needed breath. More than she needed a business contract. More than she needed anything. Her nipples stabbed toward the air in a plea for relief.

"Ask me, Julietta."

She blinked and rolled her hips as another wave of need and arousal washed over her. Her heels dug into the sheets. "What?"

Sawyer lifted his head. His gaze pinned hers, probing past every barrier she'd ever erected and hitting the darkest part of her soul. At that moment, she didn't care. She let him in for that brief moment and gave him everything. "Ask me," he whispered.

A sob broke from her lips. "Please, Sawyer, please let me come."

Raw possession stamped the features of his face and

pure satisfaction emanated in waves from his body. "Good girl."

He plunged three fingers deep inside, twisting and hitting the spot he had found before with firm, strong strokes. At the same time, his lips closed around her clit and he stroked his tongue right over the top. Once. Twice.

She exploded.

Julietta screamed as wave after wave of pleasure crashed through her. Her body shook helplessly underneath the raw onslaught, the release going so deep inside of her and exploding outward in layers. She was aware of his firm grip on her thighs as he held her open and continued licking her, throwing her into a bunch of mini convulsions that stretched out for endless minutes.

She sank into the mattress, limp and sated. Her muscles shook and a haze drifted over her vision as she fought for consciousness. She had never experienced such an intense, physical experience in her life.

She finally knew what she'd been missing. How could she have imagined this type of sex was even possible? Such mind-numbing, full-body pleasure that stole her sanity and made her soul soar higher than she'd ever known?

Her brain blessedly blank, Julietta struggled to open her lids.

Sawyer stared down at her.

The angry scar on his face only emphasized the classic grace of his features. The high brow and defined cheekbones. The lush curve of lip and strong jaw. The amber heat of his eyes. He loomed over her, poised at her threshold, her legs held high in the air and close to his shoulders. Suddenly, her vulnerable position and what they were about to do snapped her back to reality.

His massive erection pulsed and threatened an invasion she couldn't handle. *Mio Dio,* she was still bound. Helpless. Julietta tugged at her cuffs and fought for breath. Panic hit.

"Easy, baby." He kissed her, long and sweet. "You are magnificent. I have never seen anyone as beautiful as you during an orgasm." His face lit with an inner light that fascinated her. "You give everything without a thought to holding back. Such a rare gift. And I will cherish it for my whole life."

His words soothed the holes in her soul and healed something she never realized was broken. Her body softened and she stopped fighting. He wouldn't hurt her. The knowledge pulsed in her gut and echoed in his face, now slightly strained as he kept his position without moving. She swallowed.

"You haven't won yet."

A delighted laugh broke from his lips. He kissed her deeper, swirling his tongue around hers and playing a game of thrust and parry. His penis pressed an inch farther. Wetness trickled down her thighs and an urgent pulsing in her core told her she was ready for another round. Was it possible? Again?

"I will." His voice changed to an arrogant demand that made her belly plummet. "Let's up the game, shall we?"

He rocked his hips back and forth as if he had all the time in the world. His features were strained, but he was solidly in control. The sheer command he had over his body and the helplessness of her own position shot fire to her pussy. The sweet ache coiled tighter with the image of that full, thick length buried deep inside of her. How long had it been? Months? More like years. But what if she couldn't climax again? What if she froze up like she normally did and disappointed both of them? The image hit her full force.

"Boring you again, am I?" Her attention snapped back. Before she could gather her thoughts, he bent his head and took her nipple into his mouth. Sucking hard on the aching nub, Julietta moaned at the delicious sensations. His cock at her entrance, his heated body pressed to hers, his tongue sliding over her nipple. The sharp scrape of teeth wrung a cry from her lips, then unbelievably, she grew wetter. "Before you drift on me again, let me set the new terms. I'll give you two more orgasms because I'm in a generous mood."

She managed a snort even though she ached for more of his delicious torture. His hand plumped her other breast, readying her. "Impossible. You got lucky with the first."

"Two more. And you will apologize for all the rotten things you said about me tonight."

"Never."

"You will. And I get a marker."

She fought for breath as he pushed in another aching inch. Her thighs clenched. "You want a marker to write with?"

"No. A marker to be used for later. When I can punish you properly for your impertinence."

The sexual buzz melted her brain cells. "Punish? You want another night?"

His teeth closed around one tight peak and tugged. She gasped. "Yes. I want you another night." He edged farther into her channel. One more strong push and he'd fill her. Suddenly, she wanted that feeling of belonging to a man, of invasion and possession, more than her next breath. More than losing. "Now say yes."

His eyes and voice demanded and refused to accept anything less than all of her.

She grit her teeth. "Yes."

Sawyer slid home.

As he buried his throbbing length between her legs, her body welcomed him like he belonged. Slick with juices, her tightness barely caused a hesitation and the fact of her complete helplessness struck again in full, crystal clear clarity.

He filled every spare inch of her, fighting for space and not allowing her any room to hide. Hands bound over her head, legs open to him, his mouth at her breast, Julietta shook with too many emotions and sensations to process, causing her a temporary sensory overload in vivid neon.

"No, no, no," she chanted, shaking her head back and forth. She fought to keep him from taking it all, but it was too late. Tears pricked her eyes.

"Julietta, look at me."

"Please, no, I can't."

"You can. Breathe, baby. Yes, like that. Another one. You can take all of me, just let yourself feel. One more slow breath. Trust me." She clung to his words—calm and strong and sure. The breath entered her lungs and the fear slowly drained away.

Suddenly, as when a movie turns from black-and-white into startling Technicolor, her body sprang to life. The restriction eased and turned to a delicious friction. He moved in tiny increments, back and forth, eliciting a rush of wetness and gripping arousal. "That's it, relax and let me take you where we both want to go." The reminder that her hands were tied and she couldn't control the pace or angle added to the ratcheting sizzle and burn of anticipation. Her muscles released and he slid even deeper.

Sawyer groaned. "Jesus, you're tight. So fucking good." He grabbed her ankles and lifted them on top of his shoulders. Her spiked heels dug into his hard muscles and a thrill shot through her.

He moved. All the way out in one slick slide. Paused. Then a slow, delicious glide back, over and over, on his own time and in his own way. Julietta had prepared for the familiar rush to the finish line. Her experiences before this had contained her lover pumping furiously while she tried to force herself to catch up and not disappoint. Orgasms were a stress she'd decided to leave behind. But not anymore.

Sawyer didn't give a crap about time. He played with her breasts with every rotation of his hips, sometimes gentle, sometimes deep and hungry. The erratic rhythms didn't allow her to anticipate or calculate a response. Suddenly, she craved more—much more. Her clit pounded in demand from the teasing scrape of his cock, and she ground her stilettos into his shoulders while she reached for more. The punishing bite of his teeth and his dirty laugh told her he knew exactly what she wanted and refused to give it to her.

"More," she moaned.

"No."

She pulled at her cuffs. His cock sank deeper into her channel until he seemed a permanent part of her. He shifted angle. Paused. And gently bit her nipple.

The flash of pain registered the same time he hit some special spot that made fireworks explode behind her closed lids. She panted. So close. She needed—

"Ah, you like that, huh? Right here?" He thrust again and an animal noise exploded in the air. Was that her? He chuckled. "Yes, that's the spot. And what if I did this?" He reached between their bodies and pressed down on her swollen clit. Julietta wondered if she could die from sexual tension, so close to release yet kept on the edge for endless minutes. He rubbed lightly, back and forth, keeping his thrusts shallow and sharp, hitting the spot where white-hot heat coiled deep, ready to explode.

"Are you ready for your second orgasm, Julietta?"

Pride and rationality vanished under the raw demand of her body. "Yes, please, Sawyer, please."

"And you'll give yourself to me for one more night?"

His fingers flicked. She cried out. "Yes! Yes, anything you want, just please."

"Open your eyes. I want to see your face when you come."

The words sent her over the cliff as much as his next hard plunge. His fingers and cock worked her faster, in perfect tandem with what she craved, and she flew apart for the second time that night.

The orgasm started from her toes and exploded through every part of her body. Julietta let go, arching under the violent spasms and giving up. Sobs broke from her throat at the excruciating pleasure that went on and on. Sawyer never broke his gaze, taking in every expression and cry as if it belonged to him. When she finally surfaced, she realized he was still buried deep inside her, fully erect.

Half drunk on a hormonal high, Julietta roused herself enough to lift her head off the pillow. "What are you doing?" she slurred.

He pulled out and coaxed another shudder. Overly sensitized from back-to-back orgasms, she felt the edge of pain and pleasure blur. "We're not done yet. You owe me one more."

Her heart rate sped up. She tried to shake her head in a confident manner, but it felt like jelly attached to her neck. "No, I can't; I don't want to."

A low laugh raked her ears. He reset an easy pace, giving her just enough rubbing motion to interest her in steady, slow peaks. Wetness leaked down her thighs, and she arched again into the biting pleasure. "*Mio Dio,* not again."

"A deal is a deal, sweet one." He pressed her legs wider and changed to short, strong strokes that buried him balls deep. Too exhausted to think or move, she could only respond to what he commanded, and he brought her right back up to the peak and kept her there. Increasing to a brutal pace, he pounded into her with a primitive energy that turned her on, the damp slapping of their bodies, the sharp scent of arousal, the sweat-slicked slide of skin. Her belly coiled and she burned.

He gently squeezed her clit. "Come for me, baby. Now."

The command hit her ears the moment her body exploded. With a roar, Sawyer pumped his hips and gripped her tightly, spilling his seed. The raw satisfaction on his face soothed, almost as if he surrendered as deeply to the experience of their lovemaking as she had. The orgasm rushed on, claiming and wracking every inch of her body, until finally he collapsed on top of her.

Completely weak and helpless, Julietta sagged against her restraints. The empty part inside that had been completely filled moments ago suddenly widened into a chasm of emotions and mess. The tears that had previously threatened sprang free, and she turned her head in shame.

Her wrists were freed and Sawyer removed the handcuffs. Rubbing her sore muscles, he worked the tension from her hands, fingers, and arms, then dragged her to him. Tucking her into his chest, he pulled the covers over them and snuggled her into his arms.

"Let me go." She tried to move away but felt like a newborn colt—all gangly legs and off balance. Julietta battled for her inner strength and fought against his embrace.

"Shh, sweet girl, you're not going anywhere." His grip was steel, and his voice and touch were gentle as he stroked her hair, murmuring soft words against her ear. "You're exhausted and need to rest. I've got you." The warmth of his skin and the comforter cocooned her in security and safety she hadn't experienced in so long, she didn't believe it had existed. Maybe just a minute. He smelled so good, and his tender strokes lured a hazy sleep to claim her muscles, dragging her down into the dark. Just one minute. As she eased into sleep, his whisper drifted toward her unconscious.

"What have you done to me?" she whispered.

Then she fell asleep.

Chapter Nine

Sawyer held her tight in his embrace and studied her face. Sweat matted the hair clinging to her forehead and cheeks. Breath rushed in and out of her swollen lips. With softly glowing skin and her long lashes gleaming with unshed tears, she reminded him of a sleeping princess waiting for her prince. A very well-fucked, satisfied princess.

His cock stirred.

What had happened?

Usually, he was always in complete control during a scene. He locked away his physical needs and concentrated on what his lovers needed from him. He had no problems holding back, no matter how sweetly they begged or cajoled or promised. He allowed release for both of them on his terms, keeping his emotions secondary.

Not with Julietta. From the moment he touched her, he struggled to remain neutral. Her pleasure stoked his, but never had he craved to dig deeper, looking to strip her both physically and emotionally for his own claim. He never doubted she could orgasm. The idiot men before her deserved to be whipped for the junk they put in her head. No, he knew she needed a man to allow her to surrender and let her body rule that powerful brain. Sawyer had an instinct that she owned the soul of a bedroom submissive, just begging for someone to dominate and take control of her body. It was the other parts that wrecked him.

The way she gave herself to him during climax. The sweet cries on her lips as she begged him to take her. The trust and bravery for allowing him to restrain her the first night together. The way her body lit up under his and snugly wrapped around his cock as if he belonged between her thighs.

She overshadowed every woman before her. Like a drug, he craved his next hit, though he just spilled his seed moments ago. He ached to take her again and again, bound her to his bed, and keep her there until she admitted that's where she wanted to be.

He expected a crash of emotion after such intensity. He usually took specific steps to contradict the crash—a blanket, a bottle of water, some soothing words and a comforting embrace. But the moment he spotted her tears, and her inner fury at such a weakness, he only longed to hold her close. Rock her, kiss away her tears, and keep her with him. Definitely not his normal reaction.

The delicious scent of coconut and musk and sex hit his nostrils. Under the lure of orgasm, he'd made her agree to another night. Why would he do that? The voice whispered the truth, and icy fear trickled down his spine.

Because he didn't want to lose her.

Already, after a few hours, he was hooked on Julietta Conte. Fascinated by her honesty and strength and vulnerability, he only wanted more. Of course, it was impossible. Working together, yes. Perhaps an affair for a limited time with both of them clear on the outcome. Long term?

Never.

The chill deepened. While she'd grown up in a loving household, he'd fought with fists and knives and wits to keep his belly full. His escape from two previous homes after his parents died pegged him as a problem child in the system. Especially because of his age—nine was the beginning of the no-touch number. Foster families and parents wanted babies, or toddlers, or even that cute seven-year-old who had a shot at normalcy. Eleven was hormones and messiness and smart-ass remarks. He knew the moment he walked into his third foster home it would be different. There was a layer of fear he scented in the air, and the man with the beefy fists, ruddy features, and bloated belly held an element of mean. The social worker hadn't given a shit. And once he was placed with his new family, the rules were clearly laid out, beginning with a beating with a belt on his bare back.

Strike. No running away. They needed the money.

Strike. No causing trouble.

Strike. No interference with disciplining the other kids.

Strike. One meal per day. Stealing any more would mean consequences.

Strike. No telling. Anyone. Ever. Penalty?

Strike.

The worst nightmare he could think of.

Dickhead threw him a towel to wipe off the blood, then made him replace his T-shirt. He remembered the raw skin sticking to the material and how with each step he battled nausea and passing out. He also knew it would set the tone for the future. If he failed, Dickhead would come after him on a daily basis. Strength and control were keys to survival. After day one of hell began, he endured for years, until he turned eighteen and finally escaped.

And realized by saving himself he had killed another.

His foster brother.

"Hey."

He blinked away the memory and smiled. Her husky voice was sexy as hell, and a faint blush stained her cheekbones. Adorable. His erection pressed against her thigh and her eyes widened.

"Hey." He ran a knuckle down her heated skin. "How do you feel?"

"Good." She rolled her eyes in self mockery. "That's a lie. I feel incredible. Like gooey caramel—all warm and melty."

His cock twitched. That was exactly how she felt when he slid into her—cloaking him in rich clingy heat. He thought about tumbling her back for one more orgasm but knew she had to be sore. Time to take care of her comfort needs first. "There's a Turkish bath and steam shower in the bathroom. I'm going to start the water for you." He pressed a kiss to her temple, then slid out of bed and padded naked to the connecting bathroom. The huge glass shower doors were framed in rich gold, and the walls boasted an elaborate mosaic of earth tones. Steam hissed from the walls and formed a thick cloud. He pulled onto another knob and warm water sprayed from the ceiling onto slate tiles and the specially carved matching bench. He laid out some snowy white towels and the hotel robes, then made his way back to the bedroom.

Humor twisted his lips. She sat on the edge of the bed, wrapped like a mummy in the sheets. Her face reflected a blend of shyness and aggravation. She'd soon remember who was in charge and lose some of her innate inhibitions. Crossing one ankle over the other, he leaned against the door. "Shower's ready."

Her gaze flicked over his fully erect dick and nakedness. Her teeth pulled at her lip, then she stood up in a flash, shoulders back, dark eyes gleaming with stubbornness. She marched across the room like the Queen of Sheba with the sheets trailing behind her. Hesitating when she got close, he refused to move aside, wondering what she'd do.

With a haughty sniff, she stalked past him, dropped the sheet, and stepped into the shower. The doors closed with a relieved click and he bit back the urge to laugh out loud. His queen would soon realize there was no hiding from him. Anywhere.

He allowed her a few minutes of privacy as he went back to the main suite area and poured glasses of water. Loading them on a tray with some crackers, cheese, and veggies, he placed it on the table next to the lounge chair. He added two flutes of fizzy champagne and headed to the shower.

The expression on her face when he opened the doors and stepped in was priceless. Trying to look dignified with her hair wet and a deliciously naked body on display, she did a half turn, trying to hide her embarrassment. Sawyer was looking forward to blowing past every social nicety she ever had about sex. Including bathing together and what he could do with a shower nozzle.

His lips quirked. "Need some help?"

"No, thank you."

This time he laughed. Grabbed the loofah sponge she held in a death grip, and poured some gel into his hands. "Too bad."

With nothing to hold, she mustered enough courage

to snort and turn her back on him, obviously picking the least embarrassing position. Her gorgeous ass and gracefully curving spine only made him thank God he was a man. There was nothing as sensual as a woman's rear, and Julietta's lean length and soft skin were made for his hands. He stepped in and pulled her hips back to rest against him. She sucked in her breath.

"I can wash myself." Her body stiffened. "In fact, I'm all done, so if you will excuse me . . ."

"Have you ever showered with a man before?" He dragged the soapy sponge over her breasts.

"Of course."

"Liar." He dipped down, making wide circles over her belly, hips, and upper thighs. His cock throbbed in the notch between her thighs. "I'm glad you haven't. I like showing you things for the first time."

The temperature dropped a few degrees. Every muscle tensed. "I'm not an inexperienced virgin, Sawyer," she said coolly. "And I'm no charity case."

He spun her around and grabbed her long, wet hair. She gasped, bringing her hands up to his chest in a halfhearted attempt to push him away. He dragged her head back and loomed over her. "Don't ever say something like that to me again." Temper bit his tone. "You're a passionate, beautiful woman who had the unfortunate experience of meeting a bunch of assholes who wouldn't know how to find their own dicks in the dark. Your comment insults both of us."

Her pupils dilated with a touch of fear that soon changed to lust. He eased his grip, noting her ragged breathing and stabbing nipples. Oh, yeah. His bossy woman liked a man telling her what to do in the privacy of the bedroom. Sawyer lowered his head and spoke against her swollen lips. "Maybe I need to keep this mouth occupied as much as your brain." He crushed her lips under his, drinking in her taste and essence and conquering her mouth. Each stroke of his tongue reminded her she belonged to him in every capacity.

She gave it all back. He groaned under her sweet surrender, her own thrusting tongue tangling with his. She grabbed onto his slick shoulders and hung on while Sawyer pressed her against his chest and dipped her back to keep her slightly off balance. When she was soft and pliable, he slowly tipped her face up and broke the kiss.

Her gorgeous dark eyes gleamed with a swirl of naked emotions. He let her process for a moment, expecting her to beat a hasty retreat he intended to halt.

"I feel stupid."

Surprise made him draw back. "Why, baby?"

She squeezed her eyes shut and reached for courage. "I'm thirty-two years old and I've never done this—this stuff before. I don't know the proper way to be."

Her honesty shook him. Something deep inside flamed to life in demand, but he didn't recognize the emotion so he pushed it back down. She was a child-woman with more courage than most men he'd met.

Sawyer pulled her to him and rested his forehead against hers. He lifted her hands and pressed a kiss to both palms. "You don't have to be any certain way. Your only job is to feel and not worry about anything. I'll take care of you."

She shuddered. A bolt of need shot through him like a stray bullet tearing through vulnerable flesh. He didn't know how to process the intensity, so he focused on the naked woman in his arms and what he could do to please her. This time, when he began the soapy trail over her skin, she allowed him full access. A rumble of pleasure purred from her throat as he washed every inch of her, using a gentle rotating motion that soothed and aroused. Her nipples were treated to the rough side of the loofah, and they peaked with interest, turning a beautiful ruby red that matched her Snow White lips.

He dropped to his knees. Her body was created to be lost in—from her endless length of leg and thigh, to the perfect patch of dark hair that masked her sex, down to her scarlet toes. He cleansed her with a tenderness he'd never experienced with another woman, urging her to part her legs for him.

With a hiss of breath, she obeyed.

Her arousal elicited a primitive rush of victory, her pink inner lips glistening from water and her own moisture. He pressed the sponge to her mound and rubbed, making sure to work back and forth in a light rhythm. She arched her back and moaned; her breasts thrust forward like a pretty present. God, he should give her a rest, but he'd already gone too far to stop. He had to make her come again, feel her splinter apart around him and surrender to what he did to her.

"Turn around."

Her pause gave him what he needed. He slapped her ass with one hard strike. She jerked in reaction, her eyes wide with outrage. Sawyer looked beyond and waited.

Yes. Her nipples tightened further and the pulse at her neck beat rapidly. He bet an erotic spanking would give her intense pleasure, but he needed to be sure it was something that didn't scare or horrify her. A frown snapped her brow, but he stared right back and repeated the command. "Turn around. Now."

She did. The lush curve of her buttocks was a beautiful flushed pink from the steam and his hand. Sawyer started at her heels and worked his way up, lingering on the backs of her thighs; hips, her lower back. He straightened and dragged the sponge over her shoulders, tickling the nape of her neck, switching back and forth from the smooth to rough side so she was constantly kept off balance. The slight tremble in her legs and the tension in her muscles told him she was ready.

He sank to his knees. Urged her legs farther apart. And pressed the loofah against her pussy.

She shook and tried to remain still, but he kept the torture up by sliding the coarse side over her sensitive clit at the same time he bit the luscious arc of her ass.

Her hands reached out to grab onto something and found the granite wall. The steam and heated spray drenched them and only added to the eroticism. Sawyer growled low in his throat, dying for more. He spread her cheeks wide and ran his tongue along her dripping slit at the same time he rotated the loofah against her clit.

She screamed as the orgasm hit hard and long. He never paused, lengthening her pleasure as her cries mingled with the hiss of steam and his tongue licked without pause. Finally, she shuddered and sagged against the wall. Sawyer rose and pulled her against him. He pressed his lips to her temple and stroked her back. Mini convulsions shook through her and she snuggled against him as if she had found her home.

"Yeah, you're a real charity case," he grumbled, trying to get his head back in the game and distract himself from his raging hard-on. Her husky laugh raked across his ears in a caress.

"And you're a bully."

"Never."

"*Sei un maniaco sessuale.*"

He lifted his brow. "Trust me. If I do my job correctly, you'll be a sex maniac also."

A cloud drifted over her face, and she tipped her chin up to look at him. "Am I a job, Sawyer?"

Her honest question demanded more from him than

ever before. He pushed past the discomfort and answered. "No." The next words dried up and he was glad. He wasn't ready for anything more.

Her features eased into relaxation and a teasing smile played about her lips. "Good. Now, what about you?"

He glanced down at his stiff member and shrugged. "Forgot the condom while we played water sports. No big deal."

"You really think I'm mouthy?"

He tugged on a wet strand of hair. "Hell, yes."

"Then maybe I should do something to keep myself occupied."

He had no clue until she knelt in front of him with a ballerina's grace that took his breath away. Sawyer reached out to stop her—the night was not about him—but the moment her lips opened and slipped over his pulsing length, he was a goner. He swore he'd only allow her to experiment until she felt comfortable, knowing Julietta was unsure of her skills and needed to learn to trust her instincts. The lesson turned on him in a heartbeat. With long, deft strokes, she sucked and licked with a heady enthusiasm and purity that left him helpless to fight. Using her hands to fist his dick and pump up and down, she continued her ministrations until he exploded, the orgasm diving deep and radiating through every pore in his skin.

When the room stopped spinning, the little minx rose to her feet. Tossed him a purely feminine, purely satisfied grin.

And walked out of the shower, her naked buttocks winking at him in sheer mockery.

Oh, hell, he was in trouble.

Big trouble.

He shook his head, shut off the water, and followed her out.

• • •

Who would've thought the ice queen had turned into Raging Nympho?

Julietta wrapped the terry robe around her. Her muscles were limp noodles and an inner peace radiated from within. Was this what great sex did to a woman? Turned her brain to mush and plastered a stupid smile on her face? This was dangerous in real life. No wonder women acted like fools under a man's spell. Sawyer only had to crook his finger and she fell to her knees. Happily.

Oddly, her reaction didn't bother her as much as before. Maybe she was so sexed out no worries were able to penetrate any brain cells. Tomorrow she'd probably wake up in a full-fledged panic attack. Maybe.

Maybe not.

Julietta watched him stalk out of the shower. He wore a relaxed expression and finally owned a limp dick. Not for long, she bet. The man was a sexual dynamo, and for a little while, he belonged only to her.

The possessive thought threw her off for a moment, but she refused to analyze it. Sawyer grabbed a towel, wrapped it around his waist, and turned.

She gasped.

His back and upper buttocks were a mass of crisscrossed scars, some faded, some red and angry. There seemed to be no logic to the marks. Perfectly formed circles marred his biceps. He froze in place, as if he had forgotten his original plan to hide his nakedness from her. Julietta flicked back to the evening. He had kept his shirt on until the last moment on the bed. And he never presented his rear to her—only his front.

Her throat tightened. Why did this seem different from the scar on his face? As if he didn't care who saw that public mark. A tattoo that gave him flavor and a bad-boy demeanor. But these hidden scars were so much more. She sensed these were the ones he hid from the world, a secret, deeper pain no one suspected. Pain he refused to share or explain.

The rational woman inside knew the proper response. Be cool. Ignore the marks, pretend she didn't care, and move on. A woman engaged in a one-night stand obeyed the rules—no attachments or emotion or sharing painful pasts. Just pleasure, orgasms, alcohol, and a hasty retreat at dawn.

She struggled to be that woman, but silly tears threatened to fall. The idea of the strong man before her being helpless and hurt by nameless people tore her soul. She moved toward him and laid her hands gently on his back. Sawyer flinched. With light strokes, she caressed and traced every scar over the broad expanse of flesh. He never moved. Didn't speak. Finally, she broke the silence.

"I'm sorry someone hurt you." Julietta made sure no pity leaked into her voice. No one could possibly pity a man who exhibited such strength and character and success. Perhaps the scars drove him to be better. She refused to cluck over him and ask a million questions, but she would never pretend she didn't see what someone or many had done to him. "I'm glad you won."

He bent his head. Sucked in a ragged breath. And spoke. "I never talk about my past, Julietta. I lived in it far too long and fought too hard to leave it behind. He was evil, and I was stuck with him for too many years. He tried to beat everything out of me, but I refused to give him that final satisfaction." His voice took on the demons of a past she couldn't even imagine. "I've done—things. I won't apologize for them either. I understand if you can't handle that right now or choose to leave. I'll release you from the contract."

She gazed at the back of the man who had commanded her orgasms and made her feel like a woman for the first time in her life. Throughout the hours, he'd never taken but had freely given and pushed her boundaries. He made her feel safe. Yet he actually believed she was so fragile she'd run at the sight of a few scars or his admission he'd made some bad choices?

Julietta pressed her lips to his back. He tensed underneath the caress, but she kissed each scar with a gentle humbleness she ached to show. "*Che idiota!* How dare you insult me with such a comment? Whatever things you had to do you did to survive. Do you really think so little of me to believe I'd run from a few physical scars after the greatest sex of my life?"

He turned and faced her. Gaze wary, he studied her expression. She cursed the telltale dampness on her cheeks and realized she'd never be good at this stuff.

Sawyer reached out and ran his thumb over her face. "Are you crying?"

His stunned tone lit her temper. "I'm not crying for the man you are," she bit out. "I'm crying for the boy who never had anyone to care." Julietta let her anger dry up her tears. "I hope he is dead. I hope whoever put his hands on you died in a horrible, painful way."

A raw longing burned from amber eyes. His fingers traced the curve of her cheek as if she was a fairy about to disappear into the mist. Slowly, he pulled back, and Julietta caught the tremor in his hand. He opened his mouth, but before the words left his lips, Sawyer bit them back. His lower lip quirked in that sexy half smile that tripped her heart. "Calling me an idiot again, huh?"

She sniffed. "That's how you're acting."

He chuckled. "Such violence tucked beneath polite civility. Remind me never get on your bad side, baby."

"I have no civility when someone hurts one of my own."

Sawyer stilled. The words had slipped out before she'd had an opportunity to censor herself. *Mio Dio,* what had she done? He didn't belong to her. Never would. This was a contract—pure and simple—and though they had extended it to one more night, there was no relationship possible.

Was there?

An array of emotions flickered over his face. His voice came out rough and gravelly. "I believe you. The man you choose as your own is one lucky son of a bitch." He cleared his throat and the crackling tension eased. "Come with me. You must be hungry."

He intertwined her fingers with his and led her back to the bedroom. They feasted on crisp crackers, creamy cheese, and sweet peppers, washing it down first with water and then champagne. Sawyer lifted her feet into his lap and massaged the tender insteps, sore from the high heels. Surprised she didn't feel awkward after the various intimate encounters, Julietta relaxed into conversation about work, then chatted about her upbringing with a protective older brother.

Swirling the golden liquid in the delicate flute, she broached her next question with care. "How long have you known Wolfe?"

His fingers paused. "About a year." She fought a groan as he kneaded the tight muscles in her hamstrings. "I never thanked you for giving him a chance. Most see his appearance and believe he's useless."

"You'd never hire an employee who didn't own incredible skills. Especially with Purity. He told me a little bit about his past."

Sawyer gave a half laugh. "Yeah, he told you he came from a tattoo parlor, didn't he? Tells everyone that story. Wolfe doesn't talk about his real past."

"He said you kept him from jail and took him in. Gave him a chance to prove himself."

He looked up in surprise. "I can't believe it. He never— he never shares."

Julietta smiled. "He admires you. Hides it behind a smart-ass attitude. He's got some incredible business skills for someone so young. No wonder you brought him to Italy."

Sawyer shook his head as if trying to clear it. "Yeah, he's a smart kid. Got lost in the foster system and was trying to make it on his own in the streets. I caught him trying to pickpocket me, and I gave him a choice. Jail or an internship at my company." A flash of pain lit his eyes. "The first few months he gave me so much shit I was tempted to throw him out. But he was so damn smart it was eerie. He has a photographic memory and knows how to talk to people once he gets over his initial insecurity. Every time I gave him a task, he finished it before my regularly paid employees." Sawyer shrugged. "So I kept increasing his workload, paid him a salary, and waited for him to run. He hasn't yet."

"You care about him."

He flinched and pulled his hands from her leg. Her skin cooled as fast as his tone. "This has nothing to do with emotion. I decided to bring him with me to test his skills. He listened to that Rosetta Stone thing and learned the language in record time. But if he fails, I'll let him go."

Julietta studied the man before her. Odd, he was able to give so much in the bedroom, but normal relationships seemed impossible for him to accept. Sawyer was lying. He obviously cared more about Wolfe than he was ready to admit. Probably had no clue how to deal with a broken teenager, and Julietta suspected they shared a similar past. But this wasn't the time or place to push.

"Understood. After all, business is business."

His gaze warmed and the ghosts receded. She sucked in her breath as the familiar heat took hold. Sawyer wrapped his fingers around her ankles and dragged her close. "Exactly. I think it's time to get back to our own negotiations."

Julietta ignored the rush of joy and chalked it up to sexual hormones. "I thought we had concluded our business. Three orgasms definitely wins the bet."

He gave a wolfish smile. "Then just call me an overachiever."

He covered his body with hers. Julietta had never known losing could be so sweet.

Chapter Ten

Sawyer paced the unfinished lobby of Purity with the team. The roar of power tools filled the air, and the scent of wood, oil, and paint rose in his nostrils. The empty building of the popular Le Méridien had been abandoned for years: a lonely, sprawling piece of architecture that created a longing in the heart of the city. After years of working on buying the building, he'd finally won. He'd taken the first step in making his mark in the world and obtaining a slice of immortality. It was the best he could ever hope for.

The structure owned the old-world grace he needed to make his mark here. The marble winged horse in front led to an elegant building with a crumbling white facade amidst the bright red doors lending distinctive character. The full restaurant and lounge would be replaced by a modernized version of entertainment and the best of technology brought in for a media suite for business. Already furnished, each room needed to be made over and renovated while decisions of what furniture and structures should remain and what should be ripped out boggled his team of designers.

Pride surged as he led the team through the slowly developed rooms. They chattered as Wolfe took notes and Sawyer guided them toward his vision, pointing out where each of their respective spaces would be housed. When he stopped in front of the bakery area of La Dolce Famiglia, he paused to direct his attention to Julietta.

She had cried for him.

The memory of her tears wrecked his concentration. Other than a few flashes of being held by his parents, he had no soft memories to hold on to. Touch usually meant punishment or something to avoid at all costs. He'd learned brutally early that tears were useless and looked upon as weakness. How many times had he been beaten bloody, starved, humiliated, or punished in various ways and not one person had given him a second glance? Even his foster siblings were too busy looking after themselves, and any kindness to him was always severely punished.

Sawyer never blamed them. He would've done the same. But the moment he saw Julietta's tears, a strange yawning emptiness rose up and tried to strangle him. She had actually cared. Kissed his scars. Yelled at him for even mentioning she might want to leave. She'd demonstrated everything kind and good and he didn't know what to do with it.

The endless women before her blurred into a line of nameless faces who'd only seemed interested in his scars to make sure he got them off. He'd never had a lover kiss him with such tenderness, let alone shed tears over something she didn't know or understand. His heart squeezed with so much emotion he couldn't process the flood. Sawyer refused to analyze the weakness. Much better to concentrate on her stinging anger and insults than on such an intimate gift. He might never recover.

A whole week had already passed, and he'd been swamped every evening with work. When he finally dropped into bed, slumber eluded him. Only the image of her naked body and wet heat rose to his closed lids until sleep was impossible. He ached for another evening, but had decided earlier on to wait. Another night spent in her company might throw him off his game—and he needed to be in control in order to keep giving her the pleasure she deserved. It was also good for his suddenly slipping emotions. When was the last time he'd actually gotten mushy over a woman? Wondered how her day was going, or what she was eating for lunch, or what television show she watched before bed?

Never.

The answer was simple. Pull back for a bit, and then go in for another night once he was solid. And to think he'd been worried about her getting attached.

Sawyer cleared his throat. "Julietta, as we discussed, we're preparing La Dolce Famiglia to take up this main space for foot traffic. You'll need to pick your team carefully for this one since we won't have the main equipment on the floor."

She nodded and examined the empty store. Her severe black suit was his personal favorite. It was the most conservative, with a pencil-slim skirt and a double-breasted jacket that covered most of her delicious assets. With her hair twisted up tight and her proper white blouse, the urge to rip away her prim demeanor engulfed him. He always loved the naughty librarian fantasy. Maybe he'd make her keep the suit on. Hike the hem up her thighs, lay her back on the desk, and rip off her panties. He'd test her control by commanding her not to make a sound, then do everything with his tongue and teeth to make her scream.

His cock rose and he quickly switched his thoughts. All he needed was Tanya to think she turned him on and he bet he'd get a late night visit. Her designer skills were flawless, but she reminded him of a female predator. Sawyer shuddered at the thought.

Julietta spun on her heel. "I can make this work. Though I'd rather have the other space we discussed."

His lip twitched. Damn, she had spunk. He'd assumed she'd pretend the erotic evening had never happened. Instead, she'd switched into full business mode without a hitch. No heated glances across the conference table or blushes when their gazes met. She treated him with the detachment of a business partner, which drove him even crazier.

"Actually, I do remember the discussion. Since I was able to clearly demonstrate why that wasn't a possibility, I'm surprised you brought it up."

"Hmm, I guess I forgot." She kept her voice bland. "Perhaps the conversation should have been more memorable."

He almost choked at her impertinence. Wolfe shot him a strange look, then went back to his notes. She also owned a wicked sense of humor. Oh, she was going to pay for that remark. Only his endless practice of hiding his emotions allowed him to press down his growing arousal. "Perhaps you're right." He pinned her with his gaze. "I'll be sure to make myself clearer in the future."

Her delighted smile ruffled his nerve endings. "Good. Practice makes perfect," she chirped. "Now, let's check out the kitchen. I want to be sure the setup is what we agreed upon."

Her heels clicked in front of him in a siren's song. Her gracefully swaying ass lured him to follow, and Sawyer realized Julietta Conte had blossomed to her full power.

God help him.

They toured the site, tweaked plans, and finally finished in the late afternoon. He made sure he escorted the other members of the team out first. Would she follow his lead and allow him some alone time? Sure enough, Sawyer spotted her lingering with Wolfe. Was she just as desperate to touch him? Like a horny teen, he wanted his hands all over her, his full week of celibacy at the limit. He did a quick sweep of the room and tried to catalogue a safe place he could get her naked without giving the construction crew a thrill.

He came up behind them and caught a slight smile on Wolfe's lips. Funny, he'd watched Wolfe interact with females and rarely saw him spare any interest. Something about Julietta allowed the boy to relax, and that was a miracle. "Thanks for your input today," she said in her usual crisp tones. "I hope you'll be able to take some downtime for yourself."

Wolfe shrugged. "Don't need much. I like the work."

"I know the feeling." She hesitated, and shifted her feet. "I want you to come to dinner Sunday. At my mother's house."

Sawyer drew back in surprise. Wolfe had the same reaction and seemed to stumble on his words. "Umm, thanks, but I'm busy."

"What are you doing?"

He paused and ducked his head. "Working."

Those cocoa brown eyes sharpened and focused on Sawyer. "I'm sure your boss will give you a Sunday afternoon off."

"Not unless I'm invited, too."

She pursed her lips in annoyance. "I invited Wolfe only."

Sawyer shrugged. "We're a package deal. I'm not missing out on homemade pasta while he chows down." He jerked his thumb. "Besides, he won't even appreciate a good cooked meal. He eats crap."

Wolfe glowered. "No, I don't. If you'd actually shop for food instead of eating at your desk every night, maybe I'd cook."

"Yeah, like you clean, right?"

"And you're from the Merry Maids service, huh? Next time work on your dunk shot. I saw the Big Mac wrappers on the floor."

Julietta gasped. Sawyer glared and tried to change the subject. "Forget it, let's just move on."

"You went to McDonald's?" Julietta whispered. "That's disgusting."

Ah, crap. He was going to kill Wolfe. "Okay. I wanted a hamburger. A reminder of home."

He struggled not to laugh at her obvious horror. "You could have eaten a real hamburger at Roberto's. He would have been happy to make one for you."

How the hell could he describe the need for that awful sauce and endless salt he occasionally craved? Sawyer remembered the first time he'd tasted it—half of it in the wrapper on top of the garbage can. He'd never tasted anything so good in his life, and each time he ate one he was reminded of how far he'd come. Of course, he'd never share such a story. And why was he suddenly cowering? He pulled himself to full height. "It's not the same. Am I invited to Mama Conte's, too?"

"Fine."

"Umm, I'll pass, Julietta. Thanks for the invite though."

Sawyer watched in fascination as she crossed her arms in front of her chest and gave Wolfe a pointed stare. "You're coming. Noon. No need to bring anything with you."

Panic lit the boy's eyes. "I, uh, made other plans. I can't go."

She never backed down. "I'm inviting you to dinner with my family, Wolfe. My mother loves to cook for guests, and this will give her pleasure."

A twinge of sympathy coursed through Sawyer. Wolfe rarely mingled with anyone other than at work-related meetings. Every time Sawyer tried to get him to join him for dinner or any type of social activity, he refused.

Wolfe lifted his head and stuck out his chin. "I don't do well with mothers. They don't like me."

She smiled, reached out, and touched his hand. Wolfe didn't even flinch. "You don't know my mother. She'll adore you. I am asking you to come as a favor to me. Mama's been lonely without her children home, and you will make her happy."

Oh, she was good. Who could possibly refuse such a heartfelt invitation? He watched Wolfe crumble piece by piece in front of him.

"Fine. I'll come."

"*Grazie.*"

Wolfe made his exit. "I gotta go. See you at home."

He rushed out without another word and finally left them alone.

The smile vanished. His ice queen reappeared and came out to play. "I see you're a bully even outside the bedroom."

He glanced at the construction crew and decided it was time to remind her who was boss. "Funny, seems like you stepped into the role perfectly. Poor Wolfe didn't know what hit him. Now, follow me."

He turned and started for the back room. Raw materials blocked most of the space, but he'd spotted a sturdy wooden table in the corner that would serve his purpose. She trotted after him, caught up in the argument. "He needs to be included in something bigger. Being isolated for too long is harmful."

"Wolfe learned early he could only trust himself. It'll take him time to come around. Watch your step."

She jumped over a cord and sidestepped a power saw. "A good meal around a table with people he trusts is important. Running to the McDonald's drive-thru serves no purpose."

He winced, grabbed her hand, and maneuvered her through the open frame. "I made a mistake, okay? Is that a good reason to try to keep me from Mama Conte's cooking?"

"I thought we agreed you wouldn't attend Sunday dinners."

"I changed my mind. Especially since Wolfe gets to go. Over here."

The room was dark. He guided her deeper into the space until her back pressed against the table. Sawdust and pieces of wood were scattered over the surface. "He uses his appearance to keep people away. Mama will see right through it, and maybe he'll realize not everyone will judge him. Where are we?"

"Or he can freak out with bad memories of his own family dinners and backslide. I'm trying not to push him too hard." He grabbed the rag near him and wiped off the table. "Sit up here for a moment."

"Replacing a good memory with a bad one is one way to heal. Believe me, I know. Why am I sitting on a construction table, Sawyer?"

Anticipation ripped through him. "Because I want to make you come."

He watched the emotions ripple over her face. Shock. Fascination. Fear.

And lust.

He stepped in between her legs and eased the hem of her skirt up. She offered no resistance, her mind evidently working into a steam of rational lectures on exactly why this wasn't a good idea. He took advantage of the pause, widened her thighs, and pushed her back so she was off balance.

Her hands gripped his shoulders. The pulse beat madly

at the base of her throat, and her scent rose to his nostrils. Coconut and a hint of vanilla. Rich coffee. He dipped his head to the naked curve of her neck and breathed deep.

She sucked in her breath and tried to push him away. "Are you crazy?" she whispered. "You can't say things like that. The construction team is here. This is a public building. You may like acting out a porn movie in public, but this is not what turns me on."

He growled and bit the tender flesh behind her ear. A shudder wracked her body. "I'm not into public displays, either. In fact, the idea of another man seeing you naked makes me want to beat the shit out of him." Her fingers bit into his suit jacket and her legs trembled. God, he loved making a liar out of her. She loved the excitement of being told what to do, and though he'd never share, the bite of danger only added to the sizzle. "I gave you time to be nice, and all you did was torture me this week."

A low moan rumbled from her throat. "I did nothing of the sort. I never even mentioned our night together."

"Exactly." He ran one hand up her skirt and found warm skin with no stockings or pantyhose to block his path. His finger traced the edge of her silk underwear and realized she was already wet. Frigid? This woman was hotter than Hades. "Did you dress like this for me? Did you hope I'd finally snap and do what I've dreamed about every day at that conference table?"

Her outrage only made his dick swell to full staff. "Of

course not." Her breath hitched as he stroked a thumb over the delicate fabric. "I—I was waiting for you to mention it. I refuse to be one of those women. Clingy and helpless and begging for a man."

The knowledge she was just as off center as he was soothed him. He'd thought giving her time and space would help. Now he realized he should've yanked her in his arms and kissed her senseless the very next day. His fault. He intended to fix it now.

"Baby, you'd never be helpless. I've been dying to get my hands on you all week but wanted to give you time."

She arched toward him for more. "That was polite of you."

"Time's up."

He took her mouth like he'd been fantasizing. Claimed her lips, stroking long and deep with his tongue, inhaling her flavor like an alcoholic on a binge. He pressed his palm over her core and rubbed, and she wrapped her legs tight around his hips and hung on. She licked fire and need and lust, and his body tightened with an urgency that fogged his brain and drove him forward to take and take and take. . . .

"Hey, boss!"

His fingers paused an inch from her dripping channel. He tore his mouth from hers and fought for sanity. Julietta stiffened, her eyes wide with worry, her wet lips slightly bruised from the kiss.

"Yeah?"

"We're gonna wrap up here for the day. You need anything else?"

He prayed his voice was steady. "Nope, I'm all set. See you tomorrow."

The sound of equipment being dragged and mutters from the men drifted into the room. Slowly, he removed his hand from under her skirt and gently tugged it down. He smoothed the stray tendrils of hair back from her cheeks and placed a gentle kiss on her pale pink lips.

"Will you meet me at the hotel again?"

"Yes."

Relief cut through him. He didn't want to remind her she owed him another night. The admission of her own desire to be with him was a sweet gift. Sawyer helped her off the table, took her hand, and led her out. Before he let her go, he bent his head and whispered in her ear.

"You may not be helpless or clingy, but you will beg. I promise."

He nipped her lobe, grinned, and took off. The curse word that drifted in the evening air was blistering, but well worth it.

• • •

"Julietta, are you feeling well?"

She paused chopping tomatoes and looked at her mother. A suspicious frown marred her brow, and her stare probed past the surface. *Mio Dio,* was it possible Mama knew she was having sex? Julietta dropped the knife and adjusted her sweater, hoping there weren't any telltale bruises or bites evident. Her second encounter with Sawyer the other night had continued to blow away all images of normalcy. He pushed every boundary she erected and took pleasure in proving her wrong about who she imagined she was. Handcuffs. Shower sex. And now toys. She fought a shudder when she thought of all the delicious ways a vibrator could be used. Soon, she'd be into orgasms into the double digits. Who would've thought?

She swallowed and refocused on chopping. "Sure. Why do you ask?"

"Your skin looks different. And you were humming."

Horror flooded through her. She did not sing or hum. This was getting bad. "Umm, no, I went to the spa the other day. Got a facial and massage. I feel better."

"Hmm."

The tomato rolled across the chopping board and she grabbed for it. Did sex actually make a woman glow? Of course, she'd been majorly backed up for years, so maybe her body needed to catch up a bit before settling down again. Made sense. Time for a subject change. "Have you spoken to Michael or Carina lately?"

Her mom turned back to the stove. The scent of garlic, onion, and escarole filled the air. "Yes, they want to come out for a visit."

"All of them?"

"*Si.* They will bring all the *bambinos*. Alexa and Nick may also join them."

Julietta smiled with pure joy. Her mother looked so happy and excited, she hoped it would happen. Imagine all of them together, with her nephews and siblings by her side. Like the old times, but even better. "Oh, Mama, that would be wonderful."

A knock sounded on the door. Her mother wiped her hands on her apron and shooed her away. "Do not keep them waiting, Julietta. Answer the door."

The two men stood side by side behind a cheerful bouquet of blooms. Sawyer's eyes darkened with erotic memories, and it took all of her control not to blush. Wolfe looked nervous, a thin figure beneath his bright blue button-down shirt and leather jacket. He shifted in his stiff, heeled shoes, and her heart broke when she realized he had actually dressed a bit conservatively for the occasion. She ushered them inside and toward the warm kitchen.

"Mama, this is Wolfe, Sawyer's assistant. He's been an amazing help in putting this deal together."

Mama Conte gave Sawyer a noisy kiss, cooed over the flowers, and approached Wolfe. He looked terrified as he stood before her, just waiting for her comment. His earring winked, and his tattoo crept past the conservative collar of his shirt and spilled black ink onto his neck. Her mom took it all in, her sharp gaze assessing, and a welcoming smile curved her lips. "Welcome to my home, Wolfe. It is an honor you took the time from your busy schedule to keep an old woman company."

She ignored his don't-touch aura, reached out, and placed a kiss on his cheek. Then turned and walked back to her station. "I hope you both brought your appetite."

Wolfe blinked and glanced at Julietta. After a moment, his aura lightened and a smile curved his lips. His snarkiness was just a shell to hide a softer center he was probably scared to deal with. He only needed someone to push him a bit to get there. She grinned back and led him into the cozy kitchen.

Big wooden bowls of freshly made ravioli with sauce came out, along with crusty bread and bottles of red and white wine. Julietta urged them to take seats at the heavily carved pine table, and they fell into a comfortable rhythm of eating and small talk.

"Tell me more of this deal." Mama Conte settled back and lingered with her usual precision and enjoyment over her plate. "I understand La Dolce Famiglia will be exclusive to Purity hotels. When is the opening?"

Julietta spoke up. "Sex months."

Silence dropped. The three of them stared at her as if she'd sprouted horns, and suddenly, she realized what she said. Holy crap. Talk about a Freudian slip of epic proportions.

"*Scusi*?" Mama Conte squinted as if her eyes were failing instead of her ears.

Sawyer tightened his lips, but those amber eyes danced with delight.

She leaned over and raised her voice. "I said six months, Mama."

"Oh. Very ambitious."

"Yes, it was an ambitious undertaking." Sawyer sipped his wine and dragged his thumb around the rim of the glass. "But quite worth the effort."

Her belly dropped. He got that same look on his face whenever he was intent on teasing her to orgasm. That talented thumb had done wicked things to her clit, her nipples, and her mouth that should have been illegal. Thank God it wasn't. Heat crept under her skin and made her itch. She crossed her legs to try and relieve the ache. "Sawyer has a way of getting what he wants," she offered. "He doesn't take no for an answer when he has a certain vision in mind."

"Your papa was like that." A soft smile ghosted Mama Conte's lips. "He believed we would make a success of the bakery, even though we started so small. When he focused on a goal, he took down any obstacle in front of him."

Julietta sighed. "I still remember being fascinated by the kitchen. I'd sit at the chair and watch Mama mix and knead dough for hours, hoping to get a taste of everything. She was always covered in white powder. When papa would go to a meeting in his suit, he always complained everyone knew he was coming from the cloud of white dust he brought with him."

Sawyer grinned. "Did he bake, too?"

Mama Conte nodded. "We all helped in the kitchen. My children learned early, but none of them had the passion for baking needed to be a chef. Venezia suffered through it, always more interested in clothes and heels and makeup. Michael did it out of responsibility. Carina was too young at the time and always attracted to her art." Her mother gazed at her from across the table with a proud glint in her eyes. "Julietta showed great talent, but she is most like her papa. They were very close and seemed to enjoy the business side of La Dolce Famiglia more than the creation of pastries."

Julietta chewed the last of her ravioli and blotted her mouth. "Papa started taking me to work with him when he finally bought the headquarters building. He always fought with Michael. Used to tell me his last hope was me, and I needed to be the rational one in the family."

"Did you start working after college?" Sawyer asked.

She shook her head. "Oh, no, there wasn't time for college. I graduated high school and went straight to work. Papa showed me everything I needed to run a successful bakery. By that time we were expanding and he needed someone to trust."

"Did you ever want to do something else?"

Julietta whipped her head around at Wolfe's voice. The boy had finished his ravioli and asked the question with a curiosity that puzzled her. She blinked, thinking about the question. Did she? No, she was never given a choice to do anything else. How many people did she know who whined and groaned about their parents choosing their future? Sure, she sometimes wished for a more carefree youth—with college dorm parties and late-night drinking. When she remembered her teenage years, most of them were taken up with learning how to cope in the big world of business. Making sure she exhibited confidence, dressed appropriately, and brought honor to her family name. Instead of going on dates, she pored over spreadsheets because Papa counted on her. There was no room for error or to disappoint her father. Michael and Venezia had already broken his heart with their refusal to work at La Dolce Famiglia. She always knew she needed to step up and make him proud. A choice?

No, there had been no choices. But she refused to disrespect her papa's memory by whining about something she never had. Her opportunities and upbringing were a gift— one that Sawyer and Wolfe never experienced.

The table quieted, and she realized her mother and Sawyer also waited for her answer. Was that a glint of regret in her mother's eyes or a trick of the light? Julietta lifted her chin with pride and spoke. "I've never been happier with my decision. And I have no regrets."

Her mother cleared her throat and rose. "I will serve *secondo corso*."

Wolfe cranked his head around. "Huh? There's more?"

Mama Conte cackled with delight. "Silly Americans. Pasta is first course only. There are three more to go."

Julietta winked at Wolfe and helped clear. As each platter was bestowed on the table, the fine tension in the young boy relaxed, and Sawyer let down his guard even more. Roasted, tender lamb with a hint of mint, bowls of escarole soaked in garlic and oil, and creamy polenta was passed around as Mama Conte talked of her youth and the antics of her children.

"Sawyer, you may get a chance to see Maximus again. He is planning a visit soon. Ah, how Carina and Julietta had such crushes on him!"

Julietta snorted. "Only for a bit. Carina was mad about him for years. They were meant to be together."

Sawyer turned his full attention toward her. "Is that so?" he drawled. "Seems my old friend Max was quite the ladies' man."

She rose to the challenge. "Oh, you don't seem too far behind. I heard Sawyer courted Carina himself in Vegas, Mama. Maybe there was even an old-fashioned duel over your poor daughter."

Mama Conte looked up from her plate with interest. "Yes, I think Max mentioned this to me before the wedding. Something about a fight."

"Did you lose?" she asked Sawyer. He lifted a shoulder in a half shrug, and Julietta clucked her tongue in mock sympathy. The knowledge Sawyer once lusted after her sibling and fought Max cut deeper than she thought. She tried to act disinterested and not embarrass herself. Now that their two nights were over, they hadn't discussed another encounter. Perhaps it was even over between them. It wasn't like they had a real relationship. Not the kind he had probably wanted with Carina. "Too bad. Though I'm sure you found a decent consolation prize in place of the real thing."

His fork clattered to the plate. She lifted her gaze. His eyes snapped with male irritation and blazing heat. Her heart clamored while she fought to remain unaffected under the magnetized sexual tension pulling her in. The naughty part of her fantasized about crawling across the table, climbing onto his lap, and riding him hard.

Mama Conte clucked her tongue. "Julietta, what has come over you? That was a rude thing to say to our guest."

She squirmed at the scolding. This man made her lose her temper in ways she'd never experienced. "Sorry," she muttered.

"Accepted." He pinned her with his merciless gaze. "But let me make something quite clear. I don't settle for consolation prizes, Julietta," he stated softly. "Understood?"

The hidden meaning behind his words soothed and aroused. Heat flooded her cheeks so she ducked her head and concentrated on her meal. Maybe this whole thing had been a bad idea. She'd only meant to invite Wolfe to a family meal, but now her complicated emotions regarding Sawyer were causing an undercurrent of tension. Even her mother seemed to notice something off, her sharp gaze bouncing back and forth as if trying to figure it out.

Julietta stood and cleaned up, keeping herself engaged with the dishes and sorting the leftover food into containers. Her mother chatted with Sawyer and Wolfe while she made the espresso and pulled out a variety of fruit, cheese, figs, and apple tarts.

What was wrong with her? Did she want a relationship with Sawyer Wells? The idea seemed impossible, but her body craved him on a regular basis. She'd never thought she'd be the type of woman to be comfortable with a purely sexual relationship, but then again, she'd never had a man able to give her an orgasm. And even if she was interested, Sawyer had clearly communicated his desire to avoid long-term commitments. It was probably best they end their whole affair now, before she got too pulled in. Julietta refused to allow herself to become one of those weak-willed women asking for affection. She had too much pride.

Getting addicted to him would be disastrous. And she was positive she'd last years on just those orgasms alone. Julietta poured the espresso and set the cups on the table, then nibbled on a plump fig. "We should get going soon, Mama. We have a long week ahead."

"Of course. May I speak with you for a moment, Wolfe?"

The boy looked surprised. "Yes, of course."

"Alone, please. Would you mind waiting in the living room, Julietta? Sawyer?"

Julietta paused. But she trusted her mother, and if she had something to say to Wolfe, it was important. She nodded. "Of course."

"*Grazie*."

She led Sawyer into the living room. The hand-braided colorful rug covered pine floors and mixed well with the comfortable earth-colored tones of the sofa, love seat, and ottoman. Delicate lace curtains covered the windows, and bunches of yarn littered the coffee table, a project in the making from her mother's love of knitting. A fire crackled and warmed the room. She wrapped her arms around herself and paced, too unsettled to sit. "Don't worry. Mama would never make him uncomfortable, I promise."

"I'm not worried about Wolfe." His body heat lashed from behind and pulled her in. The delicious scent of musk and spice surrounded her. Julietta walked faster to gain more space. "I'm more worried about what's going through that mind of yours."

She focused on straightening various knickknacks and photos on the antique chest until they were in a perfect line. "Nothing we should discuss at the moment."

"I disagree. Considering my dick was deep inside of you less than twelve hours ago, I think I deserve to know your thoughts."

She stopped and whirled around. He'd moved in like a silent predator, and her body softened into a pool of goo. She would've given money to be able to claim frigidity now.

Her ice queen status was officially trumped by a constant stream of horniness that annoyed the hell out of her. She clung to the annoyance and tried to ignore the hormones. "Don't say things like that," Julietta hissed. "We're in my mother's house."

"Who's not about to overhear us at the moment. You're trying to rationalize this thing between us, aren't you?"

She hated his astuteness. Why did he have to look so hot all the time? Narrowly cut black pants showed off all his assets, and his taupe shirt accented the gold gleam in his eyes. His hair was perfectly tousled for that right-out-of-bed look and smelled freshly washed. Her fingers curled in rebellion. She ached to drag him close and feel that delicious mouth move over hers. Taste his scent that got her drunk. Instead, she needed to have a logical conversation about not sleeping with him again. "I don't think we should continue seeing each other."

"I disagree."

Her mouth hung open. "I just told you this—this thing between us needs to end."

His lips tightened. "And I said no."

Frustration snapped her nerves. Why couldn't he just go away like most men who got rejected? "Well, too bad. Our verbal contract is over. You won. We need to concentrate on Purity and getting ready. Let's agree it's been a lovely experience, shake hands, and move on."

He tipped his head back and laughed. Julietta glowered.

"Oh, you're good. Lovely experience, huh? Shake hands?" He moved so fast she had no time to fight. He yanked her hard against him and devoured her mouth in a kiss so carnal, so outrageous, her toes curled in her boots and her nipples stabbed into hard points and she moaned helplessly beneath the deep strokes of his tongue. Sawyer ripped his mouth away and breathed hard. "Who do you think I am—one of your lackeys? Do you really believe you can control this *thing* between us by declaring it over?" Lust and greed and want carved out the features of his face. Julietta stared back at him, fascinated by the raw emotions. "I say no. I'm not going to pretend to shake your hand when I'd rather push my fingers between your legs and make you come. I'm not smiling politely when I'd rather kiss you senseless and force you to confront the woman you are."

She pushed at his chest, but he didn't budge. "I know exactly who I am," she whispered furiously. "A grown woman who makes her own decisions based on logic. A few orgasms between us isn't enough to risk this deal or my sanity."

"Tough shit," he sneered. "I'm not going anywhere, and I don't play by the rules. You want to sleep chaste and alone in your own bed, fine. But I'll be flanking your side every day, reminding you of what I can give. I don't walk away from something because it's messy and real, baby."

"Oh, yeah? Then what else are you willing to give, Sawyer?" She raised herself on tiptoes and got in his face. "When the vibrators and the handcuffs and the blindfolds are done, what do you have left to give me? You already said there's no long-term relationship possible. So don't give me this crap about you getting messy and real. *Baby*."

He released her and staggered back a step in shock. Julietta pressed her knuckles to her mouth. Had she challenged him to make this a real relationship? Was that what she really wanted?

She had no time to analyze. A noise interrupted the shattering silence.

Mama Conte stood in the doorway with Wolfe. "We are all set now."

Julietta pulled herself together and pasted on a bright smile. "Great. Let me grab the coats and my purse and we'll head out." Sawyer didn't speak, but followed her lead as they got their belongings and said good-bye. She hugged her mother tight, taking strength from the firm arms around her, and breathed in the comforting scent of home.

"Take care, sweet girl." Mama Conte stroked her cheek, her gaze sweeping over her face as if trying to find out what troubled her.

"Love you, Mama."

Wolfe stopped in front of her mother with a strange look on his face. With slow, hesitant motions, he reached out and gave her a half hug, before jerking back with an awkward motion. With a dignity way past his years, he spoke. "Thank you for inviting me into your home, Mama Conte. Thank you—for everything."

Julietta bit her lip as a tide of emotion overtook her. Her mother smiled and stroked the boy's cheek. "You are welcome. You come every Sunday now with Sawyer."

Wolfe nodded. Julietta stumbled out the door and gave a quick wave to Sawyer and Wolfe before starting her car. Like the demons pitched fiery forks at her heels, she gripped the wheel, imagined her bike, and stamped on the accelerator.

She refused to analyze the complete mess of the evening. Tomorrow she'd wake up stronger and ready to face the day. Julietta snapped the radio to a local station, cranked up the volume, and headed home.

• • •

Sawyer sat in the dark and tried to figure out what was wrong with him.

The whole way home he hadn't spoken. Wolfe seemed to be on the same level and contented himself with staring out the window. Something had changed tonight, and he wasn't sure what to do.

The moment Julietta had tried to push him away, he'd gone nuts. Her cool demeanor had challenged him to prove their connection and caused a deep-seated panic he'd never experienced before. He only knew he wasn't ready to give her up. Not yet.

Sawyer figured she'd gotten spooked. Unfortunately,

he hadn't helped matters much by acting all caveman, and she'd tossed out the relationship card. Did she want something more permanent between them? Was sex getting mixed up with real feelings?

He had nothing to base it on. He'd never wanted a woman longer than a few nights. Never craved to go deeper than the physical needs of the evening. He enjoyed being in control and bestowing pleasure. But something was different with Julietta, and he didn't know what to do.

He stared at the painting on the wall. A couple entwined on a bed. The man's foot snaked between her open legs, his bare back blocking the onlookers' full view. Shadow darkened the room and highlighted parts of her anatomy. The curve of hip. The stiff peak of her nipple. The spill of dark hair over her shoulders. The woman's face filled with a naked longing as she stared at her lover. In its complete stripping down of complex emotions to only lust and need, Sawyer touched peace. He'd always loved erotic art. For a little while, when he stared at a good piece, he was transported to a place he could actually imagine and touch something real. Something he rarely felt in a good sense.

Watching Julietta in her home with her mother soothed his soul. His meals consisted of eating alone at formal restaurants, drive-thrus, or his desk. Sharing a meal forged an intimacy between them that fascinated him.

But, of course, it could never work.

He remembered the night he'd first met Mama Conte.

God, he'd been so young and green, full of raw fury and ambition he'd barely been able to restrain himself. He'd fought viciously for the opportunity of an internship to work at the Plaza hotel in New York, and his boss was the biggest asshole on the planet. Reminded him of his foster father—a bunch of mean dressed in a fancy suit with money to protect him. Robin had hated Sawyer on sight and made his days as hellish as possible, blaming him for things that went wrong and taking credit for everything right. Still, when he got to accompany Robin to Milan on a deal, he felt as if he hit the big time. Boarding a plane, learning Italian, and getting an official passport made him feel alive. Not a ghost in society, but a man who had possibilities. Until that night.

Sawyer had made an impression on the client. His big mistake had been giving out his card in hopes of working with the guy in the future. Robin didn't seem to relish the idea of his apprentice getting ahead of him. When they both hit the bar for a celebratory drink, Robin began verbally abusing him. As his voice and fury rose, Sawyer snapped, then fought back.

And got fired.

Sawyer squeezed his eyes shut as the memory cut deep. The terror at being stranded in Italy, jobless, and having to start over. The humiliation of having everyone in the lounge stare at him, shaking their heads with pity for the poor kid.

Sawyer was dragged back to his past.

Robin stayed at the bar drinking heavily. The plan took

root as Sawyer watched him make a pass at an exquisitely dressed woman beside him. Sawyer knew she was a prostitute, and as his former boss became louder and more aggressive, he made a decision.

He left the bar. It was easy to buy the video camera. Even easier to make a deal with the hooker for the footage necessary to blackmail and ruin his boss. Sawyer watched the scene play out from the sidelines as Robin staggered and the woman took out her room key, leading him away. She nodded at Sawyer and held up a hand.

Five minutes.

He got up to nurse his beer at the bar while he waited. And heard the voice.

"He probably deserves it, you know."

His head swiveled. The woman beside him was dressed in pewter slacks and a charcoal cardigan, and had beautiful, long gray hair twisted up in a bun. The lines of her face were full of humor and grace, and her dark eyes were kind as she stared back at him.

"Scusi?"

The woman smiled and ordered a glass of Chardonnay from the bartender. "I was eating with my friend and overheard the scene. He is your boss, no?"

Sawyer drummed his fingers on the wood top and glanced at his watch. Four minutes. "He was *my boss. Got fired."*

She sighed. "Many people use power for the wrong things. What business are you in?"

"Hotels. We were meeting a client here, but I guess I was a bit too successful." The hate and bitterness twisted inside him and made him nauseous. Sawyer pushed his beer away. "Not sure why I thought it would be different," he murmured to himself. "I was stupid to play by the rules."

"No. You were brave. Believing in something good is the only thing that can hold us together."

He paused and studied her. She smelled of sugar and cakes and sweetness. What was her game? His fingers slipped to the small bag that held the camera. He gripped it more firmly and took a swig of beer. Three minutes. "Trust me, I don't live in the world of the fantastic. You need to protect yourself by using any means necessary. Only the strong survive."

Suddenly, her hand grasped his wrist. His first reaction was to jerk away—he couldn't stand anyone touching him without warning—but her skin was warm and her gaze steady as she looked at him. Not just on the surface, but down deep using those brown eyes, so Sawyer sensed she saw every one of his writhing, twisted demons. "Life is more than surviving, don't you think? Life is about choices. Hard ones. There is something bigger than us out there, something called karma. Every good deed goes back into the universe, and every bad one reaps retribution. Maybe not here on Earth, but later."

He shook from a sudden onslaught of emotion. Sawyer sneered in mockery from the slight softening. "Bullshit, lady. There is no hereafter, and happiness here means money, power, and taking what you want."

Her smile was gentle and full of so much wisdom he sucked in his breath. "You're wrong. I know what you want to do, and I don't blame you. No one could. An eye for an eye seems appropriate. But you'll only wake up emptier and needing more hate to fill you." Her fingers tightened around his sudden hammering pulse. "I'm asking you to choose different. Today. Choose to walk away from this, and everything may change."

Fear shook him like a teething puppy with a new bone. "Who are you? You don't know me, or him. You don't know anything."

"I know I see something in you that's so much more than this." Her grip eased, and she drew some euros from her purse and pushed them across the bar. Then carefully placed a business card next to him. "I'd like to help you. I know someone who runs a well-known hotel, and I think you'd fit in nicely. But you need to decide what you want more."

Sawyer scoffed at the card that held the name La Dolce Famiglia with a delicate cake sketched on the front. A fucking bakery? A crazy laugh strangled his chest. He was ready to film a porno with a hooker and blackmail his boss. He lived in the garbage because that was what he knew was true. Any attempt for anything real or clean would only disappoint him. And Sawyer had learned his lesson well.

Hope was deadly.

"Sure, lady. Whatever." He tucked her card into his suit jacket to get rid of her. "Thanks for the offer."

She closed her eyes briefly, as if he was her son and had let her down. When she opened them, her brown eyes gleamed clear and bright and sharp as the edge of a broken bottle. "I know you don't believe me. I probably wouldn't either. Still, the Lord gives us choices every day, and each tiny one makes up the framework of our life. This doesn't guarantee terrible things don't happen to good people. Innocent people." A sadness clung to her like a cloud of perfume. "Your future can be changed by one decision. One good thing can offset a mountain of bad. But you need to choose."

She picked up her wine and nodded her head with a grace that made him long for something beautiful in his life. "Thank you for listening."

The woman disappeared out of the bar as if she had been conjured up by some weird sorcerer from Harry fucking Potter. Sawyer glanced at his watch and pushed the strange encounter from his mind.

Showtime.

He drained his beer, paid, and took the elevator up to the eleventh floor. The key card to room 117 burned in his grip. He checked the hall and made sure all was quiet. No maid or foot traffic yet. Saywer hefted the camera and fiddled with the buttons, making sure he was ready to film the movie of his life. Finally. His first step of vengeance, even sweeter than beating the shit out of the boys who tried to jump him in the alley he called home or stealing from rich pricks who spent their endless amounts of money on coffee and designer clothes and fancy women.

He slid the key in the door and waited for the click.

The light blinked. Sawyer paused.

The image of Danny ripped past his vision. Of a little boy who looked up to him, who believed he was strong enough to protect him from the demons and keep him safe. His failure rose up to mock him, and years of bullshit and pain raged within his gut. His fingers trembled and he choked on nausea.

This would be his life. A life of no rules, no limits, just an endless spiral of emptiness. Panic reared, and he shook as if in a fever, his breath lodged in his icy chest.

The faint sounds of laughter drifted from behind the door. A slurred insult. The sound of spanking and a low moan. Sawyer knew he'd open the door to a scene from porn heaven. He'd get his job back, get Robin fired, and never look back.

His past blurred into the present, the future. The woman's words seared his brain until a bright light exploded in his vision.

One choice stood before him, clear and true, with precise consequences.

The other loomed ahead, fogged in mystery, ready to knock him back on his ass for taking a chance.

"Oh, yes, baby, just like that, oh, feels good!"

Sawyer staggered back from the door and fought for breath. In a drunken stupor, he moved down the hallway and shot down the stairs, running faster and faster away from the demons. He burst through the doors, into the lobby, and out

*to the sidewalk, dragging in clean air, losing himself in the
crowd of people busily shuffling past him with the goal of
work, pleasure, family, food, life.*

*He didn't know how long or how far he walked. Minutes.
Hours. Finally, he took out the card and studied the address.
He took a taxi, then the funicular into Bergamo, and finally
reached the house. His hand shook as he raised it to knock.*

*The door swung open, and the woman from the bar
looked at him.*

*"I didn't do it." His breath rushed out of his lungs. A
strange sob rose to his lips. "I didn't do it."*

*The woman's voice was wrapped in a loving strength
promising safe haven. Promising something Sawyer didn't
believe existed. "I am so proud of you. What is your name?"*

"Sawyer Wells."

*"Come inside, Sawyer Wells. We will talk. It will all be all
right."*

He stepped inside and his life changed.

The memory shimmered and disappeared like wisps
of smoke. He was betraying a woman he loved. If Julietta
had any feelings for him other than sexual, he'd destroy
her and hurt Mama Conte. Julietta was a woman with
character, strength, purpose. She was loyal to her family
and walked in the light. Deep down, he'd never be enough
for her, and the longer they spent together, the more dangerous the outcome. Better to allow Julietta the distance
she desperately craved. She deserved a man who was

whole and could give her the kind of life she deserved. Marriage. Babies. A full heart. Not someone who had nothing else to offer her other than good intentions and endless nights of sex.

No, he needed to end it now. Go back to the standard working relationship and be happy with memories.

His gut burned like acid.

"What are you doing?"

Sawyer jerked his head around. Wolfe stood in the doorway in a long-sleeved Nike shirt and boxers. His crazy hair stood straight up at wacky angles. "Nothing." Sawyer's voice was empty, as devoid of emotion as his own pathetic soul. "Go back to bed." He was about to turn away when he caught the look in the boy's eyes.

Haunted.

Ah, yes. The monsters always came at night, when you needed sleep and peace desperately. When you were most vulnerable. Sawyer motioned toward the chair next to him. "Actually, do me a favor. Sit down for a minute. I'm in a pissy mood and don't feel like being alone."

The boy moved into the living area, sat on the silver cushions, and pushed away a fancy blue striped pillow. Sawyer recognized the sheen of sweat on his forehead, the wrinkled shirt from twisting back and forth in the sheets, and the hollow cheeks. The boy finally spoke. "What's up? I thought you had a good night."

"I thought so, too." A short silence fell. Usually he disliked anyone in his personal space, but Wolfe's presence comforted him. "Had a nightmare. You get them?"

Wolfe shifted on the cushion. "Yeah." He paused. "What was it about?"

Sawyer studied the boy on his couch and realized how similar to Danny he was. Young. Strong. Mouthy. Smart as hell. But with his bare feet and his crazy hair, he seemed so damn vulnerable. So easy to . . . disappoint. Again. He cleared his throat. "Bad stuff. Getting beaten, trying to survive. You?"

Wolfe's blue eyes turned flat. "Same."

Sawyer reached for normal conversation, not wanting to torture the kid with a minefield of feelings he still tried to process. "I have to be at the site early in the morning. Can you sort through the inventory records so I'm set for delivery?"

"Yep."

"Dinner was good, huh?"

"I liked the pasta. Better than any meal in some of those fancy restaurants you go to."

"Yeah, Mama Conte doesn't fool around when it comes to a meal. How was your conversation?"

He ducked his head. "She was so nice to me."

"She saved my ass when I was a little older than you. She's good people."

"Yeah."

"The whole family is amazing. And have you tasted any of their desserts? Un-frikkin'-believable."

"Does it ever go away?"

The question shot through the room like a cannon misfire. Sawyer quickly covered his surprise and gazed back at the boy. Lips tight, chin up, something wobbling in his eyes, a gleam of desperation for normalcy, a need to hear the words that it would all go away and he'd be happy for the rest of his life.

A connection fused between them. His chest tightened, and a soul-deep need to take away the boy's pain blistered inside. God, he wanted to lie. But he knew truth was more important.

"No." The devastation on Wolfe's face choked him. "But it gets better. I swear to you, there will be nights with no nightmares or memories. You're able to handle more normal stuff. Work helps. Maybe therapy."

Wolfe sneered. "Did that. No, thanks."

"Depends on the shrink. Some are decent. I bailed, too. But we can look around and try again."

Wolfe nodded. "Okay. At least you were honest."

An image of his brother dead in an alleyway like a piece of garbage rose up and taunted him. Sawyer dragged in a breath. "I'll always tell you the truth. And I'll help in any way I can. Day by day. And I know I'm not the touchy-feely type either, but you can talk to me. About anything."

Wolfe gave a jerky nod. Some of the muscles in his body loosened. "Thanks, Sawyer."

Sawyer made a fast decision. The hell with it. There'd

be no sleep for them anyway tonight. He stood up and motioned to Wolfe. "Let's go."

"Where?"

"My kind of therapy. The gym. Meet you back here in five. Deal?"

"Deal."

Sawyer trudged to his room to change, preparing for a few rounds at the bag, some on the mat, and a vicious weight competition. His spirits lightened as he looked forward to a few hours of sweat, the blessed emptiness of mind and soul, and the company of a boy for whom he was beginning to deeply care. He grabbed his duffel and headed out.

Chapter Eleven

Julietta studied the tilt of the painting and wondered how it had gotten knocked askew. Her skin prickled as her usual OCD grabbed hold. Carina had sent it to her as a gift, and the image calmed her each time she looked up. She'd decided to put it in her office rather than her home since she spent most of her time here, especially with the subject matter.

Her papa sat at the head of the carved pine table in their kitchen. Plates of food, baskets of bread, and wine bottles were scattered across the surface. A blur of shadows made up the members seated around him, their faces not visible but the target of her father's stare. His hands clasped in front of him, dark eyes filled with a naked love as he looked at his family. Gray hair carefully combed back from his forehead, his face a mass of lines from both weariness and laughter, his long Italian nose dominating his features.

Their relationship had been different. She was definitely Daddy's girl, but it went deeper, a type of shared understanding between them that La Dolce Famiglia was the backbone of the family's sweat, blood, and tears. The respect she had for him and the way he worked to make her mother's dream a reality pushed her to consistently do better. For him. For her. For everyone.

Julietta loved looking at the painting when she was thinking over a business decision or when the employees left for the day and she stayed behind alone. As if Carina knew Julietta needed someone to look after her.

She wondered if Sawyer had ever had that experience in his life.

Julietta had stayed up all night analyzing every detail of their last encounter like a lovesick teen. The way he demanded she deal with him and her emotions. The way he never crumbled or became intimidated by her cool words, choosing instead to look beyond and find the truth. Her head said to stay away, but her body and heart cried out for more.

While she tossed and turned and waited for dawn, an odd truth finally revealed itself. She took many chances in her work world but had never taken one leap in her personal life. Over and over she walked away from complications or the threat of unrest in her safe little bubble. Now, all her siblings were happily married, starting families, and she was still alone.

Julietta drummed her nails against her desk and focused on her papa. Would he be proud of her? Or would he have shaken his head in regret at her inability to take a leap? Though he'd frown on engaging in a sexual affair with no permanence, Julietta knew she had to follow it through. Sawyer gave no guarantees, but he was truthful. For now, she wanted to throw caution away and engage in a heady, passionate affair that might lead to more. It was time she took a chance on a man who made her experience emotions she never believed possible. The next time she saw him, she'd be clear about her intentions.

With a satisfied smirk, she rose from the desk and kicked off her shoes. She'd go nuts if she had to look at the crooked angle one more moment. Julietta dragged over the cream-colored chair and climbed up. She stretched out her fingers but only brushed the edge. Hmm, the furniture was heavy enough that if she stood on the top wooden arch of the chair she'd just be able to right the painting. She yanked up her skirt a few inches for better reach. Propping one hand against the wall for balance, she stepped up, wobbled, and clutched the edge of the heavy gilded frame. One inch. Two. One more toward the right and—

"What are you doing?"

The familiar voice boomed through the room. Startled,

she scrambled for footing, slipped, and fell back into nothingness.

The automatic yell of fear died on her lips as strong
arms broke her descent. The breath whooshed out of her
as she slammed into a hard muscled chest. He staggered
back one step, two, then righted himself. She looked up and
fought the immediate urge to cover that sensual mouth with
hers. *Mio Dio,* he was physically perfect. A face straight
from heaven, with lips blessed by the demons.

"What the hell is wrong with you?" His brows drew
together in a fierce frown, and eyes as golden as buried
treasure shot sparks of anger. "Can't you ask for help with
anything? Are you so much a control freak you'd rather
break an ankle than let a man move a goddamn painting?"

Her gratitude died in her throat. Julietta found her footing and broke out of his embrace. Shoulders thrown back,
she carefully slid on her heels and shot him a glare. "Why?
Is it easier for a man to move a goddamn painting even
though he's the same height as me? Because I'm taller than
most of my employees. I don't have a penis, though, so that
must make a difference."

"Oh, for God's sake, I meant ask anyone! How about
your secretary holding your legs so you at least have a spotter? Or does that compete with your 'I am woman, hear me
roar' crap?"

She gazed back at him in icy stillness. "I was just straightening a painting, Sawyer. Not trying to prove a point for

equality of the sexes. Maybe you should ask yourself why you're so pissed off you can't control my actions?"

He spit out a humorless laugh and shoved his fingers through his hair. Of course, that only gave him the tousled, right-out-of-bed look that curled her toes in her sensible pumps. "Do you always have a smart-ass answer?"

"I always have an answer, period. Why are you so upset?"

He muttered something under his breath. "I didn't sleep well last night."

She studied the faint lines under his eyes and the strain around his mouth. Her anger burned away, and she took a step closer. "*Mi dispiace,* can I help with anything?"

She reached out to touch his arm, but he took a hasty step back. She stared at him. A cold ball of dread settled in the pit of her stomach at his inability to meet her gaze and the panic on his face. Obviously, he didn't want her to touch him. Which meant—

"I thought about what you said last night." The words seemed forced from his lips, but she made herself stand still and listen. "I think you were right."

She refused to give him the satisfaction of letting him believe he meant something to her. Julietta forced a smile. "I'm so glad. I was afraid it would be strange between us, and this deal is more important than a—what do you Americans say—a roll in the hay?"

His gaze lifted and pinned her. He looked deep, saw the

lie, and accepted it anyway. Sawyer nodded. "Yes. Thank you for putting up with me. I promise not to make you uncomfortable again."

"Of course. Are we still meeting today at three?"

"Yes."

"Excellent. Thanks for coming to say this in person."

"You are welcome."

The excruciating politeness hurt more than knives raking blood. Desperate to get him out of the office before a fissure broke in her facade, she turned and grabbed a file from her desk. "I better get back to work. See you later."

She tore through pages where words blurred and heard the door open.

"I'll never forget those two nights together, Julietta. Your gift to me was—priceless."

He left. Julietta looked at the painting, now perfectly straight, and suddenly knew why she never took risks in her personal life.

. . .

When Sawyer got the call, he originally planned to give her an excuse and say he couldn't make it. After all, he wasn't lying. His schedule was packed tighter than a woman's luggage. The last thing he needed with his sudden emotional upheaval was seeing her in the center of the storm. Hell, no. Unfortunately, she was just as stubborn as when he'd first met her, and she'd forced his hand in the only way he'd never refuse.

She'd simply told him she'd be waiting.

Sawyer grabbed for his patience while she served him a cup of strong espresso, less than twenty-four hours after he'd walked out of her home. After many minutes of polite chatter, Mama Conte finally sat across from him, took a sip of her brew, and leveled her gaze.

"I want you to marry my daughter."

Sawyer looked around for the camera. Son of a bitch. He'd seen *Punk'd* on MTV, but hadn't it been canceled? Betty White's candid camera spoof was about old people. Or maybe this was a modern day version of *Scare Tactics*? A grin curved his lips. "Sorry, I know about these shows. You're not getting me."

A frown marred her brows. "What shows?"

His grin faded. Come to think of it, why would anyone want to tape this anyway? "I'm sorry, I think I misunderstood. Did you say you want me to carry your daughter? Carry her where?"

"Sawyer Wells, do not play *stupido* with me. I want you to marry my daughter Julietta. The one you are sleeping with."

A strange squeak emitted from his lips. He'd heard the sound before—usually from weaker men who'd just realized they'd been outwitted and outplayed for food, shelter, or money. Odd, he'd never been driven to make the sound before now. Kind of pathetic. Reminded him of those mob movies like *Goodfellas* where the patsy rolled over and whined like a girl while he got the shit beat out of him. What had she said?

"We're not sleeping together." Her disappointed look at his lie made him throw his hands up in front of him. "We're not."

"You were the other night."

Jesus, this was so not happening. Time to man up and take control of the ridiculous conversation. "Okay, yes, we were. We did. But now we are not."

"Why did you stop?"

"This is really none of your business, Mama Conte." He kept his words firm as if speaking to an unruly child. "We were together and then decided it was best we continue our relationship in a strictly business format."

She spit into the air. "Bah, business. My daughter has been obsessed with her career since she was young. This was originally a good thing. It taught her goals, responsibility. She grew into a determined, independent woman we all admire. But she is losing her soul for the good of a profit."

Sawyer stood up. Whoa, this was not the time or place to dissect Julietta's life. Not with her mother. Not with the strange feelings he had for Julietta still bubbling up with nowhere to go. The hell with disrespect, he was getting out of here. "Umm, this is not my business. I'm sorry, but I have to go. I'm not sure what you're thinking, but—"

"Sit down, Sawyer."

Sawyer sat. Holy crap, was this what mothers did? Used some magic tone like a dom to make their children obey? She closed her eyes, as if trying to draw strength from above. When she opened them, a sliver of pure fear trickled down his spine. Mob bosses had nothing on this woman.

"I want you to listen to me. I am old. My heart is weak, my arthritis is strengthening, and I'm in the time of my life where I need to let go of my worries. Many things have been settled and bring me great joy. But there are two things that haunt me at night, keeping me from peace and from sleep, no matter how I try to surrender: my oldest daughter and La Dolce Famiglia."

Her words came slow, deliberate. Sawyer sat back in his chair and gave her his full attention.

"I built this bakery on sweat, blood, family, and love. I need to know it will reign for a long time, solid, without causing Julietta to sacrifice everything to keep it going. She will not delegate. She is too proud, too like her papa to believe anyone else can take care of our business. I need to make sure this merger between La Dolce Famiglia and Purity will be the key to her freedom. By signing such a contract, she is bestowing a piece of this legacy into your care. She is entrusting you to succeed, and she will have a long-term partner for support."

Saywer shook his head in confusion. "Wait a moment. We already told you the contract is signed. There's no need for a permanent personal relationship between us. We are both loyal to our word and signed a business agreement. Our respective companies will grow and expand together. You don't have to worry about this. I give my word I'll always look after Julietta and the bakery as my own."

Her mouth softened into a smile. "You are such a good man, though you still don't believe it." She sighed deeply. "I hope that will come with time. I believe you, Sawyer. But contracts are broken all the time, and when the ink dries, and time passes, distance supersedes it all. There is only one way I know of to guarantee Julietta and La Dolce Famiglia will have a partner and supporter I can trust with my life. Marriage. The sacred vows of marriage pledge a bond never to be broken. This is what I need from you."

He needed to steer Mama Conte back on course. This was crazy talk. Sawyer decided the best way to blow up the plan was to play devil's advocate.

"Mama Conte, I think you're missing some important elements in your idea. First, marriages today are more slippery than business contracts. People get divorced, leave the other, have affairs. Marriage is not what it once was. The sacredness is truly gone."

She tilted her head in thought. "Marriage is like everything else. It is what the person brings to it—whether it be a vow of celibacy, support, or profit. It is not the covenant that fails, but the people. Once you and Julietta make that decision, you will not back away from your responsibilities. This I know to be true."

His first full-force panic attack beat at the gates of his mind but he fought back. "Okay, fine. Let's talk about Julietta. We may have slept together, but we don't love each other. She has no interest in proclaiming forever with me, especially if she's forced into it. I assume you know your daughter's stubbornness?"

"I saw her with you. How she looked. How you made her feel." Memories flashed past his vision, and for a moment, Sawyer glimpsed the woman Mama Conte had been when she was younger. "There are real feelings there, but they are caught up with logic and contracts and a bit of fear. She needs a man who can be a companion, who understands how her work feeds her soul, a man who doesn't want to change her but accepts every pore of her being."

"I'm not that man."

The truth slammed through him. For a brief moment, he wondered what it would feel like to know he was the man who could give her all that. To hold her, keep her safe, finally let someone he trusted into his world. But it was only a mirage, not meant for people like him. Especially not with someone like Julietta.

"You are. You are her match, and I knew when I saw you together. Two halves of a coin that have no idea how to merge. Once you accept this, you will both be whole."

Temper bit his nerves. Enough of this bizarre vision of mergers and arranged marriages. "I'm sorry, Mama Conte, you are mistaken. I am not the man you believe me to be.

I don't have enough to give to a permanent partner. And if you truly love your daughter, you would never force her to do something like this. You'd be sentencing her to a lifetime of unhappiness. Let me ask you this. Would you pull this kind of thing on your other children? Force them into marriage like puppets without giving them a choice? Threaten or blackmail them into doing what you wanted? Or is Julietta different from the others because she chose differently? Answer that honestly."

His victory was short-lived. He expected a shamefaced duck of her head. A defensive anger at his wisdom. Instead, she tilted her head back and cackled with pure glee. He stared at her in astonishment.

"Your point is well taken. But I can honestly tell you I am not treating Julietta any differently from my other children." Her eyes sparkled with laughter. "Trust me on this."

He shook his head. "This is a moot point anyway. She'd never agree to this plan."

"She will. If you ask her."

He barked out a laugh. "Sure. And get my head ripped off in the process? No, thanks." He softened his tone. "I don't want you to worry about things. I promise La Dolce Famiglia will never falter, and I will always remain in your daughter's life. *Va bene*?"

He got up to leave, satisfied he'd done all he could. Sawyer turned toward the door.

"Do you remember your promise to me?"

The room shifted. He swayed for balance as his words trapped him in a vicious vise that echoed the squeeze of a boa constrictor around his neck. He bowed his head as his fate stepped forward and sucker punched him in the jaw. He gritted his teeth together. "Yes. I remember."

"*La devo un grande debito. Se lei mai ha bisogno di me, farò che lei chiede.*"

"*I owe you a great debt. If you ever need me, I will do whatever you ask.*"

"I need you. This is what I ask. I want you to marry my daughter."

He didn't remember much after that. The loud roaring in his ears, the pounding of his heart, the sweat dampening his palms. He refused to meet her gaze, knowing he couldn't trust himself with his emotions right now. Could he refuse? She had no idea what she truly asked of him. His acceptance of her request would set in motion a chain of events that scared the hell out of him.

Sawyer teetered on the edge, then realized there had never been a choice.

His marker had officially been called in.

He dragged in a shaky breath and accepted his fate. He might have to satisfy the debt, but he didn't have to be happy or gracious about it. Trying not to stumble, he made his way toward the door and clasped the handle in a death grip.

"So be it. But you better talk to her first. And God help you if she agrees."

Sawyer lurched out the door without a backward glance.

• • •

Julietta sat in the Piazza del Duomo. A heavy fog shrouded the cathedral's soaring, elegant lines, and a cold mist bit through vulnerable skin in an effort to nip bone. The wind whipped in late-March fury and pedestrians huddled past clad in long wool coats and hats. She stared at the gorgeous structure that had been a mainstay since childhood: the mingle of style and grace of each individual bronze carving on the massive gate; the sharp points of marble thrusting toward the sky. The gilded copper statue of La Madonnina dominating the sky.

She had loved sitting inside the cathedral, gazing at the rays of colored light as they filtered through the Gothic windows. The sense of peace and tranquility amidst great works of art and the mythical search for spiritual perfection. Afterward, Papa would take her to the square at lunchtime, where they would feast on fresh paninis and drink cappuccino, washing the meal down with pancetta and ripened grapes from the market. She'd watch the women—fashionably dressed in designer suits and heels—come and go, and wish to transform into one of them someday.

Well, she had. At least on the outside. Her wool coat

and matching fur hat bespoke a confident, stylish executive on her lunch break. Her green Prada handbag and Manolo shoes screamed refined elegance. Though she'd never left Italy to travel like Carina or her brother, she always felt safe at home. Never empty from not seeing other places. Never strangled.

Until now.

She was going to marry Sawyer Wells.

Humiliation burned in her blood. Her own mother wished to marry her off so she wouldn't become a cold, lonely spinster counting her gold coins. Their discussion had turned from amusing, to concerning, to enraging. She had shouted horrible things while her mama remained calm. Like an implacable statue, she'd repeated the same thing over and over.

You deserve happiness, my sweet girl. And if you won't do it your way, I'll do it mine. Sawyer Wells will give you what you need, though you don't believe it now.

No. She didn't believe it. Would never believe it. Somehow, Sawyer owed her mother a great debt, and he'd marry her to satisfy it. Her mother craved a clear conscience where her children were traditionally married and settled. Obviously, she didn't trust Julietta to run the business successfully alone, so she'd decided to add an extra layer of protection in the symbol of a big, strong man. Oh, how she hated both of them with a passion right now. Her mother for her betrayal.

And Sawyer for his agreement.

A shadow fell upon her. Sawyer sat beside her on the bench, keeping a polite distance between them. Her gaze roved over the shine of his Rolex watch, the radiance of his white-blond hair, the cool charcoal tones of his cashmere coat. The red scarf tucked neatly around his neck gave a hint of his boldness and ability to not care about other opinions. They sat together for a long time in silence while the wind roared and their skin numbed. Pedestrians hurried past them, tilting their heads up toward the sky to try and gauge the magnificence of the Duomo with its intricate architecture and soaring grace. A large flock of pigeons descended from the sky and clogged the piazza, their wings bright blue and heads bobbing furiously for leftover crumbs.

Julietta watched in silence as a younger couple squished together for warmth and laughed at the bird invasion. The woman was pretty, with brilliant red hair. She knelt down and put her hands out, and a bunch of the winged creatures hurried over and hopped onto her body. Her laugh was bright and tinkled through the fierce wind. The man laughed with her, knelt down beside her, and kissed her. The picture burned into her lids and reminded her of the things she'd never have.

She finally spoke. "Do you owe her that much?" she whispered. "Enough to give up your life for a sham of a marriage?"

"Yes."

Julietta nodded, already anticipating his answer. A yawning emptiness and grief roared up and pumped through her veins, looking for some type of outlet. She squashed it like an ant under the heel of her stiletto. Never again. She wouldn't let herself go back to that place of feeling, surrender. Not with him.

"I said no, of course. Walked away and swore I'd never return. I called her names. Raged at her. She just took it and said she believed this was for the best." A crazy laugh escaped her lips. "You know the worst part of this charade? She believes she's right. She's not doing it to hurt us, or make us suffer. What do they say about good intentions?"

"The road to hell is paved with good intentions."

"That's the one. Give the man a gold star. Oh, and a wife! Cha-ching!" She clamped down on the mania and struggled for composure. No reason to get wacky over a simple marriage merger. Because that was what it would be. She'd give her mother what she wanted, but in her own damn way. "Forgive me, I'm still adjusting. Even though this is Italy, I didn't know arranged marriages occurred anymore."

"I understand."

His voice was gentle, and she had a crazy impulse to grab his hand and beg him to make it all okay. Take her in his arms and say they'd work it out and ease the terrible tightness in her chest. But she did what came naturally. Sat quiet and stiff in her own cold bubble and did nothing. "It took me three days to realize she won. That everything I was so proud of becoming meant nothing because I'd still obey her like a child."

"What changed your mind?"

That part was the worst. Julietta didn't like to disappoint her mother, but there was no way she'd bend to a loveless marriage. Until she said the words that singed her ears and crippled her resolve.

"*Before your papa passed on, he made me promise two things: to make sure you solidified La Dolce Famiglia as our family legacy. And for you to marry. He loved all his children equally, but you were special to him. He worried about you the most. I do not think his spirit will rest until you give this to him, sweet girl.*"

A deathbed promise with her as the casualty. She tried to ignore the words, but they haunted her day and night. The portrait in her office stared back at her, demanding her acquiescence. Until she finally realized she had no other choice. Just like Sawyer.

She spoke with no emotion. "She said Papa would want this. For me. For La Dolce Famiglia. And I'm afraid she's right."

Sawyer made a move, almost to comfort, but she stiffened and he pulled back. She couldn't have this awful conversation with any type of warmth or she'd never recover.

"How do you want to proceed?" he asked quietly.

This she could handle. "I'd prefer to say we eloped. Like

Carina and Max. As soon as our paperwork arrives, Father Richard can marry us with just my mother in attendance. I'll tell my family it was a whirlwind affair, and we wanted little fanfare and attention. We can cite the merger and our workload to escape a honeymoon. We'll send out a brief press release, tell our respective companies in a meeting, and hopefully the fervor and gossip will die down quickly. Is that acceptable to you?"

Sawyer nodded.

The young couple before her rose to their feet, interlocked arms, and walked out of the square. She watched them leave and wondered if they would always be that happy. She shook off the thought and got back to business.

"Good. Now, as for residence, I propose we get a big place immediately. I'll rent out my apartment for now. I'd prefer Milan to be close to the office, if that's okay, and we'll split the cost equally. We'll need plenty of space so we can lead our separate lives without bothering the other. I'll put my Realtor on the hunt immediately. Agreed?"

Another slight nod.

"We'll need a prenup. Would you like to use my lawyer or yours?"

"Doesn't matter."

A family took the place of the couple and crowded in front of the bench. Two small boys ran around, laughing in delight as they chased pigeons, while the parents shook their heads and tried to rein them in. Julietta watched the man grin broadly, point up to the Duomo, and pull his mate in close. She leaned in with a naturalness that spoke of years together.

Julietta continued. "We'll need to set the terms, of course. Mama never needs to know our intention to end it after a certain allotment of time. If it's acceptable to you, I'd like to use two years as our frame. I'm afraid one year won't satisfy my mother's wishes, but two is a fair enough deal to say we both tried. Unless you disagree?"

He didn't look at her. Just stared at the young family as if they were the key to unlock the answers he needed. "Two years is fine."

"Good. I refuse to let this thing throw off our time schedule and delay opening. You have my word I'll hire help and get this transition done as smoothly as possible."

He lifted his head as if awakening from a fairy-tale sleep. "What about us?"

She blinked. "Us?"

"Yeah, us. What's the rules for that? Same bedroom? Separate? Do we share work during the day and distance ourselves at home? Are we companions who share meals and conversation? Have you planned that out yet?"

Her back went ramrod straight. His gaze probed hers, as if he were looking for some type of emotion she refused to show him. What did he want from her? She snapped out her words with deliberate precision. "Why don't we take care of all the necessary details before we subject ourselves to a heart-to-heart? Once we marry, we'll sit down and go over what each of us is comfortable with. I'm sure we can agree to a mutually beneficial compromise."

He laughed with no humor. "Spoken like a woman in complete control of the situation. Must be nice."

Her defenses split, ripped, and bled. "What do you want from me? An apology?" Her voice broke, but she pushed on. "I'm sorry. Sorry a debt owed to my mother will stick you with a charity case for two years. Sorry I wasn't enough for my family, for me, for anyone. Especially you." Her eyes burned with unshed tears. "I'm doing the best I can to make this palatable for both of us."

The shell of the civil, distant man beside her shattered. He reached out, grabbed her upper arms and pulled her against his chest. "You offer me an apology?" he tore out, golden eyes spitting sparks of fiery rage as he shook her slightly. "Goddamn you to hell. You think I'm upset because I'm stuck with you? How dare you call yourself a charity case to the man who kissed you and stripped you and fucked you for so many hours we both fell into exhaustion? You deserve a man to be whole — a man who can offer you a decent life and not tear you apart piece by piece. I'll never be able to give you what you need. Don't you understand I'm frozen inside? There's nothing left to give you except physical pleasure."

His sensual lips twisted in a sneer, and his fingers bit through the thick fabric of her coat. "But I'm not as polite or charitable as you, I guess. I don't intend to be a martyr and give you a safe little space with his-and-her bedrooms and an occasional smile as we pass in the hallway." The angel morphed into devil. Lust and rage and something completely untamable gleamed in the depths of his eyes. "Not me. I'll rip down your door when I've had enough and take both of us to hell. And I won't have a shred of regret."

She parted her lips, entranced by the powerful aura beating from him in waves. His body heat battled the wind and made her burn to let him take her as many times and in as many ways as he fantasized.

His gaze focused on her mouth. Her heart thundered. She waited for him to lower his head and claim what was already his. Instead, Sawyer eased his grip and pulled back. A bleak desolation carved the lines of his face. "But I don't want to hurt you. So I'll allow you your barriers and your own bedroom and anything else you need from me. I have only one rule. You will never talk about yourself as a charity case or someone unworthy. Not in my presence."

A stray lock of hair broke loose and lay against his forehead. Without hesitation, she reached out and tucked it behind his ear. Then ran her hand down his cheek. The rasp of his beard tickled her fingers. She caught his scent of musk and spice and lemon on the wind. "Okay," she whispered.

Like a sinner seeking penance, Sawyer bent his head and pressed a kiss to her open palm. Julietta sensed something deeper in his actions and craved to follow the path leading to a thicket of thorns, poison ivy, and endless predators poised to tear flesh. When his gaze finally pierced hers, Julietta knew this man would be the one to either complete her or destroy her.

She trembled in pure terror. He traced the sensitive line of her jaw, her chin, and slowly down her neck. His light touch caused shivers of sensation to prick her skin and tighten her nipples. Julietta ached to take the leap and damn the consequences.

He took the choice away from her and stood up. "I'll begin immediately on the paperwork. Let me know when the Realtor comes up with something appropriate. Wolfe will be over this afternoon. Call if you need anything."

He left.

She watched him walk across the square and disappear behind the building. Then she sat on the bench for a long time, in the cold, and wondered what she was going to do.

Chapter Twelve

Julietta walked into the foyer. The vaulted ceilings held a graceful elegance that pulsed through every brick in their new home. Situated in Via della Spiga, her Realtor discovered the hidden treasure of the luxurious traditional mansion. From the outside, an onlooker imagined nice apartments hiding behind the somewhat crumbling facade. Inside, a feast for the senses awaited. Boasting three stories, the parquet floor gleamed as Julietta walked over to the circular staircase and did a quick survey. The open concept living room and kitchen gave the impression of massive space, and the rustic beauty of old wood, thick walls, and lush foliage wrapped the home in elegance.

The moment she stepped foot in the house she instinctually knew she was home. Funny, letting go of her apartment she loved for so long didn't cause a pang. After boxing up all her belongings, the pathetic truth slammed into her brain. She had few personal items she loved or needed to bring. The apartment only held stray trinkets but most were work things or fancy gadgets. This house was different. It screamed of character and history. Julietta imagined stamping her own story here and finally making a permanent mark. For the first time in her life, she understood the unique characteristics of a place to live and a place to thrive.

With Sawyer.

The wedding was set. The home was bought. Various information outlets regarding their romance and decision to quickly marry were outsourced and already losing gossip potency. The past three weeks blurred in an endless stream of tasks, work, and shoring up her defenses. Each time she spoke with Sawyer, he was polite, helpful, and distant. It was almost as if she planned someone else's future and wedding, for each conversation was exactly what she wanted. Business. No mess of emotional upheaval, but a calm, focused plan of attack.

She hated it.

Footsteps echoed behind her and she pushed the thought aside. Julietta turned and caught his profile. The sunlight poured over him, accenting the clean slash of his scar and bathing his features in golden warmth. With the graceful precision that was part of his core, Sawyer walked through each room and studied the final layout.

She bit her lip. "What do you think? Anything can be

changed. We'll have to commute a bit to work, but this area completely charmed me."

He stopped in front of the glass doors leading to the terrace. Stone floors led to an extensive garden with a small lagoon pool. Julietta imagined working on her laptop and sipping espresso in the quiet space as the sound of gurgling water soothed her.

"It's beautiful."

His husky voice rippled across her ears in a caress. Relief poured through her, and a smile curved her lips. "I'm glad you like it. There's a whole extra wing I thought Wolfe could make good use of. It's like his own apartment, but not so separate he can disappear for days without us noticing." He flinched as if in pain. "What's wrong?"

"I didn't specifically talk about living arrangements with Wolfe."

She frowned. "He knows we're getting married. Where else would he go?"

Sawyer shifted his feet. "My old place. I don't think he wants to live with us. Even though he has no idea about our situation, he assumes we're honeymooners. It will make him uncomfortable."

"What type of conversation did you have with him?"

"General stuff. That we decided to get married because we're a good fit. Told him his position in the company was unchanged and we'd continue like we have been. He never asked about where we'd live, so I didn't bring it up."

Julietta watched his sudden discomfort and shifted through the possibilities. "You're afraid to talk with him, aren't you?"

"What do you mean? We've shared space for a while now. We talk every day."

She shook her head. "No, not really. You talk about work. That's it. Listen to your own words—you share space. I think you're afraid to delve any deeper in case you upset him. As long as you keep it light and uncomplicated, he'll stay." Her gut lurched with pain for him and the boy he'd taken under his care. Her voice softened. "Sawyer, he needs to know you want him. I see the way he looks at you. Wolfe would never ask, but he's looking for your approval. If he thinks he's in the way, he'll chew off his own hand to get away. He'll refuse to be a burden on anyone."

Sawyer spun around and glared. "Of course he's no burden. You don't know how it is for kids like him. They've been kicked in the teeth and emotionally tortured. I never want him to believe he's trapped or owes me to stay. If I keep it light, he won't feel any pressure. I just want him to be safe. Try to protect him."

Another layer peeled off before her. Julietta stared at the man who was about to become her husband and wondered if she'd ever be safe from him. His sexual appeal was magnetic but something she could fight. His determination to protect Wolfe snuck past every defense. He loved Wolfe, but he didn't know how to communicate or deal with it.

Julietta realized he didn't know how to care about another person in a permanent way. His past told him commitments ended in pain. God knows what he'd gone through, but she had to show him a different path. Prove in some way that there was so much more for him if he only opened up. Sawyer deserved it. Wolfe deserved it.

She fought the need to hold him and stood still. "I'm not going to pretend to have the same kind of background, to experience the type of pain you both went through. But I do know he's a nineteen-year-old kid who needs something he can cling to. Something solid. He needs you, Sawyer."

He jerked as if slapped. "I'm doing the best I can," he growled. "Jesus, why are you pushing him? If he wants his own space, I can't blame him. He can't be forced into an uncomfortable situation."

Sensing she neared a dangerous precipice, Julietta listened to her gut and pushed. Her heels snapped as she closed the distance and stood before him. Chin up, she got in his face and challenged him. "He needs the exact opposite right now. Giving him space means you don't give a shit about him. Letting him work things out in his own time translates that you don't want to be bothered. Are you that much of a coward? Do you only want to do half of the work to help him and then scurry away because it gets too messy? You got him off the street and gave him a job. But the moment emotion is involved, you freeze up and deny it's even there. Or is that something you just want to accuse me of?"

Stunned recognition filled tiger gold eyes. Something seemed to break inside him, a memory that drove him to lose control and slip into the wild, animalistic persona always shimmering beyond his surface. He gritted his teeth. "You think a hug and heart-to-heart chat can fix what's wrong with us? We're way past that, baby. It's a fucking miracle he doesn't jump anymore when someone touches him, let alone share some fun memories. How about the nights spent on the street in freezing temperatures under dirty newspapers and smelling like shit? Fighting over a half-eaten hot dog in the garbage? Watching a kid get the shit beaten out of him and not lifting a finger to help?" The darkness rose up and claimed him. His body shuddered and she knew it wasn't about Wolfe any longer, but his own dreadful past rearing up. "Whenever I tried to protect someone, I made it worse. I learned to step back and not get involved, because it was safer for everyone."

"Not now," she said firmly. Julietta grabbed his hands and squeezed. He stared at her with eyes half focused. "That was before, because you needed to survive. Now you need to live, Sawyer, and so does Wolfe. You need to give him more of yourself even though you're scared. Wolfe has a chance because you got to him in time. Do you understand?"

"What if I make it worse? I don't want him to . . . leave."

Her heart shattered, and she stepped into his arms. Laying her head on his chest, she buried herself deep in his warmth and bled for the little boy who never had anyone to help him. He responded to the embrace and hugged her back hard and clung. "He doesn't want to leave you," she whispered. "He just needs to know you'll fight for him. That you care enough and that he's not a charity project you pick up and play with."

Silence fell between them. Julietta stayed in his arms for a long time and let her words sink in. When his heart stopped hammering, and his grip relaxed, she eased out of the embrace. His gaze probed her face, searching for something she was terrified of. "Why do you care so much?" he asked.

She took a shaky breath. "Because I see him in you." Julietta turned and took a few steps back. Waited for him to grab her and challenge the statement. Push her to cop to the emotion like he did all those hours in the bedroom, wringing out every honest response her physical and emotional body hid from him. But he said nothing. Disappointment flooded her, but she told herself it was a good thing. Better to keep the relationship on neutral ground or they might destroy each other. "We'd better go. I have a meeting at noon."

He followed her out in silence.

. . .

Sawyer rapped on the door and tried to ignore his sweaty palms. Un-fucking-believable. He'd gotten dragged into parental hell without the benefit of any previous experience.

But Julietta was right. Time to grow some balls and take control of this situation.

The kid opened the door. "I'll take one of those meat-ball subs."

Sawyer snorted. "I'm not here to take your dinner order, smart-ass. I have leftovers from yesterday we can heat up."

"Cool. What's up?"

Wolfe wore one of his usual long-sleeved cotton shirts, a pair of jeans, and white sport socks. His headset fell around his neck, and the echo of some loud type of rock music pinged in the air. The crazy spikes of his hair were damp and soft, falling into thick curls that told Sawyer the kid had once had a nice set of locks before he decided to torture them. "I wanted to talk for a minute."

A wall dropped between them. The easy manner disappeared, and a gleam of resolution pierced through turquoise eyes. "Sure. Umm, listen, I was gonna say this to you later, but I figured you had a lot going on with the wedding. I'm heading out."

Sawyer moved into the room, causing Wolfe to back up. Dread settled in his stomach, but he kept his tone light. "Heading out where?"

Wolfe shifted his feet. "You're getting hitched, and I've got itchy feet. Figure I'll help you finish out this deal and move on. Maybe back to New York."

"You don't like working for me anymore?"

"No, I like it. Let's be honest, man. We never spoke

long-term arrangements here. I've been saving my money for a while, and I think I can support myself now. After all, you paid me a great salary. You've helped me a lot, and it's time to get on with your life. Do you think you could give me a recommendation? If you want to, of course."

Sawyer took a deep breath. His nightmare was coming true. Perhaps Julietta was right. Behind Wolfe's blank expression, a glimmer of misery and anxiety shone in his eyes. He'd normally agree with Wolfe in an effort to make him happy, let him carve his own path in life. But Sawyer realized he was just a kid who had no direction. No one cared enough to ask him to stay.

He was taken back to that night in a flash.

"Please don't go, Sawyer." Danny's face was full of fury, pleading, rebellion. It was dark, and a sliver of moonlight leaked from the broken blinds and played upon the mattresses. "I'm coming with you."

He stuffed the few clothes and belongings he had in the bag and kept his head averted. He was afraid to leave Danny alone with Asshole, but the sooner he got out, got a job and a place to stay, he could come back and get him. If he stayed here, his foster father could still use Danny as leverage. If he left, maybe the kid would fall off the old man's radar and he'd get some peace.

The plan was simple. Get out, get successful, and save Danny. Then go to the authorities and nail the son of a bitch. His time had finally come.

He reached out and squeezed the boy's shoulder. The sharp thrust of bone met his palm. Sawyer ignored his foster brother's trembling lower lip and forced a smile. "Listen, dude, it's going to be all right. I'll get a job and come back for you, and we'll leave this shithole behind. In the meantime, keep low. Don't push him, and when he drinks, lock yourself in the bathroom; there're weapons in there in case you need them."

"Okay."

The flat acceptance told him Danny didn't believe him. When he left, he swore he'd make it right, but a few months later, his opportunity was gone for good.

Sawyer stared at the boy before him, the past and present mingling in a strange psychedelic haze. He'd failed Danny. If he let Wolfe walk away without a fight, he'd never forgive himself. Something deep inside him broke open and oozed out in a big mess he usually refused to deal with. His instincts screamed for him to run away and not look back. Instead, he crossed his arms in front of his chest and stared hard at the boy.

"I don't want you to go."

Wolfe jerked. Ran a hand through those damp curls. "I told you I'd stay to finish the deal."

"I'm not talking about the deal. I'm talking about you." He took a ragged breath and tried to say the words. "You do an incredible job for me with Purity. When I first took you in, I just wanted to show you another way to go. I was your age and barely surviving when a guy did me a favor and helped me. Changed my whole future. That's what I originally wanted for you, but I never thought about how long you'd stay or what would occur. I never say it because I suck at mushy crap. But I got attached. I like having you around. I like the man you're becoming. And I don't want you to leave."

The vulnerability of exposing himself made him want to bolt for the door, but he forced himself to stand still. The shock on Wolfe's face was almost worth it. His mouth hung open in an almost comical way before he realized it and snapped his lips closed. "But—but you're getting married."

Sawyer shrugged. "So what? Julietta wants you to come live with us, too. We got a big-assed mansion where you can have plenty of space and privacy. Plus Julietta cooks. And we get to go to Mama Conte's house on Sundays if we want. No maid, though, and I have a feeling women get pissy about that sort of thing, so you'll need to be neater."

The boy bit at his cuticle in the nervous gesture Sawyer noted meant he was thinking hard. "I don't want to get in the way. Don't want to be a charity case."

His voice flicked like a lash. "Don't say that. You're no charity case to me, damnit. I care about you. I think you're an awesome kid, and I want you to stay." He paused. "Please."

Sawyer caught the gleam of delight in the boy's bright blue eyes at the admission. Finally, he had done something right. "Okay."

Sawyer grinned. He had won. "Get your crap packed, because it has to be done by Saturday. And you're coming to the wedding. We'll have dinner afterward and then go to the new digs."

"No honeymoon?"

"Nah, too much work. Are we good?"

Joy bloomed when Wolfe slowly nodded. A banked relief carved out the features of his face. For a crazy moment, he ached to give the boy a hug, but he kept his reaction muted, sensing it would be too much emotion for both of them to handle at the moment.

"Okay. We're good."

"Cool." Sawyer walked out of the room, shut the door, and leaned against it in relief. Once again, his ice queen had been right. He hadn't wanted to delve into the snake pit with Wolfe, but it had been worth it. He wanted him in his life for the long term and if Julietta hadn't challenged him, the boy would be walking away and leaving them both unhappy.

He wondered what other type of surprises his wife-to-be had in store for him.

The dominant part of his makeup roared to shove past both of their barriers and take her to bed. Once he put his hands on her, she would melt and allow herself to give up control. But after only two nights, he already craved more. Going into a marriage with a woman who threatened his sanity wasn't smart. How would he handle the intimacy of seeing her on a daily basis? Sharing meals? Evenings? He needed time to find his balance, and that meant no sex. For now. Companionship. Work. Simple rules. Simple emotions.

As long as she never wanted more from him.

Two years. He needed to bear down and last two years before he'd be able to walk away, knowing his promise was technically fulfilled. He wondered what it would be like to be a real husband to her, to build a life with children and family and fullness. But the empty place inside him was too cold, an endless landscape of Arctic ice.

Yes. It was too late for him.

He accepted the fact and trudged into his bedroom.

Chapter Thirteen

Julietta gazed down at the diamond on her finger. Three carats, princess cut, flawless in clarity. The setting was platinum gold with no other diamonds fighting to compete. Her husband knew her taste well—simplicity and elegance. Too bad he wasn't real.

The ceremony was exactly what she'd wanted. Thank goodness Venezia and Dominick were in London for business. She wanted no family members there to witness the sham occurring before a Catholic priest. She'd always dreamed of getting married in Colleoni Chapel with its famous rose window showing off the flanked carved medallions of Caesar and Trajan. The intricate detail and intimacy of the small church in Bergamo provided the perfect backdrop. Her elegant Rivini wedding dress was exquisite with detail, from the tightly fitted strapless bodice to the spill of chiffon of the fuller skirt, fluid with movement in a deep creamy white color. The diamond combs held her hair up in a classic upsweep and flashed bright within her dark hair. Her shoes were custom-made, with encrusted diamonds over the four-inches heel and toe, playing a game of hide-and-go-peek as she walked down the aisle.

When she moved to the high altar, the rich murals and frescoes etched on the walls exploded with images of color and sacredness. Her mother and Wolfe stood by their sides as light streamed through the stained-glass window and Julietta waited to see if God would send down a thunderbolt in a sign that this marriage was doomed.

Instead, the day was mild and spring warm, and the singer lent a haunting note of beauty as she sang, her voice along with the organ's chords lifting and echoing toward the arched dome ceiling and stirring emotion Julietta refused to recognize. Her mother beamed with pride and a satisfaction that ripped at Julietta's heart. When she recited her vows, she wondered if her father's spirit was finally pleased.

Unlike her sisters, she'd rarely dreamed about weddings and had never imagined walking down the aisle with anyone. When she gazed into those shattering golden eyes, her heart lurched in a beautiful agony of need. The truth whispered deep inside her in mocking tones.

She wanted it to be real.

What would it feel like to be the woman Sawyer loved?

The one who opened up all those dark, dusty corners of his soul and let fresh, clean air blow through? He'd possess his mate with a fierceness and primitive air that no man could equal. But there was also a sweetness in his soul that called out to her. She remembered him bathing her so tenderly, the gentle touch of his finger across her cheek, the passionate way he'd ordered her never to demean herself.

"Julietta? Are you okay?"

She shook herself out of her musings and looked up. The object of her thoughts stood in the doorway of the room she claimed as her office. After dinner, they'd headed to their new house, and both of them had immersed themselves in work, retreating to their separate space. Wolfe had long since gone to bed. The quiet, impersonal environment mocked the idea that a wedding had taken place just hours ago. It was business as usual, with iPads and laptops and furious text messages to business associates. The house roared up and seemed to demand more personal contact from its inhabitants. "Sure, just wrapping up some loose ends."

Sawyer stretched and rubbed the back of his neck. He'd changed into a pair of loose khaki slacks and a clean white T-shirt, and he sported bare feet. The intimacy of sharing a house suddenly loomed before her. Seeing him in all forms of undress, but not feeling she had the right to touch him. Panic lit. What if she couldn't play this charade? It was their honeymoon night, and she had no idea how to act. Cool and sophisticated? Warm and friendly? She ached to crawl under the covers and hide for the night, but wouldn't that look pathetic at this point? He spoke with no idea regarding her looming attack. "Yeah, me, too. I have to get up early to go to the site tomorrow. Are you finished up?"

"Yes."

"Wanna join me for a quick drink before bed?"

Her nerves shrieked and her body jumped to come out and play. She deliberately squeezed her thighs together in rebellion. "Sure. Wouldn't mind a taste of cognac before sleep. I've got an early morning, too."

She followed him down the winding staircase, her fingers lightly tracing the smooth mahogany as they walked into the library. Julietta took a soothing breath of lemon, paper, and leather. Between both of them, they'd filled up the mounted bookcases with a variety of fiction, biography, business, and cooking. She'd been fascinated by his eclectic reading taste and found he could hold a conversation on practically any topic. She took a seat close to the fireplace and tucked her feet underneath her. It was important they set a precedent for the future. Julietta decided she'd be friendly, but distant.

He handed her the snifter of amber liquid and sat beside her. The warmth of the fire enveloped them in a comfortable haze, and she relaxed a bit. "You looked beautiful today," he said.

Julietta smiled. "*Grazie*. You didn't look too bad yourself. And Wolfe was quite handsome. He even took out his many piercings."

Sawyer laughed and sipped his drink. "Yeah, he cleans up nice. I never got to thank you. For your advice with Wolfe." He lifted his gaze and pinned her with sheer intensity. "He was going to walk, and if I hadn't asked him to stay, we would've both been alone. How did you know?"

She swallowed past the tightness in her throat. "I saw the way you look at each other. Respect. Admiration. Care. You may have met as strangers, but he's part of you now. That's how family is. They drive you crazy, push you to the edge, but family stands true."

"I always had the opposite."

"I know. But family isn't about blood. It's about sticking and loyalty and sacrifice. I didn't want you to let Wolfe go because of pride."

"And that's why you agreed to marry me. Right?"

Julietta stiffened, afraid he might guess too much of the truth. Yes, she'd done it for family. For Papa. For business. But the secret part inside told her she'd only marry someone she cared about, felt safe with. Sawyer was both. "Yes, that's right."

"Did you ever think of marrying before?"

His probing surprised her, but she decided to answer. "No. There was one man I got close to. We worked together. For a little while, I wondered what it would be like to come home to him at night. Share meals, a bed, a life. But I started to realize things were flat between us. We made a good connection on paper, but he never sought time with me. I was like his conferences—scheduled in." She remembered that feeling of inadequacy as she craved to forge more of a connection before realizing he wasn't interested. He'd been calm and rational in what he wanted—a wife for business, a companion for company. Her frigidity annoyed him, but he never took time to push for more of a reaction from her, which only caused more friction and numbness every time he took her in his arms. Eventually, the relationship withered and died without a speck of smoke or flame.

"Sounds like a real dickhead."

A faint smile passed her lips, but the ghosts had been unleashed. The words popped out of her mouth. "No, he just didn't want me enough. No man ever has."

The sudden focus of his attention shifted. Those hot eyes roved over her body, reminding her of all the places he'd touched and licked and bitten, and the hundreds of ways he'd made her explode beneath him. "I repeat. He was a dickhead. And a moron."

Humiliated at her confession, she laughed it off and straightened in her chair. "I agree. I rarely give him a second thought, so it was for the best." Her lie lay between them like a big fat elephant in true cliché form. "How about you? Any desire before to walk down the aisle?"

"No."

His flat admission made her cock her head. "I know you've been with many women. You seem to like companionship. What was missing?"

Darkness danced over his face. A shadow fell over his cheek and highlighted his scar. "Nothing. Everything. I'm able to have fun and have a sexual affair, but they always demanded more. Things I couldn't give. So I kept moving on."

"And now? What will you do now?"

Her challenge seemed to startle him. "I don't think I've ever met another woman as direct as you."

"I'm not sure that's a compliment."

He gave a short laugh. "It is. You're able to consistently surprise and challenge me. Is it time for our heart-to-heart?"

Her temper simmered again and she narrowed her eyes. "I don't enjoy being mocked. Why don't we do what's best for us? Work together. Share space. Respect. We'll keep those more base emotions out of the equation so neither of us loses focus. Agreed?"

He studied her mercilessly, but she refused to yield. Julietta remained still under his scrutiny. Her mind screamed for him to take the compromise. Her gut screamed for him to ignore her polite request and drag her to bed. Finally, he nodded. "As you wish."

The air turned flat and stale. Her energy drained out like a broken pipe, and she quickly finished her cognac. "I'm glad we agree. It's for the best. If you don't mind, I'm going to bed."

"I took the adjoining room just in case Wolfe gets suspicious."

"Of course." She set her snifter on the table and forced a smile. "Good night, Sawyer."

"Good night, Julietta. Sleep tight."

She left the room and headed toward bed, half relieved and half heartbroken

• • •

Sawyer refilled his glass as the door shut behind him. He still smelled her unique scent of mocha and coconut that made his mouth salivate for a candy bar. But she was much tastier, the memory of her thighs spread wide and her gorgeous honey flowing free over his lips.

Jesus, he was going to lose it.

His dick strained in a desperate effort to break free of his pants. Was she trying to drive him insane? She wanted a companion. Work partner. Friend. How could he concentrate on those aspects when he ached to strip away her polite veneer and uncover the wild, sensual woman he'd discovered in his bed? And how long would he hold out? He imagined himself exploding during a calm dinner and ripping off her clothes in a frenzy.

But would she like that?

Her words haunted him. No man had ever wanted her enough. His very tough, capable woman had her own demons. He bet the few men she'd tried to forge relationships with had wrecked her self-confidence. How else could a sexy, smart, independent woman think she wasn't good enough for marriage?

Maybe he needed to show her.

The possibility danced along the edges of his mind. He could accept her terms and they'd move forward with no messiness. Probably the best course. But the look on her face when he agreed told him a very different truth.

No man had ever been strong enough to challenge her. Push her. Seduce her. Her body melted under his instruction; her mind cracked open to allow secret entry that both humbled and inspired him. He craved her like a drug injected in his veins, and though it was unpredictable and chaotic and unplanned, he needed her.

Allowing her to sleep in her cold bed tonight would only let her build back her defenses. The right thing to do would be to leave her alone. He didn't do love. She was a woman who deserved it. But what was worse? Keeping her safe but believing she wasn't enough for a man to fight for? Or dragging her into his bed and risking heartbreak?

His brain told him clearly the only decision he could make. The path he followed since he found out he'd killed his foster brother as clearly as pulling the trigger.

But tonight all the thinking power had gone to his dick, and there was only one decision he'd be making tonight.

Sawyer set down his drink and went to claim his wife.

• • •

Julietta twisted in the pale blue sheets, kicking out one leg in an effort to cool down. For such an old house, the radiators pumped heat in massive gulps, and sweat clung to her neck and upper back. With a groan, she threw back all the covers and stared at the ceiling. Her body throbbed with a desire that wouldn't be quenched tonight. Too bad she didn't own a vibrator. Of course, she'd always been too embarrassed to try it before, afraid even a gadget wouldn't push past her icy core toward orgasm.

Amazing how Sawyer seemed to sense whenever she was pulled out of her body. He yanked her right back to the moment and refused to let her mind take over.

Stop thinking about Sawyer.

Sleep. Focus on sleep. Julietta closed her eyes and started counting. One. Two. Three. Had she approved the finance report for the quarter? Yes, she'd sent it. Four. Five. Six. Was it her secretary's birthday this week? She needed to buy a present tomorrow. Seven. Eight. Nine—

The door opened.

She sat up. Stared at the figure before her. He'd taken off his shirt, so the moonlight played over the naked skin of his chest. The cut muscles of his abs and biceps shimmered amidst the wicked scars fighting for dominance. He stood with bare feet apart, hands on hips, gaze narrowed in quiet power. In that moment, the blood roared in her veins in a pure adrenaline rush. She swayed slightly, trying to breath through the crazy hammering of her heart. "What are you doing in here?"

"I think you know."

His voice oozed like salted caramel. Smooth and rough and sexy as hell. She tried to answer but only squeaked some type of pathetic sound. He moved slowly, each graceful motion a deliberate action to pump up the sensual tension whipping through the room. She sat frozen amidst the sheets like a terrified doe about to be swallowed whole. Julietta murmured the only word with the power to stop the roller coaster of emotion she was terrified to ride on. "No."

He stopped beside her bed. His aura pumped out a raw, male scent that caused a low moan to rip from her throat. Sawyer reached out and grasped her wrist. Pulled her from the mattress so she stood. Her pale pink nightgown clearly showed the thrust of her naked nipples, the shadow of her body beneath the delicate fabric. In her bare feet, he towered over her with a domineering manner that screamed he was in charge. Of everything.

"You're my wife. It's our wedding night. I heard your proper speech and agree that keeping sex out of the equation would be the smart thing for each of us." He paused, lifting his palm to caress her cheek, stroke back the tangled wave of hair from her shoulder. "But I can't. I won't. You belong to me."

"I don't belong to anyone."

He chuckled at her shaken words and continued stroking her face, hair, throat, shoulders like he was soothing a pissed-off cat he only wanted to pet. "Jesus, you're magnifi-

cent. You never give up, and you're not afraid of anything
but this. Of what you feel like once I touch you, command
you, direct you to give me every part of that delectable
body." Her skin warmed and softened underneath his touch,
her nipples painfully hard against the soft cotton barrier.
"I'm not spending night after night with an erection that
won't go down and a need in my soul to have you. You do
belong to me, Julietta. Your body is mine for the taking, and
I'm taking it tonight."

His mouth claimed hers. She waited for brutality and
raw invasion. She got softness, heat, and a man intent on
winning. She lifted her arms, poised to push him away and
fight. His tongue sank deep between her lips, inviting her to
play, tempting her to leave safety behind and plunge into
the all the dark delights he was going to show her.

She grabbed onto his shoulders and surrendered.

His satisfied moan pushed the heat higher. Their
tongues tangled together, and his taste swamped her, the
delicious burn of alcohol and spice and a hint of mint tooth-
paste. He gripped her head and dived in, over and over, taking her mouth like he intended to thrust between her legs
with all the glorious power that left no room for thought or
decisions or approval.

Still holding tight, he guided her against the far wall and
pushed her against it, never breaking contact. Her hands
greedily ran over the lines of his chest, the roped muscles
of his shoulders and arms, the line of blond hair that trailed

down the center of his stomach and disappeared beneath the waistband of his pants. He ripped his mouth away from her, stepped back half an inch, and gave her a wolfish grin.

Sawyer grabbed the delicate collar of her nightgown in the center and ripped it straight down the middle. Wetness ran down her thighs at the raw violence of the motion. He stared greedily at her naked body, and her clit pounded in demand. Sawyer touched a hard nipple, ran a thumb under the curve of her breasts, and continued down her quivering stomach. "You didn't wear panties to bed. Why?"

His question demanded the truth. Her voice ripped from her throat. "Because it was too much. I was thinking of you, and I was too—"

"Aroused?"

She jerked her head. Lust gleamed from tiger eyes as he kissed her again, pulling her tight against his chest, devouring her piece by piece. He unbuttoned his pants and stripped quickly, then slowly turned her around. She fought to keep skin-to-skin contact, but he nipped at her neck in punishment and forced her hips to swivel.

"Hands on the wall. And don't let go, Julietta."

A shudder wracked through her. She placed her palms flat on the wall. He spread her legs wide so cool air rushed between and teased the swollen flesh. "I wish I could paint you like this," he said reverently, tracing the line of her spine, the curve of her buttocks. "You're everything beautiful and perfect and feminine in a woman. Graceful, muscular, with gentle curves and golden skin that reminds me of a goddess." He placed kisses down her back and nibbled on her nape, pushing her hair back over her shoulder. "I want to brand you so every inch of your body responds only to me. Your taste haunts me. I watch you conducting a proper business conversation and dream of lifting your skirt and burying my mouth in your pussy."

"Sawyer——" She turned in desperation but a quick smack on her buttocks stole her breath.

"Hands on the wall. You're not allowed to have an orgasm until I'm inside you. If you do, there will be consequences." He nipped at her shoulder. "And I'm going to do everything in my power so that you disobey me, baby. That way I'll be able to punish you."

His outrageous words stripped her sanity and turned her into a creature of animalistic needs. She squirmed and rested her forehead against the cool plaster, desperate for more. His low chuckle told her he knew every dark, dirty thought in her mind and intended to fulfill them all. His hands cupped her breasts and he played with her nipples, tugging, twisting, until they swelled and were so sensitive that pleasure leaked into the fine edge of pain. His tongue traced down the line of her spine and settled above the swell of her buttocks, then lower, spreading her cheeks and slipping his tongue to her dripping slit to pleasure her.

The slide of his tongue over her swollen clit, the nibble of his teeth, the strength of his hands as he held her open to everything he chose to do with her—all of it came crashing down into a raging climax that overtook her body and tossed her like a grain of sand in a tidal wave. She screamed, her hands clenching together as she bucked against him wildly, her body convulsing in pleasurable shocks. He helped her ride it out for a long time. Finally, her muscles quivered and relaxed. He supported her weight and held her against the wall, his erection pushing between her legs in pulsing demand.

"God, you're sexy. You're—everything." The soft words wrung another shudder. He lifted her and brought her to the bed. "But you still disobeyed my orders."

"I kept my hands on the wall."

He laughed. "True. I'll punish you only fifty percent for coming before I approved. On your knees."

She muttered a curse under her breath but got onto all fours on the bed. "Why do you get to make all the rules?"

"Because I said so. And it's more pleasant for you when you obey. Has anyone ever spanked you before?"

Her head rolled around to glare. "What do you think?"

His lip quirked in amusement at her sarcasm. "I think no. You get ten whacks by my hand."

"I'm not a child. That's humiliating. And if you continue, I'll make sure you lose that hand."

"Oh, I like games, baby, and I'm the master. How about me torturing you for hours without letting you orgasm?" She opened her mouth to say something smart, then snapped it shut. The idea of it tantalized her, but she was deathly afraid he was telling the truth. "Hmm, smart response. Though I may have to try that in the future; you looked way too intrigued to see if I could accomplish the feat. For now, you get the spanking."

"What could this possibly do for you or me? I've never heard of such a thing."

"I guess you'll have to tell me. One."

His flat palm hit her right cheek. A quick sting made her suck in her breath. Her ass was probably as red as her face, completely embarrassed at her position and vulnerability. Three more quick hits on the right, then he moved to the left. Julietta locked herself in position before each swat, cursing him, wondering why the heck he'd get aroused over such a ridiculous game.

Until she realized her body was dripping wet. Sensitized. Ready to go over the edge with one touch.

As if he knew, Sawyer paused halfway through to rub her heated skin. The massage only revved up her crazed response. She squeezed her eyes shut at the realization the whole thing was turning her on horribly. He continued on the left cheek for three more. Each time, instead of suffering through it, she arched against him without thought, craving more of the delicious prickly warmth that oozed through her bloodstream and sensitized every nerve ending. She held her breath for the last two.

"Widen your legs."

She pushed her thighs apart one inch. Two. Waited for the pain in horrible anticipation. His fingers settled on her buttocks, rubbed, then slipped between her thighs.

"*Mio Dio!*"

Her clit pounded for release and her nipples stabbed open air in a terrible need to have his mouth and tongue and teeth. Just as she was about to orgasm, he slid his fingers out and swatted her backside with two strong strokes.

Her arms trembled, unable to take her weight. Her arousal rose to her own nostrils, and a low animal moan escaped her lips and echoed in the air.

His control must have snapped. With an answering groan, she heard the rip of a wrapper, and suddenly he mounted her. Grasping her hips, he slid into her in one hard thrust, filling every inch of her body and claiming her completely.

Julietta surrendered. Body, mind, soul. With long, full strokes, he brought her straight to the edge and held her there mercilessly, guiding the rhythm and not allowing her to do anything but hang on and give him what he wanted. Her channel milked him, and he tortured her for what seemed like forever until she begged.

"Please, oh, please."

He paused. Held himself deep inside of her, not moving, as her body spasmed around his penis. "You belong to me. Say it."

"I belong to you, Sawyer. Take me."

He reached around, gently squeezed her clit, and plunged.

The orgasm hit hard. His dim shout told her he followed her over. She sobbed in relief and let go, giving him everything he asked for and more.

• • •

"I think I'm dead."

Sawyer kissed her cheek and pulled her closer. She burrowed under the sheets, and her silky warmth pressed against him. The scent of sex filled the air. Moonlight leaked through the window and cast shadows over the bed. "Then I've done my job for the night." He caressed her bare arm, enjoying the feel of her skin. He didn't think he'd ever get enough of her.

"Will you kill me every night?"

"Yes. I hope that's okay with you, or we'll have to play out this caveman scene on a daily basis." Sawyer held his breath and waited for her answer. Somehow, some way, this woman had crawled under his skin and buried herself there. He needed this from her, needed the connection of sex, and then he was sure the tension would finally relax between them. After all, they were married.

"No. I don't want to fight you anymore. Fight this."

"Good." They lay in relaxed silence for long minutes. He was about to drift off when she spoke his name. "What, sweetheart?"

Her tone was wary. Unsure. "I know you said you never talk about your past. I understand. But I feel as if you know so much about me. It feels unbalanced. And I feel—"

"What?"

"Vulnerable," she whispered. "I need something. Of your choice." She paused. "Please."

The memories swamped him, but her confession touched a tender part in his soul. She was so honest about her needs, even though she opened herself up to his ridicule. And Julietta was right. He hadn't given anything of himself other than his body. He reached down and sought what he could sacrifice. The words flowed out without hesitation, as if always waiting on the surface for the right person, the right time, to escape.

"My parents died when I was nine. I had no other relatives, no friends to take me. I went into the foster care system, and I wasn't prepared for what I found. No one wanted a young boy on the edge of being a teenager. I was placed a few times before I found a permanent residence. But things were bad. Worse than for someone who never had the experience of good parents I think. Like a shock to the system, I had to change my thinking about what life was in order to survive. When I finally escaped at eighteen, I roamed the streets, made a place for myself, but it was rough. I found an old hotel in Manhattan I'd been staking out and slept in the cellar. Near the janitor's room. I'd wash myself, steal food, and keep hidden. Until Jerry found me. He was a janitor—worked there for years. I waited for him to throw me out and call management or the cops, but he did neither. He let me stay."

She didn't say anything when he stopped. He refused to taint her with his criminal actions, of the violence during his years with his foster father. She'd never understand. After a while he gave her the rest.

"We didn't talk much about what had happened. He'd manage to steal me another uniform and began to show me the ropes. He told management I was his nephew and got me a job. I learned starting at the bottom of any establishment is the way to learn it all. You know the employees, the gossips, the codes, and the behind-the-scene shit that happens in all hotels. He pushed me to be more, and I finally got an opportunity at the Waldorf hotel. I traveled to Milan on an internship and stayed for a while with another hotel and finally traveled back to New York.

"He had a heart attack on a Tuesday at two forty-five p.m. I was doing okay for myself by then, but then I found out the truth. Jerry was previous military and had received a purple heart in Iraq. He also came from a wealthy family, but after the war, he dropped from sight and gave it all up. I opened my door to two lawyers who told me Jerry left me everything. I was a multimillionaire at twenty-five years old."

Her focus was almost physical, as if poised on his every word and drinking it in deep. Instead of avid curiosity, he felt only a deep peace and understanding from her, making it easier to go on. "He left me a note he'd written when I was twenty years old. It said, 'Make your mark.' I took off for a while to get my head straight. Blew a lot of money. Then decided to focus on doing exactly what he wanted— proving myself a success. When Purity opens, it's for him, because he was the only one other than my parents to ever give a shit."

He let out a breath and waited. For the questions. The probing. He didn't blame her and knew how women needed to push until it was painful and there was nothing else to give. He waited in dread, and finally, she moved.

Julietta lifted her head. Cocoa brown eyes gleamed brightly, but no tears showed. She lowered herself over him and kissed him. Thoroughly. Gently. As if he was precious glass and deserved all the care and love in the world. "Thank you," she whispered.

She rested her head against his chest, intertwined her thigh with his, and gave a long sigh. Then drifted off to sleep.

He waited for the pain to flood his conscience, the feeling of being unclean, of never being enough for the mentor who had saved him. Instead, there was nothing. A void where the rawness had once hidden. A curious wave of relief whooshed through his body, and he suddenly imagined himself lighter and more at peace.

Chapter Fourteen

"**S**trange. There're a few extra cars at Mama's today. I guess she invited some guests to dinner."

Sawyer linked her hand within his and winked at Wolfe. "Good, maybe there will be even more food to munch on."

She laughed and shook her head. "You two are amazing. I've never seen grown men eat like they've never had real food before."

"At least I help you clean up," Wolfe pointed out.

Sawyer shot him a glare. "Traitor. Wait till I get you in the gym. I'll double-kick your ass."

"'Double-kick' is a word, old man? Funny, I didn't see you going all Rocky Balboa on me when I got you in the ring. When you went down, you stayed down."

"Who's Rocky Balboa?" Julietta asked.

The men traded a shocked look. "Holy shit, you've never seen *Rocky* one, two, three, four, five, or six?" Sawyer asked.

"If there're six installments, that does not bode well for me," she said, reaching the door.

"Marathon, baby. Tonight."

"Behave, boys. I hear voices."

"Surprise!"

A roar filled the room as the door opened. Julietta looked inside in pure shock. She couldn't speak as the image before her finally registered. Her family. Crowded in one room, together.

Tears filled her eyes, and she pressed her fingers against her mouth. "*Mio Dio,* why did you not tell me you were coming?" Julietta rushed forward and was immediately clasped in a cocoon of safety and warmth. With laughter, tears, and shouting, she reached out and grabbed onto Carina, holding her in a hug that also tried to encompass her brother-in-law and Michael.

Carina laughed in delight and squeezed her back. "We wanted to surprise you! We told Mama we were coming but never thought we could pull off such a huge coup."

Michael lifted her in his arms and swung her around like she was five years old. "We all had to get off work from La Dolce Maggie, and we had to make sure the twins were finally ready to visit their aunt."

Two matching boys hid behind Maggie's legs, peeking

out curiously at the loving chaos in the room. One sported bright green eyes like her sister-in-law, and the other a deep bark that pegged him immediately as the brooding Luke, exactly forty seconds older than his brother, Ethan. She squatted and held out her arms, lowering her voice to a soothing tone. "Hi, Luke. Hi, Ethan. I'm your aunt Julietta. Can I get a hug?"

A gentle prod from Maggie caused the two to toddle over. They both wore designer jeans, T-shirts, and matching leather jackets. Sturdy walking shoes helped them keep their balance as they entered her arms. Julietta pressed her lips to soft baby locks and breathed in their clean scent like a drug. "Oh, I'm madly in love." She lifted her face to the boys, beaming. "And I love the outfits."

"You should see what your sister-in-law gets for my two. I swear Nick has a heart attack every time I open one of her gifts." Julietta rose to her knees and laughed in delight when her gaze snagged on Alexa and Nick. She'd never met them but felt as if they were already family from the stories and photos. Alexa was Maggie's best friend from childhood, and Nick was Maggie's brother. With a squee, she gave matching hugs to the attractive couple. Corkscrew curls hung wildly around Alexa's face, and her gorgeous curves reminded Julietta of Carina: earthly and sensual in a way most men craved. Nick sported blond hair in various shades and amused chestnut eyes.

"Yeah, I thought your brother would keep her in line,

but she's just as outrageous as ever. I came home one night to find Lily demonstrating the 'Gangnam Style' dance moves while Maria proudly wore a T-shirt proclaiming her 'Too Cool for Drool.'"

Maggie punched her brother in the arm and rolled her eyes. "If I left it up to you, they'd be studying Mozart and being too nerdy for high school."

"Ruin your own kids, Maggs."

Alexa sighed. "Children, please. We just arrived and you're already fighting."

Julietta pressed her lips together in amusement. "I can't believe you were able to get coverage for the bookstore. I'm so excited to finally see you here!"

"Nick is in between projects right now, and since Carina came to work for me, I'm super organized at BookCrazy. We were able to squeeze out a full week of vacation. Of course, we didn't have to worry about the hassle because we took Michael's jet, and it was completely relaxing. I just hope we didn't put poor Mama Conte out this week."

Mama Conte held baby Maria in her arms, her eyes filled with joy as she gazed around the room. Her voice snapped with command. "Don't ever say such a thing. This house has been empty much too long. It needs children and laughter. You stay as long as you like."

Julietta hugged and chatted until a strange silence fell over the room. She swiveled her head and caught her husband's gaze.

Pure discomfort and the urge to flee echoed from his eyes. Wolfe shifted his feet and looked nauseous and uncomfortable, staying as far away from the crowd as possible with his back pressed against the door. Her heart lurched, and she walked back into the foyer to slowly take each one of their hands and link them with her own.

"This is Sawyer, everyone. My new husband. And this is Wolfe, a very close friend who's more like family."

Max stepped forward, his dark good looks battling with Sawyer's smooth blond grace. The male testosterone crackled in the room and kept her transfixed. "You're a sneaky bastard, you know that, Sawyer?" Max challenged, standing in front of him. "Not a lousy phone call or e-mail to tell me you got hitched. I guess we're now related in some strange incestuous way."

Julietta held her breath, about to tell Max to back down, but a smile curved across her husband's face. "Too bad. Who the hell would want to be related to you? You suck at poker and you're butt ugly."

Max leaned forward. "But I'm taller, and I can beat your ass."

"Only when I let you." His gaze slid to Carina. "And thank God I finally did."

A short silence fell. Then the men boomed with laughter and clapped each other on the shoulder in that half hug grown men use. Totally not getting their code, Julietta shook her head and tugged Wolfe into the fray. "I love your tattoo," Maggie announced, taking control and stepping in front of Wolfe. "Serpent. Goes down the chest, too?"

"Yeah."

"Very hot. And I love the cut of your hair. Do you model?"

He narrowed his eyes as if preparing for mockery. "No, of course not."

She gave a thoughtful snort. "You'd be amazing in a cover shoot. I see you work out. Great biceps. Ever think of modeling?"

Michael grabbed onto his wife and pulled her away. "*La mia piccola tigre,* please leave the poor boy alone. He does not want to strip to his underwear for your camera."

"Why not? He'd make a ton of money. The photographs I can do would be extraordinary."

"Are you really serious? Is that something you think I could do?"

Michael groaned. "Here we go."

Maggie practically hopped up and down, ignoring her husband. "I'm working with a new Italian designer, and you're exactly what he's looking for. He needs edge. I'll call him in the morning and set up an interview while I'm here."

Wolfe straightened his posture. "Cool. Yeah, I'm up for it. Thanks."

"You're not taking my best assistant away, are you?" Sawyer called out.

Maggie smiled sweetly. "Let's see how much Victorio wants to pay him first. Then we'll talk."

"*Mi dispiace,* Sawyer. My wife cannot control herself when she sees someone to photograph."

Maggie wrinkled her nose. "I'm not cooking for you tomorrow."

"Thank goodness."

Julietta laughed at their easy camaraderie and the sexual spark that still shot like wildfire around them. As if underneath the teasing and insults lay pure combustion just ready to explode in private. Carina wrapped Wolfe in easy conversation that was such a part of her generous heart, and Julietta took a moment to immerse herself in the crazy chaos of family. She missed Venezia and Dominick, who would have completed the entire circle, but V had to dress a celebrity client for a movie premiere, and Dominick had decided to accompany her to London and stay for the week. Julietta made a note to call her so they could at least Skype.

The hours passed as they drank bottles of Chianti, played with the children, and hurried back and forth into the kitchen with platters of appetizers. Thick tomato with buffalo mozzarella, fruity olive oil and fresh basil on Italian bread. Plump mushrooms with lumps of crab, salty prosciutto wrapped around sweet, juicy melon. She kept a close eye on Wolfe, who at first didn't eat, obviously nervous about being accosted by numerous family members he didn't know. He seemed to loosen up as the evening progressed, and as his appetite increased, she noted Mama

Conte made sure to keep bowls of food near him at all times. Sawyer also seemed to relax, enjoying conversations with Max and Carina and finally meeting Max's mother, who beamed with pride at her son's accomplishments and her new daughter-in-law she'd always loved as her own.

Maggie beckoned Julietta from the door and she crossed the room. "What's the matter?"

Maggie's cinnamon-colored hair shimmered under the chandelier. Green eyes spoke volumes of worry. "I'm not cranking pasta by hand again, Julietta. It takes me forever, it always sucks, and I've completed the tradition. It's your turn."

Julietta bit her lip. "I make pasta all the time, Maggie. Anyway, I see Alexa in there. She's got it covered."

Maggie lowered her voice in a hiss. "Your mom thinks I don't cook enough and wants me to practice. I already committed to the apple cake; I do that much better than pasta. Alexa is nuts, she loves this stuff—look at her in there." Alexa beamed and listened to directions from Mama Conte, elbow-deep in dough as she kneaded mercilessly. "Besides, Mama said you can take my place because you haven't served your husband yet."

Panic fluttered and Julietta's stomach sank fast and low. The Conte tradition of cooking by hand for each new spouse in the family was unwritten, unspoken, but a known passage of intimacy. Feeding your husband with your own hand was a way to connect on a deeper level and nourish a connection beyond the physical. Not that Sawyer would know, of course. He'd have no idea if she slid a plate in front of him, but Julietta didn't think she could handle it. It had been two full weeks since their wedding night and the fragile bond formed then seemed to bloom brighter with each day. They never analyzed their new relationship. Each night, Sawyer took her into bed, made love to her in every way imaginable, and held her through sleep. Purity was taking form with the speed of light, the construction complete and all the details finalized for the unveiling in three months. Yes, she cooked for both him and Wolfe when they weren't working overtime, but it was quick and efficient. They formed their own routine as a family, but none of them looked deeper than that.

"Umm, I don't think this is a good time. I'm worried about Wolfe, and I need to help watch Lily and—"

"I'll do it; just get in there." Maggie ripped off her apron, pushed her into the kitchen, and took off.

Porca vacca.

"Where is Margherita?"

Julietta sighed and tied the apron around her waist. "Took off. You know she's like a sly fox when it comes to getting out of cooking."

Her mother cackled in delight. "I will make her do apple cake and biscotti. She will regret it. I need you. Here is your station."

Alexa grinned. "This is the most awesome thing I ever did. From now on, I'm making fresh pasta in the house. But

I think I may get one of those machines, Mama Conte. I'm not as adept as you. My fingers are getting tired."

"Push through. Machines do help, but it is the strength and gracefulness of the body that flows into the food and bestows good energy."

Alexa dug in with gusto, and Julietta enjoyed her positive energy flowing around them and relaxing her a bit. She fell into the motions used since childhood: dusting, whisking egg, sprinkling out flour, kneading, and pouring into a dough form that depended on a fresh mix of ingredients and the basic talent of the pasta maker. The movements soothed her, and an odd need to excel at making the food she would feed her husband beat inside her, an ancient instinct rising up from the ashes of years of tradition. The room fell away, and Julietta lost herself in the task, pulling and stretching the dough to a fine, thin layer like gossamer without breakage. She heard the muttered frustration of Alexa as her noodles broke one after the other, but Julietta never broke her concentration. Piece after perfect piece was pulled and laid out to dry over the racks.

She pulled a fresh loaf of bread from the oven and sliced. Carina floated in, and eventually Maggie came back. They prepared, set the table, laughed, and drank wine during various tasks while thick pots of gravy bubbled up and the smell of garlic and lemons tinged the air. Wooden bowls were placed at each setting, and the men filed in with groans of approval. The scrape of chairs against the floor rose to her ears. Steam billowed, and Julietta made sure her pasta was cooked perfectly al dente, not pausing to wonder why it was so important.

High chairs also clustered around the table with tiny bowls of pasta and sippy cups in front of them. The twins seemed fascinated by the scene before them, and Lily chatted with Maggie nonstop, giggling at her father's occasional tug on her wild curls so like her mother's.

Alexa placed her bowl in front of Nick. "Try it."

He looked up. "Did you make this?"

"Yes. Tell me what you think."

He picked up his fork and took a bite. She watched his face in sheer anticipation. Nick broke into a broad grin and shook his head. "Amazing. This is the best pasta I ever had in my life." She beamed with pride and joy and leaned over to place a kiss on his mouth. "You get a reward for that later."

His brow arched. "Is Maggie babysitting?"

His sister snorted. "Dream on. You're babysitting for us."

Carina sighed. "Would you two just stop? Max and I will take the kids for you, if you want some alone time."

Max choked. "No, we won't. I didn't agree to that." He grunted at the obvious kick under the table.

Julietta stood with her bowl in her hands. Her hands slipped on the edges, and she chastised herself for being so ridiculous. He wouldn't know. No one would. It was a silly tradition anyway and meant nothing. She set the bowl in front of him. "Here you go. *Buon appetito.*"

The sudden chatter dimmed. All gazes focused on Sawyer, who stared down at his plate and then back up in pure confusion. Damn them all. Why were they making it meaningful? "Umm, is something wrong?" Sawyer asked.

Her mother gave her the look. The look that prodded her to speak and had forced her to do many things she didn't want to do over the years. Julietta pressed her lips together. Mama Conte snorted at her daughter's stubbornness and took the reins. "My daughter has made your plate by her own hands. She has done this with the honor of serving you, her husband, for your pleasure."

Heat struck her cheekbones. This was such an archaic tradition. Sawyer was probably dying from being the focus of everyone's attention with no idea how to react. Her nerves fluttered. "It's nothing." She forced a laugh. "Just eat."

She slid into the seat beside him and laid her napkin on her lap. When he didn't say anything, she lifted her lids to sneak a peek.

He stared down at the pasta in sheer amazement. As if gazing at pure gold, he shifted his glance back and forth, staring with a strange vulnerability and need that called out to her. "You made this for me?" he asked.

Julietta gave a jerky nod.

In silence, he picked up his fork and twisted the noodles

around the utensil. Placed it in his mouth with a reverence that stole her breath and her heart. She watched his every movement, his profile a portrait of angelic grace, even with his scar. Sawyer swallowed, then slowly placed his utensil down. In front of all witnesses, he reached over and took her hand in his. The warm strength of his grip settled her nerves and caused a pure joy to flood every crevice of her body.

"Thank you for this gift. It's simply the best thing I ever ate in my life."

Julietta smiled and squeezed his hand. "*Prego*," she whispered.

As if knowing the tension had dissipated, Lily burst out, "More pasta, please!"

Nick tapped her nose and refilled her bowl. Chatter resumed, stories were shared, and Julietta ate. But she knew something had changed between them. Something that couldn't be undone. Something that broke all the rules.

She pushed the thought away and focused on her family.

• • •

She cooked for him.

Sawyer ate with a methodical precision as the scene at the table faded to the background. Odd, when she laid the plate in front of him, he sensed something different. Like he'd reverted to an alternate time and place where certain actions masked deep emotions that were experienced but unspoken. His wife had prepared a dish with him solely in mind. Served him with a humbleness he didn't deserve. And looked at him with a banked fire in her eyes that drew him to her like a homing pigeon on a mission.

Food was survival. When he'd become rich enough for it to be a pleasure, he dined at gourmet restaurants. Culinary chefs had prepared meals on yachts and in endless hotel rooms. He'd ordered room service for women he slept with.

Since their wedding night, Julietta prepared simple meals for Wolfe and him that he recognized and appreciated. Lamb chops, pasta, risotto, grilled fish. He'd never had a frozen vegetable with her and was beginning to get used to the bottles of herbs on the windowsill, the baskets of tomatoes and prunes, grapes and lemons that littered the countertops.

But today was different. She offered him something of herself, as beautifully as she offered her body to him night after night. And in the way he only knew from his life, he took and took and took, giving her orgasms and pleasure but keeping himself solidly locked behind a wall that crumbled inch by inch with each day that passed.

Confusion and want swamped him in a deadly mixture. The memory caught, shifted, and dragged him under.

Thanksgiving. He sat in the closet with his foster brother and sister. One slice of turkey lay before them. Bread. Half a cup of milk. "You're gonna get in trouble," Danny whis-

pered, his eyes greedy at the sight of the meat. "Did you steal it?"

"Yeah. But I don't care. It's Thanksgiving, and we should celebrate."

"School talked about it. I learned about the Pilgrims and stuff, but the other kids talked about turkeys and stuffing and cranberries. What is stuffing like?"

His sister touched the turkey like it would disappear. "We should return it." Worry laced her voice. "You'll get beaten."

"I don't care. He won't find out. I was really careful. Here, I'll cut up a slice for each of us." He made sure to give them the bulk and take a tiny piece for himself. They ate the meal in silence, enjoying every bite of something that had actual texture and good taste. Food was another way of controlling them and their behavior, along with the beating, the solitude.

"We should say what we're grateful for."

Sawyer bit back his bitter response and desperately tried to think positive for his siblings. "Sure. You go first, Danny."

His brother took it seriously, scrunching his brows together as he thought. "I'm grateful you gave this meal to us."

Sawyer smiled. "Me, too. How about you, Molly?"

The girl was more solemn, her green eyes haunting in the sallow lines of her face. "I'm grateful we have legs and arms. I saw a man on the street who had none of those body parts. I'm really glad I have them."

"Me, too."

"How about you, Sawyer? What are you grateful for?"

Tightness constricted his throat. The path ahead was endless, strewn with pain and emptiness and the struggle to get through another day. His freedom loomed before him like the Holy Grail. Eighteen. If he made it. If he could help the others. He forced a smile. "I'm grateful for you guys. I'd be awfully bored without your company."

"And what do we have here?"

The door ripped open. Sawyer pushed the two behind him as his foster father loomed like Satan, blocking the only exit to heaven. His gaze took in the empty plate with the crumbs of turkey and he reached out with a meaty fist and dragged Sawyer out. "Think you can outsmart me, boy? Stole the combination of the lock to the fridge, huh? Think you're pretty smart?"

He kept his furious silence, knowing words only made things much worse.

"Nothing to say, huh? That's okay. I'm sure you'll say plenty later. Starting with begging for forgiveness."

"Fuck you."

He knew he'd made a huge error the moment he caught the satisfied gleam in Asshole's eyes. "Nice mouth. Since you don't seem to care what happens to you, maybe you'll think next time you pull a stunt like this." *Sawyer fought him, but the bigger man lashed out with his fists and his belt, and quickly tied him to the bedpost.*

His siblings were dragged out of the closet and placed in front of him. Sawyer met his gaze, the cold black void of evil and a lust for pain, and knew he'd made a terrible tactical error they'd all pay for. "Wanted to give them a nice Thanksgiving, huh? Too bad they now have to pay for your mistakes. You'll watch while I punish them, boy, and you'll beg for forgiveness until your throat is hoarse."

The terror on his siblings' faces enraged him, and yet another lesson was learned. He could save no one, and by his very presence he brought pain to the ones he loved the most.

He spent Thanksgiving night not seated around the table with a turkey and stuffing. He spent it watching his siblings get beaten while he screamed for mercy.

"Saywer? Are you okay?"

The voice cut through the memory, but it was too late. Nausea twisted his stomach, and sweat broke out on his skin. He gazed at Julietta with unfocused eyes and knew he had to get out of that room for a minute.

"Just have to use the bathroom. Be right back."

He half stumbled out of his chair and shot down the hallway. Sawyer locked the bathroom door behind him with shaking fingers, leaning over the toilet as he willed the sickness to go away. God, even after all these years the pain still got to him. He was in a safe place, surrounded by people who cared. He wasn't alone. He was safe.

He ran the faucet and splashed cold water on his face. Took deep, ragged breaths. He was kidding himself. He was playing at a normal life he'd never have. Every person he got close to he ended up destroying, and he'd do the same to Julietta. He ached to give her what she needed, but he'd been numb for so many years, he didn't know how to feel any softer emotions. Especially love.

He needed to get out of here. Gain some space. He'd make an excuse of sickness and go home, think about what to do, run away, get out, get lost.

Sawyer stepped out.

Wolfe stood before him.

The kid shifted his feet and picked at his cuticle. "You okay, man?"

Sawyer fought a shudder. "Yeah. Sure. Just ate too fast, you know. Not feeling good. I need to take off."

Sharp blue eyes that shredded his lies and saw too much pinned him. "I hear you. It's a lot in there." He jerked his thumb toward the kitchen. "Almost left myself. I mean, come on, are we stuck in an Italian spin-off of *The Cosby Show*? This shit doesn't happen. It's not real. Sunday dinner with homemade food. People being nice to each other. Laughing. Enjoying themselves."

Sawyer clawed for control not to spring through the door and leave it all behind. "Yeah. I know."

The boy's jaw tightened and a dark shadow crossed his face. "I hung out with this crew who knew a real good way to entertain themselves on a Sunday afternoon. We'd play the game Pick a Patsy. We each took a turn. Pick out a guy on the street. Follow him. One who looked nice, with some money. Good job. Had a great diversion tactic just like the molesters use. Asked for help with a hurt puppy down the alley. Guys fell for it all the time." Sawyer watched his throat work as if he were trying desperately to swallow. "We'd beat the shit out of him. Take his money, spit in his face, pawn his valuables. Laugh our asses off and buy ourselves something great to eat. Funny, though, we'd be at the diner or Mickey D's, all this food laid out in front of us, and I barely ate a bite. All I could see was the poor patsy's face bloodied up, wondering what the hell he did to deserve it. Yeah, those were the type of Sunday dinners we knew."

This kid clawed for his own sanity every second. Was this what Sawyer wanted to teach him? Run when something good came to you? Escape and distrust people who were kind and only wanted to help?

Wolfe needed to know there was something else out there. Something good and whole and pure. Something worth fighting for. Living for.

The realization slammed through him. He had a choice. But even more important, he held both of their choices in his hands, and damned if he'd let another person down. He wasn't that boy any longer. He wasn't helpless or afraid, and he wasn't about to abandon Wolfe because of a few nightmares.

A deep calmness settled over him and smoothed out the jagged edges. Sawyer nodded and clasped the boy around the shoulder. Wolfe jumped, startled out of his own memory, and waited.

"I think this a way better way to spend a Sunday, don't you?" He didn't let go, sensing this time that touch was needed to ground both of them. "And I think I can eat more than you today. Just like I can outlift you."

A smile ghosted Wolfe's lips. "Bullshit. I already had two bowls to your one."

"Then I'd better get my ass back and get to work."

He walked Wolfe back to the table and took his seat. Julietta stared at him with a worried look he was beginning to savor. How odd to have a female care about him and his welfare. "Are you okay?" she whispered.

"Yeah. Now I am." They smiled at each other and the room slammed into vivid neon color. Same type of thing that always happened when his wife walked into a room. He lifted his empty plate and raised his voice. "More pasta, please!"

Lily giggled.

• • •

Most of them settled into the living room for coffee and dessert. Maggie remained in the kitchen, grumbling at the task of having to help bake two desserts. Alexa sat Lily on top of the counter to watch the process and offer occasional assistance. Julietta noticed the sparkle in her mother's eye. Mama loved a woman with fire and had taken a complete shine to Maggie the moment they met, though she seemed the complete opposite of what his brother searched for in a wife. Alexa slid seamlessly into the family without a hitch, her laughter and kindness a perfect fit for the Contes. The twins were put down early to bed, and Julietta rocked Maria in her arms.

The six-month-old fit snugly in her arms. She enjoyed the hefty weight of diapered baby booty, the little toes that curled in pleasure as she slept. Julietta propped herself against the cushion and settled in while the fire roared. "So, what's the plan for this week? Sightseeing? Relaxing? You know we'll have to invite all our cousins over."

Carina snuggled next to Max. She noticed her baby sister never strayed too far from his side, and they still acted like a pair of newlyweds, their hands constantly all over each other. Tears pricked the back of her lids. *Mio Dio,* she hated acting like such a girl. But Carina had grown into such a strong, independent woman with a fire Julietta had never noticed. Her erotic art had taken off huge in Manhattan, and now she did shows while helping Alexa with the bookstore. Max still burned with banked sexual energy, but all that delicious focus was on his wife. His blue eyes lit with such love and gentle humor when he looked at her. Her family had finally found their happiness.

She looked up. Sawyer watched her with a heat that caused her to suck in her breath and shift her weight. The way he commanded her with his gaze or a bow of his head completely mystified her. How could she have gone from frigid to nymphomaniac? Her fingers itched to tear off his clothes and press her body against his naked skin. Skim the rippling muscles, fist his erection, and guide him into her heat.

Color flooded her face. Sawyer dropped a lid in a naughty wink, acknowledging her fantasy. Promising to give it to her later. And more.

Michael sipped his sambuca and stretched his legs out on Mama's coffee table. "Maggie has a shoot in Milan this week. Maybe we can come and see the progress of Purity? I'd love to see it, Sawyer. And kudos on such a huge business maneuver. Combining an exclusive luxury chain with La Dolce Famiglia was brilliant. I knew my sister would put our name on the map."

Julietta smiled at the pride in her brother's voice. It had been a long, hard road to finally get him to back off and trust her to run Mama's empire. Maggie had nudged him in the right direction, and finally Julietta felt as if he truly let her go on her own to run the business as she thought fit. "*Grazie,* Michael. That means a lot to me. Purity is simply amazing. The vision, the plans, the marketing. Everything fits seamlessly together. We're lucky he wanted us to join him."

Sawyer gave a half laugh. His face showed a touch of embarrassment at her praise. "Just call us the mutual admiration club."

Her brother's gaze sharpened. "Yes, things moved quite

fast between you two. I wish you had waited for us to attend your wedding."

She cleared her throat. "I guess we followed Max and Carina on that path. Elopement seemed the best choice. We wanted to be together quickly but decided we didn't want to sacrifice work at this point in the deal."

Michael nodded, glancing back and forth between them. "Of course. I guess business and pleasure do mix sometimes."

"We'll have you over to the new house," she offered. "You'll love it."

Carina snorted. "How come the women are always cooking and the men are always eating? I want to go out to dinner."

Maggie's voice echoed from the hallway. "Yeah, me, too. Why don't you take your women out? Or are you a bunch of billionaire cheapskates?"

"I agree!" Alexa shouted.

Max laughed. "We have children to disperse. Who's going to watch the *bambinos*? Mom?" He looked over and his mother let out a chiding stream of Italian.

"Maximus, do you really need to ask? We would be happy to watch our grandchildren."

Carina gave a whoop. "Tomorrow night then? We'll meet here early. Five? We can go to Botinero, I love the food there."

Julietta looked at Sawyer, who nodded. "*Si*. It is a date."

Maggie's whoop floated past their ears.

"How about we meet you down at Purity tomorrow afternoon beforehand?" Max asked. "We'll get a tour and do some catching up."

"Sounds good to me," Sawyer said. "Michael, can you join us?"

"*Si.*"

Julietta smiled at Maria's sleepy grunt. "We better skip out on dessert and get going. We have a ton of stuff for tomorrow. I think—what's that? *Mio Dio,* is that Dante?"

A massive form of black fur prowled into the room. His body reminded her of a small dog set on gobbling up his next snack. Narrowed green eyes took in the crowd, his gaze assessing each member of the family and then snobbily dismissing them. The once-stray cat who had lived in the wild had been tamed and now lived with Michael and Maggie, but his cranky nature had not disappeared. Julietta bit back a laugh when Carina jumped from her seat and crouched in a kneel on the floor. "Here, Dante, come to Aunt Carina. I'll give you a treat." She did her animal-whispering mantra, a haunting tone that usually had any feline or canine falling over in ecstasy. Dante took a step forward and Carina's face lit up.

The cat bared his teeth and hissed with sheer menace.

Carina's shoulders slumped. "I see him all the time, and he just doesn't like me." Her tone held a slight whine. "I don't think I'll ever be satisfied until I can win him over."

"That's what he wants, sweetheart," Max said. "Let's

face it. We all hate that cat except for Maggie. He's mean, snarky, and greedy as hell. Lives to be served."

"Leave Dante alone!" Maggie bellowed. "He's perfect just the way he is."

Michael snorted. "I wanted to leave him behind, but she absolutely refused. We take him everywhere. I swear, sometimes I get into bed and I'm afraid to touch my wife. He looms over her with menace. When we lock him out, I have to check my shoes constantly for my punishment."

Julietta laughed. "I'm glad he finally found someone to love."

Nick eased himself from the chair. "Be right back. I need to make a call."

Alexa suddenly appeared with a powdered Lily on her hip. She frowned. "Nick, you just called my mother a few hours ago. They're fine."

Pure indignation beat from him in waves. "I'm not calling your mother. I need to check in with work. Just a second." He disappeared, and Alexa gave a long sigh.

"Why is he calling your mom?" Julietta asked. "Is she feeling okay?"

Alexa rolled bright blue eyes. "My mom's just fine. She's babysitting precious cargo on this trip, and he's been a complete wreck."

Carina giggled. "I've never seen a man so attached to two animals before. It's adorable. Even Max and I haven't checked in on Rocky."

Alexa faced her. "My husband is worried over our dogs—Old Yeller and Simba. We left them with my mom because he refused to board them, and now he checks in on them every few hours. I swear, the man went from an animal hater to extreme animal parenting."

The idea of a man loving his family, even his dogs, so completely left Julietta with an empty hole in her gut. Suddenly, it seemed too much. And the truth was becoming harder to fight with every passing day.

She wanted the same thing with Sawyer.

Julietta stood and gave Maria to Alexa, stopping to press a kiss to her forehead. "We really have to go," she whispered.

Alexa searched her face with a touch of worry. "Sure. Thanks for taking care of her."

"Wolfe, are you ready? I need—"

She stopped and watched the scene unfold before her.

Dante had stopped an inch before Wolfe and was studying him with a half-cocked head, as if sensing something deeper that could never be scented from the surface. Wolfe had one ankle hooked over his knee and was slumped into the cushions like any teen. She was opening her mouth to shoo Dante away, afraid he might try to bite poor Wolfe, when the unthinkable occurred.

With one graceful leap, Dante soared through the air and landed on Wolfe's lap.

The cat wiggled his butt. Leaned his furry head close to

the boy's jaw and sniffed. Circled once. Then plopped his entire weight smack in the middle of his thighs.

"Oh. My. God."

Alexa stared, openmouthed. Maggie must have sensed something huge happening, because her footsteps echoed and paused in the doorway. Her gaze took in her mean cat purring like a chain saw, completely content in Wolfe's lap as though they had been soul mates for centuries.

Wolfe seemed hesitant at first, but his hand finally lifted and began stroking Dante's back. The cat purred louder and made an orgasmic sound of pleasure.

Julietta looked at her sister-in-law. A big smile curved Maggie's lips and satisfaction oozed from every pore.

"Told ya Dante is smarter than any animal on the planet. He only likes the cool ones. Welcome to the club, Wolfe."

Wolfe smiled.

• • •

Julietta gazed out the window. Darkness soaked every inch of the night sky. The tiny sliver of moon emitted a weak trickle of light. Crooked tree branches swayed in spooky shadows, and frost glittered on the grass. She pressed her cheek to the cold pane of glass and wondered what she was going to do.

She was in love with her husband.

The knowledge rose up and mocked everything she'd

thought she was. Everything she thought she'd wanted. The rocky, littered path to this moment stunned her. First business. Then sex. She'd been so cocky, believing she could compartmentalize her feelings like a work deal. Somehow, emotion had mixed up with the physical and had snatched away any rational thought.

Sawyer was the perfect man *not* to fall in love with. He offered shocking bodily pleasures, but clearly stated he'd never be hers. He did not believe in love. Was not able to gift that emotion because of fear. He was honest about his limitations. Within two short weeks of marriage, did she expect to change him?

She glimpsed the man he was hiding behind walls—the walls of his past he refused to share. Julietta thought about the night he'd confessed some of his past. She knew how difficult it was for him to revisit the nightmares. The precious gift meant more to her than anything. He recognized her broken vulnerability and tried to give her something to ease her. Sawyer had an amazing capacity to give, but it was twisted up with so many bad things, he'd learned to run away.

Setting the plate of pasta in front of him had changed her. In such a simple act of servitude, she realized how much more she wanted from him. How much more she craved to give.

She wanted to be the woman he leaned on, laughed with, trusted. Being in the midst of her family, surrounded by relationships that were real, tempted her to reach out for more. Did he want more, too? And if she was finally brave enough to give him the truth, would he reject her? As long as nothing was spoken aloud, they'd be able to continue. She could still have his companionship and his physical attention on a daily basis. Why screw it up by saying three lousy words? She wasn't as brave as her siblings. Her awkward experience with relationships only confirmed her inability to connect with men. Maybe that's why her mother had to force her into this marriage under the guise of business, because she sensed Julietta's inward cowardice in regards to love.

Pathetic.

She never heard his footsteps. His hands pressed down over her shoulders and pulled her into his chest. Julietta breathed in his scent, her hands wrapping around his while she clung to what he could give her. His body. Night after night. Some part of him would always belong to her, as much as she belonged to him. He made her say the words before he slipped inside her, words she'd give freely, without sensual torture.

She'd give Sawyer Wells her very soul if he asked.

The sexual chemistry burned and sizzled between them. Her body softened, her thighs parting to allow him immediate entrance. She sensed his nakedness; his erection nudged the cleft of her buttocks in demand for more. She waited for the games to begin—the dark twisted world she craved, of dominance and submission, of raw nerves and bared lust.

He turned her slowly. Cupped her cheeks. Took her mouth.

His tongue claimed her with slow thrusts that began the dance. She opened and allowed him to tug off her robe. The fabric slid to the floor in a pool of silk. His hands cupped, caressed, but she didn't need any foreplay—the whole evening spent in his company had weaved its own spell. His finger sank into her swollen wetness and dove deep.

Sawyer lifted her without breaking the kiss. Her legs wrapped tight around his hips and with one slow slide, he buried himself inside her.

Home.

She welcomed him, clenching around his shaft. This time, there was no play, no teasing nips or confessions wrung from her lips. There was only the hitch of his breath, the rock of his hips, the strength of his hands, the sweep of his tongue. She shattered around him, never breaking her grip or the connection, and he spilled his seed inside her without the barrier of a condom, his teeth bruising her tender lips in a primitive masculine claim of possession.

Still inside her, he walked to the bed and eased them down, never breaking contact. The truth hovered on her lips, but she was too afraid to speak. The whisper of her name was the last thing she remembered.

Chapter Fifteen

Sawyer lifted his beer and clinked it against Max's. The frosty brew slid cold and clean down his throat. "*Salute.* Been too long, man."

"Yeah, since Vegas. When you tried to seduce my wife."

"If I hadn't pushed you to make a move, you never would've been married. Just call me Cupid."

"Yeah, I'm still not feeling all warm and fuzzy with that one." His friend slid two more beers down for Michael and Nick, who were embroiled in a lively debate of Gucci versus Prada. He jerked a thumb at them. "They're going to ruin our reputation as real men. What the hell happened to football versus baseball?"

Sawyer gave a wicked chuckle. "Let's just call them metrosexual. They'll want to kick our asses."

"What's that?"

"You don't want to know, man."

The Brera district held an eclectic mix of hot clubs, bars, and restaurants. The real night crowd began coming in around ten, but the after-work crowd poured in around five for an aperitif to celebrate the end of the day. Sawyer rarely put in time for socializing, especially at the local hot spots, but after touring Purity and spending a few hours sketching out his plans, it felt good to relax and hang with his old friend. Max was one of his closest male acquaintances, and Sawyer recognized an honesty in the man along with the dry humor that spoke to him. After a fight on a Greek yacht over some random woman, they'd forged a bond that had only strengthened since Max had met and married Carina.

"How's married life treating you?" Max asked.

The loaded question gave him pause. "Good."

His friend raised a brow. "Why do I think there's something deeper going on here? You're not the type to rush into a wedding, since the word *commitment* used to give you a nasty rash. Love at first sight?"

He wished he could confess the truth. He was one hot mess. Making love to his wife last night had transcended their usual bedroom games. Things were changing, fast, and the slippery slope kept inclining in a mad rush to toss him off. Sawyer took another sip of beer. "Something like that."

His friend stared at him long and hard. "You know you can talk to me, right? I know Julietta is Carina's sister, but if I thought you were a piece of shit I would've boarded the plane ASAP to break it up. I saw you together. She's the one."

Sawyer raised his gaze, startled. "What makes you say that after a few hours?"

Max shrugged. "A connection. The way you look at each other. And you seem different. Less—"

"What?"

"Haunted."

Sawyer jerked. He opened his mouth to respond, but Michael and Nick slid into the booth with their beers. "What are we talking about?" Michael interjected.

Max rolled his eyes. "Women. What else?"

"Bunch of pansies," Nick muttered. "Hey, speaking of women, aren't we running late? We're supposed to pick them up at five, right? Who has a watch?"

The other two men glanced at their designer Zannetti watches. "Yeah, we'll finish our beers and head back," Michael noted. "I never go out anymore. Do you?"

Max and Nick shook their heads. "Nope. Not that I partied hard before, but after the kids came, it's too crazy. I'm lucky to have some quality time with Alexa."

"Same thing with Maggie. Those boys are a hell of a lot of work. Worth everything, though. How about you, Max? I bet you're still hitting fabulous parties and living high."

Max snorted. "Are you kidding me? We're not planning to have kids till next year, and we're already exhausted. Our work schedules are insane, and we tire out at ten. Pathetic."

Sawyer grunted. "Look at you. Finally out for a few drinks with the guys, and you're whining. Let's enjoy it. Live it up a bit. Hell, for my excitement, I'm looking forward to a *Rocky* marathon with Julietta and Wolfe."

"I love Balboa. Italian Stallion. Never gets old," Nick said.

"Nah, anyone see *Road House*? Now that's a quality movie," Max ventured.

Sawyer bobbed his head and drained his beer. Put up a finger for another. "Women don't get the real gist behind that movie. A shame."

"I'm a Tarantino convert," Michael said. "He's a genius. *Reservoir Dogs. Django.*"

"Alexa gives me a hard time. Says he's too violent."

The men all groaned in agreement. And ordered another round.

When they finally got to Mama Conte's house, Sawyer sensed trouble. He knew they were late but figured the women would be flexible. After all, how often did their husbands get out for some quality male conversation?

Michael paused before opening the door. He blinked and swayed a bit on his feet. "How late are we really?"

Nick laughed. Seemed like Nick was laughing a lot lately, and the guy wasn't the giggly type. "Just an hour. Or two. I lost track after the third extra round. That damn funicular should have a warning sign. I almost got killed."

Sawyer did a quick body scan. Definitely a bit off, but

not drunk. No one was really drunk. Why was Michael just standing there? "Dude, aren't you going to open the door?"

Nick pressed his ears to the heavy wood. "I don't hear anything. How come the kids aren't screaming?"

Max rubbed his forehead. "I have a bad feeling about this. This stinks of a setup. Do you think they'll be unreasonable because we're a little late?"

Michael groaned. "Maggie's probably stirring them up."

Sawyer let out a breath. "Guys, get it together. Let's go in, tell them we lost track of time, and then take them to dinner. Are you afraid of your own wives?"

The looks on their faces screamed yes, but male pride forced them to grunt. Michael pushed open the door.

The scene was not good.

Maggie, Carina, Alexa, and Julietta all sat in the living room facing the open hallway, dressed in killer heels and little black dresses. The sweet scent of musk and spice drifted in the air along with another, fainter smell.

Female rage.

Their expressions all matched. Accusation peppered the men like ammo from a paintball gun, stinging and reminding them that hell hath no fury like a woman scorned. Or a woman waiting to be fed. Sawyer glanced at the male crew. The magnitude of their error seemed to hit them all at once. He stepped forward to try and smooth things out.

Julietta met him halfway. The long naked length of her

legs got him dizzy. Her hair swung in a rich cloud of dark waves over her bare shoulders. The tiny scrap of fabric hugging her hips and stopping midthigh was an intricate mixture of black lace that played a wicked game of hide-and-go-seek that he desperately wanted to win. She wore a deep red lipstick that plumped her lush mouth and gleamed moist and wet under the light.

"Don't." She put up a hand. "We've been waiting for three hours. Max's mother finally left. Mama finally got the kids settled, but the twins keep waking up because it's a strange place, and Lily peed the bed and we had to refix our hair and makeup at least three times."

Alexa narrowed her eyes and pinned Nick to the wall. "You're drunk."

"No not."

Sawyer closed his eyes. He guessed the man was not used to eight beers in three hours. "Do you know much I was looking forward to this? All of us going out for a real adult evening? Why are you so late?" Alexa asked.

"Not no," Nick said.

Michael stepped up to the plate and directed his words to his wife. "I'm so sorry, *cara*. We ended up having a drink, and our watches stopped and we lost track of time."

Maggie pointed to the piece of expensive jewelry on his wrist. "That watch? The one that never loses power, works underwater while scuba diving, and is as strong as James Bond's? The one I bought you for your birthday after you lusted after Max's? That thing cost a fortune and resembles a spy unit. It stopped?"

Out at first base.

Max raised his hands, his gaze roving over Carina's low-cut top with blurred lust. "You look beautiful, baby. I'm sorry. Let's go now, and we'll make it up to you. Look, we're ready. The kids are asleep. It's early."

Carina pursed her lips. "We ate already, Max. We were starving, so Mama made us dinner. We can't leave her alone with the kids at this point; she's resting in her room after a long day of serving her family and babysitting her grandchildren. So, no, I'm not going to do that to my mother at this point."

Out at second.

Nick gave a hearty laugh. "We're all together now. Let's open a bottle of wine, start the fire, and spend a relaxing evening in. We haven't done that in a while."

Alexa glared. "We do that every Friday night. After we cook and clean up and take care of the kids."

Out at third.

"What do you want us to do then?" Sawyer asked.

Four women shared glances. Smiles eased onto their lips and he nodded with relief. Good, they'd salvage the evening, and he'd be able to drag Julietta out early so he could show her the many ways her outfit could be used for bondage purposes.

They all stood in one uniformed mass, grabbed their beaded bags, and dragged on their coats.

Alexa said, "Maria needs to be fed within the hour. Bottle's in the fridge. Check on Lily, she's been up a few times. Bye."

Maggie grinned. "The twins should pop back up in a few. Good luck."

Carina and Julietta didn't speak. Just gave their men a look and eased past them toward the front door.

Sawyer glanced around, not understanding. "Wait. Where are you going?"

Julietta winked. "Out. Don't wait up."

In a cloud of sensuality and mystery and pissed-off hormones, they shut the door behind them.

Out at home.

. . .

"Stood up by our own husbands." Maggie ran a finger over the rim of her glass and sucked the salt off her finger. "Pathetic."

Alexa sighed and stared moodily into her chocolate martini. "I shaved. Waxed. Bikini wax!"

Carina clucked in sympathy. "You know how men are when they get together. Probably talking stupid violent movies and sports. Remembering the good old days when they were young and free and drunk."

Julietta looked at the depressed women in front of her. She took charge and spoke in a crisp tone. "Enough. Yes, we missed out on romantic dinners, but when was the last time any of you went out for ladies' night?"

Maggie shrugged. "Too long."

"Exactly. So let's stop whining about our husbands and enjoy ourselves."

Alexa perked up. "Julietta's right. This is just as good. Shopping at Marc Jacobs and eating at the café is a dream. Promise no more complaining. Look at this place!"

Julietta glanced around the familiar café. She'd stopped many times along the way to grab a drink or do some shopping, but seeing it through Alexa's eyes made her appreciate the sleek design of illuminated glass, sprawling bar, and tiered ceiling. The bar hopped, music blared, and their table looked out over all the action.

"Agreed," Maggie said. " But we have to stick together on one point. They need to be taught a lesson."

"Absolutely. What do you think we should do?" Carina asked.

Her sister-in-law grinned. "It's what we don't do. No sex tonight."

Silence.

Julietta knew how they felt. Sure, she was mad at Sawyer, but she still looked forward to climbing into bed with him after girls' night out.

Alexa sank back into gloom. "Good-bye painful bikini wax."

Carina pursed her lips. "Couldn't we just torture them a lot in bed?"

Maggie shook her head firmly. "No. It will drive the lesson home. Just tonight. Hell, by the time we all get home, we'll be exhausted, and they'll be sleeping anyway. We won't suffer at all. But this needs to be a united agreement."

Julietta rallied. After all, it would be the easiest for her. And a night alone might be the best thing for both of them. "Agreed."

Carina and Alexa chimed in.

Maggie rubbed her palms together, green eyes sparkling. "Great. They have music starting in a few, so we can dance. Now that we're not having sex, let's talk about sex." Her gaze swung around like a radar. "Starting with Julietta. Spill."

"Me?" She ducked her head to fight the color in her cheeks and took a sip of her Kahlúa. "Uh, it's good. We're good."

Carina giggled. "You're blushing. That says it all."

Curiosity made her face her sister. "Hmm, since you could have been in my place, maybe I should ask you. Didn't you spend some time with Sawyer before Max?"

Carina made a face. "I didn't fool around with my new brother-in-law, Julietta! We shared a short kiss that meant nothing. He was a nice distraction while I trying to make Max jealous. But he had all this brooding, sexual energy that seemed quite yummy for the right woman. It wasn't like that at all between us." Her dark eyes sparkled. "But with you he's so different. Calmer. Happier."

Julietta jerked back. "Really? How do you know?"

The women shared a worried glance. "Why do you seem surprised?" Carina asked gently. "You got married. You're obviously madly in love. Is something else going on?"

Odd, she'd always been close to her sisters but had never shared her personal secrets. Venezia was too different to understand, and Carina was always too young. The girlfriends she hung with were always chosen from work and rarely scratched the deeper surface of sharing thoughts, dreams, and fears. Her innate loneliness had become such a part of her makeup, she'd never thought to question it. But since Sawyer had stormed into her life, she craved more. Including friendship.

Her heart pounded and she dragged her sweaty palms down the length of her skirt. "We didn't elope like we told everyone. We had to get married."

Carina gasped. "Are you pregnant?"

"No. Mama made us."

A short silence fell over the table. The sounds of the band starting up, glass tinkling, and laughter rang out. Maggie cleared her throat. "Umm, Julietta, I think you need to tell us everything."

Julietta did. When she was done with the whole story, a lightness tingled through her body. For the first time, she didn't feel so isolated. How silly of her to be so afraid of opening up. The serious looks on their faces told her how much they cared about her, and that her fight was theirs.

Carina took her hand and squeezed. "I'm so sorry,

Julietta. I had no idea you were going through this. Meanwhile, I was telling the girls we finally had proof the love-spell book worked."

The memory of creating the love spell and burning her list in the fire shimmered before her. Such an odd coincidence. "Nope, I guess this time it didn't have the power. At least not compared to Mama."

Carina took a deep breath. "I have my own truth to tell. Mama made me marry Max."

Julietta gasped. "What are you talking about? You married in Vegas."

Her sister nodded. "We slept together. Mama came to visit and found us. She threatened Max and me, and we ended up eloping."

Maggie drained her margarita in one long gulp. "You guys are starting to freak me out here. You're making her sound like some crazy mob boss."

"Her reasons were solid, and Mama is very strict on traditional values and doing the right thing. She also told me she knew I was in love with Max and that she would never have forced me to marry someone I didn't love."

"Weird. Two forced marriages in one family." Maggie frowned, as if a thought flickered past. "You know, I'm not sure you know this, but your brother and I weren't really married when we came to visit you guys. It was supposed to be a fake to let Venezia get married."

Julietta's mouth slid open. "No. Not possible."

"Yeah. I never planned on saying anything, but it seems this is confession time." She gave a laugh. "Of course, the fake marriage ended up real when your mother surprised us. Father Richard showed up, and all of a sudden, I was saying vows and . . ." She trailed off. "Oh. My. God. Do you think Mama knew we were faking it? She was sick, and Michael was afraid to say no."

Carina pressed her lips together. "Remember how surprised we all were when she was perfectly fine a few hours later? Like nothing ever happened. Maggie, I bet she knew and forced you to marry Michael!"

They all lapsed into quiet, analyzing the actions of the woman who'd raised them. Maggie whistled. "Damn, she *is* a mob boss. A love-mob boss. I don't know whether to yell at her or kiss her."

Alexa spoke up. "Umm, since we're all confessing how we fell for our husbands, I think it's my turn. Mama Conte wasn't involved, though. But I ended up marrying Nick for money to save my mother's home. We struck a bargain to be married for a year. No sex, no love, nothing." She grinned. "Of course, that didn't work out the way we planned, thank God. We fell in love and eventually worked it out. But isn't it strange how all of us at this table were forced to marry our husbands?"

Maggie grabbed her wallet and slid off the stool. "Wait here. I'm getting another round for everyone. We need some serious alcohol."

Carina leaned across the table. "You need to tell him the truth, Julietta. He loves you—I see it in his eyes when he looks at you. And the way he treats Wolfe? He watched over him the whole time at Mama's. Making sure he was comfortable, trying to engage him in conversation. When Dante jumped on his lap and Wolfe smiled, Sawyer looked so damn happy it was like he was his father."

Alexa nodded. "Sometimes you have to take your shot. It may have started because Mama Conte bullied you and on paper it sounded like a good arrangement, but he has real feelings for you. He's probably terrified, and you'll need to take the plunge. What do you have to lose?"

Everything.

"It could change us," she whispered. "As long as we don't push, things can stay the same. We're content. We still have each other. Maybe with more time, he'll come around. Sawyer was very clear he doesn't believe in love."

Alexa smiled gently. "Nick was the same way. Something was broken inside, but eventually we were able to heal it together. He still has some flashbacks from his lousy parents, but we deal with it. He knows I'm not going anywhere. Sawyer needs to know you'll fight for him. You deserve happiness, Julietta. A real marriage. Maybe children one day."

Carina nodded. "And if Sawyer can't give this to you, you may have to make a choice. When Max and I had trouble, I realized it became more about me. I didn't think I was worthy of him. Took a while to get my head on straight and then I got him back. Something tells me you've always avoided relationships for a very good reason. Once you figure it out, you don't have to be scared any longer."

Her sister's words crashed through her with a bone-deep truth. How many years was she going to wait to feel worthy of love? Would she spend the rest of her time working endlessly, being satisfied on paper but empty in her soul?

Maggie plunked the drinks down and grinned. "Guy tried to pick me up at the bar. So cool. Now, let's finish this group therapy session and do some dancing. *Salute.*"

The glasses clinked.

. . .

Sawyer rolled over and stared up at the ceiling. Two a.m. He didn't expect her to come to him tonight, but he couldn't seem to fall asleep until he knew she'd gotten home safe. He cocked his knee for a better position. Of course, she was fine. She was in a close-knit group, and Maggie could kick anyone's ass, but he'd expected her a few hours ago. What if she drank too much and got sick? Would Carina call him? He shifted for the hundredth time and glanced at his cell phone. Maybe he'd call. Just once. Maybe—

The sound of heels clicking echoed in the air.

Relief coursed through him. She was safe. Good. He ached to open his door to see her himself, but he forced himself to remain in bed. Time to go back to sleep. Nothing more to worry about.

Long minutes ticked by. He heard the adjoining bathroom door open. Water running. He imagined her brushing her teeth, donning her nightgown, and falling into bed. She'd probably fall into a deep slumber from a fun night out while he'd been tortured for hours babysitting, male sitting, and then waiting for her to come home.

He punched the pillow. Rolled over.

The door opened.

The hallway light splashed through and illuminated her naked body. She stood perfectly still and let him drink his fill. The high tilt of her breasts, the hard stab of strawberry nipples. Her dancer-type body was beautiful in its muscled symmetry and grace, the curve of hip, length of thigh, right to the perfectly trimmed dark mound that covered her sex.

He sat up in bed and waited.

She crossed the room, hips swaying, hair brushing her naked back in a sleek waterfall of dark silk. Her eyes were filled with a focus and purpose that stopped his heart. He opened his mouth to halt her, half afraid of her intentions, but his dick had swelled to the max and Sawyer knew he'd sell his fucking soul to claim her tonight.

She crawled, on hands and knees, across the bed. Swung her leg over him and straddled his thighs. A groan rose up and escaped. He reached for her.

"No." The velvety, dark voice of a powerful goddess

made him pause. "You're not allowed to touch me. Tonight we play by my rules." She shook out her hair and ran her fingers down his cock. "Hands over your head. Grip the head rails."

A strange panic fluttered through him. He never played sub and was uncomfortable not being in control. No way. "Baby, you know you love it when I'm in charge. Let me show you how much I missed you."

He reared up to flip her over, but those gentle hands suddenly wrapped around his erection and squeezed. Hard. The breath let loose from his chest, and arousal hit and grabbed him in a death grip. His balls tightened at her calm power. "Wrong. We play my way, or I leave. I'm not kidding, Sawyer. Think carefully before you decide."

Holy shit, her demand touched his skin with pure flame. He studied her face, looked into her eyes, and realized something else was going on, something he didn't know and didn't want to find out. He opened his mouth to call it off, but her hand did some magic stroking, and he shuddered helplessly.

Sawyer slid his arms over his head and grasped the rails.

She purred like a cat and all that silky skin poured over him like warm sticky honey. He'd play her game for a few, then wrest back control when she was too far gone. Confident in his plan, he enjoyed the shift of her body and the clench of her thighs as she adjusted herself over him. He waited for the ease of foreplay, the glide of her mouth over his, the stroke of her hands on his body.

Instead, she lowered her mouth and took his shaft deep.

He bucked up at the sudden move and gritted his teeth. Jesus, her tongue swirled around and licked with an expertise that made his eyes roll in the back of his head. Her hair spilled over his stomach and thighs, the strands sweeping and tickling his skin and wrapping him in a sensual cocoon. Completely under her spell, his fingers tightened on the wooden spindles.

She demolished him. Her teeth scraped the underside of his length, while her fingers massaged his testicles. Deep moaning sounds from her mouth vibrated off his erection and tumbled through his body. He stretched to monstrous proportions until his skin was pulled so tight he didn't think he could hold off any longer.

Every stroke of her tongue and lips and teeth bespoke a pure giving of herself over to him. This was more than sex, more than a woman who wanted to receive pleasure. She continued to drive him toward orgasm at a heart-stopping pace he couldn't seem to control.

He released his hold on the rails. "Wait. Baby, wait, let me—"

She lifted her head. "No." Cocoa brown eyes seethed with arousal, lust, and a need that stripped him of any rights. "Don't make me punish you." She reached up and cupped her breasts, running her fingers over her tight nipples, taunting him. "Or you don't get to touch me at all."

The monster he'd created took charge. His body shut

down his mind, and with a muttered curse, he returned to his original position. He feasted on the lush curves of her ass, the way the hall light played over her body, the delicious up and down motion of her mouth as she sucked him. He hung on to his control with his last rasping breath, but it didn't stop, never stopped. She kissed every part of him, his legs, hips, stomach. Moved up his chest to play with his nipples while her hands massaged and rubbed his erection, keeping him iron hard. When she finally reached his mouth, he was starved for her taste. She nibbled his bottom lip, running her tongue lightly over the seam, until he groaned and opened for her.

She dove in, claiming him as he'd claimed her endless nights, knowing he was completely at her mercy. She tasted of sweet chocolate, crisp mint, a touch of Kalúha. Her musky arousal assaulted his nostrils and made him crazed for more. His fingers gripped with all his strength until he was afraid the posts would snap in two.

"You taste so good. Feel so good," she breathed against him, diving in deep with her tongue. "I'll never get enough of you."

Time to finish. He eased his hold and got ready to take what was his.

But she sensed his shift and slid down his body in one graceful motion. Parted her legs. And buried him to the hilt inside her.

He cried out. Her silky, wet channel clenched around

him and squeezed tight. She adjusted her position, shimmying her hips as she took control and began easing up and down on top of him. Within pleasure, a glimmer of fear took root in his gut. He fought for rational thought and began to flip her over.

"No." Her eyes were wild, her lips soft and slightly bruised. "Let me do this. Let me love you."

The words stung like wasps. He lost his breath. "Don't." She arched, and ripples of pleasure shot down his dick. "Julietta, please."

"Let go. Just this once."

She didn't wait for his response. She rode him hard and wild and deep. His need to come, to give to her, roared up and washed away the last of his control. He watched her as she neared the edge, held herself there, her fingers digging into his hips, hair streaming down her back, face completely open to him.

"Tell me you belong to me."

Her demand singed his nerves. Sawyer gritted his teeth, and the orgasm shimmered before him in all its haunting glory. "I belong to you."

"Come for me, Sawyer."

With a shout, he let go. His seed shot inside of her, but she never stopped the frantic pounding rhythm. She drenched him with her own climax, and aftershocks of pleasure hit and convulsed his body. The orgasm went on and on with so much intensity it blurred into pain. Sawyer took it all, humbled by her beauty, and a wave of emotion washed over him in violent splendor.

Her body folded over. Her breasts pressed into his chest, and he stroked back her damp hair. She gave him the words in the darkness with no hesitation.

"I love you, Sawyer. This is more than sex. More than business or companionship or something on paper. This is about how I feel when I look at you. About the way you protect Wolfe, and how you respect me, and how you make me a better person. A whole person. It's about the man I see every day. I believe he has everything to give; he's just afraid to take it. I'm not going to be afraid anymore. I'm going to be brave enough for both of us."

The stunning words crashed through his barriers and pierced his heart. His thoughts whirled in a jumbled mass of confusion and need and fear he'd never experienced. Unable to speak, unable to do anything but breathe and remain frozen, Sawyer did nothing.

A while later, she fell asleep, never asking for his answer.

Chapter Sixteen

Two days later, Sawyer punched the button for the intercom. "Is Wolfe back yet?"

His secretary's voice came out crisp and sharp. "He just arrived, Mr. Wells. Should I send him in?"

"Please."

He pushed back from his chair and paced his inner sanctum, stopping by the few erotic pieces he displayed on the wall. He'd begun to notice his new wife had a touch of OCD and constantly needed to straighten paintings, pictures, or knickknacks to a perfect line. Especially when she was stressed. It was another tic he enjoyed getting to know about her.

Sawyer studied the paintings. They were subtle enough for an office, yet still retained the aura of sensuality he enjoyed studying. The woman lay her head on the man's chest, her eyes closed, her face reflecting a peace and satisfaction of a recent orgasm. The man held her in a possessive gesture that always fascinated Sawyer. When he took women to bed, he had never experienced the need to hold them close afterward or the roar of his inner primate to claim them on any more than a physical level. He soothed, comforted, supported. He pleasured. Never, ever did he actually feel.

Until Julietta.

They'd gone riding yesterday again. Taking advantage of the lure of spring, they'd actually played hooky on their lunch hour and taken to the streets. He loved the wild freedom of watching her take off on the sexy bike, her laughter and challenge echoing in the air around them as they roared through the city.

He still hadn't responded to her comment of love. He'd prepared himself for a dreaded conversation where he once again explained his emotional limitations, but instead she hadn't said a word. Just continued as if the event had never happened.

He didn't even know if he was overjoyed or pissed off.

The door opened behind him, but he didn't turn around. "About time you got back. Don't tell me we had more problems on the site."

"No. Remember I told you I needed a few hours to meet with Maggie?"

"Oh, yeah, the modeling thing." Sawyer shook his head in

amusement. "You won't even wear the designer clothes I got you, let alone get in front of a camera. But I thought it was really nice you let Maggie drag you over there." He twisted to face Wolfe with a grin. "How'd you get—holy shit!"

He blinked, not recognizing the boy in front of him.

He looked more man than boy. His crazy spiked hair had been completely shaved off so he sported the popular look preferred by today's youth. Without hair, nothing deflected from the strong lines of his face, the stinging blue of his eyes, the strong jaw with the slight dimple that he never noticed because of the facial jewelry. A bit of stubble hugged his chin.

His basic shirt and tie had been replaced by an Armani suit that seemed to have been custom-made for him. Snug lines emphasized his height, and the double-breasted jacket with a red tie gave him a dashing aura that would have women dropping their panties. Crap, his shoulders and biceps were huge, evident in the way the material stretched. All that working out had given his apprentice another benefit.

A hot bod, as the ladies would say.

His gaze kept roving over the boy's figure but his mouth wouldn't work. Wolfe scowled and thrust out his jaw in familiar rebellion. "What's the matter? Don't you like the hair?"

Sawyer struggled for words. "You look so different."

"Different how? Do I look like a nerd, dude?"

He shook his head in awe. "Hell, no. You look awesome. How did Maggie talk you into this? What happened?"

Wolfe shifted his weight. "I had a consultation with the designer. He was a trip. Loved my look, but said we needed to soften some of the edge. Maggie suggested I go for the shaven style, and I figured it would be good for business, too. I mean, I can't keep meeting big clients with this appearance anymore. It's just not fair to you."

Sawyer remained mute, feeling as if he'd been dropped into an alternate universe. Was this the kid who sneered and challenged and refused to bend?

"So, we got it done, and the guy booked me for a shoot next week. But listen, I don't want you to think this is going to pull me away from Purity. It's a Saturday session, and I'll make up the hours. Is this cool with you?"

Raw emotion rose up and choked him. "It's very cool with me. Jesus, Wolfe, you look amazing. So . . . grown up. And you're gonna be a fucking cover model? Women will be dropping at your feet."

Wolfe grinned and again, Sawyer was struck by how the boy seemed to have changed. "Yeah, we can hope. Listen, I gotta catch up with Julietta on a few things. You need me for anything?"

"Not now. We have a four o'clock meeting I'll need you to sit in on."

"No problem. Thanks, Sawyer."

Sawyer watched the door close behind Wolfe. Pride surged and tingled through every vein in his body. Somehow, someway, Wolfe was going to be okay.

• • •

Later that night, Sawyer watched the credits roll past on the massive TV, and he pulled his wife's feet into his lap. She groaned as he massaged her insteps. "I can't take any more," she moaned deliciously. "No more *Rocky*. I'm burnt out. How does he always manage to come from behind when he's so much smaller than his opponents?"

Wolfe snorted. "Wait till you see the final installment. Five sucks bad so we're skipping it, but he brings it home in the sixth."

"But how old is he? I thought his brain was fried in three?"

Sawyer gave a patient sigh. Women. "He pushed through it. Wolfe's right, five's a tragedy. But the last one wraps the whole series up. Poor guy."

"Yeah, it's sad how lost he seems without Adrian."

Julietta swung her head around. "What? Adrian dies? That's terrible! I don't want to see it."

Wolfe stuffed another handful of popcorn in his mouth and adjusted his blanket. Clad in flannel pants and a long-sleeved shirt, he propped his bare feet on the edge of the chair with a bowl settled in his lap. "Come on, Julietta. You're usually not so girly. Suck it up."

She sputtered a laugh, which turned into one of those yummy moans when Sawyer worked her toes. She had pretty feet, with delicate bones and fire-engine-red nails.

"Fine. But this is the last one. It's almost two a.m.. I'll be dreaming about knockout punches."

Sawyer pressed a kiss to the top of her head and eased off the sofa to slip in the last DVD. When Wolfe arrived home from work, Julietta always greeted him with a kiss and a huge. Sure, Wolfe usually looked awkward and ducked his head, but the flash of pleasure in those blue eyes told him the truth. He'd gotten quite attached to Julietta and allowed her liberties most couldn't claim. Like touches, smiles, and even the occasional laugh.

After dinner, Wolfe announced they should have a movie marathon with the old classics. Since his collection included all of the *Rocky* movies, they'd convinced Julietta to watch the original *Rocky*. Of course, this morphed into most of the series, so they all looked like a bunch of vegetables like poor Rocky.

"Bathroom break," Wolfe announced. "Don't start without me."

Julietta shook her head in amusement, the obvious adoration on her face for him making Sawyer's heart lurch. Odd. They acted just like a family would. The scariest part of all?

He loved every moment.

He gazed at his wife, who was cuddled under a cream-colored afghan. The conflict raging inside grew more violent. Sawyer knew he was hurting her by not being man enough to even admit he'd heard her confession. Once again, the confirmation he sucked at dealing with real emotions dragged him down.

Julietta loved him. The truth was in her eyes every time she looked at him. His ice queen was really a woman full of passion and goodness, opening her arms to a man who had once lived in garbage and walked in darkness. All he had to do was take her hand and take a chance.

Maybe he could. Maybe, just once, this time it would work.

"I forgot to tell you, some mail came for you today. It's on the kitchen counter," Julietta said.

"Probably a bunch of bills. Let me check, be right back." He walked into the kitchen and scanned through the envelopes. Then froze. The return address was stamped FISHKILL CORRECTIONAL FACILITY.

His fingers numbed and dread slithered through his veins. The past rose up from Dante's Hell and entered Earth.

"I have to check something out real quick on the computer," he called out. "Be right back."

He headed toward his office, shut the door, and ripped open the envelope. He unfolded it and read the words from his hated foster father.

Dear Sawyer,

Did you think that by changing your name and running to Italy you'd avoid me forever? I know ev-

erything about you since you locked me up in this hellhole. You always did think you were better than anybody else. I took you in, gave you shelter, food, and you threw it back in my face. You should be in jail for killing Danny. You were such a pussy, you couldn't stay for your little brother. He trusted you to care for him, but you left. Left him knowing what would happen. You're at fault, too. Does that bother you at night, or have you forgotten him and moved on with your perfect little life?

I'm coming up for parole. You may have put me in this place, but you're going to help get me out. I need you to recommend my release, which will help me in court.

I can hear you laughing now and asking why you'd do that. And I'll tell you why. If you don't, I'll find a way from prison to destroy your reputation. We have a lot of time to think and plan in here. I'll destroy everything you've built. I'll leak the story to the press. Tell your sweet little family the shit you pulled, the way you killed your brother because you didn't take care of him. Or have you just replaced him with that kid in your house and moved on?

I'll use my last dying breath to drag your past into the open. I've got nothing to lose. Do you?

Send the written letter in care of the parole board address below.

Sawyer shoved the letter back in the envelope and threw it in the desk drawer. He despised his automatic fear, a boy's fear, and reminded himself he was a grown man. That it was over. He'd never give the asshole a way out of prison, a way to hurt other kids.

The best memory of his life was the one of his foster father going to jail. Once Sawyer lost Danny, he went straight to the social workers and exposed what had been going on for years. Within months, the piece of shit was behind bars for a long, long time. It was the only justice that allowed him to sleep at night.

Now he was back.

The other memory shoved its way into his brain and carved him in raw, bloody pieces he knew would never heal. An innocent boy on the streets was ripe for anything to happen. Danny had been looking for Sawyer, trying to find him, believing he was old enough to make it on his own. Instead, he'd fallen into one of the local gang traps and was caught stealing their food. There was a price to pay on the streets, and his brother paid the ultimate price.

Sawyer's fault.

He stared sightlessly at the floor. His heart beat and air filled his lungs. Blood pumped through his veins. But inside, he was empty, a soulless being with a past that would never go away and that would continually remind him he was nothing.

His fingers lifted and he traced the scar on his cheek. A reminder of what he'd almost forgotten. He was better alone.

Julietta and Wolfe would be dragged into a mess, and poor Wolfe didn't need that type of exposure. Not when he was just beginning to heal. He thought over the options for a long time before returning to the living room.

Wolfe sat on the chair with the remote in hand. "Ready, man?"

His tone was wooden. "Sorry, guys, I gotta hit the bed. You two finish it up. My head's starting to hurt, and I need some sleep."

Julietta studied his face, probing for answers. He forced a smile and left them.

When she finally came into bed and slipped in beside him, Sawyer pretended to be asleep. He lay still for hours, throughout the night, and wondered what he was going to do.

. . .

Julietta sat in her office and stared at her sister. "Something's wrong. Really wrong."

Carina put down her coffee cup and looked at her with concern. "What's the matter?"

The itchy restlessness drove Julietta to stand up and begin pacing. The nugget of worry had now blossomed to a full-fledged attack. A few nights had passed since their movie marathon, and her husband was no longer the same. A faceless, nameless ghost haunted every moment, evident in the preoccupied look in his eyes, the distance carved out on his features when he spoke. He cited work and refused to eat dinner at home. He sidestepped her request to speak with him alone, ready with a list of excuses, and kept himself locked in his office or endlessly talking on the phone. He canceled an outing with her family and kept away from her mother's house. When he wasn't working, Julietta caught him staring at the wall, as if another place was on his mind. She'd tried to be patient and understanding. Tried speaking with him. Even tried sex, but by the time he came to bed, it was the middle of the night, and she'd fallen into an exhausted sleep.

"I think he got spooked. I told him I loved him the night we went out. During sex."

Carina swiveled her head around. "Hey, you weren't supposed to have sex that night. We agreed, remember?"

"Did you jump Max when you got home?"

Her sister sighed. "Yeah. You know I did. Alexa admitted her failure right away. And Maggie was pretty quiet and tame the next day, so I think Michael apologized properly. They definitely did it, too."

"See? Drunk women get horny. So, anyway, I told him how I felt after I seduced him, and even though he didn't answer, he changed. He was more open before, happier. We were starting to gel as a family." Back and forth she walked, her heels tapping. "But suddenly, during our *Rocky* marathon break, he came back in the room and acted funny. He's withdrawn completely. I'm worried about him, Carina."

"I love those *Rocky* movies."

"Focus."

"Sorry. Have you tried to talk to him about it?"

"Several times. He completely shut down. Wolfe is worried, too. They used to work out together every day, but he's missed all their sessions."

"Did you try sex?"

"Yeah, he's been avoiding me."

"This is serious." Carina nibbled on her lip. "Maybe Max can talk to him? They're close. Maybe it's a guy thing."

Julietta adjusted the photos of her nieces and nephews so they were lined up perfectly straight. Why couldn't the cleaning person put them back in their proper place when she was done? She held back an impatient sigh and refocused. "When do you guys leave?"

"Two more days. I'll talk to Max tonight. Try to get Sawyer to come to the house. Mama wants to have a big farewell dinner, and we want both of you there."

Julietta stopped. The doubts assailed her; the sheer rawness of her emotions screamed something was wrong but she didn't know how to fix it. "What if it's me? What if he doesn't love me the way I need?"

Her sister got up and pulled her in for a tight hug. "He does. Give him some time. I don't think he ever had anyone believe in him the way you do. And I think it's the opposite. I truly believe he doesn't think he's worthy of you."

Juliettta hugged her back. "Thanks. I have a meeting in a minute. Meet you at Mama's tonight?"

"Yes." Carina got her coat. "Trust your gut, and do what you think is right."

After her sister left, Julietta pulled herself together and headed toward the conference room. She needed to be calm. Cool. Allow him to work it out on his own and be patient. She clicked off her earpiece, grabbed her files, and took her place at the table. The department heads trickled in, laughing and joking. She fell into her role without hesitation, automatically bringing business back to being the main focus, challenging her directors on various questions, pushing for more efficiency, better production, bigger sales, always more.

Her fingers gripped her pen, eyes unfocused on the screen. The PowerPoint slides flashed with fury in an endless rhythm.

She needed to talk to her husband.

The little voice inside whispered, growing louder as the meeting droned on. Julietta stood in front of her team and knew in that moment nothing else mattered except preserving the precious gift she had found in a simple business merger.

Love.

The pen rolled from her fingers. She pulled off her

headset and threw it on the table. Her employees stared at her, startled at her sudden jerky motions. "I have to go."

Her assistant, Elena, raised her voice. "We'll wait if you need to take a call. Marcus can pass out the new marketing statistics."

She shook her head hard. "No. I need to leave. I have to go talk to someone. Meeting dismissed."

She fled the building without a glance back.

. . .

The door slid open soundlessly and she entered the office.

He stood with his back toward her. Dressed in a custom designed black suit, the cut of his pants and tight jacket showed off the hard lines of his body. His hair was loose, and blond waves hit the tops of his shoulders. His stillness reminded her of someone separate from civilization, as if he drew in the world's energy and locked it up inside himself. Her heart lurched in pain and a wanting that would never go away.

"You need to talk to me. Tell me. I deserve that."

He turned. Those piercing tiger eyes met her gaze and shredded past the surface to her soul. Slowly, he inclined his head. "Of course. You're right. I apologize for avoiding you. I just don't think this is working out."

She swallowed past the fear and remained still. "Care to explain?"

He spoke as if he wasn't in the room with her. A wall surrounded him, reminding her of a pod who spoke human and acted human but owned no soul. "I told you from the beginning I wasn't good at this. I think spending so much time together, and being married, blurred the lines. I don't think you're in love with me, Julietta. If we take a step back and concentrate on why we did this in the first place, we can go back to the way things were. I can't risk Purity because of emotions that aren't even real."

Her temper snapped. She closed the distance, moved past the wall, and made bodily contact. He jerked as she grabbed his biceps and dug her fingernails into his jacket. "Don't you dare patronize me about my own emotions," she hissed. "Do you think I throw words like that around? I love you. It's not going away, and it's not neat and tidy. Now, cut the bullshit and tell me what happened. Did something from the past come up?" She paused. "Or someone?"

The surprised gleam in his eye confirmed her suspicions. "Exactly what I thought. If it was that bastard who put those marks on you, I'll kill him myself. What happened? Did he or she dredge up the past? Remind you of all the reasons you don't deserve to be happy?"

She struck a nerve. Rage and grief battled for dominance, and he grabbed her arms, shaking her slightly. "Why are you doing this? I'm not good for you, never was. Don't ruin this between us. Let's step back, get our footing, and try to focus on why we did this in the first place. To settle a debt. To make your mama happy. To solidify La Dolce Famiglia."

"Fuck that," she growled. He was in front of her but hovered on the edge of nothingness. Julietta was afraid if she let him slip over, she'd never get him back. "I don't care about work or La Dolce Famiglia or anything I once believed in. Right now, all I want is you. Now tell me the truth."

"My foster father contacted me. From prison."

The words were ripped out of his mouth in a snarl. He let go of her and stepped back, as if he couldn't stand the thought of touching her. He shook his head and rubbed his forehead. "Tell me," she said softly. "I deserve to know, don't you think?"

"The bastard's up for parole, and he wants me to write a recommendation on his behalf. If I don't, he said he'd leak out to the press what happened, who I once was."

The air pulsed with electricity as if a tornado hovered, ready to strike. In the quiet of the center of the storm, she took a deep breath. "And who were you?"

"I lost my parents when I was nine. Went into the system. Got picked up by him and his alcoholic wife. They liked to take the older ones since no one wanted them. Always had a few kids going in and out, but I became his favorite. He liked to beat the pride out of me, as he used to say. I learned early not to tell, or the others got hurt. It's funny when you hear stories like that: The first reaction from people is always the same. Just tell the social worker. But a lot of them aren't like in the movies, where they want to help. Many of them just need to get their placements done and turn a blind eye to a bruise now and then.

"Anyway, there was a little boy named Danny. Looked up to me. As I grew older, Dickhead liked to use the younger ones as bait. You know, if I didn't do what he asked, he'd beat the shit out of them instead of me. I could take being beaten, but they couldn't. I counted the days till I was eighteen and legally free. By that time, I'd promised Danny I'd take him away. But I needed to get myself fixed up with a job and a place first. I told him to wait for me."

An agony of grief poured through her, but she kept her tone even. "Is that when you found Jerry?"

"No. There's no job for an eighteen-year-old with no diploma and no money. The shelters were almost worse than the foster home. Almost. I started to learn the rules of the street. Found places to sleep, people to steal from, restaurants to haunt. I learned the gangs who ruled and how to survive. But Danny was getting restless, and he didn't want to wait any longer. I stopped checking in with him as much, and I think he thought I'd abandoned him."

A shattering silence fell over the room. "What happened?"

"He came looking for me. Packed his shit and snuck out at night. But he didn't know where to find me. Gossip came from the street that there was a young boy who tried stealing food from a rival gang. They beat him to a pulp. He didn't survive. I found out it was Danny."

Julietta closed her eyes, fighting the nausea that ripped at her stomach. "Did your foster father get blamed?"

"Nah. He told the worker Danny ran away and that I sicced the gang on him. They found me and brought me in for questioning. I saw it in their faces, the knowledge that I'd killed him by not keeping my word. I promised I'd get him out, keep him safe. Instead, I killed him."

The woman who loved him wanted to cry and rage and comfort. But he was past that and spiraling down a pit of blame he'd been nurturing since his foster father planted the idea in his head. She snapped her voice like a whiplash. "And how is that your fault, Sawyer? Did you beat him up? Did you deliver him to the gang who killed him?"

"No. But if I had gotten him a message beforehand, he would've waited."

"Bullshit. His father was beating him daily. He would've tried to run away before he did, and I don't think any message of yours would have stopped him. He'd had enough, and he ran into the wrong crowd, and he got killed. But you didn't kill him." He stared as if surprised she was still there. "How did you get your scar?"

He rubbed his cheek. A small smile touched his lips. "I went after the gang. It was me against six, but I managed to put three in the hospital. They knifed me. It never healed right." The energy seeped out of him, bone by bone, and all she glimpsed was a man who had surrendered his hope. "The next two years were a blur until I finally found my way to Jerry. There was a little girl, Molly, who I also tried to help. She ended up hooking on the streets rather than live with him. Ended up dead of an overdose before I could get to her. You know the rest."

"And your foster father? How did he finally go to jail?"

"I finally went after him. All those years, he'd poisoned me to believe no one would think I told the truth. I was worried about the others. After Danny and Molly, nothing mattered. I just knew I couldn't let him hurt any more kids. One social worker listened to me. I exposed the truth and testified in court. Of course, it was too late for the ones he had already ruined, but at least they locked him up for a long time."

Julietta gathered all her strength and walked over. Tilted her head to gaze up at him. His beautiful face looked down at her in puzzlement, not understanding why she wasn't leaving him or cringing in disgust. She didn't know if he'd ever heal his wounded soul, but she refused to walk until she knew this man couldn't give her the love he held tightly under wraps in the mistaken impression he'd hurt someone he cared about. She traced the line of the scar with tenderness.

"This scar reminds me of your bravery. That you're a man who protects the people who belong to him. A man who will fight for what he believes in and what is right, even against the odds. This is a man who deserves everything.

Happiness. A home. Me. Wolfe. A family. That's what I want with you, Sawyer Wells. Your broken past means nothing to me; it only reminds me of what you've become in spite of everything that tried to rip you down. You're not getting rid of me. Until you can look me in the eye and tell me I mean nothing to you, I'm fighting for both of us." She raised herself on tiptoe and pressed a kiss to his lips. "I want you to come to Mama's tonight. My family's leaving soon, and it's a good-bye dinner. They all want you there because you're a part of us now.

"I love you. Deal with it."

She left him with her words echoing in the air.

• • •

He wasn't coming.

Julietta stared at the door with a sinking heart. Wolfe stretched out next to her, stroking Dante's back as the cat purred madly. The kids sat in a circle playing with a puzzle, the twins rolling and giggling while Lily played the little mother and kept them in line. Alexa was in the kitchen with Mama helping to clean up, and Maggie and Michael had escaped for a walk. The house had been full of cousins and uncles and relatives. Now, the last of the guests trickled out, leaving an exhausted clean-up crew and a quiet vibration through the villa.

Julietta refused to accept defeat. She'd spent her whole

life hiding from anything messy or real. It was finally time to fight for her future, but Sawyer might not be ready. The first test had failed. The path ahead might be a losing battle, but she wasn't going to step neatly aside and let the man she loved isolate himself because he was afraid he had no emotions left to give.

Screw that.

Wolfe watched her face with a deep worry she ached to soothe. Each step Sawyer took away from them, the boy suffered. They'd formed a bond within this short time period, and she sensed Wolfe's constant premonition that anything good would eventually be destroyed. Julietta swore if Sawyer walked away from them, she'd never let Wolfe go. She'd cling to him like a fierce mama bear and spend the rest of her days proving her devotion.

Max took a seat next to her. "I haven't seen Sawyer since our night out. Working round the clock?"

Julietta slid a glance over to Wolfe and pasted on a bright smile. "Yeah, the opening for Purity is coming close. We're all putting in extra hours to make sure we don't miss the deadline."

Wolfe paused midstroke. His gaze assessed her face as if he knew there was a deeper problem. Dante sensed something amiss and pushed his head into the boy's palm, bumping his attention back to the task at hand. Wolfe looked down at the demanding cat and gave a half smile. "Pain in the ass," he muttered under his breath. "Want some milk?"

Dante jumped down in perfect understanding and stalked toward the kitchen, not bothering to look back to confirm Wolfe followed. She watched the boy disappear and turned toward her brother-in-law. "Something's wrong, Max. Do you know anything about his past?"

Max shook his head. "No, it's obviously a closed subject. I never pried."

Julietta struggled between needing help and not wanting to disrespect her husband's privacy. "There's someone who's come back from his childhood. It's dredged up a mess of memories, and he's distancing himself from us."

"Do you think he just needs some time to process?"

She clenched her fists. "Maybe. But my gut says the more space I give him, the more he'll slip away from us. This person is trying to blackmail him."

"Bad stuff?"

"Yeah. Nothing that he did wrong, though. But he doesn't believe that."

"Sawyer doesn't take crap from anyone. He'd never buckle from a threat. I'll visit him tomorrow."

"Thank you." Julietta didn't know if she was making a bigger mistake recruiting Max. Her husband could lose his temper and slip even further away from her, but she trusted her gut. It had never failed in business. Time to put her instincts to the test in her personal life.

Max gave her shoulder a squeeze. "Sawyer is one tough son of a bitch. He's going to be okay. You probably knocked him sideways with his feelings for you. He's obviously fallen hard, and he's never committed to anyone before, let alone marriage."

She forced a smile. "I hope you're right."

Please don't leave us, Sawyer. We need you.

Chapter Seventeen

Sawyer made his way toward the basement and followed the sounds of grunting. Three a.m. The time of night terrors and ghosts that took flight. He pushed open the door and found Wolfe in the middle of the mat, going at the punching bag like Rocky in the final round with Apollo Creed.

Sweat gleamed from Wolfe's skin. His focus told a deeper story, and Sawyer felt a pang at how distant he'd been lately with the boy. He'd missed workouts this week, not ready to face him while he wondered about the status of his marriage. Wolfe didn't deserve to be around emotional conflict or deal with his whiny shit. He deserved more than that.

Sawyer dropped his bottle of water and towel, waiting for him to finish.

Wolfe tore off the gloves and panted for breath.

"Nice jabs. But your hooks still suck." Sawyer waited for his smart-mouthed comeback, but the boy ignored him. He turned his back and grabbed his own bottle of water, chugging it down. "Hard night?"

Wolfe wiped his mouth and glared at him. "What do you care?"

Sawyer jerked back. "Listen, I'm sorry I missed a few of our sessions. You know work has been killing me. Purity has to come first."

"Got no problem with that. Just don't like lies."

He frowned. "I'm not lying. I can't let up until opening, and even then the first year will take everything I got. I thought you were on board with that."

Blue eyes glittered with banked rage. "You think I'm stupid, man? You think I don't know you're thinking of taking off?" He gave a bark of laughter. "I'm the king of that move, so don't try to pretend it's about Purity. It's about Julietta. Me. Us, together. This whole thing is not working for you, and you got itchy feet. Fine, I don't give a shit. Just be a man and tell us to our faces instead of this bullshit about work."

The ground roared up and swallowed him whole. Sickness churned his stomach. Dear God, Wolfe believed he was cutting out on him, just like everyone did in his life beforehand. He shook his head hard and took a step forward. "Listen, Wolfe, you're wrong. Dead wrong. I am not leaving you, and I never will. We're a team going forward. I'm just going through some shit with Julietta, but I'll figure it out."

Wolfe made a low growl deep in his throat and backed off. "Lie. I see the way you look at me now, at her. Like you can't wait to get away from us. We remind you of something we'll never be able to fix. It's just a matter of time before you bolt. But I'm not waiting around for it. I like Julietta; she's given me more respect than I ever had, other than you. She makes me want to do better. I'm not going to hang around while you tear her apart and then start on me. I've been down this road, man. I'm done."

Panic hit. Sawyer scrambled for balance. "You're important to me, damnit! I don't want you to leave, and I'm not going to bolt. Even if this thing doesn't work out with Julietta, I'll never let you down. I can't let anyone else down again!"

The boy studied him in the dim light. Foo Fighters blared in the background. In those endless blue depths, Sawyer saw a deep truth that shook him. An understanding and disappointment so ingrained there was nothing he'd be able to utter to wipe away the doubts.

Because Sawyer knew the boy was right.

He was a liar. He couldn't live in his own skin any longer, especially with everything he loved and dreamed of and hoped for right in front of him. A wife he loved. A son to care for. A home and a family. Everything he'd never believed in, so he was taking off before it could blow up in his face.

Wolfe twisted his lips and hung the towel around his neck. "I understand, man. You're not letting us down; you're just doing what we all do. Coping. I was wrong to believe there was something more. Not your fault." He walked past him toward the door. "I'll finish up until Purity opens, then I'm going back to New York. Don't jerk Julietta around anymore. Not when you already have your mind made up to leave."

Wolfe disappeared.

Sawyer dropped to the bench and slumped against the wall. His instincts roared at him to go after Wolfe and prove the boy wrong. Drag Julietta out of bed and admit his cowardice, tell her he'd fight for her, for Wolfe, for all of them. But all he heard was his foster father's taunting words reminding him over and over he'd never be enough. Gossip would be gleeful, especially considering his current limelight with his new hotel chain. The press had been trying to hook him up for years, and any negative story would involve Julietta and eventually La Dolce Famiglia. And what about Wolfe? What if they discovered the boy lived with them and they began prying into his past? He couldn't risk it.

Letting them go might be the biggest gift he had to offer.

They deserved everything.

Sawyer rose from the bench and headed toward the

free weights. He wouldn't come out of the room until his body was completely drained and shaking with exhaustion. Maybe then he'd find a sliver of peace.

. . .

He walked the site and took note of the new developments with a tingle of pride. His vision shimmered before him, almost complete. The details were finally coming together to complete a portrait of exotic lushness paired with an environment that welcomed travelers home, with all the modern luxuries, from a dedicated technology and video room for business executives needing to Skype and hold online meetings, to the pampering spa, pools, hot tubs, and steam rooms. The rich textures of polished marble, glittering crystals, plush velvet, and rich mahogany conjured old and new worlds. He'd used his private art collection to make sure the main rooms inspired, like a high-class art gallery for his guests.

Sawyer closed his eyes for a moment and pictured the hotel full, his dream finally complete. And wondered why the culmination of his goal beat like a hole in his heart. Empty. Void. Dead.

"Hey, it's looking good, man."

Sawyer turned toward Max. A flicker of guilt trickled through him. Blowing off the family dinner had been a visible slap in the face to Julietta and everyone else. Wishing he knew a different way to handle it, Sawyer shook Max's hand and forced a smile. "Thanks. Listen, sorry I couldn't do dinner last night. Got caught up in the office. Hope you understand."

"Sure. We've all been there, especially around a new opening. Can I talk to you a sec?"

Warning bristled his nerves. "Sorry, got a meeting. Maybe later."

"Just a minute. Please?"

Coldness seeped through his veins. "Okay." He led Max up the stairs and into the shell of what would be his private office. The empty room was devoid of furniture and details, confirming it couldn't be a long talk. "What's up?"

"Julietta told me what was going on with you. Blackmail. Not any details, just the bare bones of some asshole with threats. Wanted to see if you needed any help."

"Appreciate the gesture. But I got it handled. Thanks."

He began walking out, but Max didn't move. Sawyer's heart stuttered in an uneven rhythm. "Not done yet," Max said. Sawyer stiffened in preparation. "See, I don't think you have it handled. I think you believe you're in this alone and need to fix something from years ago that you had no control over. Problem is, you're married to Julietta now. You're stuck with a family, and we don't let one of our own deal with this shit alone. You probably know as many people as I do, but not the same type. I know a guy. So this is how it's gonna work. You give me a name. And you don't get contacted again. *Capisce*?"

In the *Twilight Zone* of the conversation, Sawyer's lip quirked with humor. "Did you really say the words 'I know a guy'? Have I been recruited into a bad episode of *Mobsters*?"

Max didn't smile. "I'm not fucking around, Sawyer."

He realized his friend was dead serious. "Thanks for the offer, but I'm handling it."

"By pulling away from your wife? From Wolfe? By torturing yourself with what-ifs you can't change?"

"How much did she tell you?"

Max shrugged. "Not much. But I've known you for a long time. We've been friends awhile, and though we don't talk about your past, I'm not an idiot. I know shit happened. I know who you are today and what type of man you became. That's what matters."

The truth hit him in the face like a belly flop. "Jesus, I didn't expect this heart-to-heart." His nerves rubbed raw against the look on Max's face. A need to share and to trust him rose up. "You were wrong, Max," he said softly. "I'm not good enough. Julietta needs someone who can make her happy. Love her the way she deserves. Keep her safe. It's not me."

"Yes it is. But you gotta believe it before it can happen." Max leaned against the empty wall. "When Carina and I finally got together, we had a lot of work to do. We played this ridiculous game of back-and-forth. I didn't think I could ever be good enough for her. She was a woman meant for family, marriage, a commitment. But she never let up until I caved. When we got married, I realized it's not about being good enough. It's just about loving them enough to want to be good enough. We all deserve that shot. Especially you. By the time I got my act together, Carina had gone through the same thing. Not believing in herself or who she was. It took a while, but she got there, and I waited. See, there's no perfect person out there for Julietta, dude. You're already screwed. She loves you, and when one of the Conte sisters falls, you don't get away. You can run as far and fast as you want, but I bet she'll be waiting for you when you get there." Max shook his head. "They are some seriously scary women when they want someone."

Max's words dived deep and latched on. A crazy flicker of hope lit. "I don't know."

"I figured. Listen, we leave for the airport tonight. Would be nice for you to see us out. I know Michael and Nick wanted to say good-bye. Flight's at six. Come on by real quick when you've had some time to think about it. See, we take care of each other, no strings attached. Whether you want the help or not, Sawyer, you got it. Not only do I know 'a guy,' but I have some excellent lawyers, too. Hope to see you later."

Max walked up and gave him a brief hug.

Sawyer watched him disappear, the words frozen in his throat. Fear and want mingled in a flood that drowned him. Max had thrown him a lifeline.

Now he just had to decide whether or not to use it.

. . .

Julietta waited while her sister hung on to Mama with the fierceness the baby in the family always experienced. Carina blinked away tears when she finally separated herself. "I don't want to let you go yet," she whispered, clinging to her hand.

Mama Conte squeezed her in one last tight hug. "I know, sweet girl. But your life is back in New York, and it's time to return. Will you send me one of your latest paintings? One with no nakedness in it?"

Carina sniffed. "Yes. Promise. Michael's working on getting you to the States for another visit soon."

"Sounds wonderful."

Julietta watched as Maggie and Alexa got their hugs and headed out toward the car. "Are you coming to the airport with us?" Maggie asked.

"Yes, I'm not ready to say good-bye yet. I'll follow you and leave from there."

"I'll go with you."

She turned toward Wolfe and smiled. "Thanks. I know Dante will want to give you a last purr before he leaves." She watched as the boy petted the cat through the carrier.

Carina hooked her arm through Julietta's and pulled her away. "Tell Sawyer we said good-bye. I'm sorry he couldn't come."

Grief sprang up and choked her. "I know Max tried to talk to him. I'm not giving up. I've spent my whole life waiting for a man like him. I'm going to fight as hard as I did when Luigi's Bakery tried to steal our recipes and put us out of business."

Carina laughed. "They never had a shot against you. Neither does Sawyer. Make sure you keep me up to date, okay?"

"As long as you don't bother me with any more love spells."

Carina sighed. "I don't know what happened; it's the oddest thing. Worked with all three of us."

"Just goes to show I'm always the fluke."

Her sister punched her lightly in the arm. "Not true. Your road to true love just took a few hard turns. I love you."

"Love you, too. Let's get you guys to the airport."

They climbed into the car and took off.

• • •

Sawyer stared at the door. They were probably gone. Still, he'd tried. Max's words had beaten in his head like a mantra all day. He'd struggled about taking the step to come here today, but he still didn't feel as if he should belong to such a group.

Sawyer turned and decided to go home. Stay with his first instinct to remove himself. It would be easier.

Mama Conte opened the door. "You missed them. They left for the airport."

He dragged his feet like a child in trouble. "Sorry, Mama Conte. I'll catch Julietta later at home."

She opened the door wider. "Not yet. Come in for a moment."

"Umm, I—"

"Now."

He walked in. The house was still and perfectly clean. She led him into the kitchen, and he took his usual seat. She brewed him a cup of espresso in silence, set it in front of him, and slid into a chair. Sawyer sipped the steaming brew and hoped to God she wasn't going to give him a hard time. He couldn't take any more.

"Do you know why I made you marry my daughter?"

He looked up. "For La Dolce Famiglia."

She waved a hand through the air. "I couldn't care less about the bakery. Yes, it's important, but not as important as my children's happiness. No, Sawyer Wells, I did it because I knew you were meant to be the one she loves. I also knew neither of you would have entertained the idea unless I forced it. Both stubborn. Both workaholics. Both convinced love is an illusion and marriage an impossibility."

All the doubts reared up. His words came out clipped and hard. "You were wrong. I told you before when you first hatched this crazy plan. I've done things. Failed people. I'm not who you believe I am, and Julietta and Wolfe deserve better."

She spat in disgust. "Crazy talk. We all have a past, some harder than others. We all have scars, either physical or emotional or both. Do you remember when I met you at the bar and I told you about karma? You had a choice to make that night. Your life could have gone in either direction. You could have argued you were forced to take the wrong path because of your past—because of what you thought you deserved. But in that moment, you reached for more. Nothing held you from that except your own belief. Not others. Today, you face the same decision. You can fight for my daughter, the woman you love. You can fight for Wolfe and watch as he grows. Or you can take the other path and talk about what you are destined for, because of this past that you say owns you."

Her words hammered home and splintered the crumbled wall behind his heart. Halfway torn down by Julietta, chipped away by his friend's words, the final blow smashed the last obstacle. All that remained was a mess of rioting emotions, raw and vulnerable and pulsing with scars.

His voice broke. Sawyer bowed his head. "I don't know if I can."

She rose and came to him. Strong arms held him with no apology, no hesitation. She stroked his hair like a mother

would, soothing him with her warmth and safety and be-
liefs. "My sweet boy, yes, you can. Your life is your own.
You were a child and could not protect the ones you loved.
None of us can. So instead, we choose to love as much as
possible, and that needs to be enough."

She pressed a kiss to the top of his head. Tears stung his
eyes as he hugged her back. "My daughter does not choose
wrong. You are who she wants, and she will not let you go
easily. Let her choose you, and know you are enough."

The seconds ticked by. The wounds scabbed over, and a
strange peace radiated from his gut. Once again, he was in
front of that door in the hotel, a video camera gripped in his
hands. A choice. His choice.

"Where is she?"

Mama Conte pulled back and smiled. "She went to the
airport to see them off. You can still catch them."

"Thank you."

"*Prego*. Now go."

He stood up and hugged her again. Then raced out the
door.

• • •

Michael's jet was fueled and ready to go. Heart heavy to see
her family go, Julietta milled in the main lobby section before
the security checkpoint and said her final farewells. Michael
gripped her hard and raised her off the ground. "Stay strong,"

he murmured in her ear. She figured Max had given him a heads-up, but his strength and support eased her heart.

"I will. Take care of my nephews."

"*Si*."

Alexa shifted Maria in her arms; she had fallen fast asleep on the drive over. "Thank you for your hospitality, Julietta. I can't wait to go home and try out all these new recipes."

"Perhaps I'll take a trip to New York to see your home. I'll see what I can do with my schedule."

"I'd love that."

Maggie and Carina gave her another hug. "Bye, sis. We love you."

"Love you, too."

"Call if you need us. For anything."

"I will."

They turned in a mass group and began moving toward the checkpoint.

"Wait!"

Everyone stopped. Sawyer ran through the crowds, dodging and whizzing past strollers and luggage and security. He skidded to a halt in front of them, out of breath, his cashmere coat and bright purple tie symbols of stylish civility. His face reflected the opposite—a mass of naked emotion, his scar highlighted under the garish airport lighting.

Joy exploded through Julietta. "You came."

Her family moved toward him, but he put out his hands. "Stop. I have something to say."

Julietta stilled. Wolfe stiffened beside her. Amidst the chaos, a frozen silence clouded around the group, half terrified of the words that would finally be spoken aloud. Her heart exploded in rapid beats that choked her breath. She fought through the fear and hoped that by sending Max, she hadn't broken him.

His beautiful tiger eyes lit with uncertainty. His gaze skimmed the group as a whole, then came to rest on her.

"I can't do this anymore. To my wife. To Wolfe. To everyone."

"Please." She cleared her throat, desperate to stop him. "Please, don't."

"I have to. I have to do this now." He dragged in a lungful of air. "I'm a complete asshole. I pushed you past your limits and promised I'd be there to help you. But I wasn't. The first sign of real intimacy, of honesty, and I run like I've been taught my entire life. Except you wouldn't let me. Somehow, you saw past the bullshit and loved me anyway. You wrecked me, Julietta. You tore me apart piece by piece and then put me back together. I love you. And though I don't think I'll ever deserve you, I choose to try. I choose you. All of you. If you'll still have me."

A sob tore from her throat. She recognized the leap he had taken to confess his feelings in front of her family—a naked unveiling in public that scared him to the core. She stumbled forward, and he rushed to meet her.

His arms held her tight against his massive chest. Drunk

on his scent and his touch, she clung to him, afraid she was in a dream and she'd wake up.

"I love you. Every part of you, and you were mistaken if you ever thought I'd allow you to leave me. You belong to me. To us. And I'll spend every day making you believe it."

Alexa sniffled. "Oh my God, he gave her an airport scene! Just like in the books I read and all those movies. He followed her to an airport and confessed his love before she could board the plane!"

Nick laughed. "Sweetheart, she wasn't boarding the plane."

"Close enough."

Maggie sighed. "Damn, that did rock. Almost as good as you wearing the Mets cap with Old Yeller in BookCrazy."

Nick winced. "Uh, can we not talk about that, please?"

Max grinned. "Hmm, I didn't hear that story. Good, I need a little entertainment on the flight."

"Screw you."

Michael grinned. "Should we leave them alone to finish their scene in private?"

Maggie snorted. "Hell, no. I say we go in for a group hug. As Sawyer stated, he's stuck with all of us."

Suddenly, Julietta was surrounded by her family, laughing and sniffling while the men held back to retain an element of coolness. When they finally pulled away, Wolfe stood off to the side, a half smile on his lips. "You guys are nuts."

"And you're a part of it. Part of us," Julietta said.

Sawyer walked toward the boy. Clasped his shoulders. And looked into his eyes. "You were right, Wolfe. I was going to run, because that's all I knew. But not anymore. And you're not either. When you get something good and right and pure, you stick with it. Got it?"

Wolfe grinned. "Got it."

Sawyer pulled him in for a short, hard hug.

This time, Wolfe hugged him back.

. . .

Sawyer's hand drifted over her belly to cup one of her breasts. A playful tug at her nipple heated her back up, and she let out a groan. "I need a break. Too many orgasms."

He chuckled and nibbled on the sensitive curve of her neck. "Quitter."

"Those are fighting words."

"Hope so." His tongue licked up toward her ear, and his hot breath shivered moist and warm, causing goose bumps to break out on her skin. "I got a lot to make up for."

She turned her head and kissed him deep and long and sweet. "You already did."

"Do you think Wolfe will forgive me?"

"Yes. You never left. You ended up choosing him. That's what he'll remember."

"I'm thinking of sending him back to New York. After Purity opens, of course, and he settles in a bit. I want him to have the experience of college. He's so smart; he should have a degree behind him. Get a glimpse of what a normal teenager goes through."

"Wolfe will never be normal. I like him that way. But I agree. Michael, Nick, and Max can look out for him. But I'm not ready to let him go yet."

"Me either. We'll see what happens."

"And your foster father?"

Sawyer stroked her long hair, which rippled over their naked bodies. "He gets nothing from me, not anymore. The letter is proof of blackmail, which will block him from parole. And as for letting my past out, there's nothing to be afraid of anymore. Besides, Max knows a guy. And he has lawyers."

"I do love my ruthless male Italians." She pressed her lips to his. "And us?"

He grinned at her playful question, sliding her up and over him. He guided himself deep within her, rocking his hips until the light of lust lit her cocoa eyes. "We live happily ever after. One day at a time."

She rode him until the orgasm shattered them both. He watched her, hair streaming down her back, face open with pleasure and love and generosity. And Sawyer thanked karma for finally giving him the woman who loved him enough to fight the darkness and save him.

Epilogue

"What a mess." Julietta walked through the condo, tagging boxes and packing up last-minute stuff. They'd finally found a buyer and had spent most of the weekend moving the last of her old belongings. Thank goodness for Wolfe. He'd been spending the last few nights sending things back to their house and a bunch of extra items to charity.

She walked into her old bedroom where only the headboard remained. Made a quick survey of the empty room to make sure nothing was left behind. Turned her head. And caught a flash of white.

She bent down and picked up the piece of white ledger paper that was tucked behind one of the posts on the floor. Frowning, she opened it up.

The list.

The love spell.

Julietta shook her head. How embarrassing if Wolfe had discovered it. She remembered putting the second paper under her mattress before burning the first copy. She began to crumple it up and toss it away, but she took a moment to glance at the list.

The numbers shimmered before her.

1. A man who can give me orgasms.

2. A man who respects and encourages my career.

3. A man strong enough to fight for me.

4. A man who understands my soul.

5. A man who carves out his own path in life.

6. A man who gives me everything of himself.

Her fingers fisted on the paper. She closed her eyes, and the room suddenly swayed. How was this possible? Sawyer had been brought to her by Mama, not a crazy list. Right? But why was every quality a part of the man she married? She quickly reread the list and realized the items fit her husband perfectly. As if he had been created just for her.

She raced out to the living room and scanned her empty bookshelves. Where was the book? The clatter of footsteps on the stairs interrupted her thoughts.

"What's the matter? You look like you've seen a ghost?"

Julietta stared at Wolfe. "Did you pack up all my books and send them to the house?"

"No, you told me to box up those shelves and send them to the used bookstores. I sent a few boxes to different areas. I hope you didn't lose something important. Would be a bitch to try to find one of the books."

Could it be possible? They'd all created the spell and found their soul mates. Was it just coincidence? After all, there was no such thing as a love spell. Or at least a love spell that actually worked. She stared down at the paper, then quickly crumpled it up. "No. It was nothing. Probably better to let it go."

"Cool. Movers are coming for the rest of the stuff. Ready to go?"

She looked around, then slid her hand into Wolfe's. He'd started to become much more used to touch. "Yeah. Let's go home."

They walked out of the room together.

• • •

Mama Conte pulled the shawl tight around her shoulders. She sat on her favorite rocker, book in hand, espresso on her right, and gazed out at the sprawling landscape outside her home. Though spring loomed, the temperatures had dropped and frost had settled and crusted the grass. The day chilled her bones and sent a fierce wind to rattle the bare trees, but she was cozy and warm and didn't have to go out for the rest of the day.

She flexed her gnarled fingers and wondered where the years had gone. Just yesterday she had been building her family and her company. Now, the new generation would take over the legacy. Her grandchildren would thrive—some in Italy, others in America—and the Conte name would never be forgotten.

Smiling, she thought of her late husband. How he would have loved watching his children grow and develop their individual personalities. He loved them all so fiercely, with a devotion that only a parent could understand, but he always worried a bit more about Julietta. She was so like him, with a fierce independence and brilliance for business that trumped any personal relationship. Finally, her daughter was complete with a man meant to match her soul.

So many times she was afraid she'd pushed too hard. Made mistakes. But she'd trusted her gut to guide her children into love, and she could never regret her choices. Not now.

A deep satisfaction and peace settled over her. She felt her husband's presence beside her. First Venezia. Michael. Carina. And now Julietta. All had found love. All had been properly matched.

Time for a new chapter, one she wouldn't be a part of any longer. She hoped the path wasn't as difficult for the others, but she already knew that only through pain could great pleasure be attained. Appreciated. Savored.

She smiled, enjoying the silent presence of the man who had been her love match.

Her work had finally been done.

Mama Conte smiled, rocked back and forth, and enjoyed the moment.

Acknowledgments

I feel as if I could write an entire book acknowledging all the people who helped me get to this point in my career. But, alas, that would not entertain my readers, so I will allow myself a short section of praise for the wonderful people in my life.

For my kick-ass, amazing editor who I adore—Lauren McKenna. You simply bring out the best in my work and I am forever grateful.

For my agent, Kevan Lyons, who helps guide me into the future.

For the amazing Probst Posse and my faithful readers who wouldn't rest until Julietta got her own happily ever-after. You all inspire me. Special thanks to Elena from Bookish Temptations who answered my questions about Milan.

Writers need support. People to trust. And lots of laughs. For the group of writers in my life who offer all of these, especially Wendy S. Marcus, Aimee Carson, Abbi Wilder, Jen Talty, Bob Mayer, Alice Clayton, Elisabeth Barrett.

Thank you.

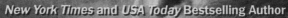

New York Times and USA Today Bestselling Author

JENNIFER PROBST

"Destined to steal your heart."
—*New York Times* bestselling author Lori Wilde

THE MARRIAGE
Bargain

It was the perfect arrangement—
then love broke all the rules. . . .

"ONE OF THE MOST EXCITING BREAKOUT NOVELISTS." —*USA TODAY*

The sizzling first book in the *New York Times* and *USA TODAY* bestselling Marriage to a Billionaire series by "one of the most exciting breakout novelists" (*USA TODAY*).

New York Times and USA Today bestselling author of
The Marriage Bargain

JENNIFER PROBST

THE MARRIAGE
Trap

A sexy billionaire seeks a faux fiancée—
but what's it worth without love?

"ONE OF THE MOST EXCITING BREAKOUT NOVELISTS." —*USA TODAY*

The sizzling second installment in the *New York Times* and *USA TODAY* bestselling Marriage to a Billionaire series by Jennifer Probst.

JENNIFER PROBST

THE MARRIAGE
Mistake

A one-night stand leads to a shotgun wedding . . .
but is it too late for love?

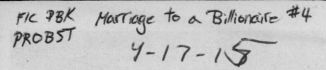

First in a hot new romance series by Jennifer Probst

Author of the *New York Times* and
USA Today bestselling
Marriage to a Billionaire novels

Searching for Someday

Matching passionate partners is her business . . . but the
power of love is pure magic.

Coming November 2013 from Gallery Books!